SILVER

SILVER

Graham Masterton

W.H. ALLEN · LONDON
1986

Phototypeset in Linotron Palatino by
Input Typesetting Ltd, London
Printed and bound in Great Britain by
Mackays of Chatham Ltd, Kent
for the Publishers, W. H. Allen & Co PLC
44 Hill Street, London W1X 8LB

British Library Cataloguing in Publication Data

Masterton, Graham
  Silver.
  I. Title
  823'.914[F]   PR6063.A834

  ISBN 0–491–03840–2

Prologue

In the second week of January, when the snow was falling as thick as a thousand burst-open pillows, and the thermometer had dropped fifteen degrees below freezing, a boy came into the lobby of the Imperial Hotel with a bright red nose and a message in a snow-blotched envelope.

He waited by the cast-iron stove while the porter went upstairs to fetch the lady to whom his message was addressed. On the other side of the lobby, a weeping-eyed Labrador regarded him soulfully; as if winter at the Imperial Hotel were a tragedy in itself.

Outside the snow-clotted windows, the town of Leadville had taken on a silent ghostliness. Horses and sleighs moved through the storm as dimly and quietly as memories; and it was impossible to see further than the bank building on the corner of Mackay Street. The boy pressed his hands in their wet grey woollen gloves up against the stove's hot chimney, until his fingers tingled and the wool began to scorch. He had been told not to come back without an answer. No answer, no dime, and that was why he continued to wait.

The outside door swung open again, and snow whirled pell-mell across the hall. A man in a thick raccoon coat and a snow-covered top-hat was trying to manoeuvre his way through the entrance with a large brown suitcase and a photographic tripod which kept misbehaving itself. The boy went over and helped the man to wrestle the tripod inside, and then together they slammed the door shut again.

The man took off his hat and a lump of snow dropped off the top of it on to the damp-stained carpet. He was brown-bearded, round-faced, with small pince-nez spectacles which had already steamed up in the heat from the stove. He shook the boy's hand vigorously.

'Well, well,' he said to himself, looking around. 'Welcome to Leadville, hey?'

'Yes, sir,' said the boy, but only because he felt he ought to.

'Anybody at home?' the man asked, jerking his thumb towards the unattended reception desk. It was a magnificent piece of furniture, the reception desk: carved out of solid mahogany with angels and sea-shells and curlicues; and behind it, on the wall, there was a gilt-framed portrait of the celebrated Emma Abbott, whose main theatrical claim to fame was that she had introduced a trapeze performance into *Romeo and Juliet*, thereby winning for ever the hearts of Leadville's less than classically-minded audiences.

The boy said, 'The porter's coming down again, by and by.'

'Well, good enough,' replied the man, tugging off his gloves. 'Cold out there, wouldn't you say? Freeze your extremities off in half an hour. By the way, my name's Sam Cutforth, *Rocky Mountain News*. Taken me just about a week to get up here.'

'David,' said the boy solemnly, and shook Mr Cutforth's hand once more.

'Know this hotel, do you?' asked Mr Cutforth, pacing around, inspecting the crimson flock wallpaper with its spreading damp patches; and the half-collapsed horsehair sofas. He lifted the wilting leaf of a potted aspidistra, and said, 'This could do with some water.' He wrung out his gloves, one after the other, over the dried-up soil.

'The Grand's better, sir. Newspaper folks usually stay at the Grand. Either that, or the Clarendon.'

'Ah, do they? Well, I suppose it depends on their expenses. On their tastes, too. I prefer a simple room and plenty of money left over for some of life's other diversions. Faro, for example. Do you play faro? How old are you, eleven? No, I suppose you wouldn't.'

At that moment, down the dark curve of the mahogany staircase, the porter came hurrying, brown-jacketed, like an anxious squirrel. He nodded back towards the landing, and said to the boy, 'She's just coming down, son; won't be a moment. Know what she's like; stands on her dignity, even now. Can't go rushing her, everything's got to be dignified, no matter what.'

6

Mr Cutforth pinged the tarnished brass bell on the reception desk.

'Yes, sir, coming to you, sir,' said the porter. He hauled out a huge leather-bound register, and banged it down in front of him. 'Room for the night, sir; the week; or maybe the year? Leadville's pleasant as Eden itself, in summer.'

'The week will do me,' Mr Cutforth replied. He was polishing up his pince-nez with his handkerchief. 'You might tell me what's for supper, too. The last meal I ate was cold corned-beef hash, at Fairplay; and nothing to wash it down with.'

'We're serving a good beef pie today, sir,' said the porter. 'And all the Coors you can drink.' He peered forward as Mr Cutforth signed the register, and asked, 'Come to see the ice-palace, then? Taking some pictures?'

'They told me you people in Leadville were sharp,' said Mr Cutforth, winking at David.

David grinned, pleased to be sharing a grown-up joke.

But he turned then, because a woman had appeared on the staircase, and was slowly descending towards the lobby as if she were making an entrance at a society ball. He saw her feet first, in frayed silk slippers that had once been as pink as roses; then the hem of a cream-coloured skirt, sewn and re-sewn, but recently redecorated with pink ribbon. Around her shoulders the woman wore a thick woollen shawl, and on her head was perched a broad-brimmed hat covered in flowers and feathers. But the crown of the hat had long ago been crushed out of shape, and the flowers were broken and soiled, and the feathers had lost their plumes.

The woman reached the foot of the stairs, and stood for a moment with her hand on the banister, small and middle-aged, pausing for effect, with all the shabbiness of someone who has been poor so long that she finds it hard to remember just how grand the grand times had really been. Nonetheless, she was still extraordinarily fine-looking; and Mr Cutforth stopped cleaning his spectacles and carefully clipped them back on his nose so that he could take a clearer look at her.

It was her eyes that were the most remarkable feature of her face. They were dark, and deep-set, with slightly hooded lids, as if they were expressing what Mr Cutforth would later describe as 'sensuousness and femininity in their most alluring and mysterious aspect'. Her cheeks were rounded but well-boned, and her mouth had the curves of an angel-bow. She

7

wore very little in the way of cosmetics; a touch of powder, a thin crimson gloss for her lips; but it was obvious that once upon a time she had been a great beauty; the kind of woman whose face makes kingdoms; and whose desires sway the self-control of even the most adamant men.

She came forward, and Mr Cutforth for some reason found himself stepping back. With a catch in her throat, she said to David, 'You have a letter for me?'

David held the letter out, and the woman took it. Before she opened it, she glanced across at Mr Cutforth, who snapped his head forward like a cast-iron Sambo money-box and blurted out, 'How d'ye do? Cold day, don't you think?'

The woman allowed the briefest of smiles to cross her lips, the smallest acknowledgement that etiquette would allow. Then she tore open the envelope while the boy and the newspaper photographer and the porter and the weepy-eyed Labrador dog all watched her with unabashed interest.

She read the message quickly. The boy and the photographer and the porter and the dog all examined her face to see if they could guess what it might have said. But she folded the letter up without any expression of surprise or emotion, and tucked it back into its envelope.

'Mrs Roberts said I wasn't to come back without an answer,' said David.

'What?' asked the woman, distractedly. She turned away, the letter clutched more tightly in her hand, and now it became apparent to Mr Cutforth that it had affected her more than she had tried to pretend.

'Mrs Roberts,' David repeated. 'She said she had to have an answer; and that I wasn't to come back without one.'

'Well, then,' the woman breathed, 'I suppose you had better give her one. You may tell her – '

She hesitated, and looked at Mr Cutforth again, almost puzzled, as if she wondered what he was doing here.

Then, in a rush, she said, 'You may tell her *yes*, if you wish. If that is the answer she wants. Well, plainly it is. So, you may tell her yes, and that I shall be there. But you may also tell her that I want no charity, nor any hint of it. Tell her to search inside her soul before she meets me; ask her if the kingdom of Heaven is any more open to those who seek revenge than it is to those who seek love that may be forbidden to them. No, don't tell her that. I shall tell her myself. Tell her simply yes.'

8

David stood, in his cap and his wet woollen gloves, waiting, with the unembarrassed patience of a ten-year-old boy, to receive a small gratuity for going. 'One come and one go at ten cents the went,' as his black friend Walter would have put it.

The woman was flustered. She opened her purse, but Mr Cutforth knew before she started searching inside it that it must be empty. He drew back his raccoon coat, and reached inside his waistcoat pocket for a nickel, which he handed to David with great solemnity.

'Off you go now,' he admonished him. 'And tell Mrs Roberts that it's yes.'

The woman snapped her purse shut, and stared up at Mr Cutforth with hotly-coloured cheeks. Close to, Mr Cutforth could see the forty-year-old wrinkles around her eyes, and the tightening of the mouth, but there was no question that she was still a most magnetic lady. She frowned briefly towards the door as David stepped out into the whirling snow; then looked back at Mr Cutforth, with both dignity and humiliation.

'I suppose I should thank you for your generosity,' she said. 'The fact of the matter is that I left my money in one of my other purses.'

'Of course,' said Mr Cutforth, and bowed his head to her. 'It was a pleasure to oblige.'

'You're Mr—?' she asked, very quickly, as if she wasn't really very interested.

'Mr Sam Cutforth, ma'am. Roving photographic correspondent of the *Rocky Mountain News*, Denver. City founded 1858, newspaper founded 1859.'

The woman took his hand. Mr Cutforth had thought that his own fingers were cold, after sitting on the box of a struggling buggy all the way from the railroad depot on the outskirts of Leadville. But this woman's touch was as chilled as ice, and without thinking, he protectively sandwiched her hand between both of his, a gesture far too intimate for a mere introduction. She withdrew her hand at once, and tightened her shawl around her shoulders.

'I apologize,' said Mr Cutforth. 'I didn't mean to be fresh. It was just that your hands were – well, they were a little cold, that's all. I'm sorry.'

'I have been – somewhat unwell,' the woman told him.

'I'm sorry,' Mr Cutforth repeated. Then 'Is there anything I can do? Perhaps I could go get some medicine for you.'

9

'There's no need, really, thank you very much. I have to go and change. It was pleasant to meet you, Mr Cutforth.'

'You still haven't told me your name,' Mr Cutforth smiled. He was trying to sound friendly and reassuring, but there was a quality about this shabby, grand, chilly-fingered woman that had undermined his usual broad self-confidence. The trouble was, he actually *wanted* something from her. He wanted to know her name, and who she was, and why she was living in such straitened circumstances in Leadville's most threadbare hotel, in winter, in snow that had turned the whole world into a timeless, soundless, suffocating theatre of white.

'My name is Pleasance,' replied the woman. She nodded almost imperceptibly to let him know that their conversation was now over, and then she turned and walked away towards the staircase. She looked back once, as she raised the hem of her skirt to climb the first tread; but she neither smiled nor acknowledged him; and soon she had disappeared up into the darkness.

'Well,' said Mr Cutforth, after she had gone.

'Some *lady*, hunh?' the porter remarked, without looking up from the register. He sniffed. 'Guess you'll want to see your room now. Number three, right in back. Fine view of the mountains, when it stops snowing.'

'Think it will?' asked Mr Cutforth rhetorically, still staring at the shadows into which the woman called Pleasance had vanished with such exaggerated hauteur.

'Think it will what?' queried the porter. Then, 'Care for your vittles now? Pie should be just about baked. Less'n you want to wash up first. There's water in the washstand on your bureau, and a hammer on the wall to break it with.'

Mr Cutforth shook his head. 'I think I'll eat first. What is it, Miss Pleasance or Mrs Pleasance?'

''Taint neither.'

'What do you mean?'

'Exactly that. 'Taint neither. That woman's name ain't Pleasance at all; neither Mrs nor Miss. Name's Roberts. Mrs Elizabeth Roberts.'

'But the woman who sent her the message was called Roberts, too.'

'Sure enough. They're both called Roberts. Mrs Elizabeth Roberts and Mrs Augusta Roberts.'

Mr Cutforth raised his eyebrows. 'Well,' he said again. He

10

didn't want to sound too inquisitive; even though Mrs Roberts had stirred up in him an extraordinary and inexplicable curiosity; and also, quite absurdly, when he thought how offhandedly she had treated him, and how briefly he had known her, a feeling of great sympathy, and concern, as if he ought to do whatever he could to take care of her.

Perhaps that was the magic of beauty, he thought: beauty always demands to be taken care of.

The porter led Mr Cutforth through to the hotel dining-rooms. They were bare, cold, deserted, and smelled of damp. There were twenty tables laid with red gingham tablecloths, and an elk's head on the wall, and a huge domed carving-trolley in which the porter and Mr Cutforth, as they walked across to the far side of the floor, were reflected like two distorted dwarves.

'Like a fire?' the porter asked. 'Kind of chilly in here.'

'You can bring me a whiskey first,' Mr Cutforth suggested. 'And I'll keep my coat on, until you get the logs burning up.'

He had to wait for almost ten minutes before a German-looking waitress with blonde braided hair came in through the door from the kitchen with a measure of whiskey on a tray.

'Are you having the pie, sir?' she asked him, her eyes as bright and inane as a china doll's.

'Is there any choice in the matter?' queried Mr Cutforth.

'Well, there's ox-cheek stew; and I think there's some pickled fish.'

'In that case, I'll stay with the pie. And bring me the bottle that goes with this whiskey, would you, there's a good girl? It's too darn cold for one small tot at a time.'

The porter came in with an armful of logs, dropping four or five of them on the floor with a loud barking clatter. He blew the ashes away from the grate, sneezed, sneezed again, and then began to stack up the fire.

Outside, it was growing dark; the snow was still falling as thickly as before.

'What time does Mrs Roberts come down to eat?' asked Mr Cutforth. The German-looking girl came in with the bottle of whiskey, and he smiled and nodded his thanks. Old Manitou Mash, it said on the label, with an etching of a Red Indian chief. Forgive me, stomach, thought Mr Cutforth, as he poured himself another glass.

11

The porter was having trouble with his matches. At last he said, 'She don't.'

'You mean she doesn't come down here to eat at all? Never?'

'Not never,' said the porter.

'She lives here, though?'

'Sure enough. Her and her husband and two daughters, all in the one room. Number eleven, up by the attic.'

The fire was crackling now, and the porter stood up, and wiped his hands on his trousers. 'Should warm up in a while or so,' he said, reassuringly. Then he turned and regarded the bottle of Old Manitou Mash with an expression of dogged longing.

'Would you. . . ?' asked Mr Cutforth, nodding towards the bottle.

The porter almost jumped in pretended surprise. 'Well, sir, that's Christian of you. Don't mind if I do. Specially these days when it's snowing. Snow plays havoc with the alimentary tract.'

'Sit down,' said Mr Cutforth. And then, when the porter had found himself a glass and noisily scraped a chair across, 'Tell me what you know about Mrs Roberts. I'm interested.'

'Who isn't?' the porter declared. He poured himself a huge glassful of whiskey, and passed it under his nose, closing his eyes as if he were smelling the sweetest of flowers.

'Was she rich, once?' asked Mr Cutforth.

'Rich?' said the porter, opening his eyes wide. 'I'll say she was rich. They were millionaires, the Roberts. Millionaires. They used to say that Mrs Roberts was the richest woman in the world. And now look at her.'

He swallowed whiskey, coughed, shuddered, and then he said, 'The house they used to live in was a palace, I'll tell you. You never saw nothing like it. And that woman used to ride around the streets of Leadville dressed up in ermine, and that's the truth.'

Mr Cutforth took off his spectacles in astonishment. 'Of *course*. Mrs Elizabeth Roberts! But they always used to call her Baby Doe Roberts, didn't they? He pointed back towards the lobby. 'That was really Baby Doe Roberts?'

The porter finished his whiskey, and wiped his mouth. 'Baby Doe as ever breathed.'

'I didn't even realize that the Roberts were still in Colorado,' said Mr Cutforth. 'I didn't even know they were still alive.'

'Oh, you bet,' said the porter. He began to stare longingly at the whiskey again. 'Upstairs, number eleven, next to the attic. The richest folk in the world, as was; *and* their two daughters.'

'And what about Mrs Augusta Roberts?'

The porter looked around the dining-rooms, as if he were suddenly deaf.

'Care for a little more whiskey?' Mr Cutforth asked him, holding up the bottle.

The porter looked at him, shiftily. Mr Cutforth poured him a small splash in the bottom of his glass, and then said, 'Tell me about Mrs Augusta Roberts. Is she the sister-in-law?'

The porter shook his head emphatically. 'No, sir. Mrs Augusta Roberts is the first Mrs Roberts. The original, so to say.'

'Well, well,' said Mr Cutforth. 'So the original Mrs Roberts has sent a message to the second Mrs Roberts, and the answer to whatever question she might have put, is "yes".' He leaned forward on the gingham tablecloth, and asked, 'Did they get on well, the first and second Mrs Roberts?'

'Get on well? I doubt if they scarcely spoke in twenty years. Mrs Augusta hated that Baby Doe something terribly awful; there was a time that Mr Roberts warned her to keep a mile away from Baby Doe day and night, in case she was tempted to do something terribly awful.'

'So what do you think that message said?'

'You could search me,' said the porter. 'I keep myself to myself, mind my own affairs. But those Roberts are so hard down on their luck these days, well, who can say what Mrs Roberts might be thinking of; that's Baby Doe Roberts I mean, although she doesn't like people to call her that, not these days. Says it reminds her of times gone by, when they were rich. Says it makes her feel too sad.'

The German-looking girl came out of the kitchen, pink with heat, carrying a huge blue dinner-plate heaped with hot beef pie. Then she brought a tureen of boiled potatoes, another tureen of winter greens, and a steaming bowl of grits; as well as corn biscuits and a jug of gravy. Mr Cutforth heaped his plate high; then took his fork and began to eat steadily.

'Is Mr Roberts employed these days?' he asked the porter with his mouth full.

'Works at the post office, just like he did years and years ago, before he struck it rich. Mind you, it was only his friends that got him that job. He's getting pretty old now, and wandering. Just remember he was fifty years old when he

13

married Baby Doe. And when was that? Ten years ago, and a good deal more.'

Mr Cutforth forked up some more pie, and chewed, and then said to himself, disbelievingly, 'Baby Doe. How about that.'

The story of Henry T. Roberts and Baby Doe was one of the legendary and often unbelievable scandals of the 1880s, when the Silver Kings of Colorado had been at their wealthiest; when huge classical mansions had risen in the mountains of Leadville as incongruous monuments to the twin principles that money can buy everything and anyone can strike it rich. Those were the days when plain men and woman had dressed in silk and lace and fed from solid silver plates; when bored heiresses had thrown silver dollars at the birds that were pecking the seed off their lawns; when the kindliest of all the successful miners had calculated the handouts he gave while strolling around the city at a rate of $50 a block.

Mr Cutforth found himself staring up at the ceiling of the dining-rooms, and feeling the weight of destiny just above him; in room number eleven, where two of the world's unluckiest lovers must be sitting even now, without dinner, without heat; with nothing to sustain them but the memory of an outrageous affair and a life that at one time had equalled that of emperors.

'If that's it,' said the porter; meaning that Mr Cutforth should either pour him some more whiskey, or consider their conversation at an end.

'Yes, that's it,' Mr Cutforth whispered. He put down his fork.

'Your bag will go up to your room, sir,' said the porter, in one last effort to wheedle another drink. 'As well as those sheerlegs of yours, sir. The *real awkward* ones.'

'Very good, thank you.'

The porter hesitated. 'Is there anything else, sir?'

'Yes, one thing,' said Mr Cutforth. 'I want you to send four portions of the beef pie up to room number eleven; with the compliments of the management. Don't let them refuse it. Tell them it's part of the Winter Festival celebration, something like that. And don't whatever you do say that it came from me.'

The porter stared at him.

'If you would be so kind as to arrange that,' Mr Cutforth asked him, with sufficient sharpness in his voice to make it clear that he was serious.

Later that evening, the snow stopped falling, and a bitterly cold wind sprang up, blowing keen north-westerly through

14

the Sawatch mountains, pluming the snow on the rooftops of Leadville, and keeping even the hardiest prostitutes indoors. At about nine-thirty, the full moon appeared, and gleamed impassively over the frigid streets, and the curved drifts, and the deep glittering snowbanks.

Mr Cutforth, peering through a circular hole which he had scraped in the opaque frost that covered his second-storey window, felt that he was looking out over a secret and tantalizing landscape; a landscape of illusions and cruelty and buried hopes. He set up his tripod, and his heavy wetplate camera, and took several exposures of the yard behind the hotel, where icicles hung like lumps of transparent barley-sugar, and the water-pump had turned into a strange sculpture of spikes and spires.

A small fire crackled and smoked in the corner of Mr Cutforth's brown-wallpapered room, but he had decided to keep on his underwear for yet another night. There was a dark bureau, which smelled of camphor; a leather armchair that looked as if it had been savagely mauled by a bear; a cheval glass that refused to stay at any angle at which he could see himself in it; a high brass bed with white china knobs; an etching of Mount Massive, too rumpled by damp for him to see clearly; and a washstand. Just as the porter had told him, there was a hammer hanging on a nail by the washstand, for guests to crack the ice in their shaving-water in the morning.

He stood by the window, fully clothed, his raccoon coat slung around his shoulders, and thought of Baby Doe. He hoped very much that she and Henry Roberts had accepted the pie. He wondered what kind of a man Roberts could be; a king one year, a miserable pauper the next. What did that do to a man's heart, and a man's sense of being a man? Yet Baby Doe had stayed with him. He must at least have been man enough to keep her undying devotion.

Mr Cutforth drained the last of the Old Manitou Mash into his glass. Perhaps, he thought, she had nowhere else to go.

Downstairs, in the parlour, someone began to play the piano, and sing in a harsh, high voice the song of Mollie May, who up until her death in 1887 had been Leadville's favourite harlot.

'Talk if you will of her,
But speak no ill of her –
The sins of the living are not of the dead
Remember her charity

15

Forget all disparity;
Let her judges be those whom she sheltered and fed.'

Mr Cutforth smiled, recognizing the song. He reached into the pocket of his tweed coat, and found his pipe. He was 31, Mr Cutforth, but he had come out West from Massachusetts just ten years too late to have experienced the real frontier; the way that it had been when Molly May was queen of Leadville's red-light district, along with other prostitutes like Molly b'Damn and Contrary Mary and Little Gold Dollar; the way that it had been when William O'Brien and James G. Fair and all the great kings of silver had still been alive.

Leadville was still rich: altogether the town's assets were probably worth $200 million. But wealth had brought greater respectability, and a desire to impress the outside world. There were still dozens of gambling hells, and any man with the price of it could have as many women as he wanted, singly or collectively, and some of them would rinse out his underwear, too, and cook him breakfast. Yet the wildness had gone. There was music now, and theatre, and lectures from Europe. There was electric light in the streets. And some of the miners would sit in the saloons and play faro and talk about the 'good old days' when a population of only 14,000 had enjoyed the benefits of 35 brothels, 118 gambling houses, and 120 saloons, not counting 19 that sold nothing but beer.

In those days, they said, you wouldn't have known it was Sunday unless you looked in your diary.

Mr Cutforth opened his worn brown leather tobacco-pouch, and discovered that it was almost empty. He remembered now: he had allowed himself a last fill at Fairplay, after his lunch, while he was waiting for the locomotive to be dug out of the snow. He guessed that the porter would have some tobacco, even if it was only a crumbled-up cigar. So he neatly packed his camera away into its case; a precaution that he always took when he was travelling, after an inquisitive maid had once dropped a $30 Fox Talbot wetplate camera and broken it; and went down to the lobby.

He was surprised to see that, although it was well after eleven o'clock, the dining-rooms were quite crowded, and the lobby was thick with a haze of tobacco smoke. He went up to the reception desk and pinged the bell, and after a while the porter came hurrying through from the office with a dishcloth over his arm and his hair sticking up at the back.

'God Almighty, rushed off my darned two feet!' he exclaimed.

'What's all this?' asked Mr Cutforth.

'Fire at the Clarendon, that's what; fire at the Clarendon. That's what comes of employing a fancified chef like Mussewer La Pierce. Throws a temper and throws a pan of cooking-oil; and that's why half of the Clarendon's diners have come down here.'

'Do you have some tobacco?' Mr Cutforth asked him. 'Any brand will do it.'

'There's Peabody's chew-and-cheroo shop right on the corner, that should still be open. Take your coat, though, sir. It'll be a short walk, but a precious cold one.'

A smiling man in a long sealskin coat came up and took Mr Cutforth by the hand. On the other side of the lobby, two ladies of the evening in fluffy fur wraps were laughing and singing. The smiling man said, 'Shouldn't I know you from somewhere? Denver, maybe.'

'Maybe,' replied Mr Cutforth.

'This your first time in Leadville?'

'Not the last, I hope. It seems like a jolly enough place, and eccentric, too. I must say that I like an eccentric place.'

'Ah, well,' said the smiling man. 'It's too much money that makes folk eccentric.'

'I don't believe that too much money is any kind of a problem.'

'You don't?' said the smiling man, still relentlessly smiling. 'Well, maybe I could help you there.' He reached into an inside pocket, and produced two stock certificates, handsomely engraved; fifty shares each in the Matchless Mine, Leadville. 'I acquired these in settlement of a long-standing debt; a fellow who owed me for whiskey, and dynamite, and gambling.'

'Well?' asked Mr Cutforth, sceptically.

'Well, you see what it says here, in black print; the mine's assets are $4 million; and that means these shares are worth $10,000 at today's prices. But, the thing of it is, I have to leave Leadville quite shortly, on account of my health. The mountain air's too thin for me, that's what my doctor advises. So I have to dispose of these shares as soon as I can; and believe me, I'm sad to do it. But I could let you have the entire one hundred shares for $2,000 flat; here and now; signed and delivered; in cash.'

Mr Cutforth began to fasten up his raccoon coat, and open out his gloves. One of the prostitutes had begun to dance, holding up her chocolate-coloured velveteen skirts, and revealing layers and layers of beautiful Brussels lace. The man on the piano was playing a very jangly, quick-tempo version of *Swanee River*. There was more laughter; the outside door opened yet again, and blew in more snow; and the lobby began to grow almost unbearably crowded.

'What do you say then?' asked the smiling man, holding up the share certificates. 'Or what would you say to fifteen hundred?'

'I would say keep your shares to retire on,' replied Mr Cutforth. 'I happen to know that the Matchless Mine remains the property of its original owner, who was Henry T. Roberts; and I also happen to know that Mr Henry T. Roberts is not only still living in Leadville, but resides right here, in the Imperial Hotel. I would also say that even if these certificates were genuine, which I vouch they're not; then they wouldn't be worth the paper they're printed on, or else Mr Roberts and his family wouldn't be living as destitute as they are now.'

The smiling man's smile didn't even quiver. He tucked the share certificates back into his coat, rubbed his hands briskly, and said, 'Well, then, how about a game of rummy, to warm us up?'

Mr Cutforth shook his head. 'I'm going out for tobacco, thanks.'

He pushed his way out through the bustling throng; and through the door, and on to the snowy sidewalk. The door swung closed behind him; sealing off the raucous singing and the jangling piano-playing and the laughter of whores and miners and drunken tourists; and out here it was intolerably cold, but silent.

He could see the tobacco store at the end of the next block. A wooden Indian stood outside, wearing a huge head-dress of snow. Mr Cutforth buried his hands in his pockets, lowered his head, and began to trudge through the snow towards it, his boots squeaking with every step.

He passed the shuttered and frosty exterior of the Elegant Art Photograph shop, proprietor H. Needles; and a little further along The Professor of Tattoo, with a card outside his darkened window which asserted that for only $200 the professor would tattoo any heraldic device or motto 'in the discreetest of

18

locations, where they may never be detected during the normal currency of daily intercourse.'

He had nearly reached the lighted windows of the tobacco store when he heard pattering footsteps a little way behind him. He looked back and saw a woman in a dark coat and a dark shawl hurriedly crossing the street from the direction of Dr Charles Broadbent's medical clinic. Her head was lowered against the wind, and in spite of the rutted and icy tracks left in the roadway by horse-drawn sleighs, she was almost running. As she reached the wooden sidewalk, she stepped up too quickly, missed her footing, and fell. Under the frigid moon, his fur coat jostling wet against his face, Mr Cutforth ran back to help her. He held on to the closest verandah-post, caught her elbow, and said, 'Here, let me lift you up.' Her coat was smothered in snow, and one of her boot-heels had snapped off. She was quaking with cold.

She hopped gracelessly on to the sidewalk. 'I'm not hurt,' she said. 'I slipped, that's all. It's very icy.' Then she turned and looked up at him; and saw who it was that had helped her.

'Mr Cutforth. Well, my thanks for your courtesy.'

'Not at all Mrs Roberts.'

Her eyes widened a little. She looked away; out across the white and deserted street. 'You've been told, then. Mr Finney, I suppose.'

'Mr Finney?'

'The porter. He means well; but he has a susceptibility for whiskey. When he drinks, he talks. I think he's really quite proud of having us there. I can't altogether blame him.'

Mr Cutforth held his arms behind his back. The moonlight reflected from his pince-nez, making him look strangely sinister and blind. 'I really wanted to know if there was anything I could do,' he told her.

She shivered. 'Do? Why should there possibly be anything that you could do?'

'I don't know. Perhaps I'm not explaining myself too well. But you are Baby Doe, aren't you?'

'I never use that name, Mr Cutforth; and I would much prefer it if you didn't either.'

'Please, I'm sorry. But I'd really like to talk to you. Both you, and your husband.'

'What for?' she asked. Her voice was flat now, no longer interested.

19

'Because. . . well, because I feel compelled to. And because I think our readers would be really interested to find out what happened to you. . . how you're living these days. You've suffered misfortune, Mrs Roberts. I don't mean to sound as if I'm patronizing, or gloating, or trying to make capital out of you. But the moment I first saw you, I said to myself, there's a woman with great dignity and grace; and if she's here, at the Imperial Hotel, well, then, there must be a story to be told. A human story.'

Mrs Roberts looked up at him; and even though her pinched face was scarlet with cold, she was still beautiful, even then, out on that freezing night in Leadville, Colorado, ten thousand feet above mean sea-level, and a million miles away from days gone by.

'I must get back,' she said, with quiet composure.

'But, Mrs Roberts – '

'No,' she insisted. 'I am no longer an object of interest; not to anybody at all, save to my poor husband and to my two poor daughters. My husband is unwell, it is better that you forget you ever saw me; better still to forget that you even knew my name.'

'The paper could pay for your story. Ten, maybe fifteen dollars.'

'Mr Cutforth, the diamond necklace that Henry gave me on the morning of our wedding cost $90,000. I am done with money; done with bargaining.'

Mr Cutforth rubbed the rime away from his beard. 'Well, then, I apologize,' he said. 'I didn't mean to offend you. That was the very last thing I wanted to do. I'm sorry. Goodnight, and I promise not to make a nuisance of myself any more.'

'Please,' she said, more softly. 'You haven't been a nuisance at all. You were gallant enough to help me when I fell.'

'It's, uh, well, it's nothing,' said Mr Cutforth. He backed away. 'I have to go buy myself some tobacco, that's why I was out here.'

'Mr Cutforth – '

'No, no,' he said, raising his hand. 'You don't have to say anything. All I can tell you that makes any sense is that I'm usually a loud, opinionated, confident kind of a man; but that when I first saw you, this afternoon, I was lost for anything intelligible to say. How can I explain it to you? I'm sorry, I can't explain it. I took one look at you and felt that I wanted to help you, take care of you; do something romantic and drastic that

20

would change your life back to what it should have been. I felt *compelled*. Does that sound completely ridiculous?'

Mrs Roberts stood on the windy sidewalk watching Mr Cutforth for a whole chilly minute. Then she reached up and gently tugged at the sleeve of his furry raccoon coat.

'Mr Cutforth,' she said, so quietly that he could hardly hear her, 'I was born to nothing; for most of my life I lived as nothing. I have returned to nothing. The editor of the *Leadville Evening Chronicle* said that Henry and I had lived our lives in a perfect circle, from rags to riches and back to rags; and that we should be an example to everyone who thinks that wealth can be acquired by chance.'

'And what do *you* think?'

She said nothing for a moment, but lifted her head with remembered pride. Then she whispered, 'We still have the Matchless. One day, perhaps, it will all be different. One day, perhaps, I will be able to dress myself in ermine again.'

'Do you really want to?'

Mrs Roberts looked at him with those dark, hooded eyes; and for a moment Mr Cutforth saw something in her expression that he couldn't understand; an emotion of which he had no experience.

'You have never been really rich, Mr Cutforth; or you would never ask that question. Now, I have to go.'

'Mrs Roberts – '

'Goodnight, Mr Cutforth.'

She hobbled on one boot-heel back towards the hotel. He saw her open the door, releasing a burst of light and laughter. Then the door closed and the street was deserted again. The wind worried around the verandah, and feathered the snow. Mr Cutforth remained where he was for a moment or two; but it was too cold for much in the way of serious reflection; and so he turned back towards the chew-and-cheroo store, clapping his hands as he went to restore the circulation that both the freezing wind and Mrs Roberts' remoteness had constricted.

The store was warm, bare-boarded, and musky with the fragrance of Latakias and Burleys. An old grey-bearded man in a long grey duster coat was measuring out chewing-tobacco for another oldtimer sitting on a keg in a shaggy fur jacket and a shaggy fur hat that obscured everything except his plum-coloured buttony nose.

21

'Be with you in a minute, son,' the grey-beard told Mr Cutforth.

'That's all right,' Mr Cutforth acknowledged, and went up to the black iron stove and rubbed his hands over the red-hot lid. 'I'm not in any hurry.'

'You visiting, or prospecting?' asked the grey-beard, balancing his tall brass scales.

'Visiting,' said Mr Cutforth.

'Seen the ice-castle yet?'

'I plan to go tomorrow.'

'That's something, that ice-castle,' grey-beard asserted. 'You won't see nothing like it if'n you live to be twice my age; not again; it's a one-time wonder; one in a million million.'

'Well, I've heard that it's pretty spectacular,' said Mr Cutforth. He looked around at the rows of burled walnut tobacco jars, each with its own decoratively-painted label.

The old-timer in the shaggy fur hat suddenly said, in a harsh voice, 'That mine that old Jim McCorquodale was excavating down at Cripple Creek; what a borrasca *that* turned out to be. He was digging down there for a month and a half before he twigged that the Hilary Brothers must've salted it; did you know that? And that's why he hit Dennis Hilary with that three-legged stool and damn near popped his eye out, too.'

'Had an excuse, then?' the grey-beard remarked.

'What do you think? That mine was scraped so deep you could have walked through to Australia. There was nothing in it; never had been much. But Gideon Hilary, he had the notion of firing a shotgun loaded with silver pellets, slap-bang into the rockface; so that when Jim looked it over, prior to buying it, why, he thought he had the May Queen mine all over again.'

Mr Cutforth said, 'Pardon me for interrupting; but did you ever know Henry T. Roberts?'

The old man in the shaggy fur hat shifted himself around on his keg; and glared at Mr Cutforth with glittering, beaver-like eyes. 'Henry T. Roberts? What does Henry T. Roberts have to do with Jim McCorquodale? And besides, do I *know* you, sir?'

Mr Cutforth came forward and held out his hand. The old man in the shaggy hat stared at it in surprise and disgust, as if Mr Cutforth had suddenly produced a dead mine-rat out of his sleeve. 'Well, now,' he said. 'This is kind of improper.'

'Oh, don't you take no notice of Squirrel here,' said the grey-beard behind the counter, wrapping up his chewing-tobacco in

22

a paper twist. 'My friend Squirrel here thinks he's king of the mountain; won't talk to visitors; not unless he's known them for forty years; and won't talk nothing but silver.'

'In that case, I'm proud to know you,' Mr Cutforth said, and shook Squirrel's reluctant hand as if he were pumping water out of an unprimed well.

'Hope y'are,' gruffed Squirrel.

Mr Cutforth said to old grey-beard, 'How about a good two ounces of best smoking-tobacco? And maybe Mr Squirrel here can tell me something about Henry T. Roberts while you're weighing up.'

He produced a silver dollar out of his waistcoat pocket; and bit it; and looked at Squirrel, and inclined his head, as if to suggest, well, here it is, a silver dollar, you can have it if you feel like talking. He flipped it, and said 'heads' and slapped it on to the back of his hand; then peered at it, and said, 'Heads it is.'

Squirrel glanced at old grey-beard, and rearranged his buttocks on his keg. 'Humph,' he said. 'Not at all usual; this kind of thing. Asking questions, expecting answers. Not a deputy, are you? Not some kind of half-fangled kind of a lawman?'

Mr Cutforth shook his head.

'Well,' said Squirrel, 'one dollar buys a fair amount of liquor across the street; enough to get a man happy.'

'Tell him if you want to,' said the old grey-beard. He grinned and winked at Mr Cutforth as he unscrewed the tobacco jar marked Indianhead. 'But if you *don't* want to tell him, then *don't.*'

Squirrel noisily cleared his sinuses. 'Long as you never tell that it came from me. But he's a sick man, that Henry T. Roberts. Dying, I'd say. He's got that yellow look about him that Roaring George Dunn had, just before he died of the fever up at Yippee. Sick, and trembling; you go take a look at him, he runs the post office. Then you'll see. Can't scarcely hold a sheet of paper so that it don't rustle and shake.'

'And Mrs Roberts?' asked Mr Cutforth, more gently.

Squirrel snorted; thought for a while; swilled phlegm around in his mouth, and at last spat it into the tobacco-store cuspidor, leaving a glistening web trailing from his beard.

'Mrs Roberts? Is that who you're interested in?' he wanted to know.

Mr Cutford said nothing; but waited for Squirrel to reply, which he knew he inevitably would.

'Mrs Roberts is not a woman to be interested in,' he said.

'Mrs Roberts don't live for nobody excepting that dying man of hers; and on the memories of what was. Any man with any sense stays away from a woman like that.'

Mr Cutforth glanced towards the grey-beard behind the counter. Old grey-beard was holding up his packet of pipe-tobacco, and it was plain from the expression on his face that he was advising Mr Cutforth not to ask any more questions. The tragedy of Henry T. Roberts was the tragedy which every miner feared: to strike it rich, and then to lose everything. To the prospectors and businessmen of Leadville, the very presence of the Roberts family, in their single room next to the attic at the Imperial Hotel, was like a curse, an inland albatross.

Squirrel said, 'That Henry Roberts, I saw him one day coming out of the Clarendon Hotel, and he was wearing a top-hat, and a fur coat you could've mistook for a genuine still-alive grizzly, and there was rings on his fingers with diamonds like ice-cubes, and his shoes shining; and I saw one poor young prospector with raggedy trousers come up to him, and say, "Mr Roberts, what makes you a better man than me? You tell me that Mr Roberts." And do you know what that Henry Roberts told him? He said, "Luck, my boy, that's all; because there's only a regulated allocation of luck in this here universe, and some of us gets a share and others don't; and I did, and you didn't; and that's the difference, so you step out of my way, because it's nothing to do with me that I'm rich and it's nothing to do with you that you're poor, and there's an end to it." '

Mr Cutforth took off his pince-nez and looked at squirrel with watery, unfocused eyes. 'Do you think that Henry Roberts actually believed that?' he asked.

Squirrel opened up his packet of chewing-tobacco and inspected it carefully. Then he said, 'Who knows? Henry Roberts was a pretty puzzling kind of a fellow; hard to figure out. Good-looking as all hell. Drew the women like flies round a jackass; but hard to figure out. Although, who isn't?'

Mr Cutforth nodded, and handed Squirrel the silver dollar. Squirrel tucked it somewhere complicated under his fur coat, and then snorted again and sat back on his keg as if he had never heard of Henry T. Roberts, or anything to do with any-thing. He said to old grey-beard, 'Not as cold as it was in Ward-ner, when I was looking for gold. Not a damned bit of it.'

At breakfast the following morning, while Mr Cutforth was

24

eating bacon and eggs and grits, Finney the porter came into the dining-rooms and whispered confidentially in his ear, 'They declined the pie, sir.'

Mr Cutforth laid down his knife and fork, and sat up straight. He found that he was quite distressed.

Finney said, 'They said that they could never accept charity, not on any account.'

'Who said? Mr Roberts, or Mrs Roberts?'

Finney pulled a face. 'Mrs, most likely, I'd say. It's Mrs who does most of the talking. Mr, well, Mr just goes to the post office, and then comes back. There's not much spunk left in Mr; and, if you ask me, he could use a piece of pie.'

Mr Cutforth finished his breakfast without much appetite, although the bacon was crisp and the coffee was hot and strong. Several people came into the dining-rooms and said, 'Good morning,' although he had never seen them before. One fat man with a haywire ginger moustache said, 'Fine day for a snowball fight.'

Mr Cutforth left the table and walked through to the lobby, where the boiler was spitting and crackling with fresh wood, and an old man with one arm was making a fairly poor job of sweeping up last night's cigar-butts, hundreds of which had carpeted the floor like the flattened dung of some pungent herd of passing elks. Mr Cutforth went to the window, and stood with his hands in his pockets looking out at the snow, which was now falling even more thickly than it had last night. He had slept very badly. Somebody had been arguing and banging around until two o'clock in the morning in the room across the hallway; and even when they had at last decided to call a truce, and he had been able to close his eyes and doze, he had dreamed of Baby Doe; in ermine and diamonds; and wrapped in snow; Baby Doe slipping in the street without anybody to catch her; Baby Doe closing her eyes in bitter acceptance of a fate that would last for ever and ever.

At dawn he had sat up in bed and smoked a pipe of tobacco. Why should he care so much? he had asked himself. He was a newspaper photographer, a journalist. He had seen tragedies far worse than this. He had seen young children dead of typhoid, and wives with their heads half shot off. Most of the families of Colorado would have been delighted to have been able to stay at the Imperial Hotel in Leadville; for all that they would have to share a room. And nobody who had seen the shanties and shacks of Cripple Cleek and Climax and Scofield, Utah, could ever say that the Roberts family were the worst off as far as accommodation was concerned.

Perhaps it was simply that even those who have never known wealth can feel pity for those who have had it and then lost it. But was it really pity that Mr Cutforth felt?

He wondered, with a flush of embarrassment that brought two spots of pinkness to his protuberant cheeks, whether the truth of it was that he had become infatuated with Mrs Elizabeth Roberts; or worse.

He was about to ask Finney where he could find himself a newspaper when he heard the lightest of footsteps on the staircase. Down came Baby Doe, in worn brown boots, and a camel-coloured coat with dark brown frogging. She wore a large dark brown hat, with a veil, and she carried an umbrella. She walked quickly across the lobby, but not quickly enough to prevent Mr Cutforth from stepping forward and opening the street door for her.

'Good morning, Mrs Roberts,' he said, bowing his head.

She hesitated, and then she said, 'Good morning, Mr Cutforth. If you'll excuse me.'

'I'm sorry. You're going out? The weather doesn't look very pleasant this morning.'

'I haven't been out for pleasure, Mr Cutforth, for many more years than I care to remember.'

Mr Cutforth opened the street door a little wider. A keen cold wind blew into the lobby and ruffled the illustrated magazines on the sofa, and made the fire in the boiler quietly flare. A fat man in a green tailcoat looked around in annoyance, and called, 'Close that damned door, sir.'

Mr Cutforth had no option but to let Mrs Roberts push past him, and step outside. He closed the door behind her, but stood with his face against the window, watching her cross the street diagonally, her umbrella raised against the softly-pelting snow. He bit his lip. Then, decisively, he ran upstairs, unlocked his room, and took down his overcoat and his camera-case. Within two or three minutes, he was dressed up for the weather, with a long scarf wound three times around his neck; and was struggling out of the front door of the Imperial Hotel with all his photographic equipment, including his unmanageable tripod.

He crossed the street, and tried to find Baby Doe's footprints

26

on the opposite sidewalk. Only four or five people had walked that way this morning, but the snow was falling so densely that their footprints had already been blurred, and it was almost impossible to tell which were the bootmarks of striding miners, and which were the delicate feet of Baby Doe. He stood where he was for a moment, squinting against the glare, the snowflakes clinging to the lenses of his spectacles and dissolving in watery patterns of crystal.

A horse-drawn sleigh jingled past, and the driver waved a hand and called out, 'Sonofabitchofday, ain't it?' and jingled on.

Mr Cutforth thought he glimpsed a dark figure at the far end of the street; and hefting up his case and his tripod, he began to walk after it, slowly at first, but then more quickly, his feet slipping from time to time in the snow, his tripod banging awkwardly and regularly against his case.

He passed a short row of stores, saloons, and a 'Home-Cooked' restaurant. All of them looked dead and deserted, their windows dark. The restaurant was superseded by a tumble-down livery stable, its timbers protruding through the snow like the black skeleton of a wrecked ship. Then there was nothing but the whirling snow and the sky the colour of tarnished bronze, and the felty sound of his boots in the freshly-fallen fields of white.

He stopped. It was so silent that he could hear the snow pattering on to his hat, and his own gasping breath. He must have made a mistake. She couldn't have come this way. Perhaps she had gone into the restaurant for cheap left-overs, so that her husband and daughters could have some breakfast. He looked around him. The snow was so thick that now it was almost impossible to see where the town had vanished.

But as he turned, he glimpsed it again: the dark hurrying figure. And again he picked up his camera-case and his tripod from out of the snow, and went stumbling after it, as if it were some alluring will-o'-the-wisp, a dark and dancing fairy who enticed innocent newspaper photographers to unsuspected and unimaginable fates.

He struggled on for another half-mile, and then, to his astonishment, he began to make out the ghostly outline of an enormous building, gradually becoming visible through the blizzard. He almost forgot his pursuit of Baby Doe, and trudged forward with dogged, abrupt steps, nearer and nearer, and

27

with each step his frustration and his tiredness changed increasingly into awe and, eventually, delight.

He stopped, and put down his equipment, and propped his hands on his hips, and said to himself, 'My God. Look at that. My God.'

Towering nearly a hundred feet above him was a medieval castle, its turrets billowing with snow; a vast fortress with battlements and buttresses and circular towers. Frozen flags, nearly a dozen of them, flew stiffly from each turret, and at the entrance stood a massive statue of a woman bearing a scroll.

Even in the corroded darkness of a snowstorm, the castle shone with an extraordinary, unnatural translucence; a dream castle; a castle of wintry extravagance; the kind of castle that men could imagine but should never have come to be. It was constructed, as Mr Cutforth already knew, out of thousands of blocks of ice. But knowing in advance that it was constructed out of blocks of ice and actually seeing it in front of him were two quite different things. It enthralled him: the way it shone, the sheer incredible wastefulness of it, the pomp, the absurd yet wonderful imagination that had built anything so fantastic in the sure knowledge that by springtime it would melt away.

Now he saw the dark figure which he had been pursuing go to the small wooden ticket-office which stood outside the castle gates. He picked up his camera and started after her once more, convinced now that it was Baby Doe. The figure disappeared through the castle gates just as he himself reached the ticket-office, and fumbled for his entrance fee of 25 cents.

'Guidebook?' the red-nosed man behind the ticket window asked him.

'Later,' he said, and hurried towards the entrance.

Mr Cutforth had already read the stunning facts about the ice-palace. Covering five acres, it had cost $20,000 to build, making it the largest and the most expensive building ever made anywhere out of ice. Work had started on it two months ago, when 260 loggers and carpenters and stonemasons had erected wooden frames on which the blocks of ice would be supported, and then trekked out to the lakes of the local water company to hew out the ice itself.

Leadville was so cold in winter that the ice in the lakes was over a foot and a half thick. It had been chopped into blocks, 20 inches by 30 inches; and when the blocks had been constructed into towers and battlements within their wooden frames, they had been sprayed with water to freeze them solidly together.

Inside the castle, the chill was penetrating, and Mr Cutforth couldn't help shivering. All around him, electric lights were embedded in the supporting pillars of ice; and by the strange opalescent light which they cast, he saw Baby Doe quickly mounting a wide staircase just ahead of him. The staircase was carpeted with hessian to prevent visitors from slipping, but its banisters were fashioned out of perfect glacial ice. Mr Cutforth felt that he was still dreaming; a dream of panic and cold-heartedness and unrealized love.

He followed Baby Doe as closely as he dared, his breath steaming, his fingers frostbitten, even inside his gloves, but the back of his flannel shirt soaked with sweat. At the top of the staircase, he found himself in a vast enclosed skating-rink, nearly 200 feet long and almost 100 feet wide, illuminated electrically. The spiralling scratches of those few skaters who had braved this morning's snowstorm sparkled on the ice like threads of unravelling silver.

The skating-rink echoed with distorted laughter. Mr Cutforth looked urgently around, his tripod under his arm, but Baby Doe was nowhere to be seen. There was an arched entrance at the side of the rink, and he decided that she must have gone through to the next room.

He found himself in a ballroom, as large as that of the Waldorf-Astoria in New York. There was no sign of Baby Doe there, either; and so he crossed the icy floor to the dining-room, which was incongruously furnished with upholstered chairs and sofas, and heated by a pot-bellied wood-burning stove to make it tolerably comfortable to sit in. No Baby Doe; and so Mr Cutforth trailed through to the long exhibition hall, lugging his camera-case and his tripod, and growing increasingly irritable.

On either side of him, exhibits of Leadville's wealth and industry were enclosed in brightly transparent blocks of ice. Mineral samples, soap, pickles, and even a display of frozen sewing-machines. There were frozen shirts and underwear from the T. G. Underhill company; oysters and fish and bottles of beer; and from the Denver & Rio Grande Railroad, a panorama of its route from Denver to Leadville, stretching through fifteen continuous blocks of ice.

Still there was no sign of Baby Doe. Mr Cutforth propped his tripod against an icy wall, took out his handkerchief and loudly blew his nose. A guide in a thick fur-trimmed coat came waddling up to him, all fuzzy tobacco-stained moustaches and golden watch-chain, and said, 'Anything I can do to help? What do you think of her? Quite a place, isn't she? Cold, though. Need your long johns.'

'Did you see a woman pass you by?' asked Mr Cutforth. 'Brown coat, brown hat?'

'Well, *one* of them was dressed like that,' said the guide. He tugged at his nose and pointed towards a narrow ice staircase at the far end of the chilly exhibition hall; as if it were necessary to tug in order to point. 'They went up there; to the north tower. You can get a fine view of not very much at all, in this weather.'

'There were *two* of them?' asked Mr Cutforth.

'As I observed it.'

Mr Cutforth tipped the guide a dime, and gathered up his case, and made his way as hurriedly as he could along to the far door. The stairs went up in a spiral, disappearing into the cold curved translucent heights of the north tower; and as he climbed them, Mr Cutforth could hear the wind blowing sadly across the open door at the top.

Eventually, he came out on to the battlements. After 32 stairs, he was gasping for breath, but the air was too cold to be taken down into his lungs in anything but small sips; and he began to feel giddy from exertion and lack of oxygen. He sat on his case for a while by the doorway, shivering and sipping air, until he had recovered. The snow tumbled across the icy crenellations like dandelion clocks, and whirled around his feet.

After a minute or two, he felt ready to go on. But this time he left his equipment where it was, and walked cautiously around the tower to see if Baby Doe and her unexpected companion were somewhere close by.

He almost bumped into them. They were standing on the far side of the entrance; in the shelter of a small pointed turret, talking. Fortunately, Baby Doe had her back to him, and even though the other woman glanced sharply sideways and saw him, she obviously had no idea who he was, because she ignored him and carried on her conversation regardless.

Mr Cutforth retreated, and carefully negotiated his way around the tower in the other direction, until he was only three or four feet away from the two women, but still out of sight behind one of the protruding buttresses of ice. It was piercingly cold up there, and his teeth were chattering like a Gatling gun, but over the noise of his teeth and the blowing of the wind, he could still hear almost everything the women were saying to each other.

The woman who had seen him was plain, large-faced, with small severe spectacles quite like his own. She looked like the kind of woman who would complain about cigar-smoking in a railroad car; and would send back plates at a restaurant because there was dried food stuck to them. She wore a black coat piped with black braid, and a black bonnet which somehow contrived to look as if it had been put on upside-down. Her voice was clipped and sharp; but the words she was saying were surprisingly emotional. It sounded almost as if she were pleading with Baby Doe.

'You must know yourself that there are times when passion overrides good reason,' the woman declared. 'You must know that there are times when rage or jealousy or love itself can blind you to sense, and even to Christian morality.'

'You are not questioning my morals, I hope?' said Baby Doe; although quite gently. 'I did not come here for that.'

'I am grateful that you came at all,' the woman told her. 'At least I know now how seriously ill he is.' She hesitated, and then she added, 'At least I know now the true measure of my blame.'

Mr Cutforth pulled his scarf up over his mouth, and missed the next thing that Baby Doe said. But he caught the woman telling her, '. . . never face him again, not to speak to, although of course I have seen him often.'

'He would not be angry with you, if you were to see him,' Baby Doe replied.

'No,' the woman said. 'I have thought of it, but I think I have already done enough to hurt you both. I wish only for you to beg him on my behalf to forgive me, as I have now forgiven him; so that when the time comes I may go to my grave with a quiet mind.'

The wind whistled and whipped around the turrets; and even in his furry raccoon coat, Mr Cutforth felt as if all the warmth were gradually draining out of his bones, leaving him with a spine and a pelvis as icy as the palace itself. Why the two women had chosen to meet each other in such a freezing and inhospitable place, he couldn't imagine; unless there was an element of self-punishment in it. The mortification of the body, as well as the conscience.

'My dear, we both bear the same name, and have both loved the same man,' said the woman in spectacles. 'Whatever our bitterness towards each other in the past, let us at least try to

31

accept now what fate has awarded us, while Henry still lives. I ask for nothing more but a kiss.'

Mr Cutforth now retreated from his chilly hiding-place, and slid his way awkwardly back to the entrance, where he had left his camera and his tripod. He bit off his gloves finger by finger, and with bright crimson hands, opened up the catches of his case and took out his Fox Talbot camera. He wished very heartily that he had brought his Kodak, with its flexible film, but he had supposed when he had left Denver that he would be taking only large-scale scenic pictures, and well-posed groups.

Numbly, he assembled the camera and mounted it on its tripod. He loaded the wetplate into it; and prayed that in this snowstorm there would be sufficient light for a reasonable exposure. Then he covered his head with his black photographer's cape, and shuffled with his camera into a position close to the edge of the battlements.

He could hear the two women talking still; although from what they were saying it sounded as if they were close to making their goodbyes. He withdrew from his cape, twisted the camera around on its bezel so that it was pointing at the women, and called out clearly, '*Mrs Roberts!*'

Both of them turned, startled. Mr Cutforth squeezed the bulb of his camera, and the shutter gave a measured mechanical click; the slowest exposure that Mr Cutforth had dared to allow himself.

'Mr Cutforth! What is the meaning of this?' Baby Doe demanded, stepping forward with her skirts raised to prevent them from trailing in the ice.

Mr Cutforth raised his hat. 'I thank you, Mrs Roberts. I am only doing my job. Please pardon the intrusion.'

'What has he done?' snapped the woman in spectacles. 'What have you done, my man?'

'He has taken our likeness,' said Baby Doe, her angel-bow mouth pursed up in surprising bitterness.

'Well, he has no right,' said the woman in spectacles. 'Sir, whoever you are, you must surrender that picture at once!'

'I'm afraid not,' replied Mr Cutforth. 'The law is quite clear on the matter of privacy; and those who stand and talk in public places cannot seek any protection in law from being photographed, no matter how compromising their meeting might be.'

Baby Doe stared at Mr Cutforth for a moment or two, and then unbuttoned and rebuttoned her gloves in a jerky little gesture of disapproval and disappointment.

32

'I thought you were a different kind of a man, Mr Cutforth.'

'I am a recorder of historical events, Mrs Roberts, first and foremost. It is my work.'

'And you consider that this event is historical? A personal meeting between two women whose lives have already been disastrously affected by public attention?'

Mr Cutforth disassembled his camera, and knelt down to put it carefully away in its case. 'It is the end of a great story, Mrs Roberts. If anything at all that I have seen in Leadville has been worthy of photographic record, including this mighty palace of ice, it is you and Mrs Roberts here meeting on this tower together and talking of forgiveness.'

'This is *quite* outrageous,' said the woman in spectacles. 'Which is your journal, my man? I shall speak at once to your editor, and have you dismissed!'

'No, ma'am, you won't,' said Mr Cutforth. He stood up, holding his case and his tripod. He looked at Baby Doe through pince-nez that were fogged with cold. He could see, however, that there was an expression on her face of considerable sadness; a blurry look of familiar defeat.

'I'll say good day,' he nodded, and made back towards the entrance. As he started to climb down the spiral staircase, though, Baby Doe called out, 'Mr Cutforth!' and he stopped, and turned.

She appeared, with snow melting on the shoulders of her coat. In the diffuse amber light from the electric lamps that were embedded in the tower walls, she looked even more remarkably beautiful and tragic than ever; and Mr Cutforth would have given anything to have been able to photograph her as she was then.

'Mr Cutforth,' she appealed, 'I beg you not to publish that picture, if you have a heart.'

Mr Cutforth paused; and then slowly shook his head. 'It is my job, Mrs Roberts. It is what I am paid to do.'

'Is there nothing I can do to make you change your mind?'

'I don't think so.'

'But you said you wanted to help me. Surely you can see that this is the very best way that you can.'

'I did want to help you,' said Mr Cutforth. 'I still do. But you are not the kind of woman that most men are capable of helping, Mrs Roberts. You are somebody special, who is beyond my reach. I have accepted that, I think. So all I can do is do my job.'

'Mr Cutforth, please.'

Mr Cutforth looked up at her. Behind her, the first Mrs Roberts was standing now, her face big and serious, her hat collecting snow. He said to Baby Doe, 'It was I, Mrs Roberts, who sent up the pie.'

Baby Doe frowned. 'You're resentful of me, because I wouldn't accept a pie?'

'No, that's not it,' smiled Mr Cutforth, wryly. 'I'm resentful of you for quite different reasons. Reasons that a gentleman doesn't usually admit to a lady whom he scarcely knows. Feelings, you see, and longings. Things that might have been, and never were. I think you get my drift.'

Baby Doe was silent for a very long time. The three of them stood at the head of the stairs as if they had been frozen into a tableau, for visitors at the ice-palace to peer at with sympathetic curiosity. Then Baby Doe whispered as quiet as a snowflake, 'Yes, Mr Cutforth. I get your drift.'

Mr Sam Cutforth, by then a scenic photographer for the W. R. Noakes Company of San Francisco, died unmarried in 1927 at the age of 62, at his boarding-house on Divisadero Street. Among his possessions were found over 3,000 glass negatives, mostly of scenes of the mining towns of the Rocky Mountains during the 1880s and 1890s. The bulk of the negatives went to the Bancroft Library; very few of them were ever printed up. One negative, however, came to the attention of the library's historical department because it had been deliberately spoiled by having a cross painted on it.

When it was printed, it showed an extraordinary scene that nobody at the library could identify. Two women were standing in what appeared to be a blizzard on the tower of a Scottish or Norman castle. One of them looked surprised, the other angry, although her face was too blurred for anyone to be able to say who she was. There was no caption attached to the picture, nothing to indicate where it might have been taken or for what reason.

The print and the negative were mailed to the Colorado Historical Society for examination, but the package failed to arrive, and had to be considered lost.

There was no other record of the meeting on January 9, 1896, between Mrs Augusta Roberts and Mrs Elizabeth Roberts, except for an entry in Mr Cutforth's diary which simply but inexplicably said, 'How can she do this to me?'

BOOK ONE
BORRASCA

'An unproductive mine or claim; the opposite of a bonanza.'

ONE

Doris came flying down the stairs in her prettiest cream and burgundy dress, ribbons and lace, and crashed straight into the broad hound's-tooth bulge of her father's well-fed porterhouse belly.

'Hey, now! Whoa there!' her father cried out. He seized her wrist and brought her around. 'Whoa there! Where's the fire?'

'Oh, no fire, Papa, but Henry's here!'

'Henry again, is it?'

'Oh, Papa, *don't* disapprove! He's taking us down to the fairground, all of us, Cissy and Eleanor too!'

Doris' mother came bustling out of the dining-room, where she had been arranging dried chrysanthemums. 'Now, William,' she admonished her husband. 'None of your grumps on a Saturday. I promised poor Doris she could go. She's been looking forward to it all the week. And she helped Brindle to clean the silver.'

'Well, he's a dude, that boy, that's my objection,' said Mr Paterson, and pouted out his thick prickly moustache. 'He's a dude, and a prankster.'

'Please don't make that face, Father,' begged Doris. 'You always remind me of a beaver when you make that face.'

'A beaver, is it? My own daughter calling me a beaver! Well, all I can say is, a beaver's industrious; which is more than anyone can allow for young Henry, with his waxy whiskers.'

'Oh, *Father*,' flirted Doris.

'Oh, Father; oh, Father,' Mr Paterson mimicked. 'What's a fellow to do in his own house, with nothing but women to contend with? Well, you run along, if it's going to make you happy; but don't get up to any mischief, and no drinking cider, neither.'

36

Doris jumped up and kissed her father on both cheeks. 'I'll just get my parasol. Henry's in the parlour; do say hello!'

Mrs Paterson gave her husband an encouraging nudge on the elbow. He whipped his arm up as if he'd been stung. 'Go on, dear,' said Mrs Paterson, 'do try to be sociable. He's quite the politest of boys; and you never know, he might be your son-in-law one of these days. Then you'll *have* to talk to him.'

'Henry What's-his-face for a son-in-law? I'd sooner throw myself in the river. Or, better still, I'd sooner throw *him* in the river.'

Nonetheless, Mr Paterson walked through to the parlour, one hand behind his back to cock up his coat-tails, pouting out his moustache for a moment until he remembered how Doris had described him, and saying out loud, 'Damn! Beaver indeed!'

Henry was standing in the patterned Saturday-morning sunlight which shone through the embroidered lace curtains. He was holding up an ambrotype of Mr Paterson's three daughters at a summer picnic; and examining it with an exaggerated frown of interest. He was very tall and noticeably broad-shouldered; at least five inches taller than Mr Paterson, and he always made Mr Paterson feel portly and disarrayed and somehow *squeaky*. His thick brown hair was brushed straight back, and he sported a small well-clipped moustache, with waxed points which stuck up like the hands of a clock. He was dressy, all right, and Mr Paterson was quite justified in calling him a dude. He wore a buff-coloured tailcoat with maroon silk braiding around it; a high collar as stiff as cardboard with a mother-of-pearl stickpin; and his shoes were what Mr Paterson used to call *'blasphemously* shiny'. Yet, in spite of his style, there was an easy handsomeness about Henry which gave him the look of being justifiably attentive to what he wore, rather than foppish. He had a squarish, well-boned face, with a deeply-cleft chin; and deep-set dark brown eyes, with heavy eyebrows. Mrs Paterson said he reminded her of a good-looking Irish horse thief she had once seen in handcuffs at Essex Junction. Doris said he looked like Michelangelo's David. Cissy said perhaps he wore a fig-leaf in that case, instead of combinations, and her father had made her sit in her room all afternoon, with no shoo-fly pie.

'Well, good morning, Mr Paterson,' said Henry, stepping forward and holding out his hand.

'Good morning, Henry,' Mr Paterson acknowledged him, trying to be gruff. 'Off to the fair, as I understand it?'

'All the girls enjoy the fair, sir. I never knew a girl who didn't. Rides, candy, apple-bobbing.'

'I suppose you can speak with some experience, then? Of girls?' asked Mr Paterson.

Henry smiled respectfully but said nothing. He had stood in too many parlours with too many fathers to let Mr Paterson's needling put him off. Every father was the same, especially with his favourite daughter. Every father felt the need to score a point over whatever beaux she brought home; out of possessiveness, out of pride, or out of jealousy. A sensible young man kept his mouth closed and allowed himself to be bested. After a while, if he did that, the father might even grow to like him.

'How's your business, Mr Paterson?' Henry asked. 'I hear you've been doing exceptionally well this year.'

'So-so,' nodded Mr Paterson with satisfaction.

'You won the Brooks case, I see?'

'Indeed,' Mr Paterson replied. 'And quite a masterly piece of legal presentation that was; even if I do say so myself. The *Carmington Recorder* said we had no more chance of acquittal than a cow has of jumping the Hoosick; and so we didn't; all the circumstantial evidence was against us; every witness claimed that it was Brooks; no chance at all; right up until my closing address; and then I tugged at their heartstrings until they openly wept.'

'You're a fine orator, sir. I saw the headlines. "Jurors Weep As Lawyer Pleads For Clemency." '

Mr Paterson glanced sideways at Henry, pleased. 'You memorized it, then?'

Henry tried to look bashful. 'I couldn't help it, really. It was a fine speech, very moving.'

'Yes,' Mr Paterson agreed. Then, 'Yes, yes it was. Very moving indeed.'

Henry said innocently, 'I suppose that daguerreotype helped, too. That picture you produced of Mr Brooks in Schenectady, when all the witnesses had said he was here at home.'

Mr Paterson's expression underwent some complicated changes; from pleased to suspicious; and he scrutinized Henry hard and long, as if he couldn't make out whether Henry was playing him for a fool or not.

But Henry simply smiled, and made a show of admiring the

38

parlour, and all the ostentatious trappings which Vermont's most successful advocate obviously considered to be essential to his position and his place. The huge sofas, with their fringes and tassels and densely-embroidered antimacassars; the occasional tables, crowded like the rafts of a shipwrecked steamer with dozens of daguerreotypes of Doris and Cissy and Eleanor, in ball-dresses and sailor-suits and summer gowns, and of course of Mr Paterson himself, with his head cocked like President Buchanan, and his thumbs stuck rigidly into his waistcoat. Just as the timber-cutters of Montana used to say, 'You can't call yourself a logger until you own a dollar-watch and have your likeness took beside a tree,' so Mr Paterson appeared to feel sure of his legal success only by arranging pictures of himself all around the house, in suitably bombastic poses.

Mr Paterson owned more than a dollar-watch, however. The big granite-quarrying companies had paid him a $12,000 retention fee every year since 1835; and one of them, the Carmington Granite Dressing Coy., had even given him 13 percent of common stock, and a granite seat with cherubs on it for the garden, instead of a fee. He wasn't as wealthy as the Huntingdons, who lived on the hill overlooking his home; but he was wealthy enough to have a strong say in local community business, and to be able to run his life as he ordered it, pretty much; and hang his walls with French paintings of fat white women in miraculously discreet draperies; and fill his drawers with shining silver cutlery, imported from England.

That, to him, was quite sufficient reason to treat all of Doris's suitors with extreme suspicion; apart from the fact that Doris was his dearest. Doris was as pretty as her mother, petite, curly-haired, with wide eyes like smashed sapphires, and a mouth that kissed at fifty feet; or so the local telegraph-boy described it. Like her mother she was full-breasted, straight-backed, and had skin that glowed as if God had already dusted it with angel-powder.

'I hope you'll take the very best care of my daughters,' he told Henry.

'Have no fear on that account, sir,' Henry reassured him. 'I'll bring them all back safe and happy by five.'

'No drinking, if you please.'

'Me, sir?'

'Yes, sir; you, sir. I know that you spend quite enough time at the Gristmill Saloon; with the Davies boys, and that odd fellow who can't get his hair to stick to his head.'

'An occasional beer, sir, no more,' said Henry.

'Well, I wish I could believe you,' Mr Paterson pouted.

'You can, sir. You couldn't be a drunkard in my line of business; not when you need such a steady hand.'

Henry, like his own father, was a monumental mason, of Roberts & Son Tombs & Memorials; fine granite headstones carved to requirements and shipped almost anywhere. He could carve any number of sobbing seraphim and laid-open Bibles. He could even sculpt a vase of lilies.

But his greatest talent was for lettering: cutting into dark granite and white marble in Roman characters the names of the dead, and whatever permanent farewells might be required. The current favourite inscription was, 'Fell Asleep'. Second favourite, 'Sorely Missed By Those Left Behind'.

Mr Paterson said, 'She's a precious girl, our Doris. That's all I'm saying. We have to take account of whoever it is she walks out with.'

'I hope you don't find me wanting in any way, sir,' said Henry, with a slight questioning tilt of his head.

'Of course not,' sniffed Mr Paterson. 'Maybe you dress too well; but I suppose that can't be counted as a fault. And I'm afraid we can't count you among Bennington's plutocrats, can we? Nor ever will.'

'Business is good enough, thank you, sir,' said Henry. 'I make enough to keep myself, and spend a little, and save a little, too. I could keep a wife quite well. That is, if I had a mind to take one; and if she had a mind to take me.'

'How much do you make, per commission?' asked Mr Paterson, beginning to grow challenging. 'Come on now, your most expensive tomb.'

'Your full-size sarcophagus in dark Barre granite complete with sentimental inscription works out at $73.58.'

'And how long does such a sarcophagus take to cut?'

'Cut, polished, and lettered from scratch, two and a half weeks' work.'

'Well, then,' said Mr Paterson, 'even if you were to undertake such an order every two weeks, it has to follow mathematically that you could never earn more than $1,678 per annum less the cost of stone and tools and that is scarcely enough to keep a

Paterson girl in the manner which I would expect.' He beamed, and cocked up his coat-tails again.

Henry could see himself in the large engraved mirror over the fireplace. He thought he looked unduly serious, but he couldn't bring himself to smile. He knew very well what Mr Paterson was saying to him; that he would be wasting his time if he were to court Doris seriously, with a view to marriage. And even though he hadn't yet considered the possibility of asking Doris to be his bride, he found her disturbingly attractive, more attractive than he really cared to think about, and he resented being told that he didn't even have the option of asking her. He twisted the end of his waxed moustache, and said, 'There must have been a time, sir, when you were not as well off as you are today.'

'Ah, well, you're right,' said Mr Paterson. He went across to the window, parted the lace curtains with two fat fingers, and peered out into the street. Henry's carriage was tethered up there: the black varnished barouche in which his father attended funerals, when he was asked. The two black horses between the shafts had been kept occupied with black hessian nosebags with black fringes. 'A little *sombre*, for a fair, don't you think?' Mr Paterson asked, rhetorically. Then he turned around and said, 'Yes, of course I was poorer, when I was a clerk. I struggled for years for what you see here. But there is one important difference between the legal profession, Henry, and the craft of monumental mason, no matter how skilful a craft that may be. A lawyer may always ask his clients for higher fees, as his ability and his experience increase. But how can *you* ask for more money? Who are your clients? The dead, who cannot pay; and the bereaved, who wish to pay as little as possible. Not much prospect *there* of making a fortune, I'd say.'

Henry said stiffly, 'I may surprise you, sir.'

Mr Paterson grasped his arm. 'I'm sure you may. You like to think of yourself as someone surprising, don't you? We do have these vanities, when we're young. But all I can say to you is, enjoy yourself at the fair. Don't dwell too much on things that you may not have; in that lies discontent; and there is nothing more bitter than discontent. Discontent is anti-social.'

Henry managed to smile now. 'It is also the spur for great achievements, sir.'

Mr Paterson stared at Henry again. Too smart by half for a

stonemason, he reckoned; although he knew that Henry's father, Fenchurch Roberts, was very widely educated, and that Henry had stayed on two years longer at Carmington College than most of his classmates; and then taken a business course with old man Protheroe, although what good *that* could have done him, the Lord could only guess. Old man Protheroe had lost all the money he ever had made on some crackbrained scheme for selling fruit syrup formula to druggists all over the Union; so that they could reconstitute it with seltzer and sell it as 'Protheroe's Elixir', 2 cents the bottle.

Mr Paterson said, 'Each man to his allotted place, that's what the Bible teaches us. Now, that's Doris, isn't it? It's time you went. Have the best time you can, and see if you can persuade Doris to bring me back some gingerbread.'

He clasped Henry's hand, and for a moment his expression was surprisingly friendly. 'Always had a weakness for gingerbread; my mother used to bake it, God bless her. "Butter, eggs, molasses, and flour; mix it with ginger and bake half an hour." That's what she used to sing.'

His eyes gazed reflectively inward, and he held Henry's hand much longer than he had meant to. Then Doris came flustering in, with her bonnet and parasol, and cried, 'Come on, Henry, do! We're all waiting!' and Mr Paterson looked at Henry with an expression which clearly meant, 'Don't think that you can take advantage of me; or of Doris; just because you caught me in one sentimental moment.'

Cissy and Eleanor were already out on the porch; Cissy in blue and Eleanor in pink. Cissy, who was two years younger than Doris, had curly bunches of fair hair, and a pert cheeky face. Eleanor, the youngest, was darker and quieter, almost Italian-looking, but promised when she grew up to be by far the most beautiful. Mr Paterson called her 'my Mona Lisa'.

Giggling and chattering, the girls danced down the long brick path to the front gate. It was a warm mid-July day, and the sky was so blue it was almost purple, like bellflowers. Behind the maples and the dark stands of Green Mountain pines, thick and creamy cumulus clouds lazed away the morning; waiting for the cooler winds of the evening before they rose up to bring southern Vermont a summer thunderstorm, and rain.

Henry helped the girls up into the barouche. Its leather straps squeaked and protested as they climbed in, still giggling and spinning their parasols. Henry closed the door, and then went around to take the nosebags off his horses.

With Henry up on the box, they trotted briskly along Carmington's main street, past the *Carmington Recorder* and the Hoosick Hotel and Maine & Pearson's Dry Goods. The street was busy this morning with farm waggons and carriages and running children. Several passers-by waved at Henry and whistled; and one young type called out, 'Lucky dog, you, Henry Roberts! Three to yourself!'

They rattled around the graceful green with its white-spired church; where a cannon still stood as a reminder of the Battle of Carmington during the War of Independence; and where children in straw bonnets were bowling hoops down a crayon-green slope. It was then that Henry saw Augusta Pierce walking along by the side of the road with her red-faced cousin Frank, and reined his horses down to a slow walk, which they were used to, being funeral horses.

'Oh, you're not stopping for *Augusta*, are you?' Doris complained.

'Disgusting Augusta,' giggled Cissy.

'Quiet, will you, Cissy,' Henry told her. 'Augusta was all kinds of help when my mother was sick last spring; cooking and cleaning up and buying the groceries for us. She has a kind heart, Augusta; and don't you go taunting her.'

He drew the black barouche up beside Augusta and Frank, and raised his hat. Augusta smiled, although she made an obvious point of ignoring the three Paterson sisters. Cissy pulled a long face, and bugged her eyes, and giggled so much that she almost had a coughing fit.

'You two off to the fair?' Henry asked Augusta.

'We'll be coming along later,' Augusta replied. 'Frank has to take these hymnbooks back to the Reverend Jones; and Mrs Jones promised to show me that fancy French embroidery stitch of hers.'

'Pity she can't embroider her face a little,' whispered Cissy; and she and Doris clutched each other in spiteful glee, and drummed their button-up boots.

It was true that Augusta was very plain. She had a big, bovine face, topped with a tight plait of thin brown hair; and the tiny wire-rimmed spectacles she wore did nothing to enhance her fleshy nose. She was dressed in an unbecoming shade of brown, with a plain percale collar, and she carried a

43

bright green parasol. Henry had always felt desperately sorry for her; because he had known from the age of ten what a considerate nature she had, in spite of all the teasing and all the taunts. He had ripped his pants once on the way to school; and while he had hidden in a roadside ditch, Augusta had neatly stitched them for him, and never laughed at him once.

Her helpfulness had never been more appreciated by the Roberts family than during Mrs Roberts' long-drawn-out illness last spring. In April, on the brightest of days, with the air full of blossom, Mrs Roberts had died, in terrible pain, of a malignancy of the womb. Neither Henry nor his father could have coped then if it hadn't been for Augusta; who had wept as they did; but had then gone about the business of preparing the funeral breakfast, and packing away his mother's clothes. Henry's father had said of Augusta that whatever she looked like, she always possessed 'the beauty of devotion'.

Henry had agreed with him. Henry and his father agreed on most things; more like brothers now than father and son. But nonetheless he had been surprised on the evening before Augusta was due to leave the Roberts' house when she had unexpectedly appeared at his bedroom door in her long billowing nightdress, without her spectacles, a scarlet mark at each side of her nose, and asked him shortsightedly, 'Is there anything you need from me, Henry? You have only to ask.'

Henry had been sitting up in bed eating an apple and reading *The Count of Monte Cristo*; the oil-lamp had been hissing on the bedside table. He had looked at Augusta for a long time, and then folded his book, and said, 'Augusta, you have already given me your friendship; and I value it more than I will ever be able to tell you.'

She had stood in the doorway, one hand raised against the frame, and then she turned away, whispering, 'Very well,' and returned to her room. Henry had remained where he was, his apple uneaten, his book unread; feeling a tangle of emotion in his throat because he was grateful for everything that she had done for him and his father, and yet could not love her, not in the way that she wanted.

Henry said, 'Meet us up at the fair, Augusta, and I'll stand you a lemonade and a poke of popcorn; you too, Frank.'

Frank gave a nod over the top of his stack of hymnbooks, and Augusta smiled; pleased to have got one over on the giggling Paterson girls; and then Henry geed up the horses, and they trotted on, with their wheels rattling on the dry-rutted roadway, the outskirts of Carmington turning around them like a slowly-revolving carousel, past white saltbox houses with leaf-shaded yards, past Dutch barns and fenced paddocks, driving their way at last through a cool avenue of mockernuts, until the fairground came into view, on a wide tufted pasture bordered with elms.

Doris clapped her hands. 'Henry, it's so exciting! Last year I had to go with Emily Vane and all those pimply brothers of hers, and that was just *dreadful!*'

'I thought you had quite a crush on Oswald Vane,' Henry teased her. Oswald was the gawkiest of all the Vane boys, all Adam's apple and wrists, with a dark downy moustache, and he had followed Doris around for weeks, begging to buy her sodas and sending her posies of flowers.

Doris prodded Henry sharply in the small of the back with her parasol. 'I'll have my father sue you for being defamatory, if you mention that booby's name again, in connection with mine!'

Henry laughed, and steered the jingling barouche around to the side of the pasture, towards the waggon-park, where there was already a motley assemblage of farm-waggons, top buggies, family-waggons and cabriolets. A boy ran forward to hold the horses and tie up the barouche; and Henry climbed down to open the door and put down the step and help Doris and Cissy and Eleanor down to the grass.

Although it was early yet, the Carmington Annual Fair was already crowded, and they could hear the Brattleboro Silver Ensemble up on the pennant-decorated bandstand playing 'Bunch of Blackberries', and the whistling and piping of the steam-calliope. Arm-in-arm, Henry and the Paterson sisters walked up the sloping pasture towards the entrance tent, and paid their 5 cents admission, and took their lucky numbers.

The fair was even bigger than last year. There were side-shows, coconut shies and hoop-las and try-your-strength machines. Under an open-sided awning, there were tables spread with chequered cloths, where families sat with beer and sodas and heaped-up plates of bratwurst. There was a fortune-telling tent; a travelling menagerie, featuring genuine Lords of the Jungle; a sword-swallower; and a candy stall glistening with barley-sugar and opera fudge and pecan penuche, molasses taffy and fruit-leather.

45

Henry bought the girls a small bag of divinity each; and then they walked across to see the big painted swings; and the steam-calliope; and the helter-skelter.

They were acquainted with almost everyone they met, and so as they walked there was a good deal of hat-lifting and smiling and saying 'Good morning'; and Henry was complimented again and again on his pretty companions. George Davies, a broad-faced freckly boy with whom Henry spent two or three evenings a week drinking beer in the back room of the Gristmill Saloon, came across and bowed and showed them all a red India-rubber fat-boy doll which he had won on the shooting-range. He pressed its stomach and it squeaked shrilly.

'Remind you of anybody?' he winked at Henry. Doris tipped her nose into the air. She knew very well, as they all did, that George was mocking her father.

'Had any rides yet?' Henry asked him.

'I was going to try the Colossal Whirler, but there's a line for it all the way round the top of the meadow. James has been on it, though, and he reckons it's just about the most terri-ferating experience he's ever had in his whole entire life.'

'Oh, let's go take a look,' Doris begged.

'See you later, George,' said Henry, and he and the girls made their way up to the top of the meadow, where the Colossal Whirler had been set up. George had been right: there was a hot and hopeful line of candidates for terri-ferating all the way along the fence and right the way down to the meatball tent. Boys and girls and fathers and mothers, even an oldtimer or two, with their jackets over their arms, eating peanut pops and rock candy, and mopping themselves with their handkerchiefs.

'Just look at it!' breathed Doris, and Cissy giggled in fear. 'Oh, Henry, we just *have* to take a ride on that!'

The Colossal Whirler had never come to Carmington before, although every enthusiastic fair-goer had heard of it by reputation. It was a huge wooden wheel, painted gold and crimson, rather like a water-wheel, with swing seats suspended from each of its spokes. It was driven by a steam-engine, connected by a wide leather belt, and when it built up top speed, the swing seats, as they reached the top of the wheel, would fly out so that their shrieking passengers were upside-down.

A barker stood by the Whirler's ticket-office, in a purple satin waistcoat and a bright green beaver hat, collecting the dimes that were being pressed into his hand as fast as the line could excitedly shuffle forward, and rapping out, 'The experience *of* a lifetime! Guaranteed to make your blood run cold *in* your arteries! Not for the faint of heart! Not for the nervous! Genuine terror assured *or* your five cents back!'

One young man who had already taken a ride on the Whirler turned around in front of Henry and muttered, 'I wasn't scared. Not me! I was damn near pooping myself!'

Doris seized Henry's hand, and said, '*Do* let's have a ride. Please, Henry! You're not going to be a spoilsport, are you?'

Henry grinned, and squeezed her hand in return. 'Of course not. But remember the golden rule. If you're going to lose your lunch on a fairground ride, first of all you have to have some lunch to lose. So let's go around the sideshows first, and then sit down for something to eat, and by that time everybody else will start getting hungry, and there won't be so much of a line.'

Eleanor said, 'Let's have our fortunes read. Cissy? Doris? Let's ask who we're going to marry.'

'Oh, yes!' Doris enthused.

'Well, you won't be marrying *me*, if your father has anything to do with it,' Henry told her.

Doris stood on tippy-toe to kiss his cheek. 'You wait and see,' she said, kissing him again. 'Papa can always be persuaded; especially if I bake him his favourite cakes.'

They tried their hand at the hoop-la, and Henry won a tortoiseshell Spanish hair-comb, which he presented to Doris with a bow, and which she received with a curtsey.

The day was growing hotter; although there was that noticeable darkness in the air which presages a storm. In spite of the heat, a restless wind would occasionally scurry through the grass, blowing hats and straw and candy-wrappers. The Brattleboro band was playing 'Say Au Revoir, But Not Goodbye'; and as it neared luncheon-time, there was a waft in the air of sizzling sausages and grilled meatballs, all mingled with that dry-hay and cotton-candy aroma that distinguishes every meadow carnival from south Vermont to Colorado.

Arm-in-arm again, they found the small striped tent advertising Madame Waldorf's Mysteries and Intimate Futures Revealed 10 cents. Cissy went first, and came out four or five minutes later giggling and saying that she was going to marry a man of the church, and have eight children; Eleanor went in next and came out looking petulant, to say that she wasn't

47

going to marry anyone until she was thirty, and then he was going to be 'a gentleman of advanced years'. Then Doris persuaded Henry to go in. 'Go on, and then we can compare what she says.'

Henry opened the flap of the tent, and ducked his head as he stepped inside. It was dim, and smelled of stale lavender and sour wine. At a small folding table, a robust-looking woman in a tight black dress and a black sequined bonnet sat with her arms folded in front of a display of tarot cards. She looked up as he came in, and touched the tip of her finger to her lips. '*Sssh*,' she said. Henry sat down on the rickety bentwood chair facing her, his hat on his lap, and watched her for a while, without saying anything.

At last she looked up. Her irises were so dark that they made her eyes look curiously dead, as if they were all pupil. Wide dead eyes that could penetrate right inside your head, and see what you were thinking; as if your head were a model theatre.

She said, 'Why did you come here, when you know already what will happen to you?'

Henry grinned, thinking that she was ragging him, but then stopped grinning.

'You will become wealthy one day,' Madame Waldorf told him. She sniffed, and drummed her fingers on the cards. She turned one over, and then she said, 'You will not become wealthy by talent; or by skill; but simply by chance.'

Henry shifted on his chair, and asked, 'What will it be, some kind of lottery prize?'

Madame Waldorf frowned, and then she said, 'No, not a lottery prize. Something to do with two men who are looking for something. One of them speaks very little English. You will know them when you meet them, at least you will if you remember my words.'

'How about, well, romance?' Henry asked her. He knew that Doris would pounce on him as soon as he came out, and demand to know whether they were going to be married or not.

Madame Waldorf spent minutes on end consulting the cards, and Henry began to grow impatient. But at last she nodded, and said, 'You will marry the woman you want to marry. There will be difficulty; perhaps great difficulty. But, at the last, she will be yours until you die.'

'Can you tell me her name?' asked Henry.

'No. But I can tell you that she is very beautiful.'

'Not even a clue?'

Madame Waldorf closed her eyes and pressed her fingertips against the lids. She breathed deeply. Henry looked around the tent; at the shabby carpet-bag which Madame Waldorf kept close beside her, with the neck of a green-glass wine-bottle protruding from it. Oh well, he thought. Sitting in a stuffy old tent all day, telling other folks' fortunes, that must be quite enough to drive anybody to drink.

'D,' Madame Waldorf said suddenly. 'I see – I *think* I see a "D".'

'Doris?'

'Well, it could be. I'm not sure. But it's a very beautiful girl whose name begins with a "D".'

'That sounds very much like Doris,' smiled Henry.

Madame Waldorf began to collect up her cards. 'If that's who you want it to be,' she said, obscurely.

Henry didn't know what she meant; but he paid her the 10 cents, and said, 'Thank you, ma'am,' and pushed his way out through the tent-flap.

'Well? Well?' Doris demanded, jumping up and down.

'I'm going to be wealthy without even working for it, and I'm going to marry a beautiful girl whose name starts with a "D",' he announced.

Doris hugged him. 'It's *true!* What did I tell you? Oh, isn't it marvellous! Oh, Henry, I'm so happy!'

'Come on, Doris, your turn now,' Cissy coaxed her.

Doris excitedly went into the fortune-telling tent, and Henry waited outside with Cissy and Eleanor and lit up a small cigar.

'You seem quiet,' said Cissy, after a while, taking his arm, and smiling at him.

'Oh, I don't know,' Henry told her. 'I was just thinking about that fortune-telling lady.'

'You don't believe in it, do you?' Cissy asked him.

Henry shrugged. 'Not really. But how did she know my girl's name began with a "D"?'

'*I* believe in it,' said Eleanor, grumpily. 'I wish I didn't. Fancy not getting married until you're *thirty!* I'll be *ancient* by then. An ancient ruin.'

'Oh, Eleanor,' said Cissy. 'I bet you'll be married before either of us. Jack Browning is absolutely mad about you.'

'Jack Browning? That big clumsy lunk? He can't even walk across a *carpet* without tripping over it.'

Henry smoked his cigar and stood with his hands in his pocket looking around him and feeling unusually contented and pleased with himself. Inside him somewhere, there was still a small dark pocket of sadness that his mother was gone; but on this hot summer's day at the Carmington Fair he felt on the whole that life was being good to him, and that nobody could ask for very much more. Perhaps he would never be rich (not unless Madame Waldorf's prediction came true) but if he could marry a pretty girl like Doris and keep up the monument business with his father, whom he was growing to know and like more and more as time went by; and if people continued to die in Carmington at more or less the same rate as they had done for the past twenty years, then he reckoned that he would have achieved something that even Mr Paterson couldn't quibble about: and that was happiness.

The tent-flap opened and Doris came out.

'Well, now,' said Henry, smiling, taking the cigar out of his mouth. 'And did she tell you the name of the man you're going to marry? Does it begin with an "H"?'

Doris turned and stared at him. To Henry's surprise, there were tears in her eyes, and she had lost all of her colour. She was as grey as if somebody had hit her. Cissy took her hand and said, 'Doris, what on earth's the matter? You look awful! Why are you crying?'

Without a word, Doris twisted her hand away. Then she lifted the hem of her skirts and began to walk off across the grass, very quickly. Cissy glanced at Henry and pulled a mystified face; then she called, 'Doris! Doris! Come back! What on *earth's* the matter?'

Henry tossed aside his cigar and ran after her. He caught hold of her sleeve just as they passed the rifle-shooting tent; and they were almost deafened by the sharp crackle of small-bore percussion rifles.

'Let go!' shouted Doris, above the noise. 'I'm just upset, that's all!'

'Oh, come on, Doris. It's only a fairground fortune. What did she say that made you cry?'

'I'm not telling you! Now, let me go!'

'You listen here,' Henry insisted. 'I promised your father I'd bring you home safe and happy; and safe and happy is just

50

how you're going to be. Now you tell me what that Madame Waldorf had to say that made you storm off so; and by God I'll go back there and wrap that tent up with her in it and put her on the first freight-waggon out of town.'

Doris couldn't help smiling through her tears. She blinked them away from her eyelashes, and then she stood close to Henry, stroking and fiddling with his silk-braided lapels as she tried to tell him what had happened.

'She said I was unlucky, that was what frightened me so much. She said I was probably never going to get married; although there might be a chance, if I stayed away from the boy I thought I loved. I mean, that seems like such a contradiction, doesn't it? I don't understand what she was trying to say to me. I asked her *why* I was going to be so unlucky, but she said she didn't know, and that there was a sort of cloud over it, and she couldn't see. But she said I had to take very great care, or else I'd never get married and I'd never have any children of my own.'

The tears began to slide down her cheeks again, and Henry took out his handkerchief, and snapped it open as if he were starting a running-race; and then dabbed her eyes for her.

'Darn me if that isn't the silliest thing I've ever heard,' he told her, in a gentle, encouraging voice. He lifted her chin with his hand, and smiled at her, and then hugged her close. 'A fat old gypsy like that, drinking wine in a tent, and you let her upset you.'

Cissy came up and stroked her sister's hair. 'He's right, Doris. It's only superstition. Like walking under a ladder or spitting at frogs. You remember Lonnie Tremlett, when he went to see that fortune-teller last year at Williamstown? She said that he was going to have a lucky break; and what happened, he caught his hand in a baler and broke his arm in five different places. Well, *that's* how right fortune-tellers aren't.'

Doris swallowed, and nodded, and said, 'I suppose you're right. But what a terrible thing to say to anyone. And the way she *said* it was scary, too; very straightforward, like it was all true.'

'Come on,' said Henry, 'let's buy ourselves a lemonade, and something to eat; and then take a ride on the Colossal Whirler. That'll cheer us all up.'

He led Doris down to the luncheon-awning, cool and canvassy, where the girls chose a table close to the duckboard walk that was laid through the centre of the field, so that everybody could see and admire them as they walked past. Henry went up to the trestles where there were waiters in stiff white aprons and curly moustaches, speedily serving out platefuls of boiled ham, fried rabbit, chicken Delmonico, grits, salads, and sausages. Eleanor came to help him and between them they heaped up four plates with food, and collected four large lemonades on a tray, and sat down to eat. Henry could have done with a beer; but he minded what Mr Paterson had told him, and didn't think it would do his chances with Doris much good if he went back to the Paterson house smelling of Burlington pilsner.

The wind was fresher now, and more persistent. But still the crowds came bustling and shuffling into the fair, and the steam-calliope played reedy off-key waltzes; and the Colossal Whirler creaked and clanked as it started off again with another cargo of happily-shrieking passengers; and over by the saloon-tent there was lusty cheering as the boxing competitions started.

While they were eating, the other two Davies brothers, Jack and Sam, came strolling past and doffed their hats. They were all alike as triplets, Jack, Sam, and George; and even their friends had difficulty telling them apart from a distance.

'Good afternoon, fair ladies,' said Jack, to Cissy and Eleanor. 'How about a ride on the swing-boats with us? That's if your noble escort has no objection.'

'Of course not,' grinned Henry. 'But bring them back straight afterwards. We're all going for a ride on the Colossal Whirler.'

'Phew, you wouldn't get me up in that thing,' said Jack. 'Upside-down, it isn't natural.'

'Don't tell me you're a scaredy-cat,' gibed Cissy.

Jack blushed. 'Nothing to do with scaredy-cat. It's just gravity, that's all. You only to have to look at that thing. It's flat against the natural laws of gravity.'

'Then how come nobody ever falls out?' Eleanor wanted to know.

Jack stuck his thumbs in his waistcoat. 'Just lucky, I guess.'

'Just lucky!' Cissy exploded, in sarcastic mirth. 'Come on, then, off we go to the swing-boats; and make sure you hold on tight, Jack Davies. We wouldn't want you to tumble out and bump your head. It might knock some sense into you.'

Cissy and Eleanor finished up their drinks; and the Davies boys drew out their chairs for them and ostentatiously offered them their arms. Henry and Doris smiled to see them go; and Henry said, 'Growing up, aren't they? Real ladies these days.'

'Don't you start getting any ideas about Cissy and Eleanor,' Doris warned him.

'Not a chance,' said Henry. Then, 'Let's take a stroll in the woods, shall we, while we're waiting for them? I'm getting a little tired of all this bustle.'

Doris gave him a flirtatious little nod of her head, feeling better after her lunch; and so they left the refreshment awning and walked hand-in-hand to the rough edges of the fairground, and into the woods. It was surprising how quickly the clamour of the fair died away, once they were two or three hundred yards into the trees; and soon they were crossing a sun-flickered clearing between elms and scarlet oaks, and apart from the faintest of tunes from the steam-calliope, and the occasional crackling of gunfire, there was no sound at all but the birds and the wind and the sound of their own feet treading through the undergrowth.

Henry stopped, and took hold of both of Doris' hands. She looked so pretty just then, with her plumed bonnet and her hair in shining ringlets, and those intensely blue eyes of hers, that he couldn't resist leaning forward and kissing the smooth curve of her forehead, and then her soft and lightly-powdered cheeks. She raised her lips to meet his lips with an innocent sensuality that made him feel as if he were someone else altogether; that he was imagining all this, the woods, and the criss-cross shafts of sunlight, and the chirruping birds, and yet the reality of it was so detailed and intense that he was stunned by it. For the very first time he said, 'I love you, Doris,' and it was as much of a revelation to him as it was to her.

Her eyes were half-closed, her lips half-parted. He held her tight in his arms, in her beautiful dress of cream and burgundy silk, and felt the narrow restriction of her corset around her waist, and the way in which her full breasts bulged over the top of it; and she aroused him so strongly that he crushed his mouth against hers, and kissed her until she had to push him away, for fear that her lips would be bruised.

'Please,' she said, breathlessly but not upset, touching him, stroking his cheek. 'Please let's walk a little. I have to catch my breath.'

They walked deeper into the woods. Their fingertips touched from time to time, but that was all that they allowed themselves, for both of them knew what intensity of feeling they had stirred up within themselves, and what its consequences might be.

Doris asked, 'Have you ever loved anyone before? *Truly* loved them?'

'Never like this,' said Henry. He thought of Hilary Beckett (now Mrs Walter Grinsale, of Danby Corners) and of the kisses they had shared, four years ago was it, already? He thought of the long afternoons they had shared together on her narrow brass bed, under the picture of St Philip, and her small red-nippled breasts, as soft as vanilla blancmanges. Her profile against the pillow. He had loved Hilary, yes. He really had. But not like this; not both carnally and romantically; not as a young and unaffected sorceress, as Doris was.

After a while they sat against the trunk of a tall scarlet oak, and held hands, and kissed with deliberate self-control.

'It's perfect,' said Doris.

'What is?' Henry asked her, although he knew.

'The day, the fair, everything. You. You're perfect.'

'I wish I was.'

'Oh, you are, my love. You are.'

Henry sat for a while with his head back against the tree, and his eyes closed. When he opened them again he saw that Doris had been watching him, and that she looked more beautiful than ever. Her face was outlined by sunshine, the curve around her lower lip shone like a tiny bow of gold.

'We'd better be getting back,' he said. 'Cissy and Eleanor will be missing us; and I did promise your father that I'd look after them, too.'

'That fortune-teller,' Doris began.

'What about her?'

'Well, I don't know,' she replied. She frowned, and turned her head away. 'She made me feel *cold*, can you believe that? She actually made me shiver.'

There was a very distant grumble of thunder, from the direction of West Mountain. Henry said, 'It's bunkum, that's all.'

'Even what she said to you? About marrying a girl whose name begins with "D"?'

Henry kissed her, quickly, on the tip of her nose. 'Maybe not that bit.'

'Well, then?' she said.

He stood up, and brushed down his smart Saturday pants, and then held out his hand to help her up. 'Marry me,' he said.

'Yes,' she replied.

They walked a little way back towards the fairground; and then Henry suddenly took her in his arms again and kissed her until his head spun around, and all he could taste and smell and feel was Doris; and Doris's perfume; and the young disturbing softness of her. My God, he thought, I really do love her that much. I really do want to marry her; and make her mine; and give her children.

When they emerged out of the woods at last the sky behind the fairground was growing black; and lightning was fingering the distant peak of Bald Mountain.

'I think we've just got time for the Whirler,' said Henry. 'Let's go find Cissy and Eleanor; then I think we'd better get back home. It's going to rain like all Isaiah in a while.'

They found Cissy and Eleanor at the candy stall with the Davies brothers and a leering young man called Carl Bukowski whose father owned the local livery stables. Henry collected both girls, and together they walked across to the Colossal Whirler, where the line had dwindled to only four or five, while the fair-goers ate their luncheon and refreshed themselves with lemonade and beer. There was very little that could keep the people of Carmington away from their food, not even a Colossal Whirler.

'Come on now, ladies and gentlemen!' the barker was calling out. 'Not for the faint of heart! Not for the lily-livered! Genuine terror here and now!' Behind him, the steam-engine chugged and whirred, and the leather drive-belt clapped in spasmodic applause.

'I'm terrified!' giggled Cissy, and stepped up on to the Whirler's platform. The barker helped her to climb into her dangling seat, and fastened the safety-chain in front of her. Then he released the brake and allowed the wheel to nudge up a little way, suspending Cissy ten feet in the air. She screamed, and kicked her heels in glee.

One by one, they all climbed aboard. Henry went last, after Doris, and paid the 40 cents fare for all of them. He found himself dangling on a small wooden seat, turning this way and that, while the Colossal Whirler lifted him higher and higher above the fairground. He looked up and called to Doris, 'How are you feeling?' and she called back, 'Scared! How are you?'

Gradually, as each seat was filled, they rose higher and higher on the wheel until Henry could look around him and see the tops of the trees, and beyond, to Harman Hill and Prospect Mountain, the green sunlit peaks of Vermont, shadowed by rising clouds. He could even see the rooftops of Carmington itself; the church spire, and part of the roof of his own house, Roberts & Son, Monumental Masons.

And today, he thought, as he swung in his little seat; today I asked Doris to marry me, and she accepted. As simple, and as happy, as that.

Gradually, the Colossal Whirler began to pick up speed. The steam-engine chugged, and the drive-belt slapped, and the huge wooden wheel turned faster and faster. At first, the suspended chairs had hung vertically, but under the influence of centrifugal force they began to swing outwards, like the spokes of a wheel; until the first scream of horror told Henry that someone at the top of the wheel had turned upside-down. The next time the wheel went up, he heard Doris scream; and then suddenly he was pitched over himself, and the fairground spun underneath him, and he yelled out, '*Aaaaahhh!*' in a hoarse voice that didn't even sound like his own. Then he was plunging down towards the ground again, and the people behind him were screaming.

After the third spin over the top of the wheel, he was clutching the chains so tight that his hands hurt, and he was beginning very much to wish that he hadn't eaten so much bratwurst. All he could think of was bratwurst and clinging on and trying to calculate how many spins of the wheel they gave you before they allowed you to get off. Then he was up and over again, and the fairground was underneath him, ninety feet below, a blur of people and tents and flags.

Up and over they went again. '*Doris!*' he shouted; and she tried to turn and look at him as the wheel descended again; and then right in front of his eyes it happened.

Her seat swung to the side as she turned, and the link holding the left-hand chain parted like a string of molasses toffee, and with terrible abruptness Doris was flung from her seat straight into the drive-belt, straight into the cogs and the flying machinery and she didn't even scream that time.

'Oh God almighty!' Henry roared, and tried desperately to unfasten his safety-chain; but then the wheel rose again and he had to cling on, screaming, '*Stop it! Stop it! For God's sake stop it!*' while he was flung upside-down again.

The Colossal Whirler came to a shuddering, groaning halt.

56

Passengers screamed as they were thrown violently from side to side; some of them had been upside-down and fell through the spokes of the wheel as violently as if they had been dropped through a hangman's trap; to dangle and swing and collide with the wheel, and shout out in fright.

Henry's chair was left ten feet above the ground; but he tugged aside his safety-chain and dropped straight to the boards below. A crowd had already gathered around the Colossal Whirler's drive-gear, and he forced his way hysterically through them, shouldering them aside, screeching, 'Let me through! Let me through! She's my wife!'

The spectators stood aside in frightened respect; and then gathered around again to stare at him in horror and pity. Doris had been thrown legs-first between the leather drive-belt and the gears, and the massive inertia of the Colossal Whirler had snatched her even further into the machinery, between the huge black intermeshing cogs. She had been crushed and mangled all the way up her legs, right up to her hips, and she was splattered in blood and oil. A man with a thick brown beard was supporting her back, and another man was already trying to force the cogs of the Colossal Whirler's machinery into reverse with a crowbar, in order to pry Doris free. But her face was as ghastly white as the newspaper on which the story of her accident would be printed; and there was so much blood drenching her cream and burgundy dress that nobody could give out any hope at all that she would live.

Henry knelt down beside her, and lifted her hand. It was rigid, and very cold, an alabaster parody of the hand he had held such a short time before in the woods. Doris stared at him, but the expression in her eyes was peculiar and shocked, and he wasn't at all sure that she understood that it was him. The man with the brown beard said quietly, 'If you have something to say, sir, best say it now.'

'Please, get her free,' said Henry. 'Please, get her out of there.'

'We're trying our best, sir. The gears are jammed fast.'

Henry stared at him, and screamed, '*Then smash this whole damned infernal machine to pieces! For God's sake! It's killed her!*'

The man laid his hand on Henry's shoulder. 'Be calm, sir. We're trying our best.'

Doris said blurrily, 'Henry?'

Henry leaned over her. 'Doris, it's me. Doris, it's Henry. I love you.'

'Henry?' she repeated, as if she were speaking from another room. Her eyes were still clear bright blue, but they didn't seem to see him at all. 'Henry, what happened? Where are you?'

'My darling, I'm here. I'm right beside you. It's all right, my darling. There was an accident, that's all. They'll soon have you free. Please try to be brave. My darling, I love you. I love you, Doris. Oh God, my darling, I love you. Oh, Doris. Oh, God.'

Henry knelt beside her with tears streaming down his face. He raised both hands to wipe them away but then all he could do was to lower his head and sob, deeply and painfully; while the barker in the fancy waistcoat and the fancy beaver hat came up behind him and held his shoulders firmly simply to reassure him that he was not alone.

At last, three men were able to force the cogs open; and Doris's crushed body was gently lifted out, and laid on a blanket on the boards. Her eyes were closed now and she was scarcely breathing. Henry knelt next to her, staring at her in shock and grief. He was past tears now. He knelt beside her and shuddered and that was all that he could do. Someone had leaned over him and told him quietly that Cissy and Eleanor were being taken home by Mr Harman, of Harman Dry Goods; and that he wasn't to worry.

Doris said nothing else. As she was being carefully examined by Dr Bendick, who had been at the fair with his family of nine children, she silently died. Dr Bendick took off his spectacles and turned to Henry and said, 'She's left you, I'm sorry to say.'

'Left me?' asked Henry, dully.

Dr Bendick glanced upwards, towards the thundery sky. The gesture struck a responsive chord in Henry's memory; some inscription he had once chiselled on a white marble gravestone. 'Gone Beyond The Clouds, And Dearly Missed.' He understood then, all the way through his consciousness, that Doris was truly dead.

He stood up. The barker tried to help him, but Henry pushed him away. He walked rigidly down the steps of the Colossal Whirler, and across the rough grass of the fairground. People parted in front of him, allowing him all the room that his grief required. He wanted to cry but his eyes refused to produce any tears. That was why he was so relieved when it suddenly started to rain; a few heavy spots at first; and then a thick hissing downpour that scattered fair-goers in all directions, paper bags held over their heads, and drummed on the tops of the tents.

Henry stumbled on between the sideshows, his hair streaming wet, the shoulders of his jacket dark with rain. A bellowing burst of thunder broke just above his head; and people ran past him with their coat-collars turned up, screaming because they were getting wet.

He was halfway down the meadow when he saw Augusta standing beside the refreshment awning, which was crowded right to its dripping gutters with sheltering townsfolk. Augusta had put up her bright green parasol to protect herself from the worst of the downpour, but her skirts were still soaked, and there were beads of rain on her spectacles.

'Henry!' she called, as he approached.

He walked mechanically past her, as if he hadn't heard.

'Henry!' she called again, hurrying after him.

He staggered his way down towards the treeline, while the thunder banged above him again and again, and lightning jumped and danced and flickered across the fields.

'Henry!' cried Augusta, running after him with her wet parasol bobbing. 'Henry!'

TWO

At eleven o'clock, when his father came up to see him, he was still sitting by the window, staring sightlessly out over the rows of pale unfinished tombstones that shone below him in the moonlight. The storm had passed now, and the skies were clear. There was a smell of wet earth and crushed grass in the air; and over by the town square a locked-up dog was howling.

His father came and stood behind him, not touching him.

59

He half-turned his head to acknowledge his father's appearance, and smiled wryly. 'Hallo, Dad.'

'Hallo, son. How are you feeling?'

Henry shrugged. 'Tired, I think. Sad.'

'Is there anything you want?'

Henry shook his head.

Fenchurch Roberts sat down on the edge of his son's bed and watched him with all the quietness of a man who understands through his own bereavement the need for grief, the terrible importance of tears. He was a big-shouldered man, not as handsome as Henry, nor as tall; but with a rugged, open, attractive face, and curly grey hair that Henry's mother had always loved to tug, and a heavy pair of grey whiskers. He was a plain man in many ways. While Henry invariably wore fancy waistcoats to work, Fenchurch wore red flannel shirts, and baggy denim pants. But Henry respected him all the same: for his eclectic knowledge of science and philosophy, for his thoughtfulness, and above all for his unshakeable patience. Fenchurch could quote Plato; he knew what Newton had discovered about gravity; but he could hug you, too.

'Mind if I help myself to a drink?' he asked, nodding towards the half-empty bottle of whiskey on the windowsill.

'Of course,' said Henry. 'Here, let me get you a glass.'

'Unh-hunh. I'll drink it out of yours.'

Fenchurch poured himself a medicine-measure of whiskey, and sipped it, and then rolled the glass slowly backwards and forwards between his strong, stubby fingers.

'You'll blame yourself for a long time to come,' he said. 'I know that *I* did, when your mother died. I still do, in a way. I still ask myself, on some warm summer evening, when the sun's going down, and the sky's all lit up with colours, I still ask myself, what right do I have to be here when Margaret's gone?'

'But Dad,' said Henry, 'it was *my* fault. The whole thing was my fault. I shouted out *Doris!* I don't know why, for no reason at all; and she twisted around and that's when the chain broke.'

Fenchurch swallowed more whiskey, and coughed. 'No good telling you that the chain would probably have broken anyway?'

'Maybe it would have done, but not right then; not when Doris was sitting in it. She twisted around and that's what did it; and she twisted around only because I called her. I called her, and I killed her.'

Fenchurch was silent for a long time, rolling the glass, watching his son with steady and sympathetic eyes. 'All right,' he said, 'you blame yourself. At least that's a step towards understanding how you feel.'

'I feel like a murderer,' said Henry, bitterly. 'God, I feel worse than that even.'

'Do you think it's going to do you any good, blaming yourself? I mean, does it make you feel any better to think that you were responsible for killing her?'

Henry looked at his father, and then lowered his head. 'I don't know,' he said, hoarsely. 'I really don't know. All I can feel is a pain, as sharp as a hatchet. All I can think about is Doris.'

Fenchurch sat back, and poured some more whiskey. 'Want some?' he asked Henry. Henry nodded, and took the glass, and drank a whole mouthful at once. He shuddered as it burned fiercely down his throat. It was Mad River Sour; distilled up at Montpelier on the Mad River; and usually he never touched it. Fenchurch had always said it was the best thing there was for cleaning egg-spoons.

'Augusta came around earlier,' Fenchurch remarked.

'Yes,' Henry nodded. 'I saw her at the fair; after the accident.'

'She asked how you were. She said you looked pretty upset when she saw you; she was worried.'

'You told her I was all right?'

'I told her you were understandably upset.'

Henry sipped a little more whiskey. 'She's a kind girl, Augusta. She's going to make somebody a very fine wife.'

Fenchurch said, 'She asked you round to her parents' house for Sunday lunch tomorrow. She said it might help to take your mind off Doris.'

'I don't want to have my mind taken off Doris.'

'I know. Well, believe me, you won't be able to think about anything else but Doris for quite a few weeks, whether you want to or not.' He paused, and reached into his top waistcoat pocket for two cheroots, and then said, 'Still, it might be good for you to go. Better than sitting here, staring at monuments.'

They both lit up, and smoke curled around the bedroom. The Roberts family had lived in this house since Henry was eight; a fine four-cornered white-painted colonial with black-painted railings along the front verandah and black-painted shutters. At the front, there was a neat enclosed yard with two mature maple trees; at the back, there was a low wooden workshop, with a shingled roof, a stable, and then, covering over half an acre, a small city of tombstones, memorials, and grave-markers; hundreds of them, crowded together side by side; in dark Barre granite and blue Vermont marble, polished tablets and hammered monuments, some with angels and some with sleeping lambs; from the simplest $2.15 block, weighing in at 95lbs, to the greatest polished and engraved sarcophagus, almost immoveable at nearly two tons. It was a sombre sight; some of the Roberts' relatives found it too chilling even to visit them for tea; for every monument would one day mark the end of a human life. But in spite of the fact that the only garden he had ever known was a corpseless cemetery; and in spite of the fact that his father's livelihood was the commemoration of death, Henry had been brought up in a family atmosphere of cheerfulness and contentment, for the Roberts were good-natured people doing proud and conscientious work, and not beyond having some fun, too.

After Henry's birth, with Henry still crimson and grizzling in his crib, Dr Bendick had advised his mother not to have any more children. Henry had grown up as spoiled as any small boy could desire to be. His father had carved him a huge wooden rocking-horse; his mother had dressed him in lace. Both parents had talked to him from the age of three as if he were already grown-up; and although that had sometimes encouraged him to act precociously and exasperate his school-friends, it had developed within him a calmness of character and a sensitivity towards the feelings of other people that had eventually won over almost everybody in Bennington who had disliked him when he was very young. His father was proud of him. His father believed in Christian contentment. His father had engraved too many names on too many tombstones at 9 cents the letter to think otherwise.

Henry's only filial rebellion against his parents had been to spend most of his wage on clothes, and beer. He had also grown up into an incurable practical joker. Fenchurch and Margaret had decided that they could comfortably accept both of these idiosyncrasies; although Fenchurch had warned Henry against pranks involving tombstones, and funerals. A laugh was a laugh, but business was business. He should always be careful not to hurt anybody else's feelings.

Fenchurch had known how much Henry had liked Doris, although he hadn't suspected for a moment that he had liked her enough to propose to her; and it had been a shock to him when Henry had said that they were engaged. But he sympathized with Henry deeply; he could share the hurt that Henry was feeling; and he also understood from his own experience that there was almost nothing he could do.

'Do you want to try and get some sleep?' he asked Henry.

Henry shook his head.

'You should,' said Fenchurch. 'It'll make you feel better in the morning. It'll help you to cope with it.'

'Not tonight,' replied Henry. He reached out and touched his father's hand. 'Don't worry, Dad. Tomorrow, I'll sleep like a log.'

There was a long silence between them, and at last Fenchurch stood up, pressing the back of his hand against his mouth to stifle a yawn. 'I'd better get to bed. There's church tomorrow. The Reverend Jones will think I've been doing something I shouldn't, if I turn up with circles under my eyes.'

Henry said, 'Maybe it's time you did.'

Fenchurch frowned, 'What?'

'Did something you shouldn't. It's been over a year.'

Fenchurch realized that Henry was testing him; probing his grief to see how long it had lasted. And so he simply smiled, and laid his hand on his son's shoulder, and said, 'Maybe you're right. Trouble is, I only know two pretty women of the right age in Carmington; and both of those are well and truly married.'

'Mrs Gordon?' asked Henry.

'She's one, yes. Fine lady. Don't know how she stands that husband of hers.'

Henry said, 'I'm sorry.'

'What for?'

Henry reached up and grasped his father's hard-calloused hand. 'I'm sorry for making you say things that you don't want to say; I'm sorry for making you pretend.'

Fenchurch was quiet for a moment. Henry guessed that he was remembering his mother. It was strange, he thought: here are the two of us, carvers of memorials into solid marble; and yet the most enduring memories we have are deep within us;

that is where people are really remembered; that is where love and devotion really last. He thought of Doris again, of kissing Doris in the woods, with the distant thunder grumbling like indigestion, and the birds singing, and he knew there was no possible way in which that moment could be immortalized in stone.

'Goodnight, Dad,' he said, gently.

'Are you going to be all right?' his father asked him.

Henry nodded. 'I'll be all right.'

He stayed by the window, listening to his father in the bedroom next door, clanking the jug in the wash-basin, dropping his shoes on to the bare-boarded floor, and at last climbing into bed. The moon had risen high now, and the sky was unnaturally clear, and in the garden the ranks of tombstones shone like the petrified seasons of Doris' life, fewer than a hundred of them. There was one consolation, he thought, with bitterness, and that was that Mr Paterson wouldn't ask him to carve Doris' epitaph. From the conversations that he had overheard downstairs since returning from the fair, neighbours and friends and inquisitive acquaintances, it sounded as if Mr Paterson was blaming him for everything. God, he thought, doesn't Mr Paterson realize just how savagely I blame myself? 'Fell Asleep' could never be the words for Doris. But what else could you say? 'Mangled To Death by the Colossal Whirler'? 'Cruelly Crushed'? Or 'Killed by the One Who Said that He Loved Her'?

He emptied the last of the Mad River whiskey into his glass, and drank it slowly, watching the night turning around the town, the wheels of the stars, the revolving moon. The dog stopped barking; the temperature fell; the trees began to whisper amongst themselves in the early-morning wind. But Henry kept the window open, and at three o'clock, when the moon sank blandly behind the mountains, he got up from his chair, and felt around in the darkness for his discarded coat.

He opened his bedroom door. He could hear his father snoring. Fenchurch very rarely drank, and even one glass of Mad River Sour must have been enough to send him off. Henry tiptoed across the creaking landing, and down the stairs. At last he reached the kitchen, with its darkly gleaming casseroles and pans, and made his way to the back door. He drew the bolts, turned the key, and stepped outside.

It seemed warmer out in the back yard than it had in the

house. He walked through the rows of blank-faced gravestones, each one waiting for a name. He unlocked the wooden work-shop door, and went inside. He knew exactly what he was looking for.

He would have to walk to the fairground; he didn't want to risk waking up Fenchurch by leading out either of the horses. But now that the moon had gone down, it was unlikely that anybody would see him, even if they did happen to be standing by their window, sleepless or haunted or waiting for the dawn. He walked along the main street, and past the sloping green, staying close to the trees where the thickest shadows were gathering. Only the church shone out in the darkness, with its silent spire.

At last he reached the meadow. The fairground was deserted under the starry sky. It looked like the abandoned encampment of some absurd and motley army, Attila the Clown and his hundred saltimbancos. The waggons in which the barkers and the sword-swallowers slept were right over on the far side of the field, their tin chimneys smoking, and there were two or three guard-dogs chained up to their wheels. But Henry was too far away for them to take any notice of him, although a mountain lion growled as he passed the canvas-shrouded cages next to the menagerie.

His arms were aching by the time he reached the Colossal Whirler. He had carried with him, all the way from Hancock Street, a full two-gallon screwtop can of kerosene. He set it down on the steps of the Whirler, and stretched the muscles in his back, and looked up at the massive watermill machine that only a few hours ago had crushed Doris to death. Its spokes formed black interlocking patterns against the night; and in the darkness it looked like some elaborate engine of death. Henry unscrewed the top of his can, and smelled the oily vapour of kerosene on the wind. Then he mounted the Whirler's steps, and crossed the platform until he was standing right beneath the main wheel.

As silently as he could, he poured kerosene all over the platform and around the steam-engine housing, so that it ran liquidly all across the boards, and dripped from the wheel and the drive-belt. He felt nothing: neither guilty nor afraid. All he knew was that he was determined to destroy this grotesque machine forever. Even if he couldn't give Doris an epitaph, at least he could give her a memorial pyre.

He stepped back, and took a box of matches out of his pocket, and struck one. It flared up, and then he tossed it. It lay beneath the big wheel for a while, burning blue and sputtering. Henry was just about to throw another one when the first rush of flames fled outwards from the match, and across the platform. There was a breathy explosion, and suddenly the whole platform was ablaze, its railings and its steps and its crosspieces. The bunting that was strung around the front of the Whirler's entrance was caught by the updraught of fire, and whirled blazing into the air. Then the lower circumference of the big wheel began to burn.

Henry slowly retreated, feeling the heat against his face. The Whirler's supports were on fire now, and the timbers spat and crackled so loudly that he was amazed that nobody from the waggons had yet woken up. One of the guard-dogs had begun to bark, and jump on its leash; and over on the right-hand side of the field, beneath the trees, the horses began to whinny and thrash in their corral. Henry backed further and further away, until at last he had reached the edge of the fairground, where he could see the blazing Whirler in all its ghastly glory.

The fire was now so intense that it had started to boil the water in the Whirler's boilers; and the engine began to let out jerky little jets of steam. At first, the pressure did nothing but shake the Whirler's wheel in showers of sparks, because the brakes were still applied. But when the flames ate away at the wooden brake-shoes, the wheel slowly began to turn, and as it turned it burned like a monstrous Catherine wheel, shedding a hideous flickering light all over the fair.

The fire-bells began to beat; and there was shouting and screaming from the waggons. Henry watched from the shelter of the roadside as twenty or thirty fairground men went running up the hill towards the blazing Whirler, most of them still in their nightshirts. Someone was screeching hoarsely for buckets, but it was obvious that there was nothing left of the Colossal Whirler worth saving. It turned faster and faster, groaning and crackling with every revolution, until at last the supports collapsed and the huge fiery wheel dropped on to the grass and broke into hundreds of blazing pieces.

Henry turned away at last, and began to walk back home. As he passed the green, Carmington's fire-pump came rattling past, clanging its alarm bell, followed by a small crowd of running townspeople. George Davies was among them, and he called out, 'Henry! Come along! The fair's on fire!'

Henry walked back to his house on Hancock Street and went in by the back door. He climbed tiredly up the stairs; but as he reached the door of his room, he saw his father standing at the far end of the landing.

'You've been out,' said Fenchurch.

'Just for some air, yes. I thought you were asleep.'

'I was, until I heard the fire-bells, and went into your room, and found that you were gone. I heard someone shouting that the Whirler's on fire.'

Henry said nothing; but stood and waited in the doorway.

Fenchurch came forward and looked at Henry carefully. 'Once, when you were small, and your toy cart lost its handle, you tried to burn it, do you remember?'

Behind his father's head, through the circular landing window, Henry could see the sky beginning to grow lighter, and the outline of trees and houses. 'I remember,' he said.

'Then can you swear to me that what happened tonight, that Whirler catching fire, that wasn't anything to do with you?'

Henry said, 'Dad, I'm twenty-five years old. I can take my own responsibilities. I don't have to promise you anything.'

'I'm not asking because I don't think you're responsible for whatever you do. I'm asking because I'm your father.'

'Because you're my father, you shouldn't have to ask me.'

'You did set fire to it, though?' Fenchurch insisted.

Henry didn't answer. But Fenchurch turned away, and grasped the banister railings with both hands, and took a deep, steady breath. 'Well, of course you set fire to it,' he said, quietly. 'And who can blame you? All we have to be sure of now is that nobody can prove that it was you. You realize, don't you, that you'll be the very first suspect? And you realize what the penalty is for wilful arson? You won't have made yourself very popular, setting alight the biggest attraction at Carmington Fair.'

'It killed Doris, that's all I know,' Henry replied. He tried to stop his voice from trembling.

His father turned around again and laid his hands on his shoulders. 'Henry, I *know*. And if you really want to hear the truth of it, I'm proud of you. I think I probably would have done the same thing, if I'd have had the courage. But what worries me now is that you've put yourself at risk; and that you haven't learned much of a lesson, either. Never seek revenge, Henry; it's never worth it. You know what Shakespeare said, "the whirligig of time brings in his revenges." Time, and fate, have a way of making people pay. You don't have to do it.'

Henry hugged his father close. 'I'm sorry,' he said. 'I must be the worst kind of disappointment to you.'

Fenchurch said, 'You're Margaret's son. You can never be a disappointment. You're the very last living part I have of her.'

Henry rubbed his face with his hands. 'I think I'm going to have to get some sleep,' he said.

'You're going to take lunch with the Pierces?'

Henry nodded. 'I guess so. I wouldn't want to upset Augusta. I seem to have managed to upset almost everybody else.'

His father was about to go back to his bedroom, when he turned and asked, 'How did you do it? How did you burn the Whirler, I mean?'

'Kerosene. The whole can, splashed over the bottom of it.'

Fenchurch thought about that for a moment, and then said, 'Remind me to tell Johnson's Hardware to deliver some more. Goodnight.'

'Goodnight, Dad.'

Henry shut the door of his room behind him and stood for a moment with his eyes closed. Then he slowly undressed, hanging up his fair-going suit in the closet, alongside his bottle-green velvet coat and his blue broadcloth Sunday suit. He sat down on the edge of his bed to tug off his long cotton under-pants, and as he did so he saw the daguerreotype of his mother in the oval silver frame on the nightstand. The strong, pretty, smiling face. The brown upswept hair. He picked up the picture and looked at it for a long time.

'I'm sorry, Mom,' he said; but the words sounded flat and meaningless in the gradually-brightening room. He put the picture back on the nightstand. He wouldn't even have a picture of Doris to remember her by. He opened his bureau drawer, took out his white cotton nightshirt, and slipped into it. Then, with aching bones and an aching mind, he climbed carefully between the sheets of his bed, and lay there with his face against the pillow and his eyes wide open, watching the sunlight strengthen across the green and brown Brussels carpet.

The burning-down of the Colossal Whirler already seemed like a dream; and he was almost convinced as he lay there that if he dressed again and walked back to the fairground, he would find everything exactly as it had been before, with the sideshows crowded and the Whirler whirling and the animals roaring in the menagerie. The only recollection of which he was certain was that Doris was dead; and that recollection felt as hard and as cold and as uncompromising as a heart of lead. The heart of lead of the Happy Prince, which would never melt; not even in a furnace.

He was still awake when his father brought him a mug of black coffee. He sat up in bed while Fenchurch went to the window and looked out over the assembly of gravestones. The sun shone on Fenchurch's thick grey whiskers, making them shine like the bristles of shaving-brushes.

'I didn't tell you last night,' Fenchurch said, 'but Mr Paterson created one hell of an uproar when they first told him about Doris.'

Henry sipped the scalding hot coffee without looking round. 'I overheard Gregory Evans,' he admitted. 'I was out on the landing, and I heard him say something about Mr Paterson wanting to take me to the courts for manslaughter.'

'Well, he'd never succeed in that,' said Fenchurch, emphatically. 'It was an accident, even Mr Paterson himself knows that. But what I'm saying is that Mr Paterson and his wife are just as sad about Doris' death as you are; and in many ways much more so. So, if he's rude towards you, and aggressive; if he blames you for everything that happened; well, remember that she was his daughter, that's all. His eldest daughter. And remember that when you burned down that Whirler contraption last night, you probably succeeded in punishing the people who were really responsible for Doris' death, and in the most effective way possible.'

'You're trying to tell me to be content?' asked Henry, looking at his father sharply.

'I'm trying to tell you that accidents are accidents, and that most of the time you have to accept them, whether they're lucky or whether they're tragic. Who are you going to blame? Yourself, for shouting Doris? The engineer who was supposed to check the chain on Doris's seat, but wasn't given the time? The man who owns the Whirler, who has to keep the Whirler going even when it needs maintenance because he's obliged to pay out wages, and keep his family fed?'

'So everybody's to blame and nobody's to blame? Is that it?'

'Not at all,' replied Fenchurch. He was silent for a moment or two, and then he said, 'I'm just trying to make you understand that there is nothing simple in this world, nothing. Everything is complicated. People are complicated. Incidents are complicated. Most of the time, they're so complicated, that it's a waste of time looking for blame, or for reasons, or for any kind of justification. Take what life gives you, Henry, whether it's good or bad. What do you think luck is? A complicated series of circumstances that just happen to have a happy effect. And what do you think tragedy is? The opposite. That's all.'

Henry didn't really understand what Fenchurch was trying to explain to him, and so he turned away again, and carried on sipping his coffee. But Fenchurch came over and knelt down beside his bed, and pointed his finger at him and said, 'You were not to blame for Doris' death, Henry, no matter how much you may want to be. You did nothing wrong, except that you loved her and just happened to be there when she died. I know how sad you are, Henry, I know how you feel. But you were no more responsible for Doris dying that I was for your mother dying. That's the way life happens to be; and nothing you do or say is ever going to make any difference.'

Henry looked back at his father; and for the first time in his life felt that he was beginning truly to understand him, to grasp who he was. He began to perceive his father's limitations, as well as his strengths. His fears, as well as his courage. He loved his father, unquestioningly, and far from being diminished as he grew to see what his father could do and what he couldn't, his love for him was becoming deeper, less sentimental, more idiosyncratic. He saw his father now as a human being; and he was sensitive enough to realize that he, too, had human weaknesses, and limitations of his own. But he refused to agree with his father's view of tragedy and fortune. He would accept fortune, certainly; if good luck came his way, he wouldn't question it. But he would never accept tragedy. Not after Doris' death. Not after burning down the Whirler.

He took his father's hand and squeezed it hard, and said, 'I love you, Dad,' but even as his father smiled, and nodded, Henry could sense that their closeness would from this morning onwards always be subject to certain qualifications. The different deaths of Margaret and Doris would always be a shadow between them.

At eleven o'clock that morning, smartly dressed in black,

with a black tie, Henry presented himself at the front door of Arlington Lodge, the large hundred-year-old house in which the Pierces lived cater-corner from the Carmington church. Wisteria grew heavily over the curved pediments of the porch, and twined itself in and out of the shutters. The garden was softly arranged, with thick borders of forget-me-nots and basket-of-gold; phlox and Johnny-jump-ups. In the early heat of the day, bees swarmed blurrily over the flowers, and the lawns sparkled with evaporating dew. The garden had been planted by Augusta's mother; and she and Augusta tended it between them, a living testament to the gentleness of their spirits.

The door opened, and Mr Gordon Pierce himself appeared, a big angular man with a big plain face like Augusta's, and a curly brown moustache. He too was dressed in black, and he came out and took Henry's arm in a gesture of immediate sympathy.

'My dear Henry! We were so upset for you when we heard. You come along in. Mulliken – ' he said, calling to the maid, ' – tell cook that our guest is here, and that we shall want to be seated at the table within the hour.'

Mulliken was a skinny pretty girl with a slightly wild appearance caused by her fixed left eye, which was glass. Henry had spoken to her several times before when the Roberts had visited the Pierces, and each time she had told him a different story of how she had lost her eye: scratched by a cat, poked out by her father in a fit of drunken rage, blinded by tannin at a saddlery. But Augusta had said that at the age of fourteen Mulliken had wanted to be a nun; and when her parents had refused her, she had dug out her own eye with a teaspoon, to give as a gift to God; and that only the sudden intervention of her mother had prevented her from digging out the other eye, as well.

Augusta had said that there was a lesson to be learned from Mulliken's eye: and that was that you can never judge the strength of anybody else's devotion by your own.

In the sun-squared parlour, Augusta was sitting with her mother; both of them dressed in black taffeta, with white lace aprons; both wearing white lace bonnets. Augusta's spectacles flashed like an oval heliograph, a message of expectancy and sorrow.

'You heard that the Whirler burned down in the night?' Mr Pierce asked Henry.

Henry nodded. He took Mrs Pierce's hand, and bowed to her.

'I for one, am delighted,' said Mrs Pierce. She was a surprisingly small, bird-boned woman, and seeing her sitting next to Augusta it seemed almost impossible that she had once given birth to such a large daughter. 'Such contraptions should never be allowed. I had a cousin once, Edward; do you remember Edward, Augusta? No, you wouldn't you were too young. But Edward lost the tips of two of his fingers on a helter-skelter. Gordon, do get Henry a glass of sherry. Goodness knows how, but Edward always was particularly careless.'

Henry sat down on the opposite end of the sofa on which Augusta was already sitting; his knees together. The parlour was decorated in mild blues and peachy pinks, quite unlike the robust browns and greens which Augusta usually chose for her clothes; and the washed-out watercolour paintings and gilded mirrors that were hung around the walls made it seem even softer.

Gordon Pierce brought sherry. Outside, in the wide-boarded hallway, Mulliken's boots tapped and clattered as she took dishes into the dining-room. Henry sipped his drink and suddenly began to feel very tired, from shock and lack of sleep. The drowsiness of the morning affected him, too: a warm Sunday morning in south Vermont in the days when Gettysburg was just a small town in Pennsylvania and secession was nothing more than a troublesome political nightmare; the sort that a Congressman would have after too much toasted cheese.

Mrs Pierce said, 'I understand that you and Doris had talked of marriage.'

'Informally, unofficially, yes,' Henry replied. 'I hadn't gone so far as to ask her father. Her father wasn't too keen on me, as a matter of fact; not as a son-in-law, anyway. He said that being a memorial mason wasn't exactly the road to riches.'

'Well, he was always was a windbag, that William Paterson,' said Mrs Pierce. Then, when her husband frowned at her for being uncharitable, she ruffled herself and said, 'Well, he *was*. And still is. I can remember him when he was a clerk for Mr Bunning, and a plumper, inkier, noisier youth I find it hard to think of.'

'Somebody said the Whirler was burned down deliberately,'

remarked Augusta, in her lispy, flat-toned way. Henry had always felt that even when she was making a statement she was asking a question; and he felt it especially now. She turned to look at him and there was something in her eyes which said: I know you did it, didn't you?

'Well, that would be arson,' said Mr Pierce, unnecessarily.

Henry said, 'I understand they have quite a lot of accidents on fairgrounds. Fires, especially.'

Augusta reached across and touched his sleeve. 'Are you *very* sad? I did try to help you yesterday, but you must have been quite stunned.'

Henry, despite himself, felt a lump rising up in his throat. 'I still find it hard to believe, as a matter of fact,' he told Augusta, and there were tears in his eyes. 'I keep thinking that if I went along to the Paterson house, she would still be there; that I could speak to her. I did want to marry her, you know. I loved her. I think really that I always will.'

'You must have another sherry,' said Mr Pierce, consolingly. 'And you must do and say as you please. That is why Augusta asked you here today; so that you could spend a few hours among friends, and be reassured that we care for you, and that we mourn with you. Isn't that right, Phyllida?'

Mrs Pierce twitched her mouth in a variety of sympathetic positions. Henry took out his handkerchief and quietly blew his nose. That morning, his misery at losing Doris was like a hangover, it came in waves. Sometimes he could almost forget about it altogether; at other times it would take only a fragrance, a movement, a ray of sunlight across the carpet, and he would be reminded so painfully of Doris that he was unable to speak.

'Dr Bendick said that she couldn't have felt anything,' said Augusta.

'Well, I hope not,' said Henry, hopelessly.

Shortly after their regulator clock had struck twelve, the Pierces led Henry through to lunch, baked country ham and apples, chicken croquettes, and heaps of creamed potatoes. Mrs Pierce brought out her speciality, ginger and watermelon pickle; and Mr Pierce served his home-made fruit wine. Mulliken served them with one eye on Henry and the other fixed on the sideboard.

Towards the end of the meal, Mrs Pierce said, 'I lost an uncle once, you know, and I went to see him at the funeral parlour. Uncle Corey, poor fellow, died of inflammation of the ear. But there he was, lying in his casket, and I looked at him, I was only twelve, you know; I looked at him and suddenly his toupee slipped off and I screamed out loud and jumped up and I swear to God that I cannot look at a toupee not to this day without thinking of death. I wouldn't let Gordon wear one, not for the world. Better bald than creepy, that's what I always say.'

They said a grace after they had eaten, and Henry said a short prayer for Doris; to commend her soul to God; and Augusta said a graceful prayer for those left behind, those bewildered by the ways of holy destiny, and those who wept.

Afterwards, when Mr Pierce had gone upstairs to his dressing-room for 'Biblical study', which meant lying with his feet up on his leather chaise-longue and snoozing until teatime, Augusta and Henry went for a walk through the garden, and at last sat on a bench underneath a silver birth tree, knee-deep in day lilies, while up above them the fair-weather cumulus sailed through a sky like ink.

Augusta in her black dress and her lace apron said, 'It *was* you, wasn't it?'

'What was me?'

'You know what I mean. It was you who burned down the Colossal Whirler.'

Henry hesitated for a while, watching her. Then he nodded.

Augusta grasped both of his hands, and held them tightly between hers. 'Oh, I think you're so admirable, to have done that. Oh, Henry, what a gesture of love! You're so brave; I wish there was something I could do to console you, anything!'

'You've done too much for me already.'

'No, Henry, you're quite wrong. I could never do too much for you. Don't you understand?'

Henry did understand, but didn't want to say it. He gently took his hands out from between Augusta's; but fearing that he would seem too boorish if he were to let go of her altogether, he laid one hand on top of hers. Her face was flushed and eager, and she suddenly took off her spectacles, and stared at him with watery, unfocused eyes; her eyebrows thick and brown and unplucked.

'Henry,' she said, 'I have *always* loved you, ever since I first knew you. When I was small I loved you. I love you now. Not only as a friend, Henry; not only as a companion; but as somebody who cares for you completely, someone who will do anything for you, as a helpmate, as a devoted servant, as a lover, Henry!'

She got down on to her knees amongst the long grass and the day lilies, and clasped his wrists, and her face was so wrung with feeling that Henry could hardly look at her. 'Augusta,' he said; and 'Yes?' she replied, even more eagerly. 'Yes?'

'Augusta. . . .'

'Henry, I know; I understand. I know you loved Doris, I know that you must love her still, and that your heart has no room in it now for anything but sorrow. But the time will come, Henry, when that sorrow will diminish, and when you will need something fresh and living and full of hope to take its place. Oh, Henry; please let that be my love!'

Henry couldn't think what to say. He didn't dislike Augusta. Her manner was pleasant and she was hard-working, and she never complained. During those long spring evenings when they had been waiting for his mother to die, she had sat in their parlour by the fire and talked to him of St Ignatius and the Aboona of Abyssinia and the spirit of Christian forbearance. She was knowledgeable and enthusiastic; if rather too religious; but what kind of a fault was that?

'Augusta,' he said, quietly. He stroked her tightly-plaited hair with the palm of his hand. 'You've always been good to me. I owe you much more than I could ever repay.'

'You don't have to repay me. I don't expect it. Henry, I want nothing more than your consideration. Please allow me to help you, to care for you, to stay with you. I won't ask for anything else.'

He took hold of her arms and tried to raise her up from her knees, but she wouldn't. 'You must tell me your answer,' she said. 'Henry, I've waited so many years for this moment. I must know. If you deny me now, there is nothing ahead of me but loneliness and spinsterhood!'

'Augusta, you must give me time to think. Augusta, I'm tired. I'm really tired. After everything that happened yesterday – after last night – well, it's almost impossible for me to see straight.'

'Then at least say that you'll consider what I've asked you.'

Henry smiled. It was his first smile of the day. Augusta responded to it as if she had seen the first flower of spring opening up in front of her eyes, and she laid her head upon his knees, and held him close. One of her hairpins was digging right into his kneecap, but he didn't like to tell her to move, not because of that. His hand hovered over her head, over her bright red ear, and then withdrew.

'I'll consider it, Augusta, I promise.'

He went home after tea; daffodil cake and hermits. Augusta came to the front gate with him, and he realized that she expected a kiss. He kissed her cheek; she turned her face around and kissed his lips. A wasp zizzed past them, golden in the sunlight. 'You won't keep me waiting for too long, will you?' she asked him, and he said 'no,' so quietly that he didn't even hear it himself.

Three men were waiting in the front parlour with his father when he arrived home. They were all wearing their church-going clothes, dark and severe, and their hats were on their knees, which was a sign that they did not intend to stay for very long. One of them was William Paterson, white-faced, black-eyed, still feverish with rage and unhappiness; the others were Frederick Makepiece, the mayor of Carmington, and John Good, the county sheriff. Frederick was as small and rotund as William Paterson; the two of them looked like matching jugs. John Good was lean and laconic, one of the dreariest men that Henry had ever met, blue-chinned, drably spoken.

Fenchurch was pacing from one side of the parlour to the other, his hands in his pockets, and Henry could tell that he was upset and offended. 'Henry,' he said, as soon as Henry came in through the door, 'these gentlemen have some accusations to make. Accusations which apparently couldn't wait until Monday. Accusations which had to be made on the Sabbath; the morning after Doris' death; and the poor girl not even laid out yet.'

'Now then, Fenchurch,' said Frederick Makepiece, trying to be conciliatory. 'No purpose will be served by sarcasm, nor provocative remarks.'

'You don't think that your accusations against my son are provocative?' Fenchurch demanded. 'You don't think that every word you have uttered since I allowed you into my house has been insulting and unjustified? My dear Frederick!'

'Dad,' said Henry, gently. He walked to the centre of the room, and looked around him. 'If these gentlemen have anything to say to me, I'm sure that they can say it to my face. Hallo, Mr Paterson. I'm glad to see you. I haven't yet had the chance to express my regrets to you, nor my condolences.'

76

Mr Paterson turned away, his jaw steadily masticating with anger and suppressed grief. Mr Makepiece said, 'This is a serious matter, I'm afraid.'

'In that case, you'd better tell me all about it,' replied Henry. 'Have you been offered some tea? Or something stronger?'

'We didn't come here for refreshments, thank you,' Mr Paterson bristled.

'I'm afraid not,' said Mr Makepiece. 'We came because Mr Paterson here is convinced that his daughter's death was not accidental; and that it was your recklessness that was the larger cause of it; and that you wantonly put her life at risk. He is considering an action against you for manslaughter; that is, unless the county decides to prosecute you for manslaughter as a matter of public law.'

Henry said nothing at first. He looked at Mr Paterson, and then at Mr Good, and then turned to his father. All Fenchurch could do was shrug.

'You have some evidence, I suppose?' Henry asked Mr Makepiece; although he kept his eyes on Mr Paterson, defying him to return his stare.

'It is the *lack* of evidence that supports Mr Paterson's contention,' said Mr Makepiece.

'And what is that supposed to mean?' Henry wanted to know.

John Good spoke up now. 'It was your explanation, wasn't it, Mr Roberts, that the chain holding Miss Paterson's seat gave way?'

'That's correct.'

'Well, the fact of the matter is that you were the only person who witnessed the chain breaking; and that several other chains were broken when the Colossal Whirler came to a sudden stop. It was my intention to go to the fairground tomorrow and examine the chains to substantiate your story. Presumably, if you were telling the truth, at least one chain would have been found broken in the manner you described.'

'What are you saying?' Fenchurch snapped. 'Are you trying to accuse my son of lying? Why should he lie? He lost his dearest sweetheart yesterday, the girl he wanted to marry. How can you come here and suggest that he killed her deliberately?'

'That's not what we're saying at all, Fenchurch,' said Mr Makepiece. 'What we're saying is that there might have been some element of carelessness in your son's behaviour; that he might not have discharged his responsibility to look after Miss Paterson with quite the conscientiousness that he might have done.'

'Don't be so mealy-mouthed!' Fenchurch retorted. 'You're suggesting he killed her; aren't you? Or at least this excuse for an attorney is. What possible grounds do you have for making such charges? And, damn it, how dare you?'

John Good said, 'Simple criminological deduction, Mr Roberts.'

'Stop beating the bushes,' Fenchurch raged. 'If you've got something to say, then out with it.'

'Very well,' John Good nodded. 'The Colossal Whirler was burned down during the night, as you probably know; and we have to ask ourselves *why* it was burned down, and by whom.'

'It could have been an accident,' said Henry, tightly.

'Highly unlikely,' replied John Good. 'No, no. Not the way it caught fire so quickly. Two or three minutes, and it was going like a torch, so the fair people say. And that would suggest kerosene; and *that* would suggest that somebody set fire to it on purpose. What we have to ask ourselves is why somebody might have set fire to it on purpose.'

'Well,' challenged Henry. 'Why, in your opinion?'

John Good took out a damp-looking handkerchief and spent a long time investigating his nose. Then, frowning at whatever it was he had managed to dig out, he folded his handkerchief up again, and said, 'The only reason why anybody ever destroys property that might be material to a criminal charge is in order to eradicate evidence. *You* say, the chain broke, and that Doris was thrown off the Whirler inadvertently. *We* say, perhaps she was thrown off because somebody was getting up to irresponsible high-jinks; and putting her life in peril. *You* say, where's the broken chain, then? And *we* say, burned. Just one chain in a whole heap of chains, lying in the ashes. *You* say, where's your evidence then? And *we* say, here.'

With that, John Good stood up, and went to the doorway, and called out, 'Cotes! Bring that in here, will you?' Then he turned, and smiled at Henry, smoothing his hands together as if he were rolling out very thin strips of pastry.

A short bustling man in a brown duster coat appeared, and hurried to the middle of the room, where he held up a battered red kerosene can, as if he were auctioning it.

'This can was found close to the Colossal Whirler after it was

78

burned down,' said John Good, with dry satisfaction. 'And this can, coincidentally or not, bears the indented initials FR; which Mr Johnson at the hardware store tells me are the initials of Fenchurch Roberts. So, this can belongs to the Roberts. "FR!" it says, as clear as day; and that is proof enough for me that one of the Roberts was guilty of arson. Here's the very can, out of which the incendiary liquid was so criminally poured! A can marked "FR" for Roberts, and no doubt carried by a Roberts, no question at all, I'd say, for only a Roberts would have harboured such a destructive interest in the Colossal Whirler; at least if that Roberts were worried that somebody might examine the Whirler, and discover that his tall tale about the death of Miss Doris Paterson was not quite as he had told it. Wouldn't you say?'

'This is poisonous nonsense,' said Henry. 'Dad, tell these people to leave.'

Fenchurch propped his fists on his hips. 'They can say what they came here to say,' he replied. 'I want to hear for myself how low my friends are capable of stooping. You, Frederick, of all people. And you, Mr Paterson. You know how fond Henry was of Doris. You know as well as I do that he wouldn't have touched a hair of her head.'

'The evidence says otherwise,' Mr Paterson retorted.

'Evidence? What evidence? An empty can? What evidence is that?'

'I'm afraid we have a witness, too,' Frederick Makepiece said, as apologetically as he could manage. 'Henry was seen walking towards the fairground with the can; and returning without it, after the blaze had begun. It was Mrs Fairbrother; you know how sleepless she is. The eczema.'

'We have quite enough evidence to bring a prosecution,' said John Good. 'In fact, we have no alternative; especially since Mr Paterson is pressing us to go ahead. If we succeed, you see, then Mr Paterson's own case against you will have every chance of being successful, too.'

Frederick Makepiece said, 'I'm sorry, Fenchurch. None of us care for this business any more than you do. But we are all the custodians of justice; and if criminal damage has been committed, then we are under a moral obligation to punish it, no matter who the culprit might have been. You do understand our position.'

'Your position, as always, Frederick, is bent over double

79

with your head stuffed down your britches,' fumed Fenchurch. 'Now, I suggest you leave; and if you have any criminal charges to make, then make them properly, and formally, and in the accustomed fashion.'

'We did actually wish to avoid that,' said Frederick Makepiece.

'Although we can make them, and we will, if necessary,' added John Good, with dreary relish. He smiled, and kept on smoothing his hands.

'Come on then,' said Henry, tautly. 'Say what you have to.' He was very close to the brink of losing his temper; and it was only his father's hand on his arm that prevented him from shouting at all of these puffing hypocrites to get out of their house.

'The point is,' said Frederick Makepiece, carefully, 'the point is that *all* of us would rather avoid a scandal. A fuss, do you know what I mean? And Doris's death – well, I'm afraid it has all of the makings – particularly with Mr Paterson here so angry about it – and the Colossal Whirler, well, the fair people are stirring up all kinds of a hubbub. And we do have our community to think about; and our friendship, too. You and I, we've been friends for nearly thirty years, haven't we, Fenchurch? And you can't say that a friendship as long-standing as that doesn't have certain loyalties, and certain duties, each to the other, can you?'

'So what do you see as your loyalty and your duty to me?' asked Fenchurch, in a bald voice.

Frederick Makepiece raised both hands, pink, like a pig's trotters, and allowed his face to sink slowly and apologetically into his double chins. 'My loyalty, as I see it, is to give young Henry here an opportunity to make amends.'

'Make amends for *what?*' snapped Henry. 'For burning down a criminally dangerous sideshow? A damned infernal machine that actually killed the girl I wanted to marry? You want me to make amends for that?'

'Would you say that counted as an admission of guilt?' John Good asked Frederick Makepiece laconically, with one eyebrow raised halfway up his forehead, like a hairy caterpillar crawling up a pumpkin.

Frederick Makepiece wobbled his chins to say emphatically no, and to keep your smug remarks to yourself, John Good. He said to Henry, 'I've spent most of the morning talking about this, I'll have you know, ever since that oil-can was discovered, and Mrs Fairbrother said that she's seen you sneaking off to the fair. Mr Paterson here was dead set on taking you up before the court, and prosecuting you for manslaughter and criminal damage and everything else; and you can believe me that if the court didn't hang you, they'd certainly lock you up for the rest of your life. But Mr Paterson is prepared to see my point of view about duty and loyalty to old friends; and to respected and long-standing members of our community. For your own sake, and for the sake of avoiding a scandalous trial, but most of all for *your* father's sake both the county and Mr Paterson are prepared under particular circumstances not to press charges.'

Fenchurch was very silent, his shoulders hunched, his eyes smudged dark, but staring at Frederick Makepiece with continent anger.

'What then do you see as my loyalty and duty to *you*, Frederick?' he asked.

Frederick Makepiece gave him a tight, lopsided smile, and thrust his little fingers together. 'Henry should go away for a while. Maybe south. I hear Charleston is particularly pleasant at this time of year. Or west, even; to try something new. But he should go away, and *keep* away. That would satisfy Mr Paterson; after all, think of it, does Mr Paterson really want to come face to face, every single day of the week, with the man he believes was responsible for killing his daughter? No – hear me out, please, I know how you feel, but it's true. It's better all around, if Henry goes away for a while. Perhaps not for ever. But for long enough for tempers to cool down. Even John Good here will accept that solution, despite his criminal evidence; and will happily strike any record of this matter from his notebooks.'

'Exile, then, that's what you're talking about?' Henry demanded.

Frederick Makepiece blew out his cheeks in amusement. 'Exile, that's rather a strong word for it. You're not the Count of Monte Cristo, after all.'

'That reminds me,' said Henry, as sourly as he could, 'I still have your copy of that, Mr Makepiece. You can take it with you when you leave.'

'Don't trouble yourself,' said Frederick Makepiece. 'We're leaving now. Come on, gentlemen, let's give young Mr Roberts some time to think this over. But please, Fenchurch, don't let

81

him leave it too long; or Mr Paterson here may well change his mind about bringing an action; and Mr Good may not be left with any alternative.'

'You *are* the custodians of justice, after all,' Henry quoted him, sarcastically.

'Yes,' retorted Frederick Makepiece, looking at Henry sharply. 'We are.'

'Your hats are in the hall,' said Fenchurch; and with that, the meeting was at an end. Henry opened the door for them, and one by one they left, Frederick Makepiece and John Good each giving him an embarrassed and uncomfortable nod. Mr Paterson was the last of the three to leave; and he paused for a moment and stared at Henry as if he could joyfully strangle him.

Henry said, 'No matter what you believe, Mr Paterson, I loved her; and I love her still.'

'If what Doris felt was the effect of your love,' replied Mr Paterson, 'God help anyone who feels the effect of your hatred.'

Henry closed the door behind him. His father was standing at the end of the hallway, his hands clasped behind his back, watching him.

'Well?' said Henry.

Fenchurch shook his head. 'I really don't know. They seem to be quite confident that they can prosecute you; and even get you thrown into jail.'

'But why? Why should Mr Paterson want to do that? And why should Makepiece give him so much support?'

'You're underestimating William Paterson's influence,' said Fenchurch. He sat down in his chair, and dry-washed his face with his hands. Then he looked up at Henry, and went on, 'They're as thick as thieves, those two, Frederick Makepiece and William Paterson. Always have been, although they don't make much of a show of it. I'll bet you didn't know that Mr Paterson was godfather to Frederick's granddaughter Mary. And I'll bet you didn't know that they both own the old Kenley gristmill out at Woodford; jointly, as partners. So you can imagine that if Mr Paterson's riled up at something, Frederick's going to do everything he can to make sure that he gets whatever satisfaction he demands.'

'But Dad, you said it yourself. I wouldn't have hurt Doris for anything.'

Fenchurch slowly shook his head. 'Grief takes different people different ways. People like William Paterson, they have to look for somebody to accuse. That's their way of getting rid of all of those feelings of frustration. There isn't much you can do about it. He needs to find somebody to accuse, and you're the obvious culprit.'

Henry went to the oak wall-cupboard, took out a half-empty bottle of whiskey, and poured himself a very stiff drink. On the wall next to the cabinet, there was a pious engraving of Mary, at the foot of the cross. Such pain! thought Henry. And such pain exists; through human cruelty, and through human ignorance. He shuddered as he drank, partly because of the whiskey, and partly because he knew that Mr Paterson wanted him dead; as dead as Doris, deader. Sending him away in exile must have been a very unsatisfactory compromise, as far as Mr Paterson was concerned. Frederick Makepiece must have had a hard time persuading him.

'I had a good day with the Pierces,' Henry remarked, walking across the parlour with his drink in his hand, and sitting opposite his father. Outside, the sky was still light, that pale nostalgic turquoise of summer evenings, stirred by clouds.

Fenchurch looked away. 'I shouldn't have let them in,' he said.

'Dad, they're your neighbours. If you're going to go on living and working in Bennington, you can't turn them away.'

Fenchurch said, 'You sound as if you're thinking of leaving.'

'It may not be such a bad idea, when you come to consider it.'

'I don't want you to run away, Henry; and I don't want you to be chased away, either. I won't allow it. You have a right to stay here in Bennington; and if you're accused of anything, you have a constitutional right to a fair hearing. You know what the Bill of Rights guarantees you: due process of law. And that you shall have, I swear it.'

'Dad,' said Henry, tiredly. 'I really don't want the due process of law. I don't want to defend myself against any of them, not Paterson, nor Good, nor Makepiece; not on the grounds of bereavement. I know what I was guilty of, and what I wasn't guilty of. Why should I have to stand up in court and fight against Mr Paterson, just because he needs to find somebody to blame for Doris' death? Why should I have to explain to Mr Good and Mr Makepiece that I burned down the Whirler because I was sad, and because I wanted revenge, and because I wanted to make sure that the people who were really responsible for killing Doris were quickly and properly punished? I don't have to explain any of that to anyone. My grief is my own, and it isn't open to discussion, not by you, not by William Paterson, not by anybody; and especially not by the courts.'

Fenchurch watched him for a long time; judging in the way that only a father can judge his tiredness and his agitation. This boy that he had carried on his shoulders, on windy days down by Sadawga Pond; this boy that had sung to him, clear and high, while his mother sat in her rocking-chair and smiled, while the rockers went *click-clock, click-clock*, on the shining wooden floor. This boy that had said to him once, 'I love you,' and then run away, uncatchable, as all children eventually are, through grass and heat and thimbleweed, on a day that he had believed then was going to be endless. But no days are endless, and boys grow up, and Fenchurch understood now that Doris' death, whether Mr Paterson had accused him of recklessness or not, meant that Henry would have to go.

Fenchurch knew, too, that he wouldn't argue against Henry's going. It wasn't a question of running away. Henry would never run away, not from anything. It wasn't part of his nature. It was simply a question of looking for new possibilities, and new people. New passions, and new tragedies. Henry's destiny had probably never lain here, in Bennington, as contented as he was. Contentment is one thing; fulfilment is something else altogether. What had Shakespeare written? 'Farewell the tranquil mind, farewell content!' And (Fenchurch smiled wryly as he thought it) farewell to my son, too; that son who loved me in thimbleweed days.

He stood up. 'You must go, then, if you want to,' he said.

Henry raised his head, surprised. 'You won't object?'

'I'll mind,' said Fenchurch. 'But I won't object.'

Henry said, almost apologetically, 'I thought of going west. To California, perhaps.'

'You'd carry on the same trade?'

'Well, of course. But people must be dying there, as well as they do here. And perhaps we could manage a little business between us; you could send me Barre granite tombstones, and I could engrave them. Roberts & Son, nationwide monumental masons. What do you think of that?'

'I think you could do with some sleep.'

They had a quiet supper together of beef broth and barley, which Fenchurch had made the previous day. The decorative clock above the kitchen table chimed nine before they had finished, and it was almost dark. They sat on the back verandah

84

for a while, looking out over the tombstones, smoking, while moths pattered against the oil-lamps.

'Tell me about Doris,' said Fenchurch.

'There isn't much to say,' Henry told him. He tried to picture Doris' face. 'She was pretty; and sweet. She had no experience of life, though. Nor of love, either. I don't even know how much she loved me, because she had never loved anybody else. She probably didn't love me very much at all. Not as much as she could have done. But I wanted to marry her, and take care of her, I don't know why. I suppose I thought that I would never meet anyone quite like her again; and the trouble is, I don't believe that I will.'

Henry paused for a while, and then he said, 'It was only last night that she died you know, Dad; and yet it seems like a century ago.'

'Yes,' nodded Fenchurch. 'It was the same with your mother.'

There was a longer pause, and then Henry said, 'I won't go if you don't want me to.'

'Are you frightened of going?'

'A little, if you want the truth. And I shall be sad at leaving you.'

'Never be sad at leaving your parents.'

'I shall be sad at leaving you, no matter what.'

There was nothing else that either of them could say. The moon was very bright and full, and they sat on their verandah as if they were sitting on a floodlit stage. After a while, Henry lowered his head, and Fenchurch could hear from his muffled sobs that he was crying for Doris.

THREE

He decided that he would leave on Friday morning, after Doris' funeral. Jack Davies had offered to take him over to Troy in his surrey; and from Troy he would catch the four o'clock train south to New York. The Patersons had not invited him to the funeral, and they had ordered their headstone from Wallace's, over at Brattleboro, but Henry was nonetheless determined that he should be there. They weren't going to bury his bride-to-be without his having the opportunity to say farewell; and to throw a flower on her casket.

He spent a quiet week, packing and tidying up his room, and finishing off his outstanding orders. On the headstone of old Stuart Keene, a tobacco-spitting reprobate who had spent most of his last years dead drunk in the back of the Hayloft Saloon, he chiselled 'Seated With The Saints', although he could imagine the saints all shuffling along a little to get as far away from Stuart Keene as politely possible. He also finished a small marker for Ellie Manson, died aged eleven months, of the croup, 'Happy With God'.

Very little conversation passed during the week between him and Fenchurch. It seemed as if there was no point in starting up new arguments, because they would never be able to finish them; and somehow the old arguments didn't seem relevant any more. From the moment that Henry had decided to go, he had detached himself from Fenchurch, and from Carmington, and from all of those years of boyhood. He walked around town, down to the orchards, along by the river. It was so hot that week that the banks of the river were cracked and dry, and a violet haze hung over the mountains, and the fields were noisy with the chirping of crickets.

'Are you really going to California?' George Davies asked him, over a cold beer in the Gristmill Saloon. 'I hear they've got some really fancy women in California, San Francisco especially.'

Henry sat in his favourite chair, its back legs tilted, watching through the saloon window while carriages and waggons rattled backwards and forwards along Main Street, their harnesses ringing, the spokes of their wheels catching the afternoon sunlight.

'Yes,' he said, 'I'm really going to California.'

'And what are you going to do there?'

'Same as I do here. Carve epitaphs.'

'Don't you want to make your fortune? Get rich? Maybe you could dig for gold.'

Henry turned to George and shook his head. 'I want to be content, that's what. Let me tell you something, I could have

86

been content here, with Doris, if things hadn't happened the way they did. But contentment's worth more than all the money you can think of. Did you ever hear of anybody rich, and contented, too? There's no such man.'

'Well, I'd like to be rich,' said young Amos Duke, twisting his neck around in his high starched collar to ease the soreness. 'Then I could give up working in that darned bank; and go fishing all day; and spend all night fornicating with girls.'

George swung a friendly cuff at him. 'You don't even know how to *spell* fornicate, let alone do it.'

'I do too,' Amos retorted hotly. 'Fawn like in deer, ick like in sick, and eight like in seven plus one.'

On Thursday, there was a fierce electric storm, although it didn't rain. Henry was walking back to the house after lunch at the Hoosick Hotel when he met Augusta, hurrying the other way. She was carrying a carpet-bag; and when she saw him she said, 'Oh!' as if she were disconcerted.

'Augusta,' he said, taking off his hat. Behind him, over the top of Prospect Mountain, the thunder grumbled and echoed, and lightning flickered like electric snake's tongues.

'Oh, Henry. How are you? I hear that you're off tomorrow.'

'Right after the funeral. Jack's giving me a ride over to Troy, and then I'm taking the New York Central, down to New York.'

'Yes, your father said. I think he's going to miss you. We all will.'

'I'll come back to visit sometime, when I've settled myself down in California.'

Augusta patted nervously at her plaits. 'Well, yes. But California's a very long way, isn't it?'

Henry said, 'I shall think of you all, don't worry. And I'll write, too. We'll still be friends, won't we, in spite of the distance?'

'I hope so,' said Augusta, a little breathlessly.

'Well, I'll see you before I go,' Henry told her, and leaned forward to peck her cheek. She blushed, and then she hurried on her way. Henry watched her go, his hands in his pockets, and shrugged.

The day of Doris' funeral was hot and clear. She was to be buried at the far end of the cemetery, where most of the Patersons had been buried over the years, under the shade of a twisted old brittle-willow, one of hundreds that had been planted in New England before the Revolutionary War, for basket-making. The willow's leaves rustled sadly in the warm morning breeze; the congregation in the church sang 'Rock of Ages'.

Henry waited by the gate until all the mourners had left the church and followed the pale oak casket up through the winding cemetery paths towards the grave. Mr Paterson was one of the leading pallbearers, red-faced and grim, his bald head gleaming in the sun. Cissy and Eleanor accompanied their mother, in long black taffeta dresses sewn with black velvet ribbons, their faces hidden by long black veils. When they were all assembled around the grave, Henry came closer, standing by the Thomas mausoleum about thirty or forty feet away, his hat in his hand. He could hear Cissy sobbing.

The Reverend Jones said a prayer for Doris, that she should find peace and joy in Heaven. He spoke of the martyrdom of the young, that Heaven should have its share of youth and beauty. 'There is a reason for every death; God does not gather his children without purpose.' Cissy wept so much that she had to turn away. Henry stood in the sunlight with tears running down his face.

At last the casket was lowered into the grave. It was then that Henry walked quickly forward, through the assembled mourners, right to the edge of the grave; and before anybody could protest, tossed on to the casket a single white wild rose, which he had cut only an hour before in the meadows where he had played as a boy.

To him, it was an unchallengeable symbol of everything that he had felt for Doris; and a tragic recognition of her purity.

Mr Paterson made a noise like an injured dog, but Mrs Paterson caught at his sleeve, and prevented him from pushing his way forward and creating a furore. Henry turned away and left the graveside as quickly and as unobtrusively as he had come; and there was nothing that Mr Paterson could do; not unless he was going to turn his beloved daughter's funeral into a brawl.

Henry walked down the sloping path of the churchyard. Jack Davies was waiting for him outside the gate in his surrey, reading a copy of the *Arable Farmers' Gazetteer*. All Henry's trunks and bags were stacked in the back of the surrey, along with a canvas roll containing all his stonemason's hammers, chisels, and mauls.

'Ready, then?' asked Jack.

Henry climbed up on to the surrey's front seat. 'Yes,' he said, quietly. 'I don't think Mr Paterson was particularly pleased; but there you are.'

'He'll get over it,' said Jack, snapping his whip.

'I wish I could,' Henry replied.

It was a good twenty-four miles from Carmington to Troy; and even at a moderate trot, Jack's chestnut mare could only manage about eight miles an hour. Given that they would stop at Boyntonville for lunch, they would only just make the four o'clock New York train in time. But Henry wasn't sorry that he had gone to Doris' funeral. It had somehow made his feelings about her more complete. It had made him realize, too, that she was really dead; and that she could never come back to him, no matter what.

Jack said, 'Everybody thought you were so damn lucky.'

'What do you mean?'

'Well, with Doris and all. She was so damn pretty.'

'Yes,' said Henry.

They rolled slowly through the Taconics, along the winding rutted road, sometimes out on a dusty ridge, sometimes plunged into the shadow of overhanging trees. They talked very little; just as Henry had talked very little to Fenchurch; although Jack did say that his father was dead set against Lincoln, and all those fanatical Republicans who wanted to abolish slavery. 'My father says live and let live; if the south need their niggers, then let them keep them, there's no harm in that. And what would the niggers do, in any case, if they weren't slaves? They're fed, and clothed, and given honest work, and that's as good as any man can expect, black nor white.'

Henry was very subdued. He was, after all, leaving all of his life behind. At Boyntonville, they stopped at the Inn for pig's feet and a panful of Great Northern white beans. They ate in the open air, on a wooden table, and drank a pint of ice-chilled beer. Jack said, 'We're going to miss you, you know, back at the old Gristmill Saloon. Won't be the same without you.'

'I'm going to miss you, too,' said Henry, and meant it, although his mind was already looking forward to New York, and beyond, to California. He clasped Jack's arm. 'Drink a toast to me, won't you, when you get back there? Wish me luck. And say hallo to Augusta for me, whenever you see her. Tell her I always thought well of her.'

'Augusta?' asked Jack.

'Don't say one bad word about Augusta, ever,' warned Henry. 'She has a heart of gold, that girl; and she never did wrong by anybody. So just make sure that she's taken care of, and that she gets whatever she needs.'

'When you say "taken care of", you don't actually want me to step out with her, do you? Or marry her?'

Henry punched Jack in the arm. 'No, I don't. Don't be so darned ridiculous. She's going to make someone a wonderful wife, one day. She cooks well, and she's always good-humoured. Someone like Olaf would love her, if he could only pluck up enough courage to ask.'

'Olaf's in love with Cissy.'

'Everybody's in love with Cissy,' smiled Henry. But as he smiled, he pictured his white rose falling on to Doris' casket; and he knew that he would dream about it for the rest of his life; the polished oak; the golden coffin-plate, with Doris' name etched on it; and the white rose falling like a bird, or like a memory.

They travelled westwards towards Troy through the sultry afternoon. Occasionally, Jack sang.

'I want to go where the fishermen go
Out beyond Nantucket;
I want to be surrounded by the prettiest girls
Eating oysters and spitting out the pearls.'

They drew up at the railroad at Troy just ten minutes before the New York train was about to leave. The station yard was bustling with waggons and lumber-carts and businessmen in heavy side-whiskers who had just come up from the city. The train itself was ready; a big burnished Amoskeag locomotive with a bell-shaped stack, and a short but comfortable consist of four passenger-cars, a restaurant-car, and a red-painted caboose. A porter helped Henry to load his trunks on to the train; and then he bought some cigars and a newspaper, and said goodbye to Jack Davies.

'Carmington won't be the same, now you're gone,' said Jack.

The day was still warm. A news-butcher called out, 'Wide Awake rally in Albany! Read about it, read about it!' Dust floated across the station yard like golden muslin. Henry took Jack's hand and clasped his elbow and from that moment on could never remember what Jack looked like; although Jack would always remember Henry, in his grey travelling-cape, and his smart grey suit, and flourishing black necktie, his hair combed back from his forehead, and those earnest-intelligent eyes.

'He said that all he wanted was contentment,' he would remark about Henry, many years later. 'But all I can say about that is, some men don't know what they want, even the most ambitious. They have to find what they want before they know that they want it. They have to have it presented to them, on a silver platter.'

At five after four, the conductor blew his whistle, and the train pulled slowly out of Troy, on the Schenectady-Troy track which had now been incorporated in the New York Central. Henry sat back on his bench seat and watched the sidings jumble past him, then the outlying buildings of Troy, and eventually the trees and fields of Rensselaers county. The afternoon sun shone in through the clerestory windows in the roof of the railroad car, and gilded the mahogany woodwork. Henry lit a cigar, and opened up his newspaper. There was a long speech by Abraham Lincoln about the right to strike. 'I am glad to see that a system of labour prevails in New England under which labourers can strike whenever they want to. I wish such a system might prevail everywhere.'

'Going to New York?' a sharp voice inquired.

Henry lowered his paper, and found himself face to face with a thin pointy-faced man in a tight green coat and tight chequered britches. The man raised his hat, and said, 'Alby Monihan, glad to know you.'

'How do you do,' said Henry, guardedly.

'Mind if I take a seat?' asked Alby, taking a seat without waiting for an answer. 'First time in New York? You'll like it. Well, like it or hate it. Some like it, some hate it. You have to know the right places to go, the right people to meet.'

'I'm only travelling through,' Henry told him. He was amused by Alby's long wilting hair, and his small pursed-up eyes. He thought to himself that if a man were to dress himself up deliberately to look like a card sharp, or a confidence trickster, then he could count himself successful if he looked even half as untrustworthy as Alby Monihan.

'Me, I love New York,' Alby enthused, crossing one bony knee over the other, and leaning back as if he were used to reclining on luxurious sofas. 'I lead the life of Riley. All the best parties; all the best restaurants. I had supper with the Astors not a week ago; and played a game of rummy with Sarsaparilla Townsend.'

'Well, well,' said Henry. 'And what have you been doing in Troy?'

'Visiting my aunt. She's sick, you see, had the phobia for years. Sick, but very rich. Every time I visit, she heaps money and bonds on me as if she were stoking a fire.'

'So you yourself must be reasonably comfortable,' Henry suggested.

'Comfortable enough to lead the life of a gentleman.'

'You'll have to excuse me,' said Henry. 'I'm going to the restaurant car for something to drink. I've been travelling for most of the day.'

'Well, I'll join you,' said Alby.

They went through to the restaurant car, where afternoon tea was being served on scores of clinking cups and saucers. They took a seat in the plushly-decorated bar, with its mahogany tables and its brown velvet curtains and its engraved-glass windows; and a black bar-boy in a sharp white cutaway jacket brought them two glasses of whiskey, and a small dish of salted almonds.

'Do you have a place to stay in New York?' Alby asked, splitting an almond with his sharp front teeth.

'I was recommended the Collamore, at Broadway and Spring Street.'

'Oh, the Collamore, that old place. Fine hotel once, not so plushy now. Still, if you're travelling on a budget.'

'Where would you recommend?' asked Henry. He finished his whiskey and beckoned to the bar-boy for another.

'The Fifth Avenue, between Twenty-third and Twenty-fourth streets, no question about it. The newest, and the finest. Opened only last year.'

'That's where you're staying, I take it?'

'My dear fellow,' said Alby. 'I wouldn't dream of staying anywhere else.'

'Would you care for another drink?' Henry asked him, as the bar-boy came up; and Alby beamed, and raised his glass for a refill.

As the train rattled southwards at twenty miles an hour, through Rhinebeck and Poughkeepsie, its shadow lengthening across the fields and cuttings beside the track, Henry and Alby sat at a table in the restaurant and ate supper together, fried fish and boiled kale, and the sun burned through the blinds, bloated and red and almost intolerably hot.

After the meal, they shared a bottle of wine out on the observation platform, smoking cigars. The breeze lifted Alby's hair like a damp string mop.

'You know something, my dear fellow,' Alby remarked contentedly, 'there is nothing to compare with travel; and in particular there is nothing to compare with travel in the company of excellent friends.'

'I'm flattered,' said Henry, with a cautious smile. He had been trying to work out what Alby's angle was; what he was fishing for with all this talk of luxury and fine hotels; and the graces of comfortable living. So far Alby hadn't given him any indication at all. There had been no talk of cards, or women, or buying plots of land in Nebraska. Still, Henry remained on his guard; the last thing he wanted to happen was to be taken for a Rube on his first day away from Carmington. He recalled that George Davies had gone to Manchester once, to stay with a friend, and lost all of his $17 spending money on a shell game, on the train.

It was plain that Alby wasn't everything he said he was. The cuffs of his coat were shiny with wear, and his collar looked as crumpled as a month-old newspaper. Even if his story of having a rich aunt in Troy were true, he certainly hadn't spent any of her money on clothes.

It was when the conductor came around in his smart grey uniform to collect the money for supper that Alby's game began to reveal itself. 'Don't you think they're smart, these uniforms?' Alby remarked, as he dug into his pockets for his wallet. 'Just like Central Park policemen.'

Henry paid the conductor his dollar-ninety for lunch and tipped him a nickel. Alby couldn't seem to find his wallet in its accustomed pocket, and frowned, and began to search his other pockets, one by one, growing increasingly frantic with each pocket. The conductor stood patiently beside him, his hand held out in the manner of a man who has come for his due, and under no circumstances whatever is going to leave until he has got it.

'Do you know something?' Alby asked Henry, with a worried look on his face. 'I do believe that some rascal has taken my money. I had it here, in this pocket, two hundred and nine dollars in bills! My God, Henry, I've been robbed!'

The conductor said, 'Don't you have any loose change, sir? Enough to make up a dollar-ninety?'

'I regret not. I spent my last penny at the station, buying a posy of flowers for my aunt. This is most distressing; my God, and embarrassing, too. Henry – Henry, you don't think that you could possibly. . . ?' Alby inclined his head towards the conductor.

Henry reluctantly reached into his wallet again, and produced another two dollars. 'Keep the change,' he told the conductor, and the conductor tipped his cap, and went back inside to collect what was owed from the rest of the passengers.

'My dear fellow, I really can't thank you enough,' said Alby. 'You saved my bacon. And my face, too. I shall of course repay you as soon as we get to New York.'

'Don't bother,' said Henry. 'Have the meal on me.'

'Well, that's more than generous.'

'Yes, it is,' Henry agreed. 'And stupid, too. I should have let the conductor throw you off the train.'

'I beg your pardon?' Alby looked sharply surprised.

Henry leaned forward. He had drunk rather more wine than he had meant to; and to have divined so quickly that Alby was a confidence-trickster had made him feel pleased with himself, and rather rakish. 'You have no money at all, do you?' he asked. 'You never have done; and you certainly don't stay at the Fifth Avenue Hotel.'

'I have on occasions,' said Alby, offended.

'But you have no money?'

'Of course not. I told you. Somebody stole it.'

'Ah, but you *never* have.'

Alby poured himself a brimful glass of wine; the sure sign of a man who believes that if the free drink is going to run out quite shortly, then he had better make the most of what's left. He lifted his glass, and said, 'Good health,' and Henry quickly but neatly snatched it out of his hand and lifted it up himself.

'Good health,' he echoed, with a smile.

Alby didn't look particularly upset. He was obviously used to having his winning streaks cut abruptly short. He thrust his hands into his pockets, and sniffed, and looked out at the passing landscape as if it never occurred to him to drink wine,

94

or cadge meals from strangers, or pretend that he had lost his wallet.

Henry said, 'Tell me what you're up to.'

Alby turned around and looked at him narrowly.

'I want to know,' said Henry. 'Is it a confidence trick? Or a bogus sale? What is it?'

Alby wouldn't answer, but continued to stare at Henry as if he were deeply offended.

Henry said, 'I could always call the conductor back.'

'You don't have to do that,' replied Alby. 'And, besides, I'm not doing anything wrong. I'm not a criminal; I'm just trying to make my way to Kansas Territory.'

'What's in Kansas?' asked Henry.

'What's in Kansas?' Alby retorted. 'That's like asking, "what's in Pennsylvania?" Or, "what's in Nevada?" '

'Well, there's silver in Nevada,' Henry suggested.

'That's perfectly correct, and coal in Pennsylvania. The natural resources of a rich nation.'

'And what's in Kansas?'

'You already asked me that.'

'Yes, but you didn't tell me the answer.'

Alby petulantly crossed his arms and stared out over the landscape. Henry hesitated for a moment, and then handed him back his glass of wine. 'Go on,' he coaxed him, 'tell me what's in Kansas.'

Alby regarded the wine out of the corners of his eyes. 'Well,' he said at length, 'there are certain interesting minerals. One in particular that I shouldn't mention out loud.'

'Nobody can hear us. Not out here.'

Alby shook his head, tightly. 'You never know. Anyway, you don't believe anything I say. I don't have any money; and I'm a liar; and apart from that I've just panhandled a meal, and a bottle of wine. The best thing you can do, my dear fellow, is to return to your seat and forget that you ever saw me.'

'Not until you tell me about Kansas. Come on, I do think I deserve some return for my dollar-ninety.'

Alby took a long, thin breath through pinched-in nostrils. He pouted out his lips. 'No.' he said. 'I really don't think so. I'm sorry. Leave me your address, and I shall make absolutely sure that you receive the dollar-ninety by mail, just as soon as I'm flush.'

Henry grinned. 'Listen, Alby,' he said, 'it seems to me that you've got your hook in me, and now you're reeling me in. I know what you're up to; I don't have any illusions. But I'd still very much like to know what you're playing at.'

Alby jerked his head around and stared straight into Henry's face as dramatically as if he were a woman, announcing that she was pregnant by a Russian prince. '*Gold*,' he said.

'Well, well,' said Henry. 'So that's why you're going. But don't you think that's too much like hard work, for a fellow like you? You're used to luxury, the Fifth Avenue Hotel. I can't really picture you digging in the Rocky Mountains, with a pickaxe.'

'I won't be digging with a pickaxe,' Alby replied, shaking his head mechanically from side to side. He reached into his inside pocket, and produced a folded sheet of paper. 'I have my mine already, the Little Pittsburgh. All it needs is exploiting. The gold's there already; first-grade ore. It was found by a German called Brüchner, but he lost it in a poker game to a fellow called Frost; and when I played with Frost in Omaha, Nebraska Territory, the last time I was there, I won it from him. And here it is: look, the deed of claim, legally sound.'

Henry said, 'Let's go inside. It's getting dark out here. I want to look at this properly.'

Under the gas-lamp in the bar, with two fresh whiskeys, Henry spread the deed out on the table and examined it. It was a single document, as most mining claims were, signed by a storekeeper called Tennant and marked with a cross by a man described as 'Fritz Brüchner'. The claim was 'on the western bank of California Gulch, a mile south from Mosquito crossing, in Kansas Territory'.

'This is no guarantee that there's any gold to be found,' said Henry.

'You're right,' agreed Alby, and folded up the claim again, and tucked it back in his pocket.

'But you're still going out there? To Kansas, I mean?' Henry asked him.

'I have the assay, too,' said Alby. 'Frost wouldn't take the German's note until the German had produced a sample of ore, and he could have it tested. Well, *I* wouldn't have taken the note from Frost, would I, if I hadn't been sure of its worth?'

He reached into his pocket again, and produced a certificate from W. de Kuyper's Assay Office, Denver, K.T., which read 'I hereby certify that the specimen of ore said to have been taken from F. Brüchner's claim in California Gulch in Summit County K.T. assayed by the undersigned gave the following result; Gold per ton of 2,000 lbs 7/80/100/ozs, coin value $203.25; Silver per ton of 2,000 lbs 2/10/100/ozs, coin value $5.70.'

Henry looked at the assay for a long time. The train was drawing close to New York now, and every now and then it let out a hoarse, high, drawn-out whistle.

'All you have to do is dig it out?' he asked Alby.

Alby carefully retrieved the assay, and folded it up. 'All I have to do is pay four or five labourers to dig it up for me.'

'But if you own a gold-mine,' said Henry, 'why are you struggling around in the east, in worn-out clothes, without even the price of a meal?'

'I *did* have the price of a meal, when I first came back to New York,' Alby explained. 'But, well, my luck began to run against me. I played and I lost; and then I started drinking because I was worried that I was on a losing streak; and so I started losing faster. Going up to Troy was just about my last chance. I do have an aunt in Troy; not as rich as I told you; and a darn sight meaner, too. She gave me enough for the train ride back to New York, and that was all. I wouldn't have spent my last penny on a posy for her. I wouldn't have spent my last penny on a stinkweed to drop on her grave.'

Henry listened to all this, and then sat back and smiled at Alby, and said, 'So now you're off to make your fortune. You're going to sit back while four or five hired hands dig up your gold for you; and get rich as Croesus, without even doing a stroke?'

Alby patted his coat pocket, where the deed and the assay were tucked away. 'That's the plan.'

'How are you going to get out west, without any money? The railroad fare from New York to Chicago is $78. I don't know what it costs to travel on to Denver, but it can't be very much less than $50.'

'I shall manage,' Alby asserted. 'I have friends enough, in New York.'

'Don't think that *I'm* going to loan you the fare, because I'm not,' said Henry.

'You wouldn't perhaps be interested in a share of the mine?' asked Alby. 'A hundred dollars will take me to Denver. Stake me for that much, $100 and I'll sign over a tenth of everything

97

the mine produces guaranteed. Now, that could be a bargain for you. A rare investment indeed.'

Henry shook his head, still smiling. 'A good try, Alby; but I'm going to San Francisco, and that's all there is to it. I have just enough money to get me there, and to set myself up; and I'm not risking any of it on you.'

'Well, it's up to you, of course,' said Alby, and lifted up his empty wine glass, and stared into the bottom of it as if staring alone could refill it. Henry beckoned to the waiter. It would be the last drink he would have to buy for Alby before they arrived in New York. Already the train was clanking its way through the brownish rocky landscape of northern Manhattan; and in the distance he could see the scattered lights of New Jersey, and the grainy horizon where only ten minutes ago the sun had burned its way west. Just think: in San Francisco it was still daylight.

At last the train slowed down to a shuddering crawl, and made its way past the rocky fields of Harlem and into the railroad yards of Park Avenue. Henry stood by the window, holding tightly on to the leather strap beside him, enthralled by the gas-lights and the noise, and the rows of houses and factories which passed him by. New York had been built up residentially as far north as Thirty-seventh street; but Park Avenue in the East Forties and Fifties was one of the ugliest parts of the city, with factories and garbage dumps and stock-enclosures and switching-yards. They passed the F. & M. Schaefer brewery at Fiftieth and Fifty-first streets; and the potter's field which occupied the block bounded by Park Avenue, East Forty-ninth street, Lexington Avenue, and East Fifteith street. The train let out a last steamy scream, and clanked into the New York Central terminus, and all the passengers gathered their valises and their carpet-bags and prepared to disembark.

'Well, Alby, it's been an education to know you,' said Henry.

'I wish I could say likewise,' Alby replied, holding out his hand.

'I shall watch the newspapers, when I'm out west,' said Henry. 'If I ever hear of a gold baron called Monihan, then I shall know that it's you; and I shall thoroughly regret not taking up your offer of a tenth share in the Little Pittsburgh mine.'

Alby bit his lip. 'Listen,' he said, 'I know this is barefaced impertinence, especially seeing that I've touched you for supper, and all of those drinks, but do you think you could see your way clear to grubstaking me for just $20, so that I can get into a decent game of poker? Henry, I promise you, I'm feeling lucky. I don't drink any more, well, not to excess. If I could just borrow the $20, I promise you faithfully, on my honour; cut my throat and swear to drop dead; strangle my dog, Henry, that if you come to the gentlemen's bar at the Fifth Avenue Hotel, at seven o'clock tomorrow evening, I'll pay you back the full $20, plus $5 interest. Now, is that a fair deal, or isn't it?'

'Alby,' said Henry, 'I can't spare it. I'm sorry, but that's the way it is.'

Alby ran his hand quickly through his bedraggled hair, and looked to one side, and then looked back again, and said, 'Please. I won't lose it for you. I promise. No fancy games, no risks. Just plain straightforward poker.'

Henry thought for a moment. The train was already squealing to a halt, and the conductor was walking through the aisles announcing, 'New York Central– New York Central!'

Alby said nothing more, but buttoned up his coat. Henry took out his wallet, opened it, and counted out $20 in bills, which he tucked into Alby's handkerchief pocket.

'I'm going to be there,' he warned Alby. 'When seven o'clock strikes tomorrow, I'm going to be there. And, believe me, *you'd* better be there, too.'

Alby clasped his hand over his pocket, and his heart. 'Thank you,' he whispered, almost silently. 'I knew you were regular, the moment I set eyes on you.'

'Well, I'm beginning to wish that you never had,' said Henry, testily. He considered that $20 was sufficient charity, without having to be pleasant too.

Without staying around to try his luck, however, Alby descended from the train, and hurried off into the crowds. Henry had to find a porter for all of his trunks and his bags, and a waggon to take him to the Collamore Hotel, where he hoped that he was booked. The Reverend Jones had recommended it to him because he had stayed there himself during an ecclesiastical conference, and found it comparatively free of whores. Most of the fashionable brothels had already moved northwards to the Madison Square district to take advantage of the new hotels that were being built there, like the Fifth Avenue, and the Albemarle.

From the moment he stepped down from the train, Henry

found the chaos of New York overwhelming. The terminus teemed with people, jostling and shouting and laughing. He caught hold of a porter at last, a bandy-legged Negro with a grin like a parlour piano, and counted himself lucky that he was tall enough to be able to follow the man's head as he whistled and sang, and propelled his barrow at an almost hysterical rush through the crowds.

'Busy today,' Henry remarked, breathlessly, as the porter wheeled his luggage out into the street, and whistled for a waggon.

'Busy today, busy yesterday, busy tomorrow,' replied the porter. 'Nevah standin' still, always runnin', always tryin' to catch up. The only time you ever catch up, that's when they lay those pennies over yo' eyes.'

The waggoneer was gruntingly fat, with a green Derby hat and a coat so tight that it looked as if it would burst open at any moment, and spill the man's stuffing across the street. The black porter heaved Henry's trunks on to the back of the waggon, and helped Henry to climb up on to the lumpy leather seat. Henry tipped him a nickel, which the porter flicked up into the air, caught, bit between his teeth, and then dropped into his pocket, as neatly as if he were a candy-machine.

'Well, now,' puffed the waggoneer, 'where is it to be?'

'The Collamore, please.'

'Good enough. Hold tightly, then. Some of the roads are torn up, just now, and I wouldn't want to lose you over the side.'

The Waggoneer crossed town through a series of shadowy side streets, angles and lights, and then turned southwards on Broadway. It was a humid, dusty, sweltering evening, and Henry found the brightly-lit thoroughfare astonishing. The sidewalks were crowded with brightly-dressed promenaders and hurrying clerks; pedlars and travelling musicians; and the road itself was jammed with heavily-loaded stages, carts piled high with boxes and lumber, growlers, broughams, and scarlet and yellow horse-drawn buses. The traffic was so congested that pedestrians were having difficulty dodging between the horses and the waggons; especially where buildings were being torn down, and bricks and debris had been heaped carelessly on to the sidewalks. The main street was well-swept, particularly outside the shops, but the side alleys and entrances were clogged with old boxes, split-open flour-barrels, tea-chests and earthenware jars brimming with coal ashes. The noise was deafening: the rumbling of hundreds of iron-hooped wheels and the clattering of horseshoes on the hard stone pavement, the shouting and whistling and thundering of boxes being loaded and unloaded at stores and hotels.

'You mark my word, this will all quieten down in ten minutes flat,' puffed the waggoneer, taking out his brass pocket-watch, and then snapping the lid shut again. 'This is your Friday-evening scramble; clerks and shop-assistants beetling off home; stores stocking up for Saturday's trade; clearing up and rushing about, that's all. But give it ten minutes, give it ten minutes flat, and then you won't see nothing but walkers, and fashionable varnish, and strumpets, of course, plenty of them.'

In spite of this last-minute crashing and banging and general pandemonium, Broadway presented itself to Henry as an almost enchanted spectacle. There were gas standards lining the sidewalks like the trees in an incandescent orchard; their mantles reflected by the windows of dozens of stores and houses. It seemed that you could buy anything here: from Huntley & Pargis Toilet Articles to Bartholomew's Mourning Apparel, and what you couldn't immediately buy was adver-tised in a pasted-up poster, Hobensack's liver pills, George Christy & Wood's Minstrels, as well as cures for everything from gout to scrofula.

They passed the St Nicholas Hotel, where the sofas in the lobby were covered in wild animal skins and the curtains in the ladies' parlour had cost $25 the yard, or $700 a window. And they passed the stores, the magical Italianate palace of A.T. Stewart, the first department store in America; and Lord & Taylor, five gleaming white storeys of extravagant dry-goods. Then there were Ball, Black the jewellers, whose store had been compared with 'Aladdin's cave'; and their glittering rivals Tiffany & Co at 550 Broadway, 'a blaze of temptations'.

Several times, pretty-looking girls with white complexions and pinks cheeks winked and smiled at Henry as he rode past on the waggon; dipping their bonnets in mock modesty, and twirling the layers of their bright silk dresses. It took an effort of will for Henry not to raise his hat to them as he passed, as he would have done to any young lady in Carmington, where prostitutes were unknown; even if Mrs Varick out at the old posthouse had been known to be amiable to young schoolboys for fifty cents, and to older friends for a dollar.

But the waggoneer said, 'Don't be tempted by *them*, my friend. The pretty ones come out later.'

The waggoneer waited at the curb while Henry went inside the Collamore to the high-polished mahogany reception desk, and registered. He was relieved to find that his letter from Bennington had arrived, and that they had reserved a room for him, overlooking Spring Street. The desk-clerk blotted his signature for him. A bellboy with a nose like a cranberry carried his trunks up to his room for him. 'What have you got in here?' he demanded, rudely, as he hefted in the trunk containing Henry's stonemasonry tools. 'Your own build-it-yourself locomotive?'

At last, however, Henry could close the door behind him, and sit on the edge of the bed, and take off his shoes. He fell back on to the comforter, crossing his hands behind his head, and stared gratefully up at the acanthus-decorated ceiling. It was a small room, and noisy. There was a pipe running down one of the walls which seemed to rattle and gurgle incessantly. The curtains were brown, and dusty; but then Broadway was always dusty in the summer. And no matter how modest this room was, no matter how tawdry, it was Henry's first step towards his future, and the very first place in which he had ever stayed, apart from home.

He went to the wash-basin, and turned up the gas-mantle so that he could see himself clearly in the mirror. He looked pale and sweaty, and his waxed moustache had wilted to twenty past eight. He washed his face in hotel soap, which smelled strongly of lily of the valley, and dried himself on the rough hotel towel. Then he lifted up the sash window, and looked out over the windowsill at the street, three storeys below.

Everything was clearly lit up by the bright orangey street-lamps; the man on the corner selling ices from a stall; the gathering clusters of pretty whores. The waggoneer had been right, for Broadway was much quieter now, except for the occasional grinding rattle of a horse-drawn bus, or the echoing thunder of thrown-out packing-cases. A boy in a tall silk hat was setting up a stand in a matter-of-fact way to sell indecent magazines: pornography was a thriving trade in New York, especially books with lewd engravings. And a street musician not far away had already started to play sentimental Austrian tunes on his accordion.

Henry leaned out of his window for so 1ong, tired and fasci-

102

nated, that he almost lost track of time. But when he heard a clock chiming eight, he put down the window again, and tied up his necktie, and decided to go down to the hotel restaurant for dinner. He was alone now. He had lost Doris. But he promised himself that he wouldn't be alone for long. Before he opened the door of his room, he said to himself 'Doris,' just once, and closed his eyes, and tried to think of her. Then he stepped out into the green-carpeted corridor, where a man in evening dress was laughing so much that he had to lean against the wall to support himself, and another man was saying, ' – they were all McDowell's girls, by God!'

The two laughing men waited with suppressed giggles and snorts until Henry had gone past, and then burst out again. 'He said she was ready for it, and all she could say was, "Let loose my corset first, whatever you do!" '

Henry ate a pork chop in the dining-rooms, and drank a half-bottle of California wine. Then, after coffee, he went for a long walk along Broadway, looking into all of the shop-windows, smiling at the 'peripatetic whoreocracy', some of whom were stunningly pretty, and very young, but declining them all; and at last picking up a copy of the *New York Herald*, and (rather guiltily) a magazine called *Venus Miscellany*, which he folded inside his newspaper as he re-entered the lobby of the Collamore Hotel, and climbed the stairs to his room.

He was too tired to read, however, no matter how titillating the articles. He drew back the comforter on his bed, and crawled naked between the sheets. He promised himself that he would wake up later, and brush his teeth. But within two or three minutes he was sleeping, snoring softly; and he didn't even wake up when the chambermaid came in, a young Irish girl with ringlets like curly apple-peelings, and stared at him sleeping for two or three minutes before drawing the comforter over him, and touching his forehead with her fingertips in the sign of the cross, and commending his soul to happy slumber.

He was wakened by noise: a tremendous avalanche of wooden packing-cases being unloaded on to the sidewalk outside his room. He opened his eyes and saw the edge of his brown-varnished bedside table, and his pocket-watch with the lid still raised, and his pants, crumpled across the back of his chair. He sat up, scruffy-haired, and looked around the room; and it was only then that he realized where he was, and what

103

had happened. It was Saturday morning in New York, the day after Doris' funeral, and he was on his way to California.

He eased himself out of bed, and rubbed his face with his hands. Then he tugged his flannel robe out of his suitcase, and gathered up his towel, and walked barefooted along the corridor to the bathroom; where he sat and soaked in the high-sided tub for almost twenty minutes, watching the condensation form on the polished copper pipework.

He had planned to travel by railroad to Omaha, in Nebraska Territory, which was as far as the railroad went; then to join an overland party to San Francisco. He could have reached California by sea, crossing the isthmus of Panama, but a schoolfriend of his, Bertram Willis, had tried to travel out to California that way two years ago, and had died in Panama City of yellow fever. Besides, the 30–day voyage cost well over $300; and Henry's resources amounted to $210 flat; less $20 which he had loaned to Alby Monihan.

It was one of the extraordinary incongruities of America in these days before the Civil War that a man could ride by luxury Pullman car to Chicago, feeding himself on roast duck and French champagne; and yet no matter how rich he was, could find no way to cross the plains of Nebraska and Wyoming, and scale the Rockies and the Sierra Nevada to make his way to California, except by emigrant waggon-train, drawn by horses or oxen, with no better refreshment than bread, and salted pork, and water.

Henry breakfasted on corned-beef hash and poached egg; and then went to the hotel's writing-room, and wrote Fenchurch a long letter describing Doris' funeral, and his journey to Troy, and how Alby Monihan had tricked him out of a meal. Then he went for a long walk around Wall Street and Battery Park; and eventually had lunch at Pearson's Restaurant on Dey Street, sitting shoulder to shoulder with two clerks from a silk and necktie warehouse, with the sun beating in through the fly-speckled window, and smoke curling up in the air like incense in some forbidden temple.

In the afternoon, he booked his ticket to Council Bluffs, $79.25; and then spent an hour in Lord & Taylor, particularly in the hardware department, and then walked back to the Collamore Hotel and lay on his bed and dozed until teatime, while the sun moved slowly across the wall. His train for Chicago left at nine that night, and he went down to the desk and paid for his stay, and asked that the bellboy should come up to his room at eight, to collect his trunks.

He read some of the articles in *Venus Miscellany*, but he was not in a mood for erotica, and what had seemed tempting the night before today seemed flat and lewd. 'I was as ready as if I had never spent, and we swam in a mutual emission almost immediately, both of us being so overcome by our feelings that we almost swooned in delight; the throbbing and contracting of the folds of her vagina on my enraptured prick awoke me to renewed efforts, and we were rapidly progressing towards another spend, when she checked me. . . .' He threw the paper in the wastebasket; then changed his mind, and packed it into his trunk instead. There might be a lonely time between here and California when he felt the need of it.

At a quarter to seven, he left the Collamore and hailed a cab to take him to the Fifth Avenue Hotel. A sprinkling of rain damped down the streets; and he could hear thunder in the distance, over on the shores of New Jersey. A sudden breeze got up, whirling waste-paper and grit through the sunlit evening, and the cab-horse whinnied and blew through its nostrils.

The Fifth Avenue was far grander than the Collamore, and far newer. It was the first hotel in New York to have electric elevators; and most of those who arrived in the foyer from the upper floors bore on their faces the smug delight of those who had travelled by exotic means. Henry crossed the carpeted foyer with his hands in his pockets, and went up to the stairs to the gentlemen's bar, which was dark and mirrored, and heavy with the stratified layers of cigar smoke.

There was no sign of Alby. He looked at the gilded clock above the bar, which now read seven precisely, and decided to give his acquaintance five minutes' grace, but no more. He ordered a whiskey, and sat and drank it faster than he had meant to, and wished he had a newspaper to read, and that he wasn't there at all; and more than anything else that he had declined to lend Alby his precious $20. He looked at himself in the mirror behind the bar, framed by engravings of vine-leaves and the necks of three dozen different spirit-bottles, and he thought to himself: you hayseed. You swore to yourself that you weren't going to get caught, and you did. Your very first day. That's the last you're ever going to see of those $20; forget the $5 interest.

105

At ten past seven, he beckoned the barkeep, a portly young man with a bushy moustache, and said, 'I'm supposed to be meeting a friend of mine.'

'Oh, yes?' The barkeep regarded him suspiciously. There was rather too much of that about lately; too many clandestine meetings in men's bath-houses and men's bars; particularly Pfaff's, at 647 Broadway, north of Bleecker Street. The barkeep was under special instructions not to let that kind of thing start up here, in the Fifth Avenue Hotel. It was so degrading and disgusting that it wasn't even mentioned in the newspapers, except by reference to 'disgraceful acts, nightly practised on the Battery'.

'My friend's name is Alby Monihan,' said Henry. 'Has he been here at all, left his name?'

The barkeep stared at him with bulging eyes. 'Alby Monihan?'

'That's right.'

The barkeep nodded. 'Those gentlemen over there know something about Alby Monihan. Ask them, they'll tell you.'

Henry turned and frowned through the layers of cigar smoke. Five well-built men in black broadcloth coats were sitting around a table drinking whiskey and talking to each other as if they were doing business. They were all leaning back, which showed that there was no affection between them. They were here because it paid them to be here. Henry went over and stood beside them for a moment, and then noisily cleared his throat.

'Got a cough, friend?' one of them asked, a bald man with a heavy beard and wire-rimmed spectacles.

Henry said, 'I understand you may know a friend of mine: Alby Monihan. That's what the barkeep told me.'

The five men looked at each other, one by one. There was a congested silence. Then the bald man with the heavy beard raised a hand without even looking at Henry and beckoned him nearer.

'Did you say Alby Monihan?' he said, at last.

Henry nodded.

'A friend of yours?' the bald man asked.

'Well, near enough; you see, we were coming down from Troy yesterday, and – '

The bald man grasped Henry's wrist, as tight as a metal vice,

106

and said, 'Sit down. Come on, sit down. Wilbur, bring him a chair.'

The man next to him borrowed a chair from the table across the aisle, and wedged it under Henry's backside just as the bald man forced Henry down to his knees.

'What's this all about?' asked Henry, tightly.

'Oh, you really want to know?' the bald man retorted. 'You, a friend of Alby Monihan, and you really want to know?'

Henry said, 'Let go of my wrist.'

'Who says?'

'*I* say,' said Henry. 'Let go of my wrist or I'll break your jaw.'

'Well, now,' nodded the bald man, looking around at his companions. 'These are the kind of friends that Alby can boast. "Let go of my wrist or I'll break your jaw." What do you think this gentleman would have said if I'd have shook his hand? "Stop shaking my hand or I'll twist your neck"? This is class for you, ain't it? What do you say to that?'

The other men chuckled; some of them raised their glasses.

'Let me tell you something, my friend,' the bald man told Henry, leaning forward in his chair with unwanted intimacy. 'Your friend Alby Monihan has effected his usual trick on my young cousin here; you see this young gentleman with the wispy moustache? That's my cousin Quincy. Only his second time, here in New York, and never played cards before, not with professional sharps, like your good friend Alby Monihan. But all the same he wins a game, and Alby Monihan has to concede defeat.'

'I don't know Alby well,' Henry said, quickly. 'In fact, I don't even know him at all.'

'I licked him, though,' said the young gentleman with the wispy moustache named Quincy.

'Well, good for you,' said Henry. He was already resigned to losing his $20.

'Oh, good for him, hey?' asked the bald-headed man. 'That's what *you* think. Well, let me tell you. Alby Monihan didn't have no money, not in cash, not in gold; so he persuaded young Quincy here to take in lieu of two hundred dollars this so-called mining claim, and assay. Quincy, give it here, let's show this friend of Alby Monihan what we're talking about.'

Quincy, with an inevitability that made Henry close his eyes in resignation, produced with a flourish the claim certificate for the Little Pittsburgh mine, and the assay from W. de Kuyper, and laid them on the table.

The bald-headed man watched Henry for a long while, and sniffed, and then said smugly, 'What we need to know is, are these claims worth the paper they're printed on? Quincy may have been fool enough to take them, in lieu of his two-hundred-dollar debt, but are they worth the paper they're printed on? Because if they're not, we want to know.'

Henry glanced around the table; at the beef-fed, wide-jawed faces. At the level, uncompromising eyes. Whatever he said, he knew what the answer was going to be. They were honest men, taking their due. And there was nothing more dangerous than that. Righteous anger is the very worst kind.

'I licked him, though,' Quincy repeated.

'Oh, don't you *whine*, Quincy,' the bald-headed man snapped at him.

Henry picked up the claim, and the assay. 'Mines in Colorado,' he said, flatly, and then put them down again.

'That's right,' nodded the bald-headed man. His fists on top of the polished oak table looked like twin partridges, dark, bony and plucked, full of sinew and muscle. Minutes ticked by; the whiskey glasses were empty.

'What do you propose then?' asked Henry.

'Propose?' asked the bald-headed man. 'Well, first of all, I propose that you tell us where your friend Alby happens to be hid; so that we can return these worthless papers to him, and tell him just what we think about mines in Colorado, as payment for poker debts, or for anything else.'

'Well, that's difficult,' said Henry. 'The fact of the matter is, he owes me money, too; and I don't know where he could be, apart from here.'

'You expect me to believe that?' asked the bald-headed man. 'That's the biggest excuse since the California Compromise.'

'Ah, you're Southerners,' said Henry.

'Yes, sir, we're Southerners,' replied the bald-headed man. 'And we're not particular to being taken for fools, just because we happen to come from South Carolina.'

'I'm not trying to take you for fools,' Henry told him. 'I'm just as anxious to find Alby Monihan as you are.'

The bald-headed man took off his spectacles, and stared at Henry, and said, 'I have a proposition to make, since you asked for a proposition. I propose that we give you this deed of claim,

108

and this assay; and that in return you pay to Quincy here the sum that Alby Monihan happens to owe him, which is two hundred dollars.'

'I told you, I'm no friend of Alby Monihan,' Henry insisted.

'That's not what you said when you came in here, looking for him.'

'But he owes me money as well; I'm not settling his poker debts for him.'

'You are, by Jiminy, because we say you are.'

Henry folded his arms and faced the bald-headed man defiantly. 'Would you like me to call the police, and tell them that you're a gang of extortionists?'

'We'd kill you first,' said the bald-headed man. He said it with such simplicity that Henry believed him; but all the same, he wasn't frightened of him. He pushed back the chair which they had given to him, and stood up, and said, 'If you want money from Alby Monihan, then find Alby Monihan. That's what I'm going to do.'

'I warn you not to leave,' said the bald-headed man. 'These boys are witnesses. I warn you.'

Henry grinned, and held out his hand. 'Nice to have met you,' he said. 'Next time I'm in South Carolina, believe me, I'll look you up.'

He turned, and walked away across the bar; pushing his way past a young man with hyacinthine hair who was kicking his legs up in the air to explain to his friends how his horse had been misbehaving; and then rounding the taut white belly of a whiskery man in evening dress is if he were circumnavigating a schoolroom globe. He crossed the lobby, and stepped out on to the warm summery sidewalk of Fifth Avenue, and started looking around for a cab to take him back to the Collamore.

He was still waiting, however, when two hands gripped his arms on either side. It was the bald-headed man and one of his larger friends, a purple-faced fellow with reddish side-whiskers and eyes that glistened yellow like clams that had been left open too long. 'Now, we don't wish you any harm,' said the bald-headed man, 'so if I were you, I wouldn't kick up too much of a fuss.'

They forced Henry around the corner of the Fifth Avenue Hotel into Twenty-fourth Street, and pushed him into a side doorway, where the purple-faced fellow seized hold of his lapels, and twisted them around tight. Two or three incurious passers-by glanced across and saw what was going on, but walked on without even looking surprised. There were too many violent robberies in New York these days for anybody to take much notice, even in areas which had once been considered to be safe, like St John's Park and Union Square.

The bald-headed man pressed his beard very close to Henry's face, and said, 'We'll take whatever you have, sir; and you can retrieve it if you may from Alby Monihan, when you find him; and in recompense you can have this deed, and assay; and if it's worth what Alby Monihan says it's worth, why, you'll be lucky; and if it isn't, why, then you'll have suffered no more than my cousin Quincy would have suffered.'

The bald-headed man forced his hand into Henry's coat pocket, and tugged out his wallet. Henry twisted furiously around, and punched the purple-faced fellow deep in his stomach; but it was so heavy and soft and sack-like, thirty accumulated years of whiskey and cornmeal mush and creamed crab, that all Henry could manage to do was to wind him; and force out a 'huh!' of liquor-flavoured breath. In return, the purple-faced fellow smacked Henry hard in the ear, and Henry banged his head against the architrave of the door, and cut his eyebrow.

'Well, now!' called the bald-headed man. 'Here's enough to pay back poor Quincy!' He ripped all the bills our of Henry's wallet, and stuffed them into his pocket, and then tossed the empty wallet on to the ground. 'Here's the deed,' he said, 'so that nobody can say that what we did here tonight wasn't legal; and above-board. And here's the assay, too.' He thrust the documents into Henry's waistcoat, and bowed, and said, 'Good night to you, sir, whatever your name is. And let us trust that you and your companion will think twice before trying to skin any poor Southerners again.'

Henry painfully tugged out his handkerchief, and dabbed the blood from his forehead. Then he picked up his wallet, opening it wide in the hope that his attackers might have missed at least one last dollar; but they had left him with nothing. God damn Alby Monihan, and his God-damned mine. God damn all Rubes and hayseeds too, especially himself. He left the doorway and made his way back on to Fifth Avenue, and asked the doorman of the hotel how he could find the Collamore, on Broadway at Spring Street.

It took him twenty minutes to walk back to the Collamore,

110

through the busy gas-lit streets. As he neared Spring Street, he was propositioned several times by pretty young prostitutes; one of them even linked arms with him and walked beside him along the block, a girl of no more than sixteen or seventeen, with dark eyes, and a sapphire-blue dress that rustled provocatively with every step. 'You're a fine fellow,' she cooed, 'I could have my pleasure with a fellow like you.'

Henry raised his hat at her at the corner of the street, and left her disappointed. As he dejectedly crossed over to the next block, he reflected that he might have taken her up on her offer, if he had had the time, and the money. But now he was flat-busted, and already late for his train, and without even the price of a night's accommodation at the Collamore.

He was hot and dusty by the time he reached the hotel foyer. He went up to the reception desk; and the smooth-faced clerk came gliding over and said, 'Ah, Mr Roberts.'

'I need to send a telegraph,' said Henry. 'Can you do that? To Bennington, Vermont?'

'No trouble, sir. Just write your message on the pad here, and we'll make sure that it's sent off for you instanter. And by the way, sir, your wife's here. She's waiting for you in the café.'

Henry stared at him. 'My *wife?* I think you must be mistaking me for somebody else. Another Roberts.'

'We only have one Mr Roberts staying here, Mr Roberts; and that's yourself. We have Mr Robins, and Mr Reuben, and Mr Robozsuzsi. But you are the only Mr Roberts, Mr Roberts. And this lady did present herself as *Mrs* Roberts.'

Henry frowned. Who on earth could it be? It must be a mistake. He didn't know anyone at all in New York, except for one of his old schoolfriends, Warren Peabody, and not even Warren Peabody could have successfully passed himself off as Mrs Roberts. Perhaps one of the whores who frequented the Collamore's lobby had seen his name on his trunks when he had left them with the bellman, and was trying to arrange a commercial tryst with him. Well, he thought, whoever it is, she won't have any more luck than the girl who linked arms with me in the street; not until my father can send me some more money.

He walked through the wide archway to the Collamore's small side lobby, and then through the polished glass and mahogany doors to the Spring Street café. The café was busy serving early suppers to those guests who were going across to the Bowery: to the Tivoli, or to the Odeon, or to the Thiers Concert Hall, for an evening at the play. A string quartet was playing 'Silken Ribbons' amongst the palms and trailing flowers, and waiters in yellow jackets and black trousers hurried in and out of the kitchen doors like bees flying in and out of a hive.

Henry approached the upright desk, where the café's seating arrangements were supervised by a tiny man in a tall white collar and an evening suit that would probably have fitted a nine-year-old boy. 'I'm looking for Mrs Roberts,' Henry said, cautiously.

'Aha! Then you must be Mr Roberts! The lady told me to expect you! Thissa way, if you please!'

Bustling ahead of Henry, his elbows propped neatly outwards as if they were necessary for steering, the tiny man led the way right around the podium where the quartet were playing, until at last he reached a small group of private tables clustered beneath an enormous gilt-framed mirror. At one of these tables, an elderly gentleman was being tickled under the chin by a blonde girl who was young enough to have been his granddaughter; at another, two businessmen with straining bellies and voluminous white napkins were eating stuffed squab and discussing the sorry state of the cotton business; while at the very back, right under the mirror, hopeful, tired, apprehensive, in an unexpectedly showy hat of ribbons and feathers, her spectacles gleaming like dimes thrown into a municipal fountain, sat Augusta.

Henry stood still, his arms by his sides, his mouth half-open. He had never been so surprised by anyone in his life. He said, 'Augusta!' and walked towards her with slow, mechanical steps, while she flustered and bobbed and couldn't make up her mind whether she ought to stand up or remain seated. The tiny maître d' hovered around for a gratuity, but Henry ignored him, for no other reason except that he had nothing to give him.

'Your wife, sir,' said the maître d', just to remind him of the service that he had performed. He dodged around behind Henry, and pulled out one of the chairs for him, and then held out his hand. There was always the occasional out-of-town customer who needed a really blatant reminder of what was expected in a big-city hotel.

112

Henry nodded to the maître d', then caught sight of his outstretched hand. 'Oh,' he said. 'I'm sorry. How much do you want?'

'Whatever you consider to be appropriate, sir,' replied the maître d', smugly.

Henry hesitated for a moment, and then twisted one of the gilt buttons off his cuff, and dropped it into the maître d's palm. 'Thank you,' he smiled.

'This is a button, sir,' said the maître d'.

'You asked for whatever was appropriate,' Henry replied. 'You brought us together, as a button brings two sides of a cuff together, so what could be more appropriate than that?'

The maître d' paused for a second or two, with a face as sour as a jarful of icicle pickles. Then he bustled off again, elbows cocked, and Henry could see him talking to one of the waiters, presumably to instruct him that Henry and Augusta should be kept waiting as long as possible for any kind of service. Henry didn't mind; with no money, he preferred not to order anything anyway.

Augusta said nervously, 'You must think me very forward.'

'Mrs Roberts, hmh?' Henry asked her, with a slowly-spreading grin.

'I only did it for the sake of propriety,' Augusta retorted. 'I thought it would sound rather indelicate if a strange girl came into the hotel asking for you; especially since there are so many unfortunate girls about.'

'Well, it depends what you mean by unfortunate,' said Henry. 'I don't think *they* think they're unfortunate. The girls, I mean.'

And as for the idea that you, Augusta, in your fussy country hat and your sensible brown cape and your spectacles, could ever be mistaken for one of those painted provocative harlots outside. . . well. You couldn't damage a fellow's reputation if you danced in the lobby in nothing but your unutterables, shouting 'sin for the asking!'

'When did you get here?' Henry asked. 'And why? Why did you come? I was just about to leave for Iowa.'

'I arrived at six,' said Augusta. 'The train was delayed at Poughkeepsie. I think there was a cow on the track. Or perhaps if was a pig. I was so worried that I would miss you; but, all the same, if you'd gone, I could always have caught the next train to Iowa and come on after you, couldn't I?'

113

Henry leaned forward. 'You came because of me? I mean, you didn't just come here to visit?'

'No, no,' Augusta flustered. 'I've got everything packed. My trunks are in the luggage-store, alongside yours! That was when I knew that everything was going to be all right, of course, when they told me that your trunks were still here.'

'Augusta, I'm not sure that I understand.' Although I do, he thought, God help me, I do. She's taken my friendship for something more. She's had so few kind words in her life from men that she likes that she's sure now that I really love her. Oh God almighty, what am I going to do now? She's got her bags packed, and she's bought herself a hat, and she's come all the way from Bennington down to New York, in the eager expectation that I'm going to take her with me all the way to California.

And what then? An affectionate brother-and-sister relationship? Or marriage?

Augusta swallowed, and traced a pattern on the tablecloth with her white-gloved index finger. 'I know it's very forward of me, but you always said that people *should* be forward; if they were ever to achieve what they wanted, and have all those things that their hearts desire. Well, my heart's desire was always you, Henry, and I know for certain that you're fond of me, too, for haven't you said so? And I know that you were very upset by what happened to Doris, and that you were very preoccupied, and so perhaps you didn't think of me when you left. Well, I can understand that, I truly can; but then I thought what's going to happen when Henry finally gets to California, and starts to think about me again, and suddenly realizes that he shouldn't have left me behind. Oh, Henry, my poor poor Henry, I know how much you loved and wanted Doris, but Doris is gone now, and all the weeping in the world will never bring her back.'

Henry rubbed his forehead with his fingertips, quite hard, as if he were trying to massage Dr Kleinwort's famous eyebrow-restorer into his skin. 'Augusta,' he said, 'the fact is that I *am* fond of you; but I have a new life to make for myself, too. When I go out to California, there won't be any comforts; or luxuries either. It'll be hard work for a very long time, and really those are not the sort of circumstances into which I could plunge you with a happy heart.'

'But Henry, I'm not expecting luxury! I despise luxury! I like

114

nothing better than honest hard work, and making a home from nothing at all! Oh, Henry, my dear, it's just what I'm *best* at! I can sew and I can bake, you know that already, but I know how to paint, too, and hammer a nail, and I can make myself useful in so many ways.'

She clutched his wrist, and stared at him with such anguished intensity that he had to look away, embarrassed.

'Henry,' she said. There were tiny beads of perspiration on her upper lip. 'Henry, I can japan a cabinet.'

Henry looked around for the waiter. At last he caught the fellow's eye; but after having made quite sure that Henry knew that he had seen him, the waiter turned away, and instead made a show of serving a woman in a florid green dress.

'Henry, I love you; and I always have; and I always will,' Augusta whispered. 'Do you hear me, Henry? I love you. I'll do anything at all. I'll be your slave, Henry. I promise.'

Henry held her hand, and looked at her for a long time without saying anything. She seemed almost pretty in the early-evening lamplight, and there was a radiance about her which both attracted him and reassured him. She was kind, kindness itself, he knew that already. And to have somebody with him in California, a woman who could cook and sew and keep house for him without complaint, what a boon that would be. There was nothing to say that he would have to marry her; and even when they did part, which they inevitably would, she would probably find it far easier to catch herself a husband in California than she ever would have done in south Vermont. On the other hand, did he really want the responsibility of taking her there?

'I can't go to California straight away,' he said.

'Why not? I thought you were all ready.'

'Well, I was. But only an hour ago, I lost all of my money. It's all rather a long story. But I shall have to telegraph my father to send me some more. Even then, I don't know whether he'll have enough to set up the both of us.'

'But, Henry, that's no trouble. I've got money. I brought all my savings with me!'

'You brought all your savings?'

'Oh, yes, and you're welcome to have them. Please, Henry!'

'How much?' he asked. And thought: why am I asking? What am I getting myself into? Can I really imagine travelling west with Augusta Pierce, of all people? What would Jack Davies

115

say, if he knew? He'd probably laugh himself sick. *Henry*, with *Augusta*? Self-inflicted punishment, that's what he'd call it. Jack had always said that Augusta had a face like a roadscraper, and a figure like a bag of white beans. And you want to go to California with *her*?

Augusta had opened her red leather purse and was counting out her money. 'There,' she said, 'that's all of it, and you may have it. One hundred and sixty-eight dollars, and some cents.'

Henry took out his watch. 'The train leaves at nine. That means we have only sixteen minutes to call a waggon and get to the station.'

'You'll take me?' asked Augusta, breathlessly. It was the first time that she had betrayed any fear that he might refuse her.

Henry hesitated for seconds on end; and then took her hand; and nodded; and said, 'I'll take you.' For after all, he thought, here is the money to replace my lost capital, without having to ask my father for more; and here is a friend who is more than willing to help me set up my business; and keep my house; and there is no obligation to love her, is there? No obligation at all.

The waiter came across at last and said, 'Are you eating, sir?' his pencil poised.

'What does it look like?' Henry challenged him. Then he turned to Augusta, and said, with exaggerated formality, 'Shall we go, my dear?' and offered her his arm.

They left the café with the poise of Fifth Avenue socialites. But as they passed the maître d's desk, Henry stopped, and approached the little man, and said, 'You said that you would leave the service charge to me. Well, there has been no service, not to speak of; and therefore I think I will have my button back.'

The maître d' said contemptuously, 'I have thrown your button away, sir.' And with that, he turned to greet a party of large red-faced people who looked as if they were more than eager to get themselves stuck in to broiled buffalofish and puffed potatoes. Augusta said, 'Come on, Henry, it doesn't matter. I'll find you another one to match.' But Henry took hold of one of the black silk buttons on the maître d's tailcoat, and wrenched it off before Augusta could stop him or the maître d' realized what was happening.

Henry held up the button and smiled to the maître d' and

116

said, 'Thank you,' and felt that at least he had got a small revenge on the unprincipled city of New York.

FOUR

It was Thursday morning before they arrived in Chicago. They had missed the train on Saturday evening by only three or four minutes; and so they had spent two more nights at the Collamore Hotel before leaving for the west on the New York Central Railroad. They came in through the Chicago stockyards as the day broke, grey and overcast, and all around them, this sprawling 200–acre 'city of the beasts', with its miles of stock-pens and warehouses and railroad sidings looked to Henry like a gigantic and complicated puzzle, slats and fences and boarded avenues. The fetid smell of thousands of cattle and sheep penetrated the railroad car's ventilators and even seemed to taint the coffee which Henry was drinking.

He buttoned up his collar. Beside him, with his mouth open, the young piano salesman with whom he had shared his sleeping accommodation still snored, his spectacles and his reservoir-pen resting neatly on a copy of the Beckwith piano catalogue; dreaming no doubt of perfect middle As, produced by strings humming at 435 vibrations per second, and of mouse-proof pedals, and of veneered back-frames, and of sounding-boards.

Henry was at last beginning to feel discouraged. When they had arrived pell-mell at the New York Central terminus on Saturday night, their waggon bouncing and rattling with all of their trunks and cases, he had been in a high state of hilarity, and he had hardly minded that they had missed the train. He had taken Augusta to dinner (on Augusta's money) to Taylor's Restaurant at 365 Broadway, where they had admired the sparkling chandeliers in the ladies' dining room, and the crystal

117

fountain in the stairwell, splashing so high that the bubbling top of its jet could be seen from the floor above; and they had eaten bluefish and melon, and drunk sweet white wine. Then they had gone back to the Collamore, and Henry had extended his room reservation until Monday morning, this time signing the register as 'Mr & Mrs Henry Roberts' and trying not to speak too artificially to the smooth-faced clerk. They had agreed, he and Augusta, that to ask for separate rooms would not only be wastefully expensive, but would arouse suspicion about their 'married status'; and Henry had volunteered to sleep on the couch while Augusta slept in the bed. 'We will no doubt be forced together in all sorts of circumstances as we travel out west,' Augusta had asserted. 'We may as well get used to the idea from the very beginning.'

Augusta had locked herself in the bathroom for almost a half-hour; and then returned hot and rosy in her floral cotton robe, without her spectacles, and wearing a poplin mob-cap so low over her forehead that she reminded Henry of a gentle imbecile woman who had lived at the back of Mrs McSkillett's place on the Arlington road; and who had nodded and smiled bashfully at everyone who looked curiously into her doorway, just as Augusta had been smiling bashfully then.

She had smelled of ashes of roses; and it had been plain that without her spectacles she could see Henry only blurrily. She had walked towards him with that distinctive diagonal gait of the very shortsighted, afraid of colliding with unseen furniture head-on, and she had grasped his arm as if she were drowning, and then let out a little smiling gasp of relief.

'I've never done anything like this before,' she had told him, still smiling, still trying to focus with swimming eyes.

He had bent forward to kiss her on the forehead, but only succeeded in kissing the shirred band of her mob-cap. 'Well,' he had reassured her, there's always a first time.'

The couch had been lumpy and uncomfortable, and Henry had woken up several times during the night, feeling stiff and impossibly cramped. Each time he had listened for Augusta's breathing, and scarcely heard it; and that was because Augusta had still been awake, tense with fear and fantasies that Henry could only guess at. In his mind, he had turned over again and again the thought that it had been wrong of him to ask her to come to California with him. He would probably end up hurting her, or hating her, or both. Yet the idea had such practical attractions that it was difficult to dismiss it; and he felt somehow responsible for her following him; almost as if he had invited her.

On Sunday, they had gone to St Bartholomew's Church at Lafayette Place and Great Jones Street, although the steady movement of New York's fashionable development uptown had meant that St Bartholomew's was no longer a fashionable place to worship. They had prayed for Doris, and for each other, and for all the folks they had left behind in Bennington. Especially, they had prayed for themselves.

In the small hours of Monday morning, Augusta had suddenly said, 'Henry?'

Henry had opened his eyes. He had been dozing, and he hadn't been sure if he had heard his name called or not. But Augusta had repeated, 'Henry? Are you sleeping?'

'What is it?' Henry had asked her.

'Henry, I feel so lonely.'

Henry had stared up at the darkness of the ceiling. After a while, he had said, 'You don't have to feel lonely.'

'But I do. I feel that we're together; but somehow I feel all alone. Henry, do you like me, Henry?'

'Of course I like you. I wouldn't have asked you to come along to California with me if I didn't like you.'

'But could you love me?'

Another pause. Henry had bitten his lip in the darkness. What could he tell her? Something that wouldn't put her off; something that wouldn't upset her; and yet something that wouldn't commit him too deeply. He might be an opportunist; and a practical joker; but he wasn't a liar.

'Augusta,' he had said, 'I'm still grieving for Doris. You'll have to allow me that much.'

'I'm sorry,' she had told him. Then again, 'I'm sorry. That was very insensitive of me. I shouldn't have asked you.'

'Don't blame yourself,' he had told her. 'I'm sorry that you're feeling lonely. There isn't any need for you to feel that way. You've got me here, after all.'

'Yes,' she had said, in an unconvinced voice.

They had lain there in wakeful silence for another five minutes or so. Outside the window, the dawn had been breaking, and the rattling of drays on the straw-strewn streets had been joined after a while by the pattering sound of foot-steps along the sidewalk, as early shift-workers had hurried to the stores and warehouses of Broadway to stack up the shelves and mark up the goods and prepare the counters for opening at half-past eight. A hoarse steam-whistle had sounded from the Battery, and someone had walked across Spring Street tolling a handbell. New York was never silent. As Walt Whitman had once remarked, 'What can New York – noisy, roaring, rumbling, tumbling, bustling, stormy, turbulent New York – have to do with silence?'

But there had been silence of a special kind within Augusta's heart. And she had broken it herself by saying in an offkey, tremulous voice, 'I would care for it very much, Henry, if you could at least lie with me, and hold me. For I do feel so very lonely.'

Henry had said, 'Augusta?' but Augusta had replied only, 'Please, Henry. I ask no more of you.'

With great uncertainty, Henry had climbed off the couch and walked across to the bed. Augusta had been lying on her back staring at him myopically through the granulated light of dawn. She had reached out her hand, and Henry had taken it, such a different hand from Doris', rounder, plumper, with shorter fingers and close-cut nails. Then he had lifted up the covers of the bed and eased himself in next to her, and curled his arm around her waist. Her stomach had felt plump beneath her cotton nightdress, girdled with fat, and the smell of ashes of roses had been cloying. But he had remained dutifully next to her, comforting her as best he could; and it had been almost seven o'clock before it had been light enough for him to see that her eyes were glistening with tears.

'Augusta,' he had told her, quietly. 'I cannot give you any more of my affection; not yet.' Or ever? he had asked himself, silently; guiltily.

'My dear Henry, I know that,' Augusta had sniffed. 'And I ask no more. Please, do not think badly of me for loving you so. I cannot help my heart. And do not think badly of me, either, for asking you to lie with me. It was just that I felt so very much alone.'

She had wrestled herself into a sitting position, and looked down at him, stroking his forehead; an attention which for some reason he had found excruciatingly irritating, like being tickled when he had absolutely no inclination to laugh. She had said, flatly, 'I was brought up to believe that every girl should go to the altar without knowing a man. It is ingrained

120

in me, Henry, I'm sorry. I must be married before we have any knowledge. I didn't mean to disturb you; it was selfish of me to arouse your feelings purely for my own purposes; but believe me you have made me feel so much calmer, so much more wanted. To be wanted, Henry, that is everything, and to know that you feel want for me, well, that is the acme.'

Henry had at last been obliged to hold her wrist, to stop her from stroking him. 'Augusta,' he had begun, 'the very last thing I wish to do is disillusion you, but – '

'Hush, now, say no more,' she had said, and kissed him on the cheek. 'I know the practicalities of life; my mother told me them all. I am not a prude, Henry; even if I am determined to keep myself for my wedding-day, in purity. And there are ways of expressing physical attachment which do not involve, well, knowledge in the *complete* sense.'

She had been blushing very pink, and her voice had been breathy and wavering. To save her any more embarrassment, Henry had climbed out of the bed; but then he had felt churlish for not kissing her; bent forward to kiss her; and painfully knocked his mouth against her forehead. They had looked at each other: Augusta holding her head and Henry clasping his mouth; and then they both had burst out laughing.

'Well, this is not very auspicious,' Henry had smiled.

'Perhaps not,' Augusta had replied, and reached out her hand to him. 'But wonderfully romantic. Really, Henry, it's like a story; and I adore you. Thank you for being so understanding. Thank you, Henry, for everything.'

They had caught the Chicago train at nine o'clock on Monday evening, in a terminus billowing with smoke and golden sunlight, and they had been travelling ever since; through shadowy forests, along by the banks of glittering rivers, and for miles and miles across windy plains, where birds were blown. There had been no opportunity for Henry to find out while he was on board the train what Augusta had meant by 'ways of expressing physical attachment which do not involve knowledge in the complete sense', because they were unable to afford a private sleeping-compartment for two. On the other hand, Henry wasn't at all sure that he wanted such an opportunity, ever. He had dreamed about Augusta as he had slept in his narrow upper berth in the Pullman car; he had dreamed about her glutinously smiling, like a spoon drawn slowly through molasses; he had dreamed about her stroking his fore-

121

head; and he had dreamed again and again that she was turning towards him with her spectacle lenses catching the light, and saying, 'It's wonderfully romantic, Henry. It's like a story.' And then he had woken up and lain in the joggling darkness feeling the wheels bang incessantly over the track, and he had felt that his life had become nothing more than a series of theatrical incidents in which he was obliged to act whether he wanted to or not; an endless progression of pointless playlets which were taking him nowhere at all.

He did not understand yet how much Doris' death had changed him. Nor was he ready to see that it was not really Mr Paterson who had exiled him from Carmington; any more than it was Alby Monihan who had lost him his money; or Augusta who had persuaded him to take her to California. It was his own sense of destiny. It was his own newly-disturbed awareness that life could be very much better or very much worse than he had ever expected; and the urgent but still unrealized need to find out just how much better; just how much worse.

The train at last drew into Chicago, its brakes squealing like four dozen slaughtered pigs. Henry and Augusta stepped down from their car, and then pushed their way through a jostling crowd of passengers and porters and stockmen to find their trunks. Henry had been told in New York that there was a connection that morning on the Chicago and Rock Island Railroad for Council Bluffs; or on the Chicago and Northwestern later in the day. They waited by the baggage car while the trunks were unloaded, feeling the first spots of an early-morning shower.

Henry said, 'You look a little tired. Didn't you sleep well?'

'Not a wink all night,' Augusta admitted. 'I don't know why. My mind kept racing and racing and wouldn't be still.'

'Maybe we ought to stay here in Chicago for a night, and go on to Omaha in the morning,' Henry suggested. 'We could leave our trunks here at the depot.'

Augusta was quite white; and her appearance was very little improved by the beige suit she had decided to wear, all hung around with floppy beige ribbons.

'Would you mind terribly if we did?' she asked Henry; and then suddenly she burst into tears.

'Augusta, what's wrong?' he asked her, taking her wrists in his hands. 'What's the matter?'

'It's nothing,' she said. 'Please, it's silly of me. I've just suddenly wondered if I'm doing the right thing. Not just for me, but for you. Oh dear Henry, I haven't forced myself on you, have I? I haven't made a fool of myself? I couldn't bear it if you felt I was a nuisance.'

'Augusta,' he soothed her, 'I asked you to come along with me because I wanted you to come. Now, here, dry those tears. How can you possibly think that you're a nuisance?'

Gently, he lifted off her spectacles, and dabbed her eyes with his handkerchief. She smiled at him as bravely as she could, and then lowered her head, and blushed. 'I'm not really very pretty, am I? And worse without my spectacles. I always look so starey when I take them off.'

He kissed her on the forehead. 'Don't think so meanly of yourself. I like the way you look.' He gave her back her spectacles, and she wound them around her ears again. 'You're a fine girl, Augusta; I've always thought so, and I've always said so. Now haven't I?'

They left their trunks at the maroon-painted offices of the Chicago and Rock Island Railroad; and then hailed a cab to take them into Chicago itself. The cabbie was a thin-backed dreary man with moustaches like two skeins of wet grey wool, and he kept up an interminable complaint all the way from the railroad station until they were rattling alongside Lake Michigan. It had begun to shower more heavily now, and so Henry's first impression of Chicago was of the inside of the hansom's leathery black hood, the drumming of rain, and the droning commentary of their driver; with an occasional glimpse of crowded, water-slicked streets, and intermittent views of the lake, grey and vast and flecked with foam.

'This town is all going to the dogs,' said the cabbie. 'Stinks in the summer, freezes in the winter; drains all clogged and water not fit for a rat to wash out his stockings. You should have seen it in May; that's when you should have seen it, when Abram Lincoln was balloted for Presidential candidate; city was packed tight to bursting, not an hotel room to be had nowhere; and the Wide Awakes marching up and down the streets with torches and all. That building there, you see it? That's the Wigwam, that's where they held the convention, full to bursting that building was, and you can see the size of it, and the streets outside was full to bursting too; and you couldn't drive a cab downtown if you was urgently required to or not;

and a dratted bad time it was too, with drunks and harlots and malcontents of all possible kinds, you can believe me. And when they said that Abram Lincoln was nominated, and Hannibal Hamlin on the ticket with him, the whole darn town shook with cheering.'

'You're not a Republican, then?' Henry asked him.

The cabbie turned around in his seat, the rain dripping from his wide-brimmed hat. 'Mister, I don't take no interest in politic-king whatso-never and all I care about is making my living; as a few more of them politicians ought to. Less wind, more work, that's my flavour.'

Henry had asked him for a reasonable hotel; and he drew up outside a small but comfortable-looking timber-framed building on Portage Street, the Union Hotel, red-painted with wet red awnings, and a sign which announced 'Clean Sheets & Hot Water'. The sun was beginning to break through the clouds as Henry paid off the cabbie, and the sidewalk was glistening gold as they carried their bags up the steps to the hotel's swing doors, and into the gloomy lobby. An old man in an eyeshade was sitting behind the counter with his high-polished shoes up, reading the Chicago Tribune. He looked up as Henry and Augusta came in, and said conversationally, 'Know what it says here? They found a baby at Stickney, with its stomach full of pounded window-glass, enough to front up a middling-sized dry-goods store.'

'Well, I'm very sorry for it,' replied Augusta. 'What agony it must have suffered.'

'Less agony than living, some might say,' the old man replied, in a cheerful tone. He folded up his paper, and stood up. 'I guess you good people are looking for someplace to stay.'

Henry said, 'Mr and Mrs Henry Roberts. Just for one night.'

A black bellboy carried their cases upstairs for them, and along a narrow corridor between rows of cream-painted doors. Their room, number 5, was at the very end, and beside the door was a small window overlooking the backs of Portage Street, and part of the Wigwam, and a large hoarding which said, Oakland Dining Room Good Steaks 50 cents. Henry could see the rain clouds moving away towards the southwest, and the surface of the lake suddenly transformed into dazzling silver.

The bellboy unlocked their door for them, and said, 'This is it, folks.' It was a small room with a dark varnished wardrobe, brown floral wallpaper, two heavy armchairs, a washstand, and a massive sawn-oak bed, covered with a rose-patterned comforter. Over the bed was a sampler, with peonies on it, and the legend, 'The Lord Is My Shepherd.' Out of the window, with its dusty brown curtains, there was a view of Chicago's rooftops, still glistening, and the Chicago River; and in the distance a hazy line of hills and forest.

Henry tipped the bellboy, and then closed the door and sat down on the bed. Augusta came up to him and rested her hands on his shoulders. 'I feel somehow that I have grown so close to you,' she said. 'I hope with all my heart that you feel the same for me.'

'You must get some rest,' he said. 'Have a sleep on the bed for an hour or two, and then we'll go find ourselves some lunch.'

While Augusta slept, Henry went downstairs to the hotel's parlour, and read the newspaper. The day was waxing warm now, and the window was open so that the breeze from the lake could blow gently in to stir the curtains and the magazines on the table. Several people came and went; an agitated woman who kept twisting her gloves around and around as she waited for somebody who didn't show up; a fat Italian couple who were supposed to be going to a wedding; a travelling salesman in a creased linen suit, with a portmanteau crowded with clothes-line reels and stove brushes. Henry dozed himself for a while, and woke up only when the clock in the lobby struck noon, his mouth feeling dry and coppery.

'Do you know of anywhere good to eat?' he asked the old man behind the counter.

'There's the Wabash Chop House, two blocks down; or the St Vincent Restaurant just across the street. Personally, I don't eat meat. My grandfather always used to say that it poisons the blood. He was a great man, my grandfather. Listen, I'm seventy-one; my grandfather was there at Cambridge in 1771, when Washington took command. And my father was introduced to John Adams once, when he was a young man.'

Augusta was still asleep when Henry went upstairs, covered by the comforter. Henry gently shook her shoulder, and said, 'Augusta,' and she opened her eyes and blinked at him. 'Oh, Henry,' she said, with a smile. 'I couldn't think where I was for a moment.'

'If you want to change, we'll go and have something to eat,'

Henry told her. He went to the looking-glass and brushed his hair back, and tweaked up his moustaches. He thought he looked rather drawn; but it was nothing that a sound night's sleep wouldn't be able to remedy. The hardest part of their journey to California was still ahead of them: the rail trip to Omaha, and then the long Emigrant Trail out towards the west. He just hoped that Augusta would have the stamina for it.

The St Vincent Restaurant was noisy and friendly, with polished circular tables and potted palms and waiters in floor-length aprons and extravagant whiskers. Henry ordered a glass of raisin wine for Augusta, and a foaming glass of German beer for himself; then out of a plain menu they chose roast ribs of beef and Swiss chard, with melted cheese on it. Augusta ate with nibbling precision: cutting up each piece of meat neatly and tinily, and eating it with hurried little bites.

Henry said, 'We could take a walk by the lake later.'

Augusta simply smiled.

'We still have two thousand miles to travel, you know,' said Henry. 'I hope you feel that you can manage it.'

'With you, dear Henry, I can manage anything.'

'Well, you mustn't become too dependent on me.'

'Henry,' said Augusta, setting down her knife and fork, 'I have always been a dependent person, you must know that of me. I depend very heavily on those closest to me, both morally and emotionally, and I can't make any pretence of it. But in return I can be dependable; and reliable; and I have never shied away from good hard work.'

Henry said, with a mouthful of beef, 'Augusta, you mustn't worry yourself so. I can give you all the looking-after you need. Now please, enjoy your meal, and think of this as nothing more than a great adventure.'

Augusta looked at him fondly, and tears began to cluster in her eyes again. 'I shall,' she said. 'Dear Henry.'

They walked that afternoon beside Lake Michigan, saying very little to each other, but closer with every moment that they were far away from Carmington; and with every second that brought them nearer to the west. A warm but persistent wind blew off the water; and Augusta's beige scarf flapped like a signal. Henry walked with his hands in his pockets, his mind jumbled with half-formulated decisions about what he was going to do when he reached San Francisco; and how he was going to set up house with Augusta. He watched her as she stepped along the gritty shoreline in her brown buttoned-up boots, how the slack waves rippled on to the mud; and then he looked northwards up Michigan Avenue, at the smug and wealthy cream-coloured terraces, at the privately-financed Illinois Railroad trestle crossing the lake, at the factories and railroad sheds, at the smoking factory chimneys. Something is happening here in this country, he thought to himself; there is money here, and influence, and manifest destiny.

Augusta held out her hand for him; and they walked together through the breezy afternoon. 'I think our lives were always meant to be woven together,' said Augusta. 'I think somehow that you and I were made for each other in Heaven.'

Henry said nothing, but stopped, and frowned, as if he thought that he had heard somebody calling his name. Augusta held his arm tight, and pressed her cheek against his shoulder, and said, 'I have never been happier.'

Afternoon settled into evening. They ate supper at the Checeago Dining Rooms on Division Street, whitefish with sesame seeds; and then returned to the Union Hotel. Tonight they began to feel the enormous distances surrounding them: a thousand miles to Carmington, two thousand miles to San Francisco. And as the sun began to burn its way down toward the prairies of the West, Henry went out into the corridor and stood for a long time staring at the wharves, and the depots, and the litter of timber and packing cases, and the noisy yards of the Illinois Central railroad.

Augusta came up behind him and wound her arms around his waist. 'Come to bed with me,' she asked.

He turned his head. 'I was looking at the lake.'

'I know,' she said. 'But come to bed with me.'

They closed the door of number 5 behind them, and Henry locked it. Augusta carefully unwound her spectacles and laid them on the bedside table. Then she unfastened her dress, and her corset cover, and turned her back to unhook the corset. Henry sat on the edge of the bed meanwhile and undressed with the elaborate care of a man who is preparing himself for the inevitable. He folded his pants, and wrapped up his shirt for the hotel to take care of, and set his shoes side by side. Someone in the room below was singing a sentimental song that was popular that year, 'My Misty Reminiscences Of You'.

'Where woodbine grows and where the swallow sings
We walked in summer and exchanged our rings. . . .'

Augusta said, 'Henry,' and Henry turned, and there she was, kneeling on the opposite edge of the bed, nude, with a curving stomach like a heavy child, and small diagonally-slanting breasts, and her hair let down. She lifted her arms for him to hold her; and although he had still not taken off his cotton underwear, he did, and kissed her bare fat shoulder, and squeezed her close to him, thinking, God, this is all my responsibility; I let this happen by default. I failed to tell her firmly at every turn that I didn't love her, and every time she asked me if I loved her and I didn't reply, she took it to mean that I did. And this is the ultimate punishment for it; to have to make love to her, to have to pretend that I want her, and that she's beautiful. Because this has all gone too far, through no fault of hers, and if I tell her now that I find her plain, and unexciting, then God knows how much I'm going to hurt her.

She whispered in his ear, 'You may have me, Henry; but not in the way that a husband takes his bride.' Her words sounded both lewd and ludicrous; and Henry frowned at her.

'I'm sorry,' he said. And downstairs, the amateur tenor placidly sang,

'Now all the winter through
I walk through shadows blue. . . .'

Augusta, quite pink, said, 'I have some cream. It's what my mother used to do, with Father, before they were married. She said that it was quite all right, that it was clean, and that it didn't count as actual knowledge. She said that it was commonly practised among the Highland Scottish, and considered quite usual.'

She turned away suddenly, and started to weep. 'Oh, Henry, how can you! The very first time that I have dared to give myself to anyone, and you have made me speak to you like a whore! Henry, have you no romance? You said that everything was going to be so roma-hantic, ohh. . . .'

'And all I have is misty reminiscences of you. . . .'

Henry sat baffled on the edge of the bed, and then reached out and clasped her shoulder; as gently but as firmly as he could.

128

'Augusta, perhaps we're not quite ready. Perhaps we're not completely sure.'

'I'm sure!' Augusta retorted, her face hot with tears.

'Yes, but if we can't conduct ourselves as man and wife – if we have to resort to – well, different things – I mean – '

He found himself looking at himself again in the mirror on the washstand, skinny and glum in his underwear, with shoulders like broomsticks. He couldn't even make himself smile. He felt unhappy, that was all; and sad for Augusta; and what was worse, responsible for everything she did. She was quite right: she was a completely dependent person, and already she had come to depend on Henry for amusement, for shelter, for conversation, for every decision in her daily life from what time to get up in the morning to where shall we eat at lunchtime, and what. Now she was offering herself as a sexual dependent, too; with one important sanction; although Henry felt that this was just one more ploy in Augusta's complicated repertoire of emotional gambits. He would be able to take her, sooner or later, if he wanted to; or even if he didn't.

Augusta's strength was that she was completely absorbed in him, in nothing and nobody else, and that she needed him desperately. Her unrelenting need was like an addiction to morphia; and, just like an addict, it made her crafty and manipulative beyond even her own understanding. Henry was too amiable and too straightforward to realize how much Augusta wanted him; and to understand that if he wanted to be free of her, he would have to forget his politeness, and his natural sense of responsibility, and speak to her with harshness and complete finality.

They lay together in bed for almost two hours, like waxworks. It was not yet completely dark, and the sinking sunlight moved across the ceiling of their brown-papered room like some carefully-devised clock, reaching the top of the sampler when the chimes in the hallway outside struck seven; reaching the rose-transfered water-jug when the chimes struck eight.

At last, mutely, Augusta reached across to the bedside table, and picked up a jar of Eastman's Violette Cold Cream. Scooping into it with her fingers, she lifted out a large white fragrant lump; which she then massaged between the cheeks of her large white bottom. She kept her back to Henry: that long white back with a mole on the right shoulder-blade, her dark hair

129

spread across the pillow. And then she said, 'You may have me now.'

'Augusta – ' Henry began. But then she clutched her buttocks in her own hands, and spread them apart for him; and the blatant obscenity of what she was doing aroused him, so that his penis rose, and he found himself thinking: if I had gone with any of those Broadway prostitutes, would they have been any better? They certainly wouldn't have been so friendly; nor so clean; nor, God damn it, so compliant.

He shifted himself nearer towards her on his left hip, and held his erection in front of him in his fist. Augusta had her eyes closed; but she demanded, 'Stroke my hair.' Then, 'Feel my breasts.' And Henry did what she told him to do, knowing how much he would hurt her if he didn't. At last, Augusta said, 'Don't hurt me,' and that he knew was the final instruction to penetrate her. Not complete knowledge, of course, not full consummation; she kept her hand firmly cupped over any possibility of that. But a pushing, violent, eyes-squeezed, lips-bit, grunting intrusion into her bottom; until she quivered and said, 'Oh, Mary,' and Henry could lean away from her a little to see himself buried inside her, between her large curved, curd-like buttocks, tugging and thrusting at the crimson-pink clench of her anus.

When he came, which was quickly, he felt as if he had been hit on the back of the neck with a black cinder brick. He pulled himself out of her at once, and she was right, it was clean, but she lay there motionless for what seemed like a very long time, offering him nothing more than the broad white landscape of her shoulder, and the forest of her hair, even when he said, 'Augusta? Are you all right?'

She was sobbing, of course. It was probably agony. She sobbed and buried her face in the pillow, letting out whispered exclamations every now and then which Henry couldn't quite hear, although they sounded like 'oh, Mother, how could you!' and 'please, Mother, please.' Henry clutched her shoulder a second time, and said, 'Augusta?'

Augusta at last turned over, and looked at him with a watery smile. 'I love you, Henry, forgive me.'

'I hurt you,' he said.

She clutched him, her small breasts wobbling like twin blancmanges. 'I know, but it doesn't matter. You can hurt me all you want to. I don't mind being hurt as long as it's you.'

They said very little more that evening. They lay side by side on their backs looking up at the ceiling while the room darkened and the sun glided around the other side of the world. They slept. Augusta snored. In the morning, before it was light, she reached across for him, and held him as if she were bearing a sceptre; and she guided him up between her buttocks yet again, so that he could sodomize her a second time. He tried once, jerkily, unsuccessfully, to slip out of her bottom and penetrate her vagina, but her hand remained unremittingly clutched over the entrance which she regarded as the gateway to Christian knowledge. In revenge, perhaps, or in frustration, Henry pushed himself right up inside her as far as he could go. He knew he was hurting her, but he kept himself there, snarling in the dark, thrusting and thrusting until he finally ejaculated, deep inside her bowels.

The experience shook him. After ten minutes or so, he got out of bed and tugged on his britches, and buttoned up his shirt. Augusta stirred and said, 'Henry?' but all he replied was, 'It's all right. It's only six o'clock.' Then he pulled on his shoes and left the room and went downstairs to the parlour.

The old man in the eyeshade was down there already, drinking coffee out of a large blue china pot and sorting out mail and newspapers.

'Help yourself,' he said to Henry, nodding towards the cofee-pot.

Henry brought over a cup from one of the parlour tables, where breakfast was laid out, and poured himself a half-cup of coffee, and sipped it.

'You're travelling on today, aren't you?' the old man asked him.

'That's right. Omaha. Bound for California, eventually.'

'Well, it's a long trail,' said the old man, reflectively. Then he nodded towards the stairs and asked, 'That your wife?'

'Of course,' said Henry; and then, when the old man continued to stare at him from underneath his green-tinted eyeshade, 'Well, no, not exactly.'

'Didn't think you were,' the old man said, dryly. 'Seen too many. Get to know them, those that are suited, and those that aren't. You two don't go together at all, you two don't. Nothing between you, is there, except for someone to travel with?'

'Well,' Henry replied, 'I don't really think that's any of your business.'

'Didn't say it was,' the old man grimaced, scratching the criss-cross creases at the back of his neck.

Henry finished his coffee, and then went outside. Although he was wearing only a shirt and britches, the morning was already warm enough for him not to feel chilled. He walked across the street towards the lake-shore, and then sat for a while on the gunwales of a small fishing-boat.

A small raggedy boy came up and said, 'Got a penny, mister?'

'I'm sorry, I don't have a bean,' Henry told him.

'I didn't ask you for a damned bean,' the boy retorted. 'I asked you for a damned penny.'

'You want to go to Heaven or not?' Henry shouted after him.

'Not if you're there!' the boy yelled back.

Henry was beginning to wonder what Heaven could actually be; especially when a plain, religiously brought-up girl like Augusta could indulge herself so fiercely in what Henry had always thought of as an unnatural act, just for the sake of keeping herself 'pure' for her wedding. He had heard that there were girls who would sometimes permit it. George Davies had told him 'on first-hand authorization' that Willard Noakes had been occasionally allowed by his pretty fiancée Pamela Woodnut to have 'tea and cakes in the back parlour'. Willard and Pamela's engagement had been unusually prolonged by the death of Pamela's father, and the year-long mourning which had followed it, and Pamela was a wilful, vivacious girl who must have found it difficult to wait.

Henry supposed that for some families sodomy must have become the modern alternative to the old-fashioned ritual of bundling; and that 'tea and cakes' was probably better for some young couples than an unwanted infant. But while he could understand girls like Pamela Woodnut doing it, girls who were deeply in love, and engaged to be married, he found it hard to accept Augusta's urgent enthusiasm for it. She had wept the first time. It must have hurt her badly. Yet she had wanted more. Perhaps that was the reason why Augusta wanted him so much, and why she had followed him. Perhaps she had known that he would always give her the satisfaction of being hurt.

He went back to the Union Hotel in a thoughtful, dislocated kind of mood. The old man behind the counter grinned at him as he came in, and winked. 'Your wife's been up, and had some morning tea,' he remarked.

132

'Thank you,' Henry had told him, and gone upstairs.

Augusta was standing in front of the washstand, in a cream nainsook blouse and a frilly brown skirt, brushing her hair out into the sunlight and humming the tune that the string quartet had been playing when Henry had met her at the Collamore, 'Silken Ribbons'. Henry came in and closed the door behind him and stood with his hands in his pockets watching her.

'You went for a walk,' said Augusta, brightly.

'Yes,' he said. 'Down to the lake.'

'You should have waited for me. I would have come with you.'

'I wanted to think.'

'I had some tea in the parlour, and a muffin. I felt such a pig, eating on my own! Aren't you hungry?'

'I had some coffee, thanks.'

'It's still very early. Perhaps we should go to a coffee-house before we go to catch the train.'

'Augusta – '

She turned, and looked at him, her head a little to one side, and smiled. It was the same smile that he had dreamed about on the train, slow and drawn-out; the sort of smile that made Henry feel as if he couldn't breathe, as if someone was forcing a soft feathery pillow up against his face.

'I'm sorry,' said Augusta, and came over and put her arms around his neck. 'Here I am, chattering on about food, and muffins; and saying nothing to thank you for all of your care, and all of your dear consideration. You're such a darling, Henry. You look after me in every way. I ask so much of you, don't I? And yet you always give me everything I need, without any recrimination.'

She brought her lips close to his left ear, and whispered, in three or four bursts of hot breath, 'And last night, my lover, you were not only strong, but understanding, too; and that is why I will love you for ever.'

'Augusta,' said Henry, 'I'm not in love with you.'

'Henry, I *know* that. You made that plain to me right from the very beginning; and I don't expect you to be, not so soon after losing dear Doris. But even if you have no room inside your heart for me just at the moment, please allow me to love you the way I really want to. At least *accept* love, even if you can't give it. It's the only way in which your wounds will ever heal.'

133

He clasped her wrists, and lowered her hands away from his neck. 'It's more than that, Augusta,' he told her, as steadily as he could. 'The thing is, I don't think we should travel together any further. It's my fault; but I think the idea of us going to California together, well, it wasn't as clever a notion as I first thought it was. I'm sorry.'

Augusta looked pale, and slowly crossed her hands over her breasts. 'I don't understand you,' she said.

'I'm trying to say it as gently as I can, Augusta. I simply don't think that you and I are particularly suited. It would really be better, it would really save both of us a considerable amount of embarrassment and pain – well, if we were to call a halt to it here in Chicago, before it goes too far, before we end up committing ourselves too completely. Augusta, do you understand me? I don't want to hurt you.'

Augusta sat down smartly on the end of the bed. She looked quite shocked: her mouth open, her eyes roaming the room as if she were searching for some rapidly-escaping animal called logic.

'Augusta,' Henry repeated, 'what happened last night – '

She stared at him through spectacles beaded with tears. 'I love you, Henry. I'm so sorry about what happened last night; but I couldn't give you everything, not before we're married. Please, Henry, we must go to California together. We can't go back now.'

'Did your mother really tell you that you could do that, and that it wouldn't make any difference?'

'What do you mean?'

'What we did together last night. Do you really believe that you can do something like that and still remain pure? I mean, Augusta, how can you reconcile Christian purity with – well, what we did?'

'It was very painful, you know,' she said, with great gravity.

'Well, I'm sure that it was; but just because you suffered, that doesn't make it right; and it certainly doesn't make you innocent. Augusta, by doing that, you have given up your virginity just as surely as if we'd made love together properly.'

She glanced at him, a curious sly sideways look, and shook her head emphatically. 'If you were to kiss my lips, I would still be a virgin. If you were to put your arms around me, and caress me, I would still be a virgin. Henry, you know that's

134

true. Henry, how can you say that I'm not a virgin? How can you say that? Henry!'

Without warning, she dashed herself off the edge of the bed on to the floor, and began to hammer at the carpet with clenched fists.

'How can you say that!' she screeched. 'How can you say that!'

'Augusta!' Henry shouted. He knelt down beside her, and grappled with her, but she beat furiously at the carpet, and then at him, her eyes staring with hysteria, thrashing out at everything around her. 'How can you say that! How can you say that! Henry! How can you say that!'

Henry shook her, and shook her again, and at last she was quiet, panting and rolling her eyes like a floppy Silesia doll. 'I can't bear it,' she whispered. 'I love you, Henry; I can't bear you to leave me. Henry, please Henry don't leave me; don't make me go back. It would kill me, Henry, if I had to go back. Don't humiliate me, Henry, please.'

Henry held her close to him, and she guffawed in anguish against his shirt. Oh God, he thought: have I really become responsible, me, for this weeping ugly girl with her tiny spectacles and her big white face and her pear-shaped body? Is it really up to me now, me alone, to calm whatever fears she has, and to satisfy all of her lusts? Do I have to be the one who listens to all of her eccentric ideas about morality and purity and love; do I have to feed her insatiable appetite for reassurance and approval? God, how on earth could I have allowed this to happen? How did I get so ridiculously entangled? And how on earth, now, can I summon up the courage to send her packing back to Bennington?

'Augusta,' he said stroking her hair. 'Augusta, you have to go back.'

'I'll kill myself first,' she told him, in a muffled voice. 'I'll drown myself, or cut my wrists.'

'Augusta, I'm trying to be kind to you.'

'I don't *want* you to be kind to me.'

'Augusta, this cannot continue. This whole expedition is turning into a farce.'

Augusta knelt up straight, and cast off her hysteria as deftly as a riding-cloak. She fixed Henry with those bland myopic eyes of hers, and said coolly, 'It wasn't a farce last night. Not for you.'

'Augusta – '

'No, Henry; let's be truthful. It wasn't a farce when you really wanted me; and don't try to deny it, you did. No man could have done what you did to me unless he wanted to. You took me with love, no matter what you say. You were strong and gentle and you cared for me, and I was aching with all of my being to give in to you. I know that you're not quite ready for me yet, I know that you don't want to give me everything, not all of yourself, not until you've forgotten Doris. But I gave you as much as I dared, Henry, and you know that when you marry me, you can have all of me, without reservation, to do with me whatever you will. I shall be your slave, Henry, don't doubt it, and all I ask in return is the honour of a loving master.'

Henry let his arms drop, and knelt on the carpet in defeat, his head bowed. Augusta immediately hugged him, and kissed him, prodding her spectacles uncomfortably into his cheek; and cooed, 'My darling Henry; my dear darling Henry.'

Henry said nothing, but freed himself from her arms, and went across to the window, and looked out over the rooftops, the tilted chimney-stacks, the boarded facades, the signs advertising hotels and restaurants and patent pills. The Martin Patent Long-Reach Bull Snap, keeps your bull at bay, reduces to a minimum the chance of being gored, 14-cents. Kowalski's Hardware. Schmidt's Beer.

Augusta came up behind him and tenderly put her arms around his waist. 'I know that you feel uncertain, Henry; but I will be patient for as long as you need. It is true love, Henry, that beats in my heart, and I am devoted to you. Whatever happens, you can always count on that.'

Henry slowly nodded, with the somnolent certainty of a man in a dream. Over the city, a flock of black scoter ducks circled, like the ashes of a burned newspaper, and then vanished.

'The common scoter,' said Henry. 'Inappropriately named, because it is in fact one of the least common ducks; and the male is the only all-black duck we know of, in America.'

Augusta said, 'You know so much.'

'Well, my father made sure I had a good education,' said Henry, more to himself than to her. 'The trouble is, I don't seem to know very much about women. Not as much as I had thought, anyway.'

'Don't decry yourself,' said Augusta, although there was a noticeable lilt of satisfaction in her voice.

Henry replied, 'No, I'm not. But it strikes me that women are a good deal more complicated than men.'

'Complicated?' asked Augusta, and squeezed him hard.

He decided then that he would wait for a day or two; just long enough to give Augusta the time to settle down; but that he would definitely send her home as soon as they reached the terminus at Council Bluffs. No matter how fiercely she protested, not matter what she said about loving him, he would send her back. 'This is the very end, Augusta.' He could silently frame the words with his lips, even now. 'Goodbye, Augusta.' And what a sense of relief, to be alone. At least she could say when she returned to Bennington that she had seen Chicago, and the Mississippi River, and the prairies of Illinois and Iowa. At least she would have a romance to remember for the rest of her life; something to dream about when she lay in her bed at night, in Bennington, while Henry was sitting in whatever yard he might eventually own in San Francisco, surrounded by stacked-up tombstones, with wine, in sunlight, and free.

Henry smiled at Augusta, and she smiled back at him, and the sun came around a drainpipe on the corner of the building and lit up the room as if they were standing in church.

Augusta said, 'We ought to go, Henry. We don't want to miss the train.'

FIVE

Henry was taciturn for the rest of the day; smoking too many cigars and drinking too much whiskey; and staring out at the fields and houses of Illinois as the train clattered gradually westwards, at 20 miles an hour. They had left Chicago just after nine o'clock; and made sure that the baggage-handler loaded their trunks on to the ten o'clock special headed to Joliet, La Salle, and Rock Island, handing them five brass tags to identify their baggage when they eventually arrived at Council Bluffs.

It was a hot, deaf day, and the train moved like a mirage through the wavering green and yellow landscape. In the club car, swearing men in straw hats were playing cards and drinking Fish House punch. In second-class, tired middle-class women were staring out at the endlessly unwinding fields and wondering if they would ever stop travelling, if they would ever be able to unpack their cases and set up a home, even a vase of daisies would have been something, perched on a mantelpiece. The insects droned in and out of the windows, and babies squalled, and the engineer leaned out of his cab with a wheat-stalk twirling between his teeth and whistled 'Sweet Maria'.

While Henry drank, and dozed, and paced up and down the train, Augusta maintained a calm that was too beatific to be real; poised on her seat reading her book; or amusing her hands with a little crochet; smiling at children who ran up and down the aisles of the passenger-cars; and talking to harassed mothers about God, and changing diapers. Henry stood at the far end of their car once, and watched her, and realized that he could very easily grow to hate her; and for the very first time in his life he began to understand how men could beat women, or even murder them. If there was ever a murder victim waiting for a murderer, it was Augusta. He could picture her now, glasses crazed where the perpetrator's heel had stepped on them, blood on her corset-cover, eyes white as a steamed cod's. He turned away, and looked instead at the passing scenery of Bureau County; trees, fields, an occasional farmhouse, and children in smocks waving out of the ripened wheat.

The train took eleven hours to reach Rock Island from Chicago, and so it was dark by the time it reached the Illinois shore of the Mississippi. They waited for almost half an hour, while the locomotive took on water, but then the whistle shrilled, and the conductor called, 'Passengers for Iowa, keep your seats,' and with a sudden jolt they were on their way again.

It was only a little over four years since the Rock Island railroad bridge had been opened over the Mississippi, and so most of the passengers were respectfully silent as the train glided slowly between the parapets. Children were lifted up to the windows so that that they could see the huge black breast of the Mississippi sliding beneath them, but few of them understood what they were being lfited up for, and it was too dark to see the river anyway.

At last, however, they reached the farther shore, where the train stopped again, and a score of passengers alighted for Davenport. Henry sat back in his seat looking at the lights of the city through the window, while Augusta snoozed with her mouth open. As the train gradually began to roll off again, into the night, Augusta opened her eyes and stared at him as if she didn't know who he could be.

'I must have been dreaming,' she said, and took out her mother-of-pearl mirror, and peered at herself.

'What were you dreaming?' asked Henry.

'I don't know. I dreamed that you left me. We were right in the middle of the country somewhere, and you just turned your back and left me.'

Henry didn't say anything; but watched her; his fingers drumming on the rosewood sill of the window.

'We're in Iowa now,' he told her. 'We just crossed the Mississippi.'

'Iowa!' Augusta exclaimed.

'Another twelve hours, and we should be in Council Bluffs.'

Augusta was silent. The train whistled defiantly as it rolled out of Davenport into the night, its headlight gleaming into the summer darkness, and nothing ahead of it but miles and miles of glistening rails, and prairie, and wind. Henry said, 'Why don't you get some sleep? It's almost nine o'clock.'

'I don't feel tired.'

'Well, I'm going to go to bed soon.'

Augusta put away her mirror, and primped her hair, and then decided to delve in her bag for her rice-powder.

'Augusta,' said Henry, even though he could hear himself saying it, 'I'm not going to leave you.'

She didn't look up at him. 'I was very frightened that you might,' she replied. 'After what you said this morning.' Her voice was tight, congested, disapproving. Henry, in response, closed his eyes.

They reached Council Bluffs on the banks of the Missouri at midnight the following night; and Henry and Augusta and thirty other passengers were taken in two smelly horse-drawn omnibuses to the Pottawattamie Hotel: a large wooden building which stood by itself on the outskirts of the town, where the wind whistled through the grass, and tumbleweed blew. The Pottawattamie was supervised by an enormously fat woman with a fine moustache called Mrs Newell, whose husband had died only two years after he had taken her out west. Mrs Newell had no children: and so she regularly embraced the tired and the disillusioned with all the warmth of a mother, finding them rooms, feeding them with corn chowder, and tucking them up like bedfuls of babies in the warm prairie night. She knew that beyond the Big Muddy, where the railroad did not yet run, there was nothing but the prairie, and then the Rocky Mountains; and then beyond the Rocky Mountains the snow-peaked Sierras. Even those who had managed to come out as far as Council Bluffs in reasonable spirits would find that their will and their stamina would be sorely tested by what lay ahead.

That night, in their room, in a bed like a huge creaking raft, 'Mr and Mrs Roberts' listened to the wind blowing across the river. At two o'clock in the morning, both of them wakeful, they watched the moon rise and illuminate their room with silver. The walls were boarded, and painted with white distemper. There was a pine chest, painted with Hungarian flowers; and a chest of drawers with a small looking-glass on top of it, one of those looking-glasses in which it is impossible to see your whole face at once, but which somehow managed tonight to catch the moon, and reflect it on to the red and green Indian rug on the floor.

August put her arm around Henry's chest. She smelled of soap. She said, 'Henry, you won't leave me, will you?'

Someone in the room next door was having jouncing intercourse on their squeaky-springed bed. Henry said, 'Let's talk about it tomorrow.'

'But you said you wouldn't.'

'Then you have your word, don't you? If I said I wouldn't, I won't. Now I'm tired, Augusta. In the morning we're going to have to find ourselves an emigrant party to travel to California with. And buy ourselves a waggon; and all the stores that we're going to need.'

'Henry,' said Augusta, and she suddenly twisted herself around to turn her back to him, and tugged up her nightgown. 'Henry, take me again, Henry; please.'

Henry lay where he was, wooden with impatience and repulsion. Next door, a woman's throat let out a cry like a wounded swan, and there was a great crescendo of springs, which abruptly stopped. Blindly, Augusta groped behind her at Henry's nightshirt, scrabbling at his thighs, and panted, 'Henry, please; *take* me, Henry. I want you so much!'

Henry pushed her hand away; but it came back again, searching for him, tugging at him, and at last he gripped her wrist and twisted her arm around until she cried out in pain.

'Henry! That *hurt-*'

Henry hurled back the patchwork comforter and leaped out of bed. 'I'm sorry! I apologize! But for the love of God, Augusta, I can't sleep with you any more!'

'Henry, what's the matter?'

'It's *you*, damn it, *you're* the matter. You've been pushing yourself at me, on and on, ever since we left New York, telling me how much you love me, and how you're going to be my slave, and when are we going to be married? Augusta, I don't love you now, and I never will love you, and if you happen to love me then I'm sorry. But I can't do anything about it, and I *won't* do anything about it.'

'But you said you'd never leave me.' Tearful, uncertain, in the moonlight.

'The way you went on at me, I would have said anything to stop you from nagging.'

'You said that you might learn to love me.'

'I didn't say anything of the kind. God damn it, Augusta, don't you listen? Don't you understand? I don't love you. How can I make it any plainer than that?'

'But when you get over Doris – '

'No!' Henry roared at her. 'Not when I get over Doris! Not *ever!* What the *hell* can I do to get it through your head that I don't love you. I don't even like you, in fact I detest the sight of you!'

She sniffed, and trembled. Somebody thumped on the wall next door and shouted, 'Shut that row, will you? Folks is attempting to sleep.'

'Shut up yourself!' Henry shouted back, still quaking with frustration and fury.

The thumping was renewed. 'You listen here, mister, we got four kids in here; and now you've woken the baby. So you just shove a sock in it, you hear, or else I'm going to come next door and shut you up for good and all!'

'What the hell's going on?' demanded a voice from upstairs,

and a pair of heels drummed on the ceiling. First one baby started crying, and then another, and then two older children started grizzling, and a woman began to scream at her husband to keep quiet.

'Now see what you've done, with that ridiculous outburst,' Augusta said, bitterly.

'Me?' Henry hissed, kneeling forward on the bed and leaning over her. 'It wasn't me. It was you. If only you'd had the grace to understand. Can't you see what kind of a position you've put me in? Can't you see just how much you've been cornering me? I'm not an angry person, Augusta; I wasn't brought up that way. I was brought up to say what I had to say clearly and politely, in English, without the need for cursing. But by God you've pushed me so far, I swear to you that I've never felt like shouting at anyone in my whole life before, not the way I feel like shouting at you. For God's sake, Augusta, help yourself. Have some strength, have some spirit.'

'I told you that I would be dependent on you,' Augusta said. Her voice was almost accusing. 'I warned you, right from the very beginning.'

'But one person can't be dependent on another, not the way you're trying to be dependent on me. I can't think for you; I can't lead your life for you. I'm not your husband, and I'm never going to be. I'm not your father, either.'

Augusta clutched miserably at the shoulders of Henry's nightshirt. 'But I'm so weak,' she wept. 'Henry, I need you! I can't manage on my own! How am I going to manage on my own, out here in the middle of the prairie? Oh, Henry, I knew my dream was right. You're going to leave me, aren't you? You're going to leave me here.'

Henry squeezed his eyes tightly shut. He felt such rage within him that he couldn't stop himself from shuddering. And all the time Augusta mewled and pawed him and begged him not to leave her, please don't leave me, Henry; you know that I love you; Henry, I promise I won't nag you any more; you don't even have to sleep with me; you don't have to do anything, Henry; but please don't leave me.

He opened his eyes unexpectedly; and in unnerving contrast to the entreaty in her voice, her face was completely calm, and her eyes were staring at him with a look that disturbed him deeply, even frightened him. There was adoration there; he could see that. But there was something else: a calculating avarice, as if she could have eaten him alive. He was beginning to understand now what she really was, a cannibal, with an insatiable appetite for reassurance. A woman whose self-esteem was so low that it had to be fed on the constant approval of everybody she liked; and on the jealousy of those that she didn't. Henry had always been the dude of Carmington; and now she, Augusta, had won him for herself. And there was no doubt that she would write back to everyone in Carmington as soon as they were settled in California, and crow about it. She would go through any kind of humiliation; she would submit to anything at all; as long as she could boast that she had won Henry.

Henry was about to say, 'I hate you,' but his anger had been quelled by his realization of what Augusta needed from him. Instead, he tugged his sleeve away from her clutching hand, and stood up, and quickly dressed.

'Where are you going?' she asked him, in a ghostly voice. Always the right voice for the right moment. Anger one second, pleading the next.

'I'm going out, that's all. I think it's time we gave the rest of the guests a chance to get some sleep.'

'You won't leave me here, will you?'

'Oh, for Christ's sake, Augusta.'

He fumbled his way down the corridor, and creaked down the stairs, and then out through the unlocked hotel doors into the windy, moonlit night. He was startled for a moment by a huge ball of tumbleweed which came bounding silently across the yard, and caught in the fence; but then he walked across the stretch of dusty real-estate that separated the Pottawattamie Hotel from its nearest neighbour, the Council Bluffs Tack Store; and made his way down to the banks of the wide Missouri.

The riverbanks here were flat and muddy, and army engineers had been laying down retainers of intertwined saplings to prevent the soil from washing away, and clogging up a river which was already brown with silt. There was an old story about a woman in Sioux City, a few score miles further upstream, who had tried to commit suicide by jumping into the river, only to find herself buried up to her knees in ooze.

Henry climbed on to the woven saplings, and sat tiredly staring at the sliding Missourie, and at the winking lights of Omaha, Nebraska Territory, on the opposite side. There were seven or eight paddle-steamers moored up at Omaha's dock, a smart new side-wheeler and half a dozen old stern-wheelers. One of them was already getting up steam for the morning, and black smoke was rising from its twin smokestacks, and smudging the moon as it drifted eastwards.

He felt desperately guilty about Augusta. It had been wrong of him to shout at her; and even worse to tell her that he detested her. After all, he had invited her to come along with him, and he had used her money; and however perverse her sexual appetites may have been, she hadn't committed the act alone.

He wasn't used to feeling guilty, and he couldn't understand why Augusta had that effect on him. All right, he accepted the responsibility of bringing her here. But wasn't it better to end it now, before she grew even more dependent on him? It would hurt her, certainly; but when she went back east, that hurt would give her a greater incentive to look for somebody else, somebody who really suited her.

He walked back to the hotel. He felt exhausted and gritty. Ever since he had taken up with Augusta, he seemed to spend half his nights wandering around the streets, sitting by lake-sides and riverbanks, chilled and disappointed. The sky was growing light now, even though the moon was still out, and a grey-haired Negro came out on to the hotel steps and started sweeping.

'You up early, sir,' the Negro remarked.

'Couldn't sleep,' said Henry.

'Well, me neither, sir. Somebody making all kinds of commotion last night, shouting and hollering, and babies scree-ching and whatnot? Never knewed a night like it.'

'Anywhere I can get some breakfast?' Henry asked him.

'Grits and bacon, if that's suitable.'

'That sounds more than suitable.'

The Negro propped his broom up against the side of the hotel, and beckoned Henry to follow him around the side. There was a small lean-to building there, next to the kitchen entrance, in which there was a table and an oil-lamp and a small pot-bellied stove. On the stove was a blackened old fry-pan.

'This is my mansion, sir,' grinned the Negro. 'And by the way, my names Dat Apple.'

Henry ducked his head to step inside the lean-to, and looked around. At the very back of it, there was a bed, heaped with

144

brown and white Indian blankets, and a rickety shelf, on which Dat Apple's treasures were all arrayed. A Bible with a cracked back; a pewter jug engraved with the initials of the Hannibal & St Joe Railroad Company; a set of augers; and a small clock with the sun and the moon painted on its face. Dat Apple opened up a small meat-safe, and produced a pound of good bacon and a bowlful of grits; and then sliced a lump of lard into his fry-pan. 'Sit down,' he told Henry. This was his home; in here, he didn't have to knuckle his forehead to anyone. 'A good breakfast is a serious business.'

'How long have you lived here?' Henry asked him, sitting down on the bed.

Dat Apple watched the lard melt, and slide around the pan. 'Coming on seven years now. I was a slave once, down in Savannah. My family all died and I runned off; but Mrs Newell took me in. She still don't pay me no wages, but she feeds me and keeps me, and this is my mansion here, safe from all.'

'Who called you Dat Apple?' asked Henry.

'Mrs Newell, sir. Previous to that, my name was William Marcus Truscott, sir.'

Henry watched Dat Apple lay the rashers of bacon in the pan; and with all the fascination of hunger and tiredness scrutinized closely the way they curled up and spat.

'I do all of my cooking in this one pan, sir,' remarked Dat Apple. 'This is my Trusty Pan. Well, that's what I call it.' The aroma of home-smoked bacon was so appetizing that Henry had to swallow his mouth-water; and then blow his nose loudly with his handkerchief.

'Mrs Newell call me Dat Apple because I was never sad, sir, in spite of seeing my good wife Julia die, and losing my boys, both of them, to different plantations. I would give anything at all, sir, if I could see those boys for just one minute, and take their hand, and let them know that their father's happy. But it won't be possible, and I have to swallow that, sir, and never despair. That's why Mrs Newell called me Dat Apple, she said Dat Apple was the opposite of Dis Pear.'

Dat Apple turned the bacon in the pan; and spooned the grits in next to it. 'I only have the one plate, sir,' he said, 'but you can have that. Me, I'm used to eating my breakfast straight from the pan.'

Henry said, 'I'm looking for a party of emigrants; any party, so long as their guide's good.'

'You're heading for California, sir? Well, you missed the best party, they left two weeks ago, with Mr Nathan Reed leading them. You don't want to leave it too much longer, sir, otherwise it's going to be dead of winter by the time you have to cross the Sierras and that can be fatal, sir. You remember the Donner party, what happened to them.'

'Yes,' said Henry. 'Is there anyone else?'

Dat Apple produced a single dinner-plate, decorated with the Bavarian rose-garland pattern, and shovelled on to it five rashers of crispy bacon and a big spoonful of grits. 'There, sir,' he said. 'Now that's a serious breakfast; and here's a serious drink to go with it.' He reached behind him, and produced an earthenware jug, which he unstoppered with his teeth. 'Go ahead,' he said, offering Henry the neck. Henry hesitated for a moment, and then hefted up the jug on his forearm, and drank. It was corn liquor, strong and clear, and he coughed a cough like a dog barking, but it went right down inside him like white fire, and warmed him and woke him up at the same time.

'Dangerous stuff,' he remarked, handing the jug back.

'You bet,' grinned Dat Apple. 'A couple of quarts of that, and they'd be calling *you* Dat Apple, too. No room for Dis Pear, not with this mixture.'

Henry picked up a rasher of bacon in his fingers, and began to eat. Dat Apple sat with the fry-pan perched on his knees, and scooped his grits with a spoon. 'Only got the one spoon, sir, if you don't object to sharing.'

Henry said nothing: but held out his hand for the spoon, and dug into his grits. They were hot and soft and cumbly, and soaked with bacon-grease. 'No chance that either of *us* is going to get to Heaven through the eye of a needle,' he remarked, and Dat Apple chuckled, and stamped his foot, and said, 'You should stay here; you and me could get on pretty good; getting fat; drinking corn.'

It could have been the liquor, but Henry found himself grinning all over his face. 'What else?' he said. 'Sweeping the steps?'

Dat Apple collapsed into cackles of laughter; and had to lay his fry-pan breakfast back on the stove, so that he could wipe his eyes. 'That's right,' he wept. 'Getting fat, drinking corn, sweeping the steps, dodging the tumbleweed; who needs anything more?'

146

Henry started to laugh out loud, and almost choked on his bacon. Dat Apple got up and slapped him on the shoulders, and then both of them sat side by side and laughed and laughed until Henry felt that he was going to suffocate. 'By God,' he said, after two or three minutes, 'you're the funniest person I ever met.'

'Me?' exclaimed Dat Apple; and they both burst out laughing again.

Eventually, they recovered enough to finish their breakfast, wiping up the last of the bacon-grease with grits; and rinsing everything down with corn liquor. Dat Apple's decorated clock said that it was seven o'clock.

'You know something,' said Dat Apple, more seriously. 'A man don't ever get much of a chance to make himself a friend; not out here; being black and all, and a runaway slave. But real friends come quick, didn't you ever notice that? When you like a body, you likes them straight away, no fussing. And I hope you don't take it as anything else but a compliment, sir, when I say that I like you.'

Henry took Dat Apple's hand, and wrung it tight. 'Call me Henry,' he said. 'But only if you let me call you William.'

'No, don't call me William,' said Dat Apple, shaking his grey curly head. 'That was my master's name, in Savannah. What my own name was, well, I never knew. Dat Apple had dignity enough for me. And I'd be proud to call you Henry.'

'I'd better get back,' said Henry. 'My wife's going to be wondering where I've got myself to.'

'You married?' frowned Dat Apple.

'Not really. She's a girl who came along with me.'

'Ah well, the same thing.'

'Do you know of any guides?' asked Henry. 'Somebody you can really recommend?'

'Well,' said Dat Apple, 'there's one; I was going to mention him before; but if you've got a woman with you; hmm; he ain't really the type. He'd get you there fast, though, just on his own, with mules; no bothering with waggon-trains. Those waggon-trains are excruciating slow; just excruciating; the way those oxen plod. Plod, plod, plod. Some of those emigrants get to California half crazy, on account of that plodding, that's what Nathan Reed says, five months from here to Sutter's Fort, that's a long time. Mind you, it's a long way.'

'Tell me about this guide,' said Henry.

'His name's Edward McLowery, not an amenable man, but knows his way to California. He's staying at the Wooding House, as far as I've heard, that's where he usually stays. But he doesn't take commissions kindly; he needs persuading when it comes to going west again; for each time he goes, he swears that it's going to be the last. But he's the best, no doubt about it.'

'Well, Dat Apple, maybe I'll go and talk to him,' said Henry. He stood up, and retrieved his hat.

'Tell him Dat Apple sent you.'

'I will. And thanks for the breakfast. That was Heaven.'

'Not through the eye of a needle it wasn't.'

Henry walked satisfied round to the front of the Pottawattamie Hotel, and up the steps, and said 'Good morning,' to Mrs Newell who was scolding one of her cleaners in the lobby.

'Well, good morning,' replied Mrs Newell, staring at him oddly. Henry hesitated for a moment, wondering if she wanted to tell him something; but she turned away, and went on reprimanding her cleaning-girl. He shrugged, and went upstairs.

'Augusta,' he said, opening the bedroom door. But the room was empty, and the bed was turned back; and even Augusta's hair-brushes had disappeared from the top of the chest of drawers. 'Augusta!' he called again, and opened the wardrobe. Her dresses were gone, so was her carpet-bag.

'My God,' he thought, 'she's done it. She's left me. She's gone back to Bennington.'

He pulled open the drawers one by one, and all that remained were his own handkerchiefs, his own collars, his own underwear. Five silk neckties, and a shrivelled pair of sock-suspenders.

He sat down on the bed. She's done it. She's gone back home, and left me. And the extraordinary part about it was, that he actually missed her; that ' large plain face, and that endlessly apologetic breathiness. You can be nagged for a week, and grow quite used to it. Augusta, he thought. What a revelation. She probably caught the first train east, the six o'clock local; and now she's steaming past McClelland, her face against the window, dreaming of what a romantic time she had; and how she can go back to Bennington and say that he had taken her as far as Council Bluffs, just to kiss her goodbye; and that he had promised to come back and get her as soon as he'd made himself a fortune. Well, he didn't mind that. She could say whatever she liked, as long as she didn't come along to California. Poor Augusta.

Mrs Newell appeared in the doorway, her hands on her hips, her face as puffed-up and yellow as a Mormon Johnnycake. 'Well, Mr Roberts; your wife has left you.'

'I'm afraid so,' said Henry, running his hand through his hair.

'You caused quite an upset here, last night.'

'Yes, I'm sorry.'

'Sorry? Well, I wouldn't go down to breakfast in the parlour, if I were you. There are two or three folks there who would pay money to see you thrashed, for keeping them awake last night. All that shouting and screeching and carrying-on. That's not the sort of house I like to run.'

Henry nodded, as if he were feeling upset. Mrs Newell stood in the doorway for a moment and then came into the room, and stood close behind him.

'She said she loved you, you know.'

'Did she?'

'She said that if you ever changed your mind, well, you'd know where you could find her.'

Henry turned, and gave Mrs Newell a vague, complex smile. 'Ah,' he said, as if he understood everything.

'Oh, I'm sorry,' said Mrs Newell, taking hold of his sleeve. 'I know it isn't easy, newlyweds like you, thrashing it out on the trail. It's hard enough for couples who have been wed for five years or more; and got to know each other well.'

Henry tried to look like a newly-deserted husband; and a disappointed emigrant; and a saddened adventurer, all at once. Mrs Newell suddenly and spontaneously hugged him; squeezing him close to her huge flower-printed bosom, and cushions and corsets; and then slapped him on the back so hard that he coughed. 'Go back and find her,' she exhorted him. 'Go on, she'll take you back; I know it.'

Just as Mrs Newell was squeezing him, however, it occurred to Henry that Augusta had been carrying all of their money; or rather all of *her* money. She may have blessedly gone, and given him his freedom, but she had taken with her all the funds he needed to set up in business in California. Worse than that, all the funds he needed just to *get* to California. It had been all very tragic for her to talk of nightmares in which he had abandoned her in the middle of nowhere at all; but now she had done it to him. Here he was, in Council Bluffs, Iowa, with an hotel bill to pay, and a stack of trunks, and no return ticket to anywhere, and no money whatsoever, nothing, not even a loose nickel in his britches pocket.

Mrs Newell smiled at him, and touched his nose with the tip of her finger, and said, 'There, now. She went on the six o'clock train. If you can catch the ten o'clock special, you should catch up with her at Des Moines, or at least at Rock Island.'

'She, er, didn't pay the bill? By any chance?'

'All she did was say goodbye, my dear; and that she loved you; and that you would know where to find her, if you wanted to.'

Henry nodded. 'I see. Well, I don't think I'm going to go chasing after her right away. I think I'm going to. . . well, think for a while. You don't mind that, do you? If I keep this room for another night? I mean, there won't be any more arguments, now she's gone.'

'That's all right, my dear,' said Mrs Newell, maternally. 'You stay for as long as you wish. And if it's advice you want; or nothing but comfort; you just come to me.'

'Well,' said Henry, 'I shall.'

After Mrs Newell had gone, Henry dressed as quickly as he could, in his smartest linen suit, and his last clean collar, and walked to the Council Bluffs depot. At the baggage counter, a laconic clerk with a drawn-out country accent and a toothpick fidgeting in the corner of his mouth told him that Mrs Roberts had claimed all of her trunks, and taken them with her on the 6:03; but that she had left her husband's trunks, all three of them, with 75 cents to pay.

'But I'm the husband,' said Henry.

'In that case, 75 cents,' replied the clerk.

Henry bit his lip. 'I couldn't owe it to you?'

The clerk stared at him as if he had to be joking. 'No 75 cents, no baggage, that's the rule. There it is, right on the wall. Chicago & Rock Island Railroad, Rules For The Depositing of Passengers' Baggage. Rule Nine, no money, no baggage. Well, that's what you might call a pray-see. The real rule's written in railroad language.'

Henry said, 'I could give you an IOU.'

'I'm sorry, friend. It's 75 cents or nothing. Rule Nine.'

Henry left the depot and walked out into the street. It was

growing warmer now, although it was still windy, and he took off his jacket and carried it over his arm. He passed Deacon's Lunch Rooms, just opening up, green blinds being raised at the windows; and the Old Misery Saloon; and the Council Bluffs Druggery, with a pyramid display of Balm of Childhood and Dr Kilmer's Female Remedy 'The Great Blood Purifier and System Regulator'; and then a vacant lot; and then a small unpainted house standing on its own, a typical Iowa house with a flat false front and an outside staircase. At the top of the staircase, a young woman in a white cotton nightdress was pegging up blouses and underwear on to a makeshift line. Henry stopped and watched her, his hand shading his eyes. She reminded him of one of those imported china dolls; she was very petite, no taller than five feet; with a plump rosy-cheeked face and blue eyes that could have been painted. Her dark curly hair had been wound up into rags, although two long plaits hung all the way down her back. She was very big-breasted and chubby-hipped; but there was something about her, some natural graciousness, that caused Henry to pause.

She took the last peg out of her mouth, and then glanced down and saw him. Instead of blushing, or hurrying inside the house, she planted her hands on her hips, and said, 'What's the matter with you, Algernon? Never seen anyone doing their laundry before?' But her tone was more provocative than snappy.

Henry raised his hat. 'I'm sorry. I was just thinking how charming you looked.'

'Oh, charming, is it? Well, I've been called this and that, and even delicious, but charming's a new one.'

'I didn't mean to upset you.'

'You didn't, don't worry about it. But you're a bit early, aren't you?'

'Early for what?'

The girl blew out her cheeks in amusement. 'Early for what,' she mocked him. She opened the door of her house and then looked back at him. 'Come on up,' she said. And then, 'Early for what. Pfff.'

Henry was left in the dusty street, holding his hat. He hesitated for a moment, but then the door opened again, and the girl demanded, 'Come on then. You may be early, but I haven't got all day.' Henry climbed the stairs, and went into the house after her.

Inside, he found himself in a small lobby, with a coatstand, and an ugly brown china pot for umbrellas. Beyond that, through a curtain of red glass beads, he could see an overfurnished sitting-room, crowded with occasional tables, and red plush armchairs, and a huge chaise-longue covered in tiger-skin. In the far corner, there was a patent organ; although it was difficult to make out much else because of the density of the curtains that hung at the windows, layers of lace and swags of velvet, all beaded and bobbled and elaborately drawn up into gathers. At the opposite side of the room, the door was slightly ajar, and as he rattled through the bead curtain, Henry glimpsed the corner of a large iron-framed bed, and the interior of a bedroom that was just as excessively furnished. Plaster cherubs and lamp-fringes.

The girl came directly up to Henry in her bare feet and smiled up at him prettily. She was so small that the top of her head reached only up to his third waistcoat button. 'You must have come in last night,' she said. Her accent was very Eastern, and cultured. 'I suppose they took you to the Pottawattamie. Well, they usually do, and so they should. Mrs Newell's a very respectable lady. Most of the time, anyway. She does have her moments, though; if you like your romances on the gigantic scale.' She pronounced 'gigantic' in a deep, droll voice.

'My name's Henry,' said Henry, holding out his hand.

'Well, how do you do. My name's Annabel. Would you like some coffee now, or afterwards.'

Henry shrugged. 'I don't think there's going to be any afterwards. You see, the truth is, I can't even afford the before.'

'I haven't even told you what the rates are yet. Morning rate is more economical than evening rate.'

'Annabel, I'm sorry. I'm stony. You want me to pull my pockets inside out, and show you?'

Annabel stood looking up at him with an expression of complete disbelief. 'You don't have any money at all? A smart fellow like you?'

He shook his head.

'Well, what the hell did you come up here for?' she snapped, although she didn't seem to be particularly cross.

'You invited me.'

'I know I invited you,' she retorted. 'But not for *free*. What do you think I am, a charity for penniless emigrants? How can you possibly not have any money?'

152

Henry said, 'I could use that cup of coffee, if *that* comes free.'

Annabel let out two or three exasperated pffs, and said, 'if *that* comes free,' two or three times; and then smiled. 'All right,' she said. 'Hang up your hat, and take a seat. It should be ready by now.'

She went through to a small sunlit kitchen and made a lot of noise with a copper coffee-pot. Then she came back with a tray, on which there were two delicate demitasse cups, and a faience coffee-jug, and a plate of lace cookies, which looked home-made.

'Very genteel,' nodded Henry.

'Naturally,' said Annabel, with defiance. 'I'm a very genteel person. Gentility herself.'

She poured coffee. The steam curled up into the gloom of the room. 'Have a cookie,' she said. 'I bake them myself. All kinds, I adore them. You should taste my sand tarts.'

'I'd love to.'

Annabel sat back, tugging her nightgown demurely over her knees. 'I don't generally work in the mornings anyway. I did once, when there was a whole waggon-train of prospectors leaving for Sacramento. In fact, I worked all day. But, generally, I don't.'

Henry sipped his coffee, and looked around the room. 'Nice place you've got here.'

'Well, it wasn't expensive to furnish, I can tell you that. That chaise-longue you're sitting on, I found that by the side of the road, a little way back towards Oakland. Same with the organ. There it was, all alone, in the middle of a field, and the wind was blowing down its pipes, so that it was playing all by itself. Abandoned, you see. They carry all their prized possessions out from the east, and it's only when they start to cross the prairie that they realize that some solid oak sideboard they prized in Pennsylvania is just so much dead weight when they're trying to get to California before the snows set in.'

'And you?' asked Henry, over the rim of his cup. 'How did you get here?'

'That's my business,' said Annabel. It was quite plain from the look on her face that she wasn't going to tell him; that she never told anybody.

'You're schooled, though.'

'Certainly. Providence Ladies' College, Rhode Island.'

'And now?'

153

'I'm happy. I hope that doesn't bother you. I live by myself but I get all the gentlemen I want and nobody ever does anything to hurt me. Not inside here, at any rate,' she said tapping her forehead.

Henry sat for a while, saying nothing. Annabel nibbled her lace cookie, and watched him. Outside, two dogs began to yap at each other.

'Did somebody rob you?' she asked, at last.

Henry glanced up. 'Yes, well, you could say that.'

'Nobody here, I hope. Not in Council Bluffs.'

'It's a long story,' he said. 'You wouldn't want to hear it.'

'Well, I would, as a matter of fact,' said Annabel. She looked at him brightly, and smiled. 'You're not used to talking about yourself, are you? You think a lot, but you don't talk. Well, you should try it. I make a lot of men try it. It's as good as a fuck, sometimes, if you'll excuse my Iowan.'

Henry looked back at her with curiosity. Even Augusta had never spoken to him like this. He slowly set his coffee-cup back on the tray, without taking his eyes off Annabel, and then he said, 'All right. If you really want to hear, I'll tell you.'

He told her everything; and while he did, she repeatedly replenished his cup with fresh coffee. He told her about Doris, and how Doris had died. He told her about Alby Monihan, and William Paterson, and Augusta, and most of all about Augusta. He even told her how Augusta had encouraged him to take her from behind; and this was something that he never would have believed that he would ever tell anybody, but Annabel listened without a qualm; interested, encouraging, and unabashed.

'So what are you going to do now?' she asked him. 'Are you going to go after her?'

'I thought about it. But, no. I think it's better the way it is.'

'You're going to go on to California instead?'

Henry nodded. 'If I can raise enough money to join an emigrant waggon-train; or if I can persuade a guide to take me by mule. The nigger at Mrs Newell's said that a man called Edward McLowery was the best.'

'Ted McLowery? I suppose so. But Ted McLowery's not your usual run of fellow. I don't know whether you and he would get along very well. He charges a high price, too. *Nearly* as much as me.'

'Well, once I get my trunks out of the baggage-store at the

depot, I'll have quite a bit to sell. Stone-working tools, clothes, boots; a rotary grindstone. I should make a hundred dollars at least.'

'You're going to make a hundred dollars out of stone-working tools in the middle of the prairie? There isn't a stone for two hundred miles.'

'I'll get whatever I can,' replied Henry, a little petulantly. 'Anything's better than nothing at all.'

'I'm sorry,' Annabel coaxed him, 'I didn't mean to be smart.'

There was another long pause, and then Henry said, 'I don't suppose you could lend me 75 cents.'

Annabel burst out laughing, a high peal of a laugh, like a very young girl at a party. 'What a cheek you've got! Coming up here without a penny in your pocket, drinking my coffee and eating my cookies; and now you want a tip!'

'Well, listen, I'm sorry,' said Henry. He was past embarrassment now. 'But my trunks are in the depot, and 75 cents is what it's going to cost to get them out. I'll pay you back, I promise.'

Annabel came over, and leaned forward, and kissed him on the forehead. Henry found himself looking straight into those blue cornflower eyes of hers from very close up, and smelling coffee and cookie-sugar on her breath. He glanced down into the open neck of her nightgown, and he could see the deep cleavage of her heavy breasts.

'Henry,' she whispered, 'I'll lend you 75 cents, for as long as you like, without interest. There's only one condition.'

Henry said nothing, but stared back into her eyes, so near to her now that he could see the little flecks of brown in her irises.

'Come to bed,' she said. 'That's my one condition.'

Afterwards, he would remember that morning as if he had read about it in a book, because it seemed so separate from the rest of his life; an event that had its own beginning, its own middle, and its own ending. Nothing more crucial to the course of his career came out of that morning than 75 cents, with which he was able to redeem his trunks from the railroad depot; and yet he would never forget it. It haunted him for years to come, because in spite of its separateness, he always saw it as a painful illustration of the right people meeting at the wrong moment, of lives out of joint. Annabel had been here too long, and she had experienced too much, in spite of the fact that she was probably two or three years younger than he was. Henry on the other hand was on his way east, with a destiny ahead of him, a destiny which he couldn't afford to keep waiting. Annabel had suffered something in her past which she couldn't talk about, not on the first meeting; and while Henry had suffered enough to be able to understand it, when she eventually felt that she could trust him, that time would never come, because she had to stay and he had to go, and both of them knew it.

She knelt up on the big iron-framed bed, on the tousled sheets in which she had slept last night, and lifted her nightgown. Heavy white thighs, a dark bush of pubic hair, a soft rounded stomach. Her nightgown caught on her breasts as she lifted it, but one after the other, with a tantalizing tumble, her breasts came free, big and wide-nippled, and lightly decorated with pale blue veins.

Henry untwisted the buttons of his waistcoat, loosened his cufflinks, stepped out of his britches. Then he stood naked watching her: a tall, quite muscular young man, with just a suggestion of a belly from too much beer, and rounded buttocks. There was a white scar on the left side of his chest where a maul had slipped.

Annabel lay back on the bed and opened her thighs for him. The lips of her vulva parted moistly. He climbed on top of her, and with both hands she guided him in. She felt very hot inside, as if she were running a fever, hot and wet on the cool thermometer of his hardened penis.

Like a book, the morning had a series of its own illustrations: Henry bowing over Annabel, clasping her breasts in hands that were scarcely able to contain them. Henry and Annabel kissing, and the sun through the half-drawn curtains just catching the thin thread of saliva that joined them, lip to lip, a spider's-web at dawn. Annabel with her eyes closed; her cheeks flushed up like flowers. Henry lying on his back, with Annabel bridging his body with her thick white thighs, her neck arched back so that her long plaits brushed the bed.

It seemed to take hours and yet it took no time at all. At last Henry found himself lying alone on the bed, while Annabel clattered in the kitchen. There were sounds of splashing water. Annabel hummed, and sang snatches of popular songs, never quite finishing a line. After a while she appeared in the doorway, naked, and smiled at him. She had taken the rags

156

from out of her hair, and she was brushing it out, a huge mass of soft clean dark brown curls.

'Well?' she said, sitting down beside him, and kissing him.

'I don't think I know what to say,' he told her.

'You don't have to say anything. It's the best way. Say nothing; and do nothing; and always trust to luck.'

He cupped her breast in his hand, and lightly rubbed the nipple with his thumb, so that it crinkled and stiffened. 'You've done something very important for me today,' he said, in a hoarse voice.

She kissed him again. 'I know.'

He looked up at her, and she smiled. 'Don't worry,' she said. 'Every man has the same problem. I think they call it vanity.'

Henry slowly nodded in acknowledgement. He knew that he could never have her. He knew, too, that even if he could, he would never want her. He kept thinking of all those other men who had climbed into this bed; last night, and the night before, and the night before that; and all those other hands that had caressed these same breasts. The same would happen tonight. And, given a week, she would forget altogether the young man from Carmington in the smart linen suit who didn't have a penny; and what he looked like, and even what his name was.

'You want 75 cents,' she said. 'I'll get it for you.'

'Annabel,' said Henry.

She turned; but then she realized what he was going to say, and shook her head. 'Come back here one day,' she told him. 'Then you can pay me. Or perhaps not. Perhaps I won't let you.'

'Is it always like this?' he asked her.

'No,' she said. 'But that's no business of yours.'

'But why?'

Annabel got up off the bed again, and reached for her robe, sapphire-blue silk with Chinese lions embroidered on it, a gift from a Chinese railroad worker.

'You see this writing?' Annabel asked Henry. 'This says, "The way is like an empty bottle." '

'Do you know what that means?' Henry asked her.

Annabel shook her head. All those soft brown curls. 'No,' she said. 'But the fellow who gave it to me, he said you shouldn't have to know what it means. It's one of those things that you either understand, or you don't. Like intuition.'

He walked back to the railroad depot through the dusty, bleached-out street; jingling three quarters in his hand. Back at the baggage office, he retrieved his trunks; and then persuaded a grizzled old porter to lend him a hand-barrow on the promise of a drink when he returned it. Trundling the barrow behind him, he made his way to Seforim's Pawn Shop on Third and Quick. It was a dark, musty shop, smelling of camphor and furniture polish; and it was crowded like a bizarre indoor forest with bureau mirrors, hatstands, clocks under glass, stuffed eagles, armchairs, pianos, and chandeliers. This was all the debris of disappointed pioneers: the luxuries they could no longer afford to keep, the treasures they couldn't carry any further.

Mr Seforim sat behind his counter, a round-faced bespectacled Russian Jew wearing a red flannel shirt and a wide-brimmed cow-puncher's hat. Like so many Orthodox Jews, he had cut off his payess, his long side-curls, when he had arrived in the New World, and had turned his back on most of the old traditions. But a *mezuzah* still hung next to the door-frame which led into his living-room, a small box containing a scroll from Deuteronomy, which Mr Seforim would habitually touch as he entered that part of his shop he called home.

'What's on the barrow?' he asked, as Henry climbed over a stack of Home Doctors and Family Encyclopedias.

'Do you want to come and look?' asked Henry.

'As long as it isn't evening-wear. You'd never believe the evening-wear. I could dress a thousand people in evening-wear; the shirt-fronts I've got. The spats. What do you do in the middle of the prairie with two hundred pairs assorted spats?'

He followed Henry outside into the sunlight, sniffing and squinching up his eyes. Henry opened his three trunks, one by one, and said, 'There. Clothes, tools, books. Whatever you want.'

'What are all these tools?' Mr Seforim wanted to know, indicating Henry's chisels and hammers with an irritable sweep of his hand. 'What do you do with tools like these?'

'These are the finest that money can buy,' said Henry. 'Look at that sledge, that's crucible cast steel, worth a dollar-fifty. Then there's a whole set of chisels, and six different spalling hammers.'

'Yes, but what for? Fixing teeth?'

158

'No, stonework. I'm a monumental mason. I carve grave-markers, you know? Tombstones. Anything from a luxury granite sarcophagus to a budget-rate stump in the ground.'

'And how are you going to make a living if you pledge me your tools?'

'I'll work that out when I get to California.'

'Maybe you're going to break stone with your bare hands?'

Henry wiped sweat from his forehead. In spite of the wind that was blowing across the prairies of Nebraska, and over the breadth of the Big Muddy, it was uncomfortably hot and dusty in Council Bluffs, and he began to feel that he could scarcely breathe; especially now that his life depended on how much Mr Seforim would offer him for all of his possessions.

'You know what I have to do?' said Mr Seforim. He hauled out a large green handkerchief and blew his nose, wiping it afterwards from side to side as if he were challenging it to a duel. 'I have to say to myself, when is this man likely to come back and redeem these tools? That's what I have to say. And then I have to say to myself, supposing he never comes back, then who is going to buy them, and when, and for how much? Now, how many monumental masons do you think are going to come travelling through Council Bluffs in the next two or three years or so, looking for tools and eager to pay me their best dollar?'

'How much?' Henry asked him, irritably.

Mr Seforim walked around the open trunks, stared at with unashamed interest by two local loafers in large Mormon hats, and a cluster of four or five small boys. There was no better sport on Third and Quick than to watch an emigrant being obliged to take whatever price Mr Seforim felt like offering. In a country where hand-carved bureaux were left by the side of the trail for anybody to pick up, a pawnbroker could name his own price.

'Twenty-five dollars, all three trunks, and everything in them,' Mr Seforim suggested.

'Twenty-five dollars?' Henry exclaimed. 'The tools alone cost me three times that.'

'It's the best I can do. You want me to cut my own throat? What have you got here, hammers, a few shirts, you're lucky I'm even prepared to look at it.'

'Forty,' said Henry, belligerently.

Mr Seforim linked his hands behind his back, and tightened his mouth, and shook his head.

'Thirty-five,' Henry suggested. Again, Mr Seforim shook his head.

'Thirty, and that's as low as I go,' said Henry.

There was a long silence. Mr Seforim prowled around the trunks, lifting out coats and stretching suspenders, but Henry knew that they had a deal. Mr Seforim had probably been prepared to pay thirty right from the very beginning, if not more. But Henry needed money far more urgently than Mr Seforim needed stonemason's tools, and spare collars, and a portable rosewood writing-desk with a dried-up inkwell. Back in Bennington, before he had left, Henry had imagined writing out invoices on that writing-desk. To: *one monument block, polished and traced on the face, with fine-hammered apex cap and curved undercut; bottom base rock-faced except for fine-hammered wash bevels, £51.25.* Now he was accepting less for all of his tools and all of his possessions than the price of an ordinary family memorial.

'All right, because you look honest, thirty,' said Mr Seforim.

'I'll come back for them,' Henry promised.

'Surely you will,' nodded Mr Seforim. 'They all say that. It's a good thing for me that I don't hold my breath, waiting for them.'

Henry took the money and went to the Criterion Lunch-Rooms for a pot-pie and an Indian pudding, a meal that left him with only $28.42, but with his morale considerably improved. He still had to pay off Mrs Newell at the Pottawat-tamie, but he considered that it was more important to find Edward McLowery first, and see how much it would cost him to be guided over the Rockies and the Sierra Nevada.

He found Edward McLowery sitting asleep in the back of Wonderling's, the printers, his gaping brown leather boots parked on a table, his arms spread to either side, as if he were dreaming of being crucified; his eyes closed, and his mouth wide open. He was thin and rangy, with a thick auburn beard, and a sharp nose that could have punched holes in newspaper. He was snoring loudly; but his snoring was drowned out by the clatter of a printing-press, which was turning out posters advertising Leland's Grand Sale, Come One, Come All.

'Edward McLowery?' Henry shouted, and the printer jerked a thumb towards the sleep-martyred figure behind the table, and grinned, as if he were used to people walking in and asking for Mr McLowery, and causing trouble, too. Even when he was asleep, Edward McLowery looked like the kind of a man who might give the world some difficulty. Henry skirted the printing-press and laid a hand on Edward McLowery's shoulder, and yelled hoarsely, 'Mr McLowery!'

Edward McLowery opened his eyes, startled, and his feet dropped down from the table on which he had been resting them. 'Who the dang hell are you?' he demanded. 'Dang it, I was asleep there, and having dreams. Dreamed I was walking by the Navasota River with a lady called Philippa Paul. Now, dang it. I haven't seen that lady in thirty years, and you've spoiled it all. My great reunification.'

'Well, I'm sorry,' said Henry. 'But my name's Henry Roberts; and I was told that you were a guide, and that you could take me to California, if the price were right.'

'Oh, I don't do any of that guiding no more,' said Edward McLowery, shaking his head, and sniffing. 'I haven't taken anybody to California for three years now, not since the winter of '57, and I wouldn't do it never no more, not me. I just can't stand to see them womenfolk thirsty and suffering and almost giving up hope, and those children so bored they almost go crazy. I saw a ten-year-old boy stick a broom-handle into a waggon-wheel once, on account of something to do; and of course what happened was there was three spokes busted, and no lumber for two hundred miles, so all they could do was saw the legs off of the best dining-room table, instead of spokes. I sometimes wonder whether that kid ever lived to see eleven.'

'I haven't come on behalf of a waggon-train,' said Henry. 'I've come for myself. Me, just me, that's all. I want to go west.'

Edward McLowery tugged at his beard and twisted strands of it around his fingers. 'You?' he demanded. 'You mean, you and nobody else. No friends, no partners, no hangers-on? Just you, going off to California by yourself? No bride?'

'No bride,' Henry assured him.

'Well, I'll be,' said Edward McLowery. 'A man without ties. You know what they say about a man with no ties, don't you?'

'I have a strong suspicion you're going to tell me, even if I do know.'

Edward McLowery leaned forward and stared Henry directly in the eyes. 'I see a man that don't got ties; I seen a privy that don't got flies.'

161

'You mean you don't believe me?'

"Course I mean I don't believe you. How far do you want to go?'

'Sutter's Fort would do me.'

'Sutter's Fort, hey? Just yourself? How much baggage?'

'What you see is what there is.'

'Well,' said Edward McLowery. 'There has to be *some* baggage. A man has to eat once in a while, and wet his whistle from time to time. If you was thinking about you, and me, travelling east by mule – is that what you was thinking?'

Henry nodded.

'In that case,' said Edward McLowery, 'we'd have to take five mules minimum, along with flour and bacon and coffee and corn-meal; as well as a spider to cook in and a couple of plates to eat off of; and blankets, and ground-cloths, and lanterns; and a couple of reasonable rifles, plus powder-and-shot. And that's just supposing I wanted to do it, which I don't much.'

'What would you charge?' asked Henry.

Edward McLowery counted on his fingers, working out how many days it would take them to follow the Platte River westwards, across the plains of Nebraska, passing the landmarks that had already become familiar to nearly half a million emigrants: the severe bulk of Court House Rock; the strange attenuated spire of Chimney Rock, and the city-like peaks of Scott's Bluff, beneath which herds of buffalo ran. And still ahead of them, the Rocky Mountains, and the Great Salt Lake, and the winding passes through the Sierra Nevada. A strange, magnificent, formidable journey; along whose route scores of children and mothers and hopeful fathers had been buried, as they searched for Eden.

'Well,' said Edward McLowery, 'one hundred and twelve dollars should do it. And we could split whatever we got for the mules, once we got to Sutter's Fort.'

'I'm sorry,' said Henry, 'that's far too much.'

'You won't find cheaper,' Edward McLowery told him, reaching his hand inside the back of his shirt, and scratching his back. 'Well, you might find cheaper, but you wouldn't find your same guarantee of getting there, alive and fit and still smiling. I've known of guides take money, and then strangle their customers, once they were out on the prairie, and bury them under the sod, and who's to know? Very much cheaper, that kind of a guide. But for one hundred and twelve dollars, I'll take you personal to Sutter's Fort, and hand you over with a smile.' He smiled, to show what kind of a smile it would be.

'Well,' said Henry, hesitantly.

Edward McLowery stood up. He was almost the same height as Henry, but incredibly thin, so that Henry could have slid his arm in between his pants-suspenders and his concave stomach, without touching anything but thin air. He had a fleshy nose with two dark near-together eyes buried at either side of it, and wide lips, unnaturally red; and the usual frontier beard, all scraggle and curls and unkempt wisps, decorated with breakfast. He walked with a slight hopping limp, as if he had a chip of gravel in his boot which he couldn't be bothered to take out.

'You could make it on your own, I guess,' he told Henry, quite affably. 'There's plenty of guidebooks, to tell you the way. *The National Waggon Road Guide*, for instance. All I can say is, keep riding west until you get to Fort Bridger, then take the left-hand fork. If you take the right-hand fork, you wind up in Oregon Territory; which is fine in its way if you was intending to go there.'

Henry said, 'I have about twenty-five dollars.'

'Well, if I was you, son, I'd spend it on booze and women, and a return ticket to wherever it was you come from.'

'Listen, I have something else,' said Henry. 'Not only twenty-five dollars; but I own a gold-mine in Colorado.'

Edward McLowery squinted at him. 'If you own a gold-mine in Colorado, and it's any good, how come you've only got twenty-five dollars?'

Henry said, 'Let's go outside and talk about it. It's too noisy in here. Why don't you come across the street and have a drink?'

Edward McLowery scratched at his beard. 'That don't sound like a threatening idea.'

They crossed the sunlit street to the Cheerful Times Saloon, a dark long mahogany-panelled bar with sawdust sprinkled on the floor and rows of stools and spittoons. On the wall behind the bar was a florid painting of a fat naked woman, protecting her modesty with a fanned-out deck of cards. The title of the painting was 'Make Your Play'. Edward McLowery gave the barman an auction-bidder's wink, and the barman produced a bottle of unlabelled whiskey and two glasses. 'Dollar-ten,' he remarked, to nobody in particular, and Henry laid the money on the counter.

'Now what about this what you was talking about?' asked Edward McLowery, discreetly not mentioning the word 'gold-mine' on account of the three rough fellows standing close behind him, wreathed in blue tobacco smoke and talking in loud voices about the *Saint Susanna* steam-boat, and how she had run aground at Horseshoe Lake, and how her complement of harlots on their way to Sioux City had been obliged to lift their dresses up to their waists and wade through the mud in their bloomers.

'It was a fine sight,' one of them wheezed. 'Enough to lift a man's soul, and other parts of him besides.'

Henry and Edward McLowery sat down at a corner table, and Henry said, 'I won the deeds to a gold-mine in California Gulch in a card game, in New York.' He thought it better not to tell Edward McLowery that he had been obliged to take them by a party of outraged Southerners. 'They're in here,' he said, patting his breast pocket. 'They're genuine, just as far as I know; and if you take me to California, they're yours.'

'Why would you want to give me a gold-mine, just for taking you to California? I mean, I charge a high rate, but not *that* high.'

'Because I want to get to California, and because I don't particularly want to be a miner, not for gold nor for anything else.'

'Let's lay an eyeball or two on them deeds.'

Henry slipped the papers across the table, and Edward McLowery picked them up and scrutinized them, his head held back to compensate for chronic long-sightedness. After a while, he sniffed, and said, 'They look like the real article, don't they? Hard to tell, of course, less'n I see the mine.'

'I haven't even seen it myself,' said Henry.

'Well, then, I've got a suggestion to make,' Edward McLowery replied, leaning forward with his bony elbows on the table. 'Supposing you pay me twenty-five dollars to take you to California Gulch, so that we can take a look at this mine of yours; and then, if it's any good at all, you can transfer the deeds to me, good and legal, and then I'll take you on to Sutter's Fort, and we'll call it a fair day's work, fairly done.'

Henry sipped his whiskey. It was fierce and fiery; home-distilled; and flavoured with too much caramel. He knew that he was taking a risk, offering Edward McLowery the deeds to Alby Monihan's mine. He didn't believe more than three per cent that the mine was genuine; or that, even if it were, there was any gold to be found in it. But how else was he going to get out to California? A waggon-train wouldn't take him, not with only twenty-five dollars; and twenty-five dollars was scarcely enough to buy himself a mule and a side of bacon and a couple of sacks of corn-meal. And he would certainly need a rifle if he went on his own; there were still plenty of disgruntled Sioux and Cheyenne Indians on the trail across the plains, quite apart from bears and wolves in the mountains.

Well, he thought, even if the mine turns out to be barren, McLowery can't do very much about it. He doesn't look the kind who would shoot me, if all he got was twenty-five dollars and a wasted journey out to California Gulch. And I would get as far as Denver, at least; and that was part of the way.

'I don't reckon that we'll manage to get to Sutter's Fort till spring,' said Edward McLowery. 'By the time we get to California Gulch and take a look at that mine, we'll be running too late to beat the winter snows in the Rockies and the High Sierras, and I got the feeling in my water they're going to be early this year. But you don't mind a year, here and there, do you? I mean, you're not in any foot-burning rush, are you?'

Henry sat back, and finished the last of his whiskey. 'No,' he said. 'I don't think I am, any more.'

SIX

They took the ferry across the Missouri to Omaha on the last day of August, 1860, which was a Friday; and overcast, and very sultry. They stood under the awning on the hurricane deck, watching the coffee-brown river churn beneath them. Their four mules were tethered on the main deck below, already

165

loaded up with all their supplies. Two of the mules were bought; the other two were borrowed, with a promise of payment if they expired on the way, or had to be eaten. Their provisions were minimal: bacon, flour, sugar, and tea, although Edward McLowery had taken the trouble to bring a stone flagon of Taos Lightning, which was a distillation of wheat made in the pueblos of New Mexico, and which was guaranteed to provide 'instant obliviousness, within a minute of first drinking'. Others thought differently of it: there was a toast which ran, 'Here's to the good things that come out of Taos, but its whiskey it ain't worth three skips of a louse.'

There were scarcely any emigrant parties starting off west this late in the year. All of the larger waggon-trains had already left in mid-May; and the few straggling groups of emigrants who were leaving Omaha now would have to keep up a relentlessly tight schedule if they were to have any hope of reaching the mountain passes before the snows set in.

Omaha was an untidy collection of shacks and sheds and river-wharves, but there was a good restaurant there, the Murphy House, and before they set out, Henry and Edward sat at a scrubbed pine table with a rickety leg and ate a large breakfast of steak and beans. They said very little to each other as they walked out through the streets of Omaha, leading their mules behind them. It was eleven o'clock, and the sun was high and brassy and hot, and Henry wasn't feeling talkative. He kept thinking of Augusta, on her way back to Carmington by train, and of Doris, too. He had dreamed of Doris last night, just before morning, and he could have sworn that he had heard her whispering his name. He had seen her face as clearly as if she had been lying next to him, and when he had opened his eyes he had been sure that he could still smell her perfume.

They walked at a steady, unhurried pace. They would ride only when they were really exhausted, to save the mules. Once they had left the last few straggling outbuildings of Omaha behind, they were out on the plains alone, amidst mile after mile of short dry grass, a tawny wilderness of heat and dust, without a bush or a tree as far as Henry could see. There had been a few small possumhaws here once, but most of them had been burned down by Indians hunting game. Now there was nothing but wavering heat, and the repetitive sawing of insects, and the clattering of mules on the hard-baked trail.

'There was a real rush of prospectors out this way, last year,'

166

said Edward. 'You should have seen them, hundreds of them, with waggons and mules and buckboards and whatever they could get to carry them. They was all after the gold they found at Gregory Gulch, maybe you read about it back in the east. But that gold was so hard to dig out that most of them gave up, and came back. I seen twenty-two Gobacks lying dead by the trail, not sixty miles from Denver, all their food and water given out. Scores more died of the cholera. Well, their families buried them, whenever they could, but more often than not the wolves dug them up again. You could walk along the trail and see a human hip-bone, or a hank of woman's hair, with a comb still in it, lying right there by your feet. I saw one fellow, walking along the trail here, with his wife and baby dead in a wheelbarrow. Their eyes was all pecked out by birds; but I said to this fellow, "Good morning, need a hand, friend?" but he didn't say a word, just walked on; probably walked all the way from Denver.'

Henry would never forget his first day on the trail; the silence of it; the encroaching feeling of great loneliness; the wind that blew dust across the summer prairie. They walked and walked and the sun rose high above their heads, and then beat astoundingly at their foreheads, and at last began to sink in front of them, too fierce to look at. Edward had recommended that Henry bring a pair of green-glass goggles with him, and what with the dust and the furnace-like glare of the sun, he was relieved to have them.

By evening, they had reached the Platte River, where it curved its nearest to Omaha. The Platte was a wide, slow-flowing band of glistening silt, soaking its way in a series of lazy loops all the way from the Rocky Mountains to join the Missouri about twenty miles to the southeast of them. They had managed over twenty-three miles that day, even though they had left Omaha quite late, and Edward was pleased with their progress. They camped on the eastern bank of the river, and while Henry took the mules down to drink, Edward lit up a fire of scrub and brushwood, and fried up bacon and flour cakes. Later, they sat on their folded-up coats in the dying glow of the day, while the river shone between the darkness of its muddy banks like a silver-pink mirror, curving and mysterious and quiet.

'Are you religious?' Henry asked Edward.

'You mean, because of all this?' Edward asked him, lifting a hand to indicate the sky and the plains and the warmth of a summer evening. 'No,' he said. 'I gave up religion years ago. Bad for the chest, religion. All that singing by gravesides.'

Henry knew what Edward was trying to say. Somewhere, on these desolate plains, Edward must have lost someone he loved. And it was to become more and more evident to Henry as they travelled further west that Edward only crossed Nebraska now as an extraordinary kind of personal penance, as if he hated the plains but could never leave them; a man who had condemned himself to a treadmill of distance and tiredness and never-ending isolation. Henry guessed that Edward hadn't accepted his commission for the sake of $25, nor for the promise of a gold-mine; although he had probably been obliged to make those excuses for himself. He had agreed to come back out here because he needed to, in order to make sense of what had happened to him. These well-worn emigrant trails were the maps to Edward's whole existence.

Edward played a jew's harp after they had eaten, and then sang a song. The fire crackled and smoked in the evening wind, and the stars began to come out, thousands of them, prickling the night; and two coyotes yipped and howled at each other, across the warm breadth of the Platte Valley.

'I knew a girl and she was sure
She could grow more hair with mule-manure. . . . '

Henry lay back, and closed his eyes, and the night passed like the closing of a shutter.

For the next two weeks, they doggedly followed the northern bank of the Platte, rising at dawn and making camp at nightfall, and making do with as few stops as they could manage. On a fair day, they were able to walk forty miles; and even on days when the winds got up, and they had to mask their faces with handkerchiefs, and tug their mules behind them through the stinging dust like four reluctant pianos, they could cover thirty miles or more, and sometimes make up a little extra at night, when the winds had died down. Edward talked almost incessantly. He hated the Platte. 'A mile wide and an inch deep,' he called it. 'You can't fish in it, it's too dirty to bathe in it, and too damned thick to drink.' In places, the river's S-bends were so wide that the sun and the wind had almost dried them out, and they were able to ford their way across to banks of silt that were usually islands, and cut some of the trees that grew on them, for firewood. Most of the time, though, they gathered up buffalo droppings, 'the anthracite of the plains', and built their evening fire with those. 'Smelly and smoky, but available, and free,' Edward remarked.

It took them fifteen days to reach the confluence of the North and South Platte Rivers, 460 miles west of the Missouri – less than half the time that it usually took a fully-laden waggon-train to cover the same distance. They arrived there on the morning of a devastating storm, with lightning crackling all around them like forests of electricity, and rain sheeting across the grasslands so torrentially that Henry found it impossible to see where he was walking. Edward led the way down the slippery bank to the edge of the river, his boot-heels sliding in the mud, and then turned to Henry and shouted, 'We'll have to wait! The water's too high!' His hat was black and drooping with rainwater, and his beard had formed a bedraggled point like the tail-end of a prairie dog. There was a roll of thunder so loud that Henry felt as if the sky was going to collapse on top of him. His mules brayed in fright, and tried to pull away from him, and in trying to tug them back he fell face-first flat in the mud. As he clambered back on to his feet, he heard an unearthly high-pitched noise over the rushing of the rain, and turned around to see that Edward was laughing at him, wildly.

'Boy, you should just see yourself! Good thing this isn't a Southern state, they'd string you right up for a runaway nigger!'

They built themselves a makeshift shelter out of blankets and back-packs, and sat beneath it dripping and shivering and drinking Taos whiskey while they waited for the storm to clear. The lightning crackled and danced all around them until the air smelled like burning zinc, and the rain dashed so hard on to the ground that it set up a fine spray which covered the banks of the river like mist. It was an hour before the thunder began to grumble away to the east, and the rain began to ease off a little, and even then they could see that the river was far too swollen for them to be able to ford it. Edward took another swig of Taos Lightning and wiped his nose on the back of his hand.

'I saw a woman struck by lightning once, out on the prairie. She was cooking away on a sheet-iron stove, making her family's supper, and it weren't even raining. Then crack, and sizzle, and there was this column of lightning coming out of

169

the top of her head and I swear to God you could see her skeleton right through her skin. And it blew off all of her clothes, bang, and that sheet-iron stove flew right through the air and landed twenty feet off, still smoking. Well, we all rushed over, and there she was, pale as a ghost, and her hair all scorched off, even around her privates, and we looked up what it said to do in the medical book, and what it said was, "treatment, same as for drowning, only not of much use." '

Henry said, 'Have you ever wondered what you're doing here?'

'Is that what *you're* wondering?'

'Sometimes. I mean, I could be back in Vermont, chiselling somebody's epitaph, and looking forward to supper.'

Edward laughed, and passed over the whiskey. 'Instead of that, you're sitting under a soaking wet blanket in the middle of who-knows-where, with your face as black as Henry Brown.'

Henry smeared some of the mud away from his face. He swallowed a mouthful of Taos Lightning, and then handed the flagon back. These days, he could drink it without coughing.

'You lost somebody out on this trail, didn't you?' he asked Edward.

Edward didn't even look at him. 'Not too far from here,' he said. 'Just across the river, in fact. Ten years ago now, although it's hard to credit it. I don't suppose you would've thought much of her, but to me she was beauty incarnate, that's what she was, and her name was Elizabeth.'

He was quiet for a while, staring out over the foaming fork of the rivers, and the sandstone flats beyond with their blue-green clumps of trees. Then he said, 'I don't think I've never been in love, not before nor since, not like that. She was headed for Oregon, to be a music teacher; well, a bride is what she really wanted to be; and we met up on the trail, and got friendly. She had red hair tied around in a knot, and just a splash of freckles. And green eyes. She said I was noble. I asked her what it meant, noble, and she said, one day I'll show you, I promise. Well, that was in June, the first week in June, in Kansas, when all the wild flowers was out. But by July, when we was here, she was sick of the cholera. They was out there digging her grave even before she was dead. Well, there was nothing that anybody could do. And it was the finest day you could ever imagine, when they laid her into that grave, and most of her friends were thanking God that it was her, and that it wasn't them.'

'It wasn't your fault, though,' said Henry.

Edward looked at him. 'It doesn't matter whose fault it was. If someone dies, it's no good looking for fault. What you've got to look for is a meaning. Not *how* it happened, or who was to blame, whether it was God or man, but *why*. Can't you understand that? I have to know why. And that's why I keep on coming back here; even though I hate the place; and I hate the trail; and the sight of that river makes me cold all over. Why did she die, Henry? Why did I love her, and why did she die? Can you answer me that? Can you give me half of an answer?'

Henry hadn't told Edward about Doris. In fact, he wondered if he would ever be able to tell anyone about Doris. Perhaps if he could have guessed why Doris had died, he would have been able to say something to Edward to settle his disquiet. But the world seemed to be crowded with incidents that had no explanations, and tragedies that had no meaning, and guilt that could never be resolved. He was beginning to feel the workings of destiny in his life, but what was the point of destiny if it had no reason? Why was he here, when he couldn't help anybody, not even himself?

All he knew was that he *must* be here. It was almost like a divine punishment.

They camped that night well away from the river, sheltered by an outcropping of rock, and lit a small twig fire, and cooked themselves a sage-hen stew, with thick floury gravy. They finished the last of the Taos Lightning, although Edward kept the jug in case they needed it for carrying water. Gnawing on a leg, Edward told Henry, 'If this gold-mine turns up good, do you know what I'm going to do?'

'Tell me.'

'I'm going to find myself an artist; maybe that fellow who painted the picture in the Cheerful Times; and I'm going to sit down and tell him just how Elizabeth used to look, so that he can paint her, exactly the way I can see her in my mind's eye.'

'Well, wherever Elizabeth is, I think that she'd appreciate that,' said Henry.

'You think so?' asked Edward. He frowned at the bone he was holding in his hand. 'I hope so.'

The following morning, the water had subsided sufficiently

for Henry and Edward to ford the Platte River waist-deep to the southern bank. They would now follow the South Platte southwestwards until they reached Denver-Auraria, a mile above sea-level, on the eastern brink of the Rocky Mountains.

It was late September now, and the wind from the mountains was fresh and chilly as Edward and Henry led their mules up the steadily-rising trail that would take them into Denver. There were still signs along the trail of the Gobacks; those inexperienced prospectors who had hurried here two years ago in search of easy gold; and then, as winter approached, turned back to the east. Wooden grave-markers and broken-down waggons stood amongst the long grass by the side of the trail; and Henry paused for a while by a white-painted cross, now peeling, on which an agonized father had carved the name Laurence May, died of fever, age five.

'If you had any tears left to cry, I think you'd cry them,' said Edward; and then, under a sky the colour of black laundry ink, they carried on towards the Rockies; into the face of the wind.

They arrived in Denver on the evening of September 25, filthy and dusty, and still leading their mules, although one of them was lame in the hind leg, and had to hobble. Denver was two years old, a patchy assembly of shacks and log-cabins and flat-fronted stores, set on a breezy plain beneath the glistening splendour of the Rocky Mountains. Henry turned up the collar of his coat as they trudged slowly along Larimer Street, sniffing because of the cold; and looked around at J.E. Good's General Store, advertising with printed posters a fresh arrival of jeans, and Charley Harrison's Criterion Saloon, out of which so much tobacco smoke was blowing that it looked as if it were on fire; and Walter Cheesman's Hygienic Drugstore. Carriages and waggons rattled past them on the dusty street, their drivers yipping 'Coming through! Coming through!' and one or two people stopped on the sidewalk to watch them walk past, but otherwise their arrival was unnoticed. Edward let them to the Cherry Creek Guest House, where they took the mules around to the back, and tied them up.

'Well, I think it's time to have a wash, and get drunk,' said Edward. He clapped Henry on the back, so that white dust rose out of his coat. 'And not particularly in that order, neither.'

Henry stretched, and took a sharp sniff of mountain air. The outline of the Rockies reared up beyond the township like a jagged, shadowy wall; purple now, in the light of the evening,

172

and decorated with fingers of snow. He would one day know the outline of those mountains as well as he knew his own face in his shaving-mirror: Pike's Peak, Bison Peak, Bear Creek, Boulder Creek, Long's Peak. But tonight they looked alluring and secretive and misty; and he had a sense at last of having arrived somewhere, after a month of walking over flat prairies and flatter plains, and seeing nothing but horizons, and skies, and blowing grass.

The Cherry Creek Guest House was a boxlike, timber-framed building with a wide verandah and a balcony above, over-looking Cherry Creek itself: the muddy stream which had once divided Denver from the rival community of Auraria. There were three scrubby oaks at the back of the guest house; and across the street, the offices of the *Rocky Mountain News*. Oil-lamps were just beginning to be lit all over town as Henry and Edward climbed the steps of the guest house, and walked into the gloomy lobby.

'Well, now, it's Edward McLowery,' said a warm, amused voice. Out of the shadows a dark-haired man came forward, short, about thirty-six years old, in a smart black coat and dove-grey pants and formal necktie, as if he was dressed for a dinner-party or a wedding. He was clean-shaven, with a head that was rather too large for his body, but intelligent-looking, and friendly. He shook hands with Edward, and asked, 'What brings you back to Denver, Edward? The last time, you told me you'd given up for good.'

Edward said, 'I come up here for my health, Mr Byers. Here, meet Henry Roberts. Henry and me have just arrived from Council Bluffs, in record time, I'd say. Henry, this is William Byers.'

'How do you do, sir,' said William Byers, holding out his hand. 'Welcome to Denver. Visiting, are you, or prospecting?'

'Visiting,' replied Henry, evasively. He glanced at Edward for some clues as to who Mr Byers might be; and how he should treat him. But Edward simply grinned and made an elaborate show of scratching his ribs. 'I could sure use a bottle of Old Arapaho,' he said.

'Edward is trying very hard not to tell you that I am the owner and editor-in-chief of the *Rocky Mountain News*,' smiled William Byers. 'Last time he was here, we ran an article on the life and times of an emigrant guide, which was all about him; and good reading it was, too. Did he tell you the story about

173

the woman who was struck by lightning? All lies, of course, but marvellous copy. I just stepped over the road here to pick up Mrs Cordley's latest advertisement. You'll like it here, although I say so myself, and she's an advertiser of mine. Clean sheets, good food, and not too much interference, if you know what I mean.'

Edward said, 'You busy this evening, Mr Byers? Fancy sharing a bottle of whiskey? And a steak maybe? You could bring Lizzie along, if you were minded.'

'I'm busy this evening,' said William Byers. 'But you're welcome to come around to my house, both of you, when you're cleaned up and rested. Maybe Saturday morning.'

'I'd like that,' said Henry.

'Well, fair enough,' said William Byers. 'Come round at eleven, and I can show you the printing-presses before we have lunch. That's quite a story in itself, the way we dragged those presses all the way from Council Bluffs, as well as the stones, and the type, and two pages set up ready to print.'

'I remember what you said on one of those pages,' Edward remarked. ' "What key is it that opens the gate of misery?" that's what you said. And the answer was "Whiskey".'

William Byers gave Henry an odd, sloping smile; and said, 'Saturday, then,' and nodded to Edward, and left. Henry had the impression that he had met a man who he would either like very dearly, or hate. Whichever it might be, he had the distinct feeling, irrational or not, that Byers would play a very influential part in his life. It was almost as if the two of them had recognized each other; not from a previous meeting, but from a dream.

Perhaps he was simply tired. Perhaps Edward was right, and all they needed was a hot bath and a bottle of whiskey. Edward was certainly doing his best to expedite both: by banging with the flat of his hand on the bell of the hotel counter, and calling out, 'Now then, Mrs Cordley! How about it! No use hiding yourself!'

They heard footsteps down uncarpeted stairs, and then Mrs Cordley appeared, a plump, good-looking, big-busted woman with her hair drawn tightly back into a tortoiseshell comb, wearing a white apron and a maroon dress with printed flowers on it.

'What's all this hollering?' she demanded; and then recognized Edward, and stopped, and twirled like a little girl, and

174

came up with the coyest of smiles, and said, 'Edward McLowery, if it isn't the very same! Well, too, and then said, 'He always makes me come over pink, I shall never know why. You'd think there was something between us. But he's always so flattering. I never knew anybody so flattering; and I always come over pink just thinking of what he'll say next.'

'Mrs Cordley, you're the star of my life,' said Edward. He was so thin and loopy and droopy-whiskered, and yet when he spoke to Mrs Cordley like that, she clapped her hands to her cheeks and let out a tiny little shriek.

'I can't abide it,' she giggled. 'He always makes me so pink!'

Later, in their shared room, as Edward prized off his boots, Henry asked him, 'Why do you always make Mrs Cordley come over so pink?'

Edward shifted himself around on the bed, so that the springs squeaked. He sniffed, and said, 'I fucked her once, up against the wall in the cor'dor, in the middle of the night; and that was all; just once; and I wouldn't fuck her again, because I don't believe in it; and she's probably forgotten all about it, how it really was, but made up a story of how it should have been, and dreamed about it, and that's why she always goes pink. Nothing to do with me. It's all up here, right in her head. The way I did it was plain and simple and nothing to get pink about, not after two years.'

Henry said nothing, but unbuttoned his long johns. He was beginning to realize that Edward didn't always tell the truth. Perhaps Edward's life hadn't been quite so much of a romantic tragedy as he would have liked Henry to think. Perhaps there never had been a red-haired Elizabeth, after all; or, if there had, perhaps she hadn't died. Perhaps she was out in Sacramento even now, with her husband and children, a happy California wife, with no recollection at all of the bearded guide who had watched her balefully for mile after mile as she sat on the seat of her emigrant waggon, heading west along the Platte Valley, past Independence Rock.

Edward lay on his back for most of the night, sleeping stertorously. He had after all drunk nearly a whole bottle of whiskey, and he had complained to Henry often enough that sleeping indoors always made him play 'old Shuteye's harmonica'. It was the feathers in the pillows, he said, and all that dust, and the farts getting trapped beneath the blankets. Henry slept badly; and not only because of the snoring. At about five o'clock, just as the first light of morning began to break, he pulled on his britches and went out on to the landing, to look for the bathroom.

He went along the corridor, rubbing his face with his hands, and yawning. When he reached the stairs, however, he stopped in astonishment; and stared. A woman was standing on one foot on the newel-post at the top of the stairs, her arms outspread, balancing. She wore a tight white bodice, and a white ballet skirt, and white wool stockings, and her face was white, with dark hair that was drawn tightly back from her forehead. Her eyes were closed as if she were asleep; and her pretty, delicate features were in complete composure. Henry didn't quite know what to do; whether he ought to say anything to her or not. It seemed unlikely, but supposing she was asleep, and somnambulating? If he woke her up, she would probably fall straight down the stairwell and break her back. On the other hand, it didn't seem very wise to leave her there. He approached her slowly, and gazed up at her. She looked quite amazing, balancing there; as if she were a figure sculptured out of the finest white bisque; fragile, unearthly and infinitely calm.

He stepped closer, as quietly as he could, and raised his hands, in case he needed to catch her. When he took another step, however, she said, in a clear, French-accented voice, 'I'm not going to fall, you know. I'm just practising. I always prefer to practise with my eyes closed. It is an aid to concentration.'

Henry lowered his hands, feeling rather awkward and silly. The woman opened her eyes and stared at him, and then smiled. She had very dark, slanted eyes, almost Oriental, with sleepy-looking lids. She said, 'It was very kind of you, all the same, to think of rescuing me. The West is not exactly a hotbed of gallantry. Most of the men I have come across in the West would have tried to squint up my tu-tu first, and then thought of saving me second.'

Henry held out his hand, and the woman took it, and jumped lightly down from the newel-post. She seemed to weigh scarcely anything; like a bird, or a child. 'I should introduce myself,' she said. 'I am Mademoiselle Carolista, from the Parisian Travelling Entertainment Show. We arrived only yesterday morning, from Pueblo. Tomorrow, we are putting on a great performance in the street, fire-eating, dancing, trained dogs.'

'And balancing on banisters?' asked Henry, smiling.

Mademoiselle Carolista laughed. 'Tomorrow, it will be more

exciting than banisters. Tomorrow, I will walk across Larimer Street from one side to the other, on a high-wire, twenty feet in the air. I will not only walk, but I will dance. I call it my Ballet of the Sky.'

'Well, I shall make a point of coming to see it,' said Henry. 'By the way, my name's Henry Roberts. I've only just arrived here, too, from the east.'

'I thought you were too civilized to be a Westerner,' she said. 'What brings you here? Are you selling medicine, or looking for gold?'

'I'm halfway to California, as a matter of fact.'

'Ah, California! It can be very beautiful in California. Once, I fell in love there, in a town called Sonoma. What a man he was! Tall, handsome, and such a bastard. Are you a bastard?'

'Not that I'm aware of.'

'Well, what a pity. I always fall in love with bastards; and I think I could fall in love with you.'

Henry couldn't help grinning. Mademoiselle Carolista was so direct, yet so theatrical; and so feminine too. She was probably two or three years older than him, if he was any judge of a woman's age; but she was so fit and at the same time so self-possessed that it was hard to tell exactly. Her body was that of an 18–year-old; her mind at least 28. He had never met anyone quite like her. She lifted one leg and touched with the tip of her toe the dado rail around the landing, a graceful and elegant barre exercise; and then returned to balletic feet-apart posture and smiled at Henry with a mixture of superiority and impishness.

'Could you do that?' she asked him.

He shook his head. 'I'm not sure that there's much need for it, not in my trade.'

'What do you do? Apart from travel, and court young ladies on hotel landings?' She was teasing him again.

'Well, I cut inscriptions on gravestones.'

'Really?' Mademoiselle Carolista exclaimed. 'But how *dreadful!* How morbid! How can you bear it?'

'Chiselling a gravestone is just the same as chiselling any other kind of stone. I don't often get to see the deceased, except by special invitation.'

'*Er!*' Mademoiselle Carolista shuddered with melodramatic revulsion. 'I cannot bear to think of death. Do you know something, ever since I was six years old, I wanted to be immortal.

I used to squeeze my eyes shut and pray to God: Oh Lord, make me live for ever and ever, or at least until I am two hundred and fifty.'

'Why two hundred and fifty?' asked Henry. 'Any particular reason?'

'Of course! Why pray for anything without a particular reason? If I were to live to two hundred and fifty, I would be able to see the beginning of the twenty-first century, to the very day, and then expire.'

'"Well, I suppose that's reason enough,' said Henry. 'Would you like some coffee?'

'I think I would,' said Mademoiselle Carolista. Then, frowning a little, she added, 'You should call me Nina. That is my name. Nina Zwolenkiewicz. But, of course, Carolista is easier to pronounce. The children in my village always called me Zwonky. But, I was still the prettiest of all of them!'

They went downstairs to Mrs Cordley's kitchen. It was burnished, and immaculately clean, with rows of copper pans shining in the morning light; and a huge black-leaded range, with steel embellishments. Nina opened every cupboard until she found the coffee, and then pumped up water to fill the kettle, while Henry sat on the edge of the table and watched her.

'How long have you been walking the high-wire?' he asked her.

'All my life. My mother taught me. She was a slack-rope dancer, beautiful, one of the best in Poland. One of the best in the world. I loved her, you know. She always smelled of flowers. You know the sweet-pea? That's what she smelled like, always. We emigrated to France when I was nine; and that's why I joined the Parisian Travelling Entertainment Show. My mother died, though, when I was fifteen. Tuberculosis. On her grave, it said, *"Ne t'attends qu'à toi seul"* – and that means, never depend on anybody except yourself. That was what she always used to say to me, even when I was tiny.'

Nina spooned coffee into the copper jug, and then sat down at the kitchen table. 'An epitaph is such a final thing. Surely the dead grow wiser, even as the living do, and feel like changing their minds? One must learn such a lot in Heaven.'

Henry said, 'The strangest epitaph I was ever asked to carve on a tombstone was, "Love and Herbs".'

' "Love and Herbs"?' asked Nina.

178

'It comes from the Bible. Something like, it's better to eat nothing but herbs, as long as you've got love; than to have a whole ox, and hatred.'

'Oh, I like that,' said Nina. 'Love, and herbs. I like that.'

The kettle began to boil, and Nina made coffee. There was a calico blind drawn down over the kitchen window, and as the sun came up, Nina was silhouetted against it, her long elegant neck, her ballerina profile, her fingers poised just so, under her clear-cut chin. Henry sat with one elbow on the table watching her; and he found her so friendly, such a comfortable companion, that he felt he could have sat there all day.

'What would you like on your own tombstone?' asked Nina.

'Just my name,' replied Henry, still watching her.

Nina said, 'You didn't think me too forward? I didn't upset you?'

'What do you mean?'

'When I said that I could fall in love with you. I say that to all sorts of men. I'm only making a joke. You know, just to be friendly.'

'Do any of them ever take it seriously?'

She looked at him with those dark slanted eyes of hers. 'Some of them do, of course.'

'Should I?'

'It's up to you. Think what you want. Life is only what you make of it, isn't it? And it's the same with love.'

The clock beside the kitchen dresser struck six. Henry suddenly felt tired, as if he had been travelling without any sleep for years and years. 'What time is that show of yours?' he asked Nina.

'Three o'clock. But I don't get up on to the wire until four. I am the climax.'

Henry sipped his coffee. It was scalding hot, impossible to drink straight away. Neither of them said anything, but after a while Nina reached out her hand across the kitchen table and laid it on top of his. They looked into each other's eyes; each of them searching for something; but neither of them knowing exactly what it was. What brings two people halfway across a continent to sit at a table together? Accident, or divine design? When Henry thought of the people that he must have failed to meet; those would-be wives who had only just turned a street corner ahead of him; those potential friends who had hesitated at street corners, and never crossed over to bump into him; it

179

made him realize that the world was teeming with unrealized possibilities, from the spermatozoa which failed to fertilize an egg to the lovers who never quite managed to catch the same ferry. He had believed when he had asked Doris to marry him that they had been meant for each other; and now she was dead he felt as if there was nobody else, not at the right time, not at the right place. Except, perhaps, for Nina. The thought of it was unexpected enough for him to surprise himself. But why else had he stepped out of his boarding-house room at five in the morning, and found the woman called Zwonky balancing on the banisters? Their meeting had all the irrational ingredients of authentic destiny: an accident that, in retrospect, would seem unavoidable, inescapable, an act of fate. (Relieved lovers clasping each other's hands and saying, 'My God; imagine what life would have been like if we hadn't met.')

Henry said, 'Is it dangerous? The wire, I mean?'

Nina nodded. 'The better you are, the more dangerous it is. Because, of course, you are always risking more.'

'Do you like it?'

'I don't know. I don't like it in the way that perhaps somebody would like opera, or riding a beautiful horse, or eating oysters, or making love. It is a feeling more personal than that. It is quite impossible to describe, unless you have tried walking on the wire yourself. But it is very uplifting, very strange, as if you have managed at last to defy the laws of nature.'

'Could you teach me to do it?'

She stroked his hand carefully, tracing the whorls of his knuckles around and around; but he kept his eyes fixed on hers.

'It would depend on how much you really wanted to.'

'And if I were to say that I *did* want to, very much?'

Nina shrugged. Then the door opened, and Mrs Cordley came in, tying up her apron, and bustled around putting up the blind, and bringing down the pans she would want for cooking breakfast, and singing, and smiling.

'Glad you made yourself at home, Mam'selle Carolista. You too, Mr Roberts. Can't stand a guest who doesn't make himself at home. Too timid to ask for extra pillows, or hides his socks because he can't pluck up the courage to tell me how much they need washing. That's why I keep a dog in this place, to hunt down the dirty underwear, once the guests have gone

180

out for the day. Otherwise, this whole building would get up on its foundations and walk, I swear it, from sheer aroma.'

Henry asked, 'Anywhere I can get some darning done? Some of my socks have gone through.'

'Oh, I can fix those for you easy. Just leave 'em down on the end of your bed, Petulia will pick them up for you; and you'll have 'em back by tomorrow, darned invisible. By the way, is Edward still snoozing?'

'Last time I saw him. Do you want me to wake him up?'

'No, no. I'll do that, just as soon as I've cooked up some breakfast. Now, what would you care for? Eggs, bacon, and meatballs? Omelette, with green peppers?'

Edward spent most of the morning renewing old acquaintances, and taking Henry from one saloon to the other. Denver had boomed since he had last been here, and it seemed that almost everyone they met was eager and willing to stand them a drink. The last time Edward had been here, early in 1859, Denver had been two towns, Denver and Auraria, standing on opposite sides of Cherry Creek; but on April 3 they had merged, and taken the combined name of Denver. Now there were 29 shops, 15 hotels, 23 saloons, two schools, two theatres, and a newspaper; not to mention a Masonic Lodge and a Ladies' Union; and life had become far more fashionable and decorous.

'You won't find anything down East as sumptuous and unexceptionable as what you find here,' one banker remarked to Henry, thrusting his thumbs into his hound's-tooth business waistcoat. 'What you have here is class, with a capital K.'

Denver's chief source of prosperity was gold; not only from Gregory Gulch, where it had first been found, but from outlying mining communities in the Rocky Mountains. After the first placer deposits of free gold had given out, and the rush of amateur miners had returned despondent to the East, experienced hard-rock miners had started to hack out a fortune in gold-bearing quartz; and production had been further increased by the arrival late last year of a steam-powered stamp-mill, with four 400–lb iron hammers, which could crush the quartz fine enough for the gold to be extracted from it with chemicals. Two more stamp-mills had been ordered for delivery by Christmas, but Denver was already wealthy enough to produce its own gold coinage.

Henry said to one well-whiskered miner, 'How about California Gulch? Have you heard anything of California Gulch?

181

Somebody told me there might be rich deposits up there, if you cared to look.'

The miner winked at Henry with eyes like a weasel. 'You're right, my friend, there might be; and there is. It was Abe Lee what found the gold there first; good old Abe Lee, with the smelliest long johns ever, bar none. I used to pan for gold with Abe Lee back in '56, or was it '55, but whichever it was I couldn't stand nearer than seventy-five feet, or forty, with the wind in the wrong direction. Anyhow, he panned good dust up there, late last spring, and now you wouldn't recognize the place. But you're way too late, if you're thinking of trying to stake a claim now. I'd say that every square inch of California Gulch is taken solid. They've got shacks standing on top of shacks.'

Henry glanced at Edward McLowery and raised his eyebrows. It sounded as if Alby Monihan's deeds might not have been as spurious as he had first supposed. In fact, they might be worth a fortune. Even if the Little Pittsburgh mine had been jumped in the past year or so, by somebody else, which it probably had, Henry still held the official deeds, and could immediately evict them. It was quite possible that he was rich. It was quite possible that he was already a millionaire.

He stepped out on to the broadwalk. He had shaken hands with too many of Edward's old friends that morning, and drunk too many tots of whiskey. He didn't want to say anything foolish, or antagonistic; but it seemed to him that if the Little Pittsburgh mine was already a winner, giving the deeds to Edward was a ridiculous overpayment for nothing more than a few weeks' companionship on a well-worn trail. Of course, Henry wanted to go on to California, but not yet; especially when he had only just met a girl like Zwonky; and even more especially if he was rich. He could pay just about anybody to take him to California, if he was rich, couldn't he; and go whenever he wanted? He could pay six men to carry him on their shoulders to California.

'Or six naked women,' he remarked, out loud.

'Pardon?' asked Edward, as he came out of the saloon, and closed the door behind him.

'I was thinking, that's all.'

'You be careful, then,' cautioned Edward. 'The way this town's going, all prim and correct, saying things like that could end you up in gaol.'

182

'When are we going to take a look at that mine?' he asked Edward. 'I thought tomorrow, if we ride out early, and take a tent.'

'Suits me,' said Edward. 'Look – there's Belle McGuiness. I haven't introduced you to Belle McGuiness. Belle runs the bestest H.H. in Denver, the Mountain Dew Hotel.'

'H.H.?' asked Henry.

'Can't you *spell?*' said Edward, impatiently.

It was only as he bent forward to kiss the purple perfumed glove of the lady with the feathered hat that it dawned on Henry that 'H.H.' stood for 'Hore House'. He decided that he could use a strong cup of black coffee.

That afternoon, Larimer Street was filled by two o'clock with loafers, shoppers, gawpers, and children playing hookey from school. Henry and Edward had already secured themselves a grandstand seat on the balcony of the Cherry Creek Guest House, in two wooden sun-chairs, with a bottle of Taos Lightning and a large tin of corn crackers. The motley waggons of the Parisian Travelling Entertainment Show had been drawn up across the street, and already three or four small spotted dogs were leaping and jumping for coloured balls, while a semi-circle of bentwood chairs was set out for the orchestra.

What was attracting the greatest excitement of all, however, was the shining wire which had been attached to the frontage of the W.H. Armitage Dry Goods store, and stretched diagonally across the street to the chimney of the Pike's Peak Saloon, twenty feet above the hard, sun-crazed dirt. Everyone in town knew what the wire was for, because they had seen the coloured posters showing the beautiful ballerina dancing on tippytoe halfway across Niagara Falls, and those that could read had read again and again the legend 'Mademoiselle Carolista, Tightrope Artiste Extraordinaire! Direct From Paris, France! Defies Death! Dances The Entire French Ballet Les Petits Riens (Little Nothings)! High Above The Ground! Without a Safety Net!'

It was a hot, clear afternoon; one of those Denver days that are all blue sky and fragmented clouds and ozone, clear off the mountains. To the east, as far as Henry could see, the landscape was flat and dust-coloured and hazed with heat, not a tree for miles. But to the west, there was always that hallucinatory range of snow-capped mountains, the Front Range, and somewhere in that range his fortune lay buried. He kept turning and staring at the mountains, until he looked back and saw that Edward was staring at him suspiciously.

'Something on your mind?' Edward inquired.

Henry shook his head.

'Here, then,' said Edward, and passed him the bottle of Taos Lightning.

At three o'clock, the orchestra started playing, a ragged assembly of trombonists, cornet players, drum-bangers, and violinists; one of whom was an extraordinarily tall woman with hair as bright as a fire and a green dress that clung to her like snakeskin. Tight dresses were fashionable in New York this year, but as Edward remarked, 'not on anybody taller'n your average spruce'.

Henry began to develop a hangover in the back of his neck as the show started up. There were two fire-eaters, known as Les Deux Allumettes; one of whom managed to set a string of bunting ablaze, reminding Henry with a strange sharp feeling of the night on which he had burned down the Colossal Whirler. These were followed by Madame Pretty and her Dancing Dogs, an act which brought roars of approval and cries for more; especially from the coarser spectators by the What Comfort saloon, who particularly liked Madame Pretty's wobbling white bust and well-filled fishnet stockings, and hang the dogs. There was Ecell–0 the performing mono-cyclist, who smoked a cigar and sang 'My Dear Old Mother Ireland' while operating a glove-puppet with each hand and carrying a girl on his shoulders, all on his mono-cycle, of course. He was followed by D'Artagnan the Mousquetaire who sliced shreds of coloured paper out of the same girl's lips with the tip of his rapier, which he assured the crowd was as sharp as a 'rays air'. There was a sharpshooter called Accurate Albert who bore an expression of permanent misery; although not as miserable as his wife, at whom he was shooting. There were four hefty leg-kicking girls direct from the 'most scandalous entertainment halls of Paris'. And finally, as the crowd whistled and cheered and applauded, and small boys shinned up on to porches and balconies, Mademoiselle Carolista appeared, on the back of a buckboard decorated with red white and blue rosettes, draped in a sparkling red satin robe, sewn with red sequins, and a huge sequin head-dress. She spread her arms, opening her robe and revealing her tight red satin corset and white woolen tights. The cheers grew riotous, and hats were tossed up into

184

the air; and from the balcony of the American Hotel, one over-enthusiastic citizen fired off two pistols, and shouted, 'Hoorah for Lincoln!'

Mademoiselle Carolista ceremoniously entered the front door of the W.H. Armitage Dry Goods store so that she could climb up to the roof and begin her death-defying high-wire walk across the street. As she did so, however, Henry noticed a jostling in the crowd on the far side of the street; and saw six or seven hard-faced men in derby hats and workshirts push their way through towards the American Hotel.

'Trouble,' remarked Edward, swigging more wheat-whiskey, and wiping his mouth on the back of his hand.

Henry glanced towards the hotel. 'What's happening?'

'Well, those fellows are what they call bummers. Charley Harrison's boys, from the Criterion Saloon. Charley Harrison's a Southerner, by sentiment; and a rascal, by nature. He runs all the best H.H.'s, and three of the best saloons, and has a hold on the gambling here, too. Those bummers of his are some of the least particular gentlemen you're likely to meet; so if I were you I wouldn't say anything like "Hoorah for Lincoln!" especially not from no public balcony.'

Henry watched as the bummers elbowed their way across the street, and in through the front doors of the American Hotel. After a minute or two, the citizen who had been standing on the balcony to see the show was abruptly tugged in through the upstairs window. The orchestra was playing too noisily for Henry to be able to hear any cries, or blows; but after a moment or two one of the hotel windows was cracked, as if by a man's back falling against it; and afterwards it was smeared with blood.

'Did you see that?' asked Henry.

'Surely did,' nodded Edward. 'just goes to show that expressing your political sentiments don't pay much, not in Denver. If you was to yell out Dixie for ever, you'd probably find yourself cudgelled half to death by Wide Awakes.'

Now there was a delighted moan of anticipation, as Mademoiselle Carolista appeared on the roof of the W.H. Armitage Dry Goods store, and blew kisses down to the crowd. She had discarded her robe, but now she was carrying a red ostrich-plume in each hand, which she twirled around in the air.

'Ain't going to try to fly, are you?' one wag shouted out.

But the general laughter was soon quietened by a dramatic

roll of drums, and the appearance on the roof of the show-master, a dapper moustachioed man in a green frock-coat and a high collar, and a hat from which three small flags flew – the Union flag, the French tri-colour, and the Turkish crescent moon. He lifted his hands for silence, and then cried, 'Ladies and gentlemen of Denver! This is the moment you have been waiting for! Mademoiselle Carolista the greatest and most fear-less tightrope-walker in the entire world will walk across the street at a height of twenty-two feet without the comfort of a safety-net, and without an artificial means of balance! Not only will she walk, she will dance! An entire ballet by Mozart, or as much as time allows! Not only will she dance, she will juggle, an entertainment not usually included in Mozart ballet! This is the most terrifying tightrope act ever devised, for imagine what would happen if she were to lose her balance and fall! She would break her neck! Crack! Right in front of you! Or worse! So draw the deepest of breaths, ladies and gentlemen, and prepare yourself for the most amazing feat of balancing ever witnessed!'

Mademoiselle Carolista stepped up now on to the wire itself, testing it first with one foot, then with two, and bouncing up and down slightly to feel the tension. The crowd in the street, two or three hundred of them, were completely silent, each of them trying to imagine what could be worse than breaking your neck. Henry pushed back his chair and stood up, although Edward remained seated, his feet propped on the balcony-rail, quietly singing to himself a long and ribald song about Maggie from Maine.

'Well now, what do you think of her?' asked Henry, as Mademoiselle Carolista took her first tentative steps out along the wire.

'Too skinny by half,' said Edward. 'What I'd like to see up there is somebody substantial, a woman with some meat on her. The kind of woman who would frighten folk not just because she might fall; but because she might fall on *them*.'

'I think you're incurable,' said Henry.

Edward peered up at Mademoiselle Carolista with one squinting eye. 'You're not in love with her, are you?'

'She's beautiful. She's Polish, you know. When she was a kid, all her friends called her Zwonky.'

'Zwonky?' repeated Edward. 'How do you know that?'

'She's staying here. I had breakfast with her this morning, down in the kitchen.'

'Well, I'll be. There once was a lady named Zwonky, whose face would have scared off a donkey.'

'You keep your rude rhymes to yourself,' said Henry, and looked around at Edward with an expression which added: I mean it.

Mademoiselle Carolista had now balanced her way to the middle of the wire, arms extended, back straight, face completely serene. The only sound was the shuffling of the crowd, the faint whistling of the wind across the wire, and a low continuous drum-roll from the orchestra. Henry knew that she wasn't going to fall, but all the same he kept his teeth buried in the tip of his tongue, and his hands clenched on the balcony-rail, and when the orchestra suddenly struck up with the opening bars of *Les Petits Riens*, and Mademoiselle Carolista threw up one leg, and twirled around on her pointed toe, he let out a gasp just like everybody else in the crowd. As she jumped and danced and even *ran* along the wire, her head thrown back, the crowd began to cheer and whistle, and even Edward had to sit up and take a look.

She juggled as she danced; at last tossing the balls down to one of the members of the troupe; and then she brought her act to a stunning finale by standing perched on one leg, her back arched, her arms wide, her eyes closed; just as they had been this morning, when Henry had discovered her balancing on the newel-post.

The clapping went on and on; and there was stamping of feet and throwing of hats, and even babies. Paper streamers were thrown up from the street so that they trailed across the high-wire; and when Mademoiselle Carolista reappeared in the doorway of the hardware store, once again wrapped in her robe, the shouting and hollering and firing of pistols was deafening.

Henry said, 'Isn't she just fantastic? There isn't any other word for it, is there? She's just fantastic.'

'You be warned,' replied Edward. 'My motto is: never give your heart to itinerants. You can never count on getting it back.'

Henry hurried downstairs and shouldered his way through the crowds, getting pink cotton candy stuck to his sleeve as he did so. But at last he managed to get through to Mademoiselle Carolista, and seize her hand, shouting, 'Nina! That was magic!'

Nina was glowing and sweating and beaming with pleasure and relief. She reached up and grasped hold of Henry's hair at the back of his neck, and pulled him down quite roughly to kiss her. There was a chorus of whistling as they did so. She opened her mouth to him, so that he could lick at her teeth, and he tasted perspiration and greasepaint and gin, too. 'My marvellous fellow!' she sang out, and lifted Henry's hand along with hers, so that Henry found himself walking beside her in her tumultuous victory parade, all the way down Larimer Street, and then back again to the American Hotel, where a reception was waiting, laid on by the wealthiest and most influential of Denver's citizens in the cause of 'bonhomie, and artistic appreciation'. Everybody crowded into the hotel's dining-rooms, lined with mirrors and already thick with tobacco smoke, where there were tables laid with all the luxuries that gold could bring to a small mountain community, one whole mile above sea-level. There were heaps of fruit, oranges and apples and nectarines and early kumquats; there were crackling-baked pigs, with cinnamon apples; there was turkey and quail and sage-hen; and there were huge pressed-glass bowls full of cool custards and fruit compotes. There were oysters, too, although they were canned, and frittered mostly, with scrambled eggs and bacon. There was pâtè-de-foie; and deep shining dishes black with caviare.

Nina held on to Henry's arm as she was introduced to the bookstore owner David Moffat, who had come to Denver earlier this year, intending to remain long enough to make $75,000 and then to leave but who had already made so much money that he had decided to stay for good. Then there was Luther Kountze, all shirt-front and beady eyes, whose small gold-office had developed into a bank; and the Clark brothers, who were part-owners in Denver's first mint, along with a smooth-looking man who introduced himself as E.H. Gruber. William Byers was there, too, with a small, pert-looking woman with troublesome brown curls, whom Henry took to be his wife.

'You were startling,' Henry told Nina, when they had a moment to themselves. A waiter brought them glasses of champagne, and stuttered, 'Never seen nothing like that, Miss Carolista. That was something special.'

Nina hugged Henry close to her, and then kissed his cheek. 'They think I am not quite human, these people. They are in awe of me. That is why I am staying so close to you. It is

188

uncomfortable to be surrounded by people, none of whom think of you as real. You give me all the reassurance I require that I am real, after all.'

'I think we ought to drink a toast,' said Henry. He was aware of the envious chatter all around him; and the way in which the other men in the dining-room were thinking, you lucky hound, you, if I had two minutes with Mademoiselle Carolista, I'd show her soon enough.

'What toast?' asked Nina.

'To the incomparable Zwonky,' said Henry, touching the rim of his glass against hers.

Nina giggled. 'You say it so severely. Zwonk-ee! You should say it very soft, listen, jha-von-key.'

Henry looked down into those dark, dark slanted eyes of hers, and put his arm around her waist, such a slender waist that he could almost have lifted her up in the crook of his arm, he with his epitaph-cutter's muscles. 'Jha-von-key,' he said, gently. They kissed, and they didn't mind who was staring at them. There were more whistles, more cheers, and then the tall woman with the fiery hair suddenly began to play her violin, furiously, wildly, and some of the guests began to stamp their feet in time, and clap their hands; and before anybody knew it the dining-room was shaking with dancing.

Henry led Nina through the dancers to the back of the hotel, where there was a small dusty garden shaded by trees. In the distance, scarcely visible in the thickening heat of the afternoon, the snow that marked the summit of Pike's Peak lay like a white forgotten handkerchief. Henry clinked glasses with her again, and said, 'How long are you staying here?'

'Two more days. But we will give no more performances. Once is thrilling, twice is tedious.'

'I hope that doesn't apply to everything,' smiled Henry. 'I'd quite like to kiss you again.'

'What is a day without a kiss?' breathed Nina, and held him close, and kissed him deeply and fiercely. 'You like women, don't you?' she asked, as she let him go at last.

'I don't know many men that don't.'

'Ah, but you like them differently. I can feel it.'

At that moment, the French doors to the dining-room opened, so that their polished windows suddenly reflected the late-afternoon sky and the tracer-work of tree branches, and then a wide-shouldered man in a black coat and a low white collar stepped out, holding in his large hairy hand a half-pint tankard of champagne. He was bald, but his beard was thick and wavy and luxuriant, like the pelt of some well-groomed animal, and he smelled of expensive cologne. Henry thought that he must have been quite handsome once, before he went completely bald, and before his belly grew so huge; but it was only fair to remember that many Western women still liked their men to have enormous stomachs, and in the company of men, a mighty gut was still regarded as the most obvious sign of wealth.

'I hope you're not going to keep Mademoiselle Carolista all to yourself, friend,' the man said in a deep, amiable voice. He held out his hand to Nina, and took her hand, and bent forward to kiss it. 'You're a spark of real gold amongst the dross, mademoiselle,' he beamed. Henry wasn't at all sure whether the man was trying to suggest that he, Henry, was the dross, but he decided to hold his tongue. 'I watched your act entranced.'

'Henry Roberts,' said Henry, and held out his hand. The man shook it without even looking at Henry, and announced, 'Charles Harrison; proprietor of Harrison's Criterion Saloon and several other local enterprises; at *votre service*, mademoiselle.' He said the French words without the slightest attempt at a French pronunciation. 'Perhaps you would do me the honour of taking a little dinner with me tonight. You know, *ah derks*, as they say in Paris.'

Nina coquettishly fluttered her eyelashes. 'You are very charming, Mr Harrison. But I regret tonight that I am tired. My act always leaves me drained. Soon, I shall be retiring for the evening. A cold compress, a little ice; perhaps a spoonful of eggnog.'

Charles Harrison's thick red lips puckered up in impatient disappointment. He still didn't look at Henry. 'Well, now, perhaps you'll be rested tomorrow. Can I count on that?'

'I am not at all sure, I cannot predict. But I will think about it,' said Nina.

'Well, you're doing me an honour,' replied Charles Harrison. He kissed her hand again, and said, 'Good evening to you, mademoiselle. Good evening, Mr Whatever-you-name-is.'

He went back into the dining-room, where Henry saw him talking to Mrs Enid T. Bradley, of the Ladies Union Aid Society;

190

and then to three pugilistic-looking men in shabby suits and red neckerchiefs.

'Bummers,' he said.

'He is a powerful man, Mr Harrison,' replied Nina.

'You know about him?'

'I have never met him; not until now; but one of the girls in our troupe used to work for him, as a harlot. She said that he was very cruel, and that life meant nothing, as far as he was concerned. He shot a blacksmith once, and killed him, not long ago, because the man tried to join him in a game of poker. The things he would do to his women were unmentionable.'

Henry sipped his champagne. 'My advice to you would be to stay well away from him.'

'And you? You are a tough fellow, too, aren't you? Should I also stay away from you?'

Henry kissed her again. 'You try it. Then you'll see what a tough fellow I can really be.'

He watched her rejoin the reception, greeted by whoops and applause, and he smiled to himself. Perhaps, after all, I've struck it lucky. A woman like Zwonky, and a mine full of gold. Perhaps this is God's compensation for losing Doris. Whatever it is, I'm happy about it, and I'll take it as it comes.

That night, at a quarter past midnight, he crossed the landing with bare feet, wincing as the boards creaked with every step; and at last reached Nina's room at the far end of the corridor, and tapped. Nina said, at once, 'Henry? Come in,' and he eased open the door and went inside.

'You are late,' she smiled. 'You said midnight; and when midnight struck I was all ready for you. Perhaps I am no longer ready for you now.'

He sat down on the plain comforter next to her, and held her hand. She watched him with that curious half-Oriental look of hers, her expression giving nothing away. You could look at some women and know something about them, almost straight off; whether they were happy, or sad; whether they had loved many men, or only a few, or none. You could usually tell if they were well-travelled, how much they liked music, whether they were kind. But Henry found Nina undivinable. She smiled at him and he couldn't even tell if she was smiling at him or smiling at herself.

'Why do you still do it?' he asked her.

191

'Why do I still do what?' Her voice was as cool as water over pebbles.

'Walk on the tightrope; why?'

'Do I have to answer you?'

'There's no obligation.'

'Well . . . I walk on the tightrope because it is what I do. I am a tightrope artiste. Do you understand that? People have to do what they are. The only unhappy people you ever meet in this world are those people who are trying to work at something which is not themselves. You can distinguish a man who is a natural-born miner from an inexperienced prospector, right away. Your friend Edward is a natural-born guide. He loves to take people through the wilderness. Mr Harrison is a gambler, and a thief, and a murderer.'

'And me? What do you think I am?'

She leaned forward and kissed him. Her lips parting made a click like a cricket. Behind her, the engraved-glass oil-lamp softly flickered, and Jesus sadly looked down from the bedroom wall. I am the way, the truth, and the life: no man cometh unto the Father, but by me. He kissed Nina back, and held her shoulder; and the wild flowers fell as slowly as a memory on Doris' grave; and Alby Monihan looked up from his lunch; and the train rattled across the southern shore of Lake Michigan, still in darkness, although dawn was very near now, and the lights of America's homesteads glimmered pale. Milking time, dreaming time; time for open eyes.

'You,' whispered Nina. 'You are a man who carves epitaphs, and always will be.'

She folded back the comforter, and she was naked. Soft skin, the colour of blanched almonds, thin wrists, delicate limbs. No superfluous flesh whatsoever; a body light and fit, with a ribcage like a shuttlecock, and two small round breasts with wide crimson nipples. Henry stared at her, and then slowly began to unbutton his shirt. She knelt up on the bed, and kissed his hair, and rubbed her hands all over his face and around his back and shoulders, helping him to tug his arm out of his sleeve and then kissing him again, fire and butterflies.

But, once he was naked, he took control of her, and lifted her up in his arms, and laid her down on the bed; and climbed above her, and kissed her with the kind of urgency with which he had once kissed Doris. She sighed, and gasped, and twisted beneath him, clutching at his muscular forearms, digging her

192

nails into his shoulders and his back. But he held her so surely, one hand cradling her head, and caressing her hair; the other hand cupping the cheeks of her bottom, squeezing them, and then stroking them, and sometimes straying close to the moistened tangle of her sex; and then he bent his head foward and kissed her breasts, taking her rising nipples gently between his teeth, and she cried out something in some language that he couldn't understand, not French, not even Polish by the sound of it, 'Ah Dhe mheinnich nan dula!'

She raised both of her legs, stretching them apart impossibly, opening up for him the scarlet throat of her vagina, so that he could see deep inside her, glistening and swollen. He pressed the purple head of his erection up against her; and she hesitated, holding his shoulders with the very lightest of touches. Then with a single long thrust she pushed herself downwards, and swallowed him right inside her body, until hair intertwined with hair, and he could feel himself stretching her internally, and she quaked, and snapped at his nipples with her sharp teeth, and hurt him.

For Henry, it was the most disturbing and most revelatory of nights. Although he was always dominant with her, because she was so light and small, and he was so heavy and strong, she played with him as if he were an instrument, the Henry-forte, and brought out of him an explosion of sharp sensations and feelings that before he had only experienced foggily, or not at all. He stood up, with his thighs braced, and lifted her right off the bed; and perfectly balanced she parted her legs and slid down on to him; kissing him with pert amusement when their connection was complete. She arched herself backwards, so that he could enter her more deeply, and all he could see of her was her protruding ribcage, and her breasts. She was athletic, but also emotional, and when he had thrust himself inside her for the third time, she wept with delight, and kissed him as if she never wanted to let him go. And at the very end of the night, when the room was already grey with the light of dawn, she performed for him a finale that he could scarcely believe was real: by standing on her hands, each hand grasping one of his thighs, upside-down, her bare toes almost touching the ceiling, poised and silent, white as a statue, and then lowering herself with infinite slowness so that her long hair wound silkily around his penis and over his belly, and taking him into her open mouth, and actually into her throat, so that his penis entirely disappeared. He climaxed instantly; and so violently that he let out a hoarse, deep shout.

'I was taught to do that by Senorita Pippa, the Mexican sword-swallower,' she said, matter-of-factly, as she lay on the pillow afterwards with her hair spread out all around her, smoking a small black-papered cigarette. 'She said, *Nina*, she said, *you must always breeze wiz your noss.*'

Henry lay propped on his elbow, watching her. She held the cigarette between her full, curving lips, and let the smoke leak out all around it, in aromatic curls. Henry kissed her on the forehead, and said, 'You're somebody special, aren't you?'

'Yes,' she nodded, her eyes half-closed. Then she laughed.

Henry said, 'I have to go out to California Gulch today, to look at my mine. I may have to stay for a couple of nights. But you'll still be here on Saturday won't you?'

'Yes, I'll still be here on Saturday.'

'Nina,' he said.

She smiled at him, and ran her hand down his naked side, so that he shivered with involuntary pleasure. '*A righ nan reula runach,*' she whispered.

'What does that mean? Is that Polish?'

She shook her head. 'It's Celtic. A very ancient language, older than Christ. *A righ nan reula runach* means, "O king of the stars mysterious", and that is what I shall always call you.'

'And what were those words you said before? What did they mean?'

Nina took out her cigarette, blew a long stream of smoke, and winked at him. 'Translated politely, they mean, "O merciful God". So you can see what it is that you do to me, O king of the stars mysterious.'

'Who taught you Celtic?'

Nina looked away. 'A man. A long time ago.'

'And what did he call *you?*'

She turned back and stared at him. 'He called me, "*ailleagan cumh nan neamh*", which means "precious lady of the skies".'

'Can I call you that.'

Her eyes lost their humour. 'No,' she said. 'It has other meanings, too. And, besides, it was a long time ago.'

She sat up. The bed smelled of perfume and tobacco smoke and sex. The first bar of sunlight had intruded through the shutters, and was moving with increasing brightness across the wooden ceiling. Henry looked at Nina's narrow back, the bumps of her vertebrae, the curve of her hips. It occurred to him that he might very easily fall in love with her, unless he was careful with himself. She had a quality about her which disturbed and attracted him; and most of all, she wasn't his.

SEVEN

Edward didn't ask him where he had been all night. He was probably glad to have been able to snore undisturbed, without being continually dug in the ribs and told to turn over. Nonetheless, he was noticeably taciturn as they drove out of Denver that morning in a small rig that he had borrowed from Mrs Cordley (assuring her six times over that he would feed the horses regularly, and not attempt to raise the awning, which was broken). He didn't speak until they had left Denver itself, and started rattling up the trail which would take them another five thousand feet above sea-level between mountains that rose on all sides of them like the ramparts of Heaven itself. Then he spat over the side of the rig, and said, 'Don't get too settled.'

'What do you mean?' asked Henry.

'Just what I said. Don't get too settled. This mine may turn out as rich as all hell; but we made an arrangement, remember? Not interested in mining, you said. The deeds are for you, Edward, you said. And I'm willing to stand by my part of the bargain. You bet. I'll take you to Sutter's Fort as soon as the passes are clear after the winter. But you just remember to stand by yours.'

Henry gave Edward a quick, sideways look. Today, he was dressed in the warmest of the three outfits with which he had been left after selling all of his trunks to Mr Seforim: a three-piece tweed suit in brown dog's-tooth with thick brown woollen socks, and fancy-patterned walking-shoes. He even had a tweed hat to match, and he had waxed up his whiskers extra high, five-after-eleven, the way that most of the dudes seemed to do it in Denver. He felt suddenly dandified next to Edward, and ridiculously green.

He said, carefully, 'You don't think I'm going to go back on my word, do you?'

Edward sniffed. 'Let's just say that you seem to be making yourself cosy here, and cultivating some fancy company, like a man who thinks he's going to stay; yes, and have some ready money to pay for it, too.'

Henry let out a short, dry laugh, trying to be scornful without being unpleasant. 'You sound as if you've caught gold-fever already.'

'The only ailment I'm suffering from is the ass-itch; that and the deeply suspicious mind. I can read the way of a trail, young Henry, and I reckon that I can read you, too. You've changed, since you've been here. I've seen your eyes. You're going to be here until spring, that's if this mine is any danged good; but then you're moving on, and don't forget it.'

Henry decided not to say anything at all; because the last thing he wanted Edward to know was that he was right. Until he had arrived in Denver, Henry had never come across newly-minted wealth before: he had never smelled gold in the air, or met men who had suddenly and accidentally become million-aires, and were hell-bent on showing it. Those few people around Bennington who had owned large properties and substantial inherited incomes had been infinitely discreet about their money. Here in Denver it was champagne and diamond stick-pins and every imaginable display of good fortune, from varnished carriages to pretty women, from jewellery to grand mansions. Denver had excited in Henry the one part of his character which in Carmington had seemed like nothing more than the passing peacockery of a good-looking young man: his love of fashion, and ostentatious clothes, and all the fine and amusing things of life, like good food, and drink, and art, and attractive girls. If he had stayed in Carmington, he would probably would have grown old and sober like the rest of the community, and like his father. But here, it was flash and dazzle and pocketfuls of $10 golden eagles, and let's have another bottle of vintage wine, waiter. Nina had excited him, too, and flattered him more than any other woman he had ever met. He still felt stunned when he thought of what she had

196

done to him last night. All in all, he had decided that he had a taste for Denver: her people and her mountains and her way of life; and if the Little Pittsburgh mine was everything that Alby Monihan had said it was, he couldn't turn his back on it and trudge meekly off to Sutter's Fort like an impoverished emigrant.

Edward said, 'You and that balancer get on pretty good, did you?'

'You mean Mademoiselle Carolista? Yes, she's all right.'

'No meat on her for my taste.'

Henry shrugged. He didn't want to get into an argument.

The air grew chillier as they gradually climbed higher. It was over sixty miles to California Gulch; and another mile straight up. Hardly speaking to each other, they drove all day between high crags of rock, and stands of yellow pine; stopping once or twice for Edward to stretch his legs and wiggle his fingers and take a long swallow of whiskey. Mrs Cordly had packed for them a basket of poor-boy sandwiches made with cold roast beef and tomatoes; and fruit, and bottles of beer. Just after noon they sat on beds of pine-needles in the sharp mountain wind, and had a quick, silent lunch.

'That gold-mine better be good,' said Edward, when they had finished, wiping his nose on his sleeve. 'I don't know what Mrs Cordley's going to say if we can't pay her. Kill us, most like, or make me fuck her for three weeks non-stop.'

'That doesn't sound like a hardship.'

'You bet it isn't. After two wrassles with Mrs Cordley, it's a softship.'

At its highest point, the trail over the mountains rose above eleven thousand feet; and they reached it at evening. The sight of the sun setting over the Rockies, over Bald Mountain and Red Peak, and further into the distance, over the mystical spire of the Mountain of the Holy Cross, was dazzling. The sky was intensely clear, and the sun burned into the horizon like a crucible of molten gold. Henry sat shading his eyes, while Edward finished off the last of his whiskey, which he made a point of not sharing equally. He wasn't drunk. The air was too sharp for anyone to get drunk. But he was being erratic and irascible; and Henry guessed that he was afraid. Henry didn't quite know why. Perhaps Edward thought that if the mine proved to be profitable, then Henry would try to kill him. Then again, perhaps it was nothing more than the fear of the mine

197

being a dud, or worked-out by claim jumpers, or even not there at all. Suddenly, this deed of claim which in New York had seemed spurious and unimportant was burningly valuable to both of them. Henry had heard of gold-fever, but never experienced it, not until now. It was an extraordinary kind of euphoria, an anticipation of riches that was almost a pleasure in itself; distinguishable from every other kind of fever by the hardships which its sufferers were prepared to endure, almost happy to endure, just for the chance of picking up that nugget, or striking that glittering vug.

They tented that night, and lit a fire, and made coffee and hash. The next morning was dewy and damp, and Edward woke with a horrendous cough. After they had eaten the rest of the hash for breakfast, he went off among the trees by himself and coughed and coughed until he vomited. When he came back he was grey-faced, and even less communicative than before.

Henry said, 'Are you all right?' But Edward snapped only, 'What's it to you?'

Henry didn't answer, but felt fractured and uncomfortable. The truth was that he was creating the tension between them himself: because if he really hadn't wanted the mine, he would have made it quite clear to Edward by now that he wasn't interested, and Edward wouldn't have been in such a condition of fear and alarm.

He sang 'Sweet Josephina', and made himself sing it all the way through even though Edward scowled over the reins, and Henry's voice in the thin mountain air sounded flat and unconvincing.

'Sweet Josephina she fell ill
And they buried her down by Green Tree Hill
But her ghost it walks and it sings this song
"It was Willy O'Brien that done me wrong." '

After a long while, as the rig began to rattle along the last stretch of hard furrows that led to California Gulch, Edward snarled at Henry, 'Will you shut up, for Christ's sake?'

The community of California Gulch was a ramshackle collection of huts and timber-framed houses built along both banks of one of the streams that rushed down from the higher peaks of the Mosquito mountains. It was the longest, skinniest town

198

in the territory, because the gold washed down the gulch, and fronting the gulch was the only place where it was worth having a property. There was a grocery store, a drugstore, a pie-and-cake stall, and a grand emporium that announced itself as 'Poznainskys Gentlemans Tailor & Dry Goods Palace, Late of Last Chance Gulch, Montana'. The single street was churned and rutted and strewn with lumber, and as Henry and Edward drew up their rig outside Willard's Saloon, three dogs with mud-streaked pelts came barking and yapping around their wheels.

A young man with an immense red beard was leaning on the rail on the boardwalk, his eyes squinting against the mid-morning sun, smoking a pipe. He wore a tall-crowned hat which looked as if it had been deliberately plastered with slurry. As Henry climbed down from the rig, he lifted his pipe in greeting, and said, 'How're you doing?'

'How's yourself?' answered Henry, and stepped his way carefully through the mud until he reached the boards. The dogs kept yipping and jumping and circling around and around, until a miner on the opposite side of the street yelled out, 'Gumbo! Come here, you half-assed excuse fer a dog!'

The young man with the red beard looked down at Henry's Oxford shoes with amusement. 'Did you come to mine, or did you come to dance?' he asked, though not unpleasantly.

Henry said, 'I'm looking for the Little Pittsburgh. Any idea where that might be?'

Edward waited patiently with his thumbs in his belt, and suppressed a cough. Henry took out the deed-of-claim and unfolded it, and held it in front of the young man's face so that he could look at it. The young man shrugged and said, 'No good showing me anything on paper, your highness. I can't read fit to spit.'

But just then, a big-bellied man in a linsey-woolsey shirt and the most capacious pair of miner's jeans that Henry had ever seen came puffing out of the saloon, and said, 'What's that you was talking about? Little Pittsburgh, was it?'

'That's right,' replied Henry, and held up the deed.

The man came up, all prickly double chins and thick moustaches, and peered at the deed with watery eyes. He smelled of whiskey and fresh sweat, and that indefinable sweetness of men who haven't changed their underwear from one month to another, and haven't bathed since they came up into the mountains, on account of the water being so damned cold, and if you think I'm going to freeze my balls off in some bucketful of melted snow then you can damned well think again. The man reached into his shirt pocket, and produced an unexpectedly delicate little pair of wire-rimmed spectacles, which he hooked around his ears; and then examined the deed again.

'That's a genuine deed, by all appearances,' he said. 'But as far as I recalls it, the Little Pittsburgh was owned by a fellow called Fritz. Well, that's what everybody called him. Kind of morose fellow, not the sort that laughed too much.'

'Fritz Brüchner,' put in the red-bearded boy. 'I remember him. Lucky Fritz, they used to call him, just for a joke, because he couldn't do nothing right. Couldn't drink, always fell flat on his face. Couldn't get it going with women, paid them the money then couldn't raise it. Tried to play the jew's-harp once, when we had that dance, and swallered it.'

'Looks like he lost his gold-mine, too,' said the big fat miner, scratching at his behind.

'Do you know where the Little Pittsburgh is?' asked Henry.

'Surely do. Follow the gulch upwards, past the houses, till you crest the hill on the left hand side of the trail, and then there's an overhanging rock, and then you'll see a shack there, not much of a shack, and that's the Little Pittsburgh.'

'Anybody mining it now?' asked Edward, sharply.

'Jumpers, you mean?' the man shook his head. 'Nobody would want to jump the Little Pittsburgh, or any of them claims up there, not unless they had a pen-chant for breaking their ass for nothing. They're all borrascas, up on the hill there. Guess they thought they'd be clever, and hit the mother lode where all of this placer gold comes washing down from; but not a peep.'

Edward looked across at Henry, and his face was almost laughably miserable. 'Borrasca, is that what you say?' he asked.

'Black sand, black rock, and that's it. Poor old Fritz dug a hole deep enough to bury a horse and cart in, and that was the end of it. He always swore that there was gold there someplace, and he was always digging new holes, but he never found nothing.'

Henry held up the deed. 'So what's this worth?' he wanted to know.

'It ain't worth a light,' said Edward, in the sourest voice he could manage.

200

'Well, it's worth a *light*,' said the red-bearded boy cheerfully. 'You could always use it to get your pipe going.'

Edward ignored him. He coughed. 'That's it, then, broke,' he said.

'You wasn't counting on this mine, was you?' asked the big fat miner, rolling his eyes in curiosity from Henry to Edward and back again.

Henry gave a small, tight shake of his head. But Edward sat down on the boardwalk with his feet in the mud, and said, 'Ah, shit.'

'Well,' said the big fat miner. 'The least I can do is stand you fellows a drink, seeing as how you come out so far fer nothing. My name's 0.T. Bobbs, but mostly they call me Plumb-Bobbs. Come on in, Jack's got a special bottle for disappointments, good year-old whiskey, Disappointment Dew.'

They spent an hour or so in the small, smoky saloon, drinking small tumblers of whiskey that tasted as if it had been distilled from mountain-oak acorns and filtered through mule manure, but which was breathtakingly strong. Henry found himself the centre of attention, since he had only recently arrived from the East, and could whistle some of the latest tunes. Edward rather maliciously told the miners, too, that Henry had been stepping out with a tightrope walker; and of course they were clamouring to hear what she was like, pretty is she? and gets up to some fancy tricks, I'll bet.

Henry found the miners friendly, eager, and surprisingly gentle: very young men, most of them, who had left their families behind in search of sudden wealth. They all agreed that California Gulch was one of the richest placers they had worked; although one or two of the more experienced sourdoughs said that it didn't look like it could hold out very long. 'Make what you can, while you can, and then move on,' said one, and spat tobacco juice in a perfect accurate arc out of the doorway, and into the street.

They never talked about the risks and the hardships and the backbreaking work that they had to endure. They never mentioned the would-be prospectors, horrifying hundreds of them, who had died on the plains on their way to Pike's Peak or Cripple Creek, victims of cold or hunger or cantankerous Indians. They never discussed the tedious hours they had to spend washing placer gold in a wooden sluice, or in a rocker-box; or the frustrations of digging through gumbo; or the hair-raising danger of coyote-mining, which meant sinking one central shaft and then burrowing out in all directions along the bedrock in a wheelspoke array of unsupported tunnels.

All they talked about was gold, and what they were going to spend their money on when they were rich. In their beards and their boots and their filthy underwear, they sat in this foggy hovel of a wooden saloon, and talked about fried oysters, and handmade shoes, and going to the opera, and walking out with perfumed women dressed in silk, women with shoulders as white as swans. They shared between them, these men, a collective hallucination; a mirage that to them was more real than California Gulch itself would ever be.

To Henry, the most poignant moment of the morning was when one of the miners, a thin pale fellow with a wispy beard, started to hum a popular waltz called 'Enid Gray'; and two of his friends stood up after a while and danced together around the dusty boarded floor, big-bellied and bearded, in filthy work-shirts and britches held up with knotted suspenders, their eyes half-closed as they imagined the speckled sunlight that came in through the saloon's open door to be the light of chandeliers; and the humming to be an orchestra; and they danced with such grace and sentiment, and nobody thought them anything but elegant.

Later, Plumb-Bobbs took them up the hill to the Little Pittsburgh; and he was right. The mine was nothing more than a bald shoulder of rock, next to a high overhanging face of crumbling stone, interlaced with tree-roots. There was no sign of the shack; presumably somebody had knocked it down and used it for timber. But there were holes everywhere, some deep, some shallow, one of them nearly thirty feet from floor to lip, dank and barren and deserted. It looked as if a community of giant prairie dogs had been digging all around, and then given up, and moved away.

Plumb-Bobbs rested his huge bottom on a rock and smoked a cigar while Henry and Edward paced around their claim.

'I guess we're finished, then,' said Edward. 'Best thing we can do is flit out from Mrs Cordley's and put as much distance between us and Denver as possible.'

'I'm not leaving yet,' Henry told him.

'Why's that? On account of that balancer?'

'Edward, there's money in Denver. There's gold. And even if Lucky Fritz didn't find any here . . . well, maybe we can.'

'Are you loose in the head? Look at this place! That poor fellow must have been excavating here for months, and what did he find? Nothing!'

Edward knelt down, and broke off a lump of dry, blackish soil. 'You find gold in quartz, that's where you find it. Quartz, or mica, or iron pyrites. But take a look at this stuff; there's not more gold in here than there is in your Aunt Martha's back yard.'

'I still think that I'll stay,' said Henry.

'Well, you can suit yourself. But you owe me those twenty-five dollars for bringing you here.'

Henry counted out the money without saying a word. At the clinking of coins, Plumb-Bobbs glanced up from his rock; but quickly looked away again. Edward took the money, and said, 'Just about covers my outlay, that does; for food and mules. Least profitable trip I ever made.'

'Come on, Edward,' Henry retorted. 'If this mine had been worth something . . .'

'If this mine had been worth something, you can bet that I wouldn't have been given a look-in,' Edward countered.

'I don't understand why you're so bitter,' said Henry. 'Do we have to part so bitterly? At least let's say we're friends.'

Edward put away his money and lowered his head. 'The one thing you learn about the West is not to expect nothing,' he said.

They walked back down the gulch and the light of the afternoon was like flakes of gold itself. Henry realized as he made his way down the loose slides of rock and soil that Edward had at last come to face-to-face with the fact that this country would give him nothing; not a bride; not a fortune; not a friend. Only a few tots of whiskey called Disappointment Dew. He was flat-busted himself now. With nothing to his name but a barren patch of hard rock with holes dug in it, but at least he knew that he could work for his money. Edward had somehow expected his destiny to come for nothing, and that made his disillusionment all the more hurtful.

'Any work to be done around here?' asked Henry, as Edward untied their horses and prepared to turn the rig around.

Plumb-Bobbs said, 'Nothing that I can think of. Everybody's got all the helping hands they need; even the dry goods store.'

Henry looked around, shading his eyes against the sun. 'You don't have a bank here, though, or do you?'

'No, sir. No bank.'

'So what do you do with your gold?'

'Take it for assay; just to prove that we've got it; then hide it under the floor.'

Henry frowned. 'Do you really think that's safe?'

Plumb-Bobbs grinned, and hawked, and spat. 'Woe betide anybody I catch trying to scratch up *my* floor.'

Henry shook hands with Plumb-Bobbs, and the red-bearded boy, and two or three other miners who had come to stare at them as they left. Then Edward said, 'Hup, girl,' and they trotted back along the trail, their iron-rimmed wheels clattering and shaking and popping out pebbles.

'Are you going to go straight back to Council Bluffs?' asked Henry.

'Reckon I will,' said Edward. 'Reckon I can leave you to settle up with Mrs Cordley, the best way you can, seeing as how you got me into the goddamned mess in the first place.'

They drove between tall fragrant pines, between columns of purplish shadows, and the mountain air grew as chilly as ice. When they drove through the highest of all the passes, with the sun still shining brightly behind them, it began to snow, a whirl of flakes that blew between the spokes of their wheels and clung to Edward's whiskers. He coughed, again and again, a phlegmy, gasping cough that left him breathless; and he had to pound at his chest with his fist.

'Let me drive,' Henry urged; and at last Edward had to draw the rig to a halt and change over places. He was coughing so badly that he could scarcely speak, and all he could do when Henry asked him if there was anything he wanted was to wave his hand, and shake his head. Henry gave him his handkerchief so that he could wipe his mouth.

It was a long, difficult trail back to Denver; but Henry determined that they should get back as quickly as they could, provided the horses could stand up to the strain of the journey. He geed them up, and the rig bounced and rattled through the flickering trees, with the snow blowing all around it, as urgently and as clamorously as a waggon from hell. The rig had no suspension, and so by the time they had covered half-a-dozen miles down the stony track, Henry's back was jarred and his head felt as if it had been clapped between a door and a door-frame. Edward said nothing but coughed in thick, racking spasms; sometimes clutching hold of Henry's arm as if that were the only way in which he was going to be able to draw breath again.

Henry drove all afternoon, until it was dark; and then he halted the rig beneath a grove of ash trees, beside a stream, and lit a fire. He wrapped Edward in a blanket, and then set about brewing up some hot coffee. In two hours, the moon would come up, and they would be able to continue their journey. Right now, both of them needed a rest.

Edward coughed again; and then as Henry was spooning coffee into the enamel pot, he said, 'Oh, holy Jesus,' and Henry looked around and saw that the handkerchief which he had been holding to his mouth was dark crimson.

'Edward, you're sick,' he said, squatting down beside him and feeling his forehead. 'You're burning.'

'I feel cold,' said Edward. He coughed again, strings of spittle and blood.

'How long have you been coughing like this?'

Edward shrugged. 'Two or three years, on and off. It comes and it goes. But I guess that it's going to finish me off one day soon. It's been getting worse.'

'Have you seen a doctor?'

'Sure. Old Doc Lansing in Council Bluffs. He gave me a couple of bottles of Prickly Ash bitters and told me I was probably going to die.'

There was nothing that Henry could do. He sat on a stone and waited for the moon to rise, and listened to Edward coughing over and over, and thought about nothing at all. An owl began to scream like an affronted spinster.

Once it was light enough, they started off again, and Henry drove Mrs Cordley's horses hard, so that they foamed, but he managed to reach Denver by two o'clock in the morning, with Edward huddled up beside him, still coughing, shivering, and muttering about luck, and who had it, because it certainly wasn't him. Henry drove the rig around to the rear of the guest house, and unharnessed the horses, and by the time he had led them noisily into the stables, a light appeared at the back door and Mrs Cordley came out in a long flowery robe and a mob-cap, holding up a lamp.

'What's going on?' she demanded. 'I thought it was tinkers, or desperadoes.' Henry caught the reflection of lamplight on the barrel of a shotgun.

'It's Edward,' he told her; and she must have known already

how sick he was, because immediately she said, 'Hold this,' and gave him the shotgun, and then turned towards the boarding-house door and called out, 'Lennie! Run for the doctor!'

They managed to carry Edward into Mrs Cordley's back parlour, and lie him down on her red plush chaise-longue. He seemed to have stopped coughing now, but his eyes were closed and he was shuddering, and with every inspiration he made a harsh crowing sound. Mrs Cordley went into her kitchen and raked the fire in the range, which had burned almost down to the grate, and then stacked more wood on to it so that it would heat up enough to boil a kettle of water.

'He's had this before,' she said, sitting down next to Edward and holding his hand between hers. 'What he needs is balsam, and a strong dose of Dover's Powder.'

'You're quite a nurse,' said Henry.

Mrs Cordley looked up at him; still handsome, even in her mob-cap. 'When you run a boarding-house in a town like this, Mr Roberts, you have to be. I've delivered babies, taken out bullets with kitchen scissors, and once I cut off a poisoned thumb. I've sent Lennie for the doctor, but it's ten to one he won't come, or else he's busy somewhere else. Now, you could make yourself useful, please, and get a pudding-bowl out of the kitchen cupboard and fill it with hot water for the balsam.'

'Will he survive?' asked Henry, nodding down at Edward.

'Survive?' said Mrs Cordley. 'Of course he'll survive. He's as strong as an ox. It's his nerves that bring this on.'

'He seemed to be sure that he was going to die.'

Mrs Cordley laughed, and much to Henry's consternation, tugged Edward's hair and slapped his face. 'This rascal will outlive the both of us, you'll see.'

The doctor came briefly, a vague man who kept blinking and smelled of brandy. He commended Mrs Cordley for treating Edward with Dover's Powder, accepted a cup of coffee, declined a piece of spice cake, and left. Henry sat in the parlour with Mrs Cordley until three, and then climbed the staircase to go to bed. He unlaced his shoes and took them off, so that he wouldn't wake any of the other guests. Their snores reverberated through the house like a chorus of purring cats. As Henry was halfway up the stairs, the clock in the hallway chimed the quarter-hour, and some of the snores stopped, or changed from snores to whistles, as the chimes penetrated deep into sleeping minds.

He passed the door of Nina's room, and hesitated. He didn't want to wake her if she were asleep; but on the other hand he very much wanted to see her, and tell her that he was back. He waited for almost a minute, holding his breath and listening, and then he lightly tapped against the door-panel.

There was no response; so after a while he tapped again. A blurry voice said, 'Who is it?'

'Nina?' Henry whispered.

'Who is that? What do you want? It's the middle of the night.'

He opened the door, and stepped into the bedroom, and announced in a loud whisper, 'Nina, it's me, Henry. I just got back.'

'What the hell's going on?' a hoarse man's voice blurted out. There was a jouncing of springs, and a tussling of bedclothes, and then two faces appeared in the last of the moonlight. Nina, sparkling-eyed, in her nightgown; and Charley Harrison, podgy, tousle-haired, and naked. Henry stood still at the foot of the bed and stared at them; and they in their turn sat up side by side like a married couple surprised by a burglar, and stared back at him.

'I'm sorry,' said Henry, breathlessly; and then, with a cutting edge to his voice, 'I seem to have made a mistake.'

'You just get yourself the hell out of here,' said Charley Harrison. 'And if I ever see your face around this town again, I'm going to make sure that it never gets recognized again, not by anybody.'

'Nina?' said Henry; half-questioning, half-angry.

'You'd better go,' said Nina, very gently. 'We can talk in the morning, if you want to.'

'Just get the hell out,' Charley Harrison repeated.

Henry said, 'All right. I apologize. I only came in here because I failed to imagine that a lady like Mademoiselle Carolista could subdue her nausea for long enough to be able to spend the night with a fat unmannered hog like you. Obviously, it's all my fault; and I'm sorry.'

Charley Harrison pushed back the comforter, and climbed out of bed, and came padding on surprisingly soft little feet over to the door, and stood in front of Henry naked, his bald head gleaming, his shoulders thick whorls of hair, his belly hanging draped around his hips as if it were a bedroll. His tiny penis nested amongst the thick black hair between his thighs as if it were a fledgling cuckoo.

207

'You, my friend, have just made a serious error,' he said, softly and deeply and coldly. 'Nobody in Denver takes kindly to insults; and quite often they become shooting matters. Well, I'm not a gunfighter, although I can use a gun. I prefer to see people like you having to suffer for being so ill-mannered. And, mark my words, that's exactly what you're going to do. You're going to suffer, my friend, so bad that you're going to curse your mother for ever having given birth to you. You're going to know what pain really means, believe me.'

Henry felt as if all his blood were shrinking in his veins, but he replied, in a completely expressionless voice, 'I'm really frightened, Mr Harrison. Believe me.'

Nina said, 'Henry, please go. Don't make things worse.'

'All right,' Henry nodded. And he remembered the words she had spoken to him two nights ago, because he had repeated them over and over in the back of his mind, all the way to California Gulch. '*Ailleagan cumh nan neamh*. Precious lady of the skies.'

He closed Nina's door behind him and stood in the darkness of the corridor listening to the irritated grumbling of Charley Harrison; and the soft conciliatory murmurings of Nina; and the steady tireless ticking of the boarding-house clock.

'. . . walks in and wakes me up like he owns the place . . .' '. . . didn't mean any *harm*, Charley, and nothing happened . . .' '. . . sure you didn't fuck him, I can't believe that, not the way he walked in here . . .' '. . . he's a *boy*, that's all, no more than a boy, and I *like* him . . .' '. . . going to make damned sure he doesn't grow up to be a man, believe me. . . .'

Henry stayed where he was until the clock struck the half-hour, and the springs of Nina's bed began to squonk and squirrel again; and then he thrust his hands into his trouser pockets and walked disconsolately back to his room. He sat on the end of his bed and felt lower and more alone than he had since Doris had been killed. He was tired, too, after that hard drive all the way back from California Gulch, more than seventy miles since yesterday morning. He lay back on his bed, fully clothed, and closed his eyes; and within a minute he was asleep.

He dreamed dozens of short, vivid dreams; in bright colours; full of hurried activity and worried conversation. Somebody was telling him to come as quickly as he could, something was wrong, somebody needed his help. The shack was gone, that

208

was the trouble. The shack was gone. He felt that if he knew where the shack had gone, he would know the answer to everything. Then he was running for a train, he had to catch it so that he could see his mother. He knew she was dead, but if he caught this train he would be able to meet her and talk to her. He had a sudden feeling of intense sadness, and he knew that he was weeping in his sleep, but somehow he couldn't wake up and stop himself. A soft voice said, 'She wishes you were never born,' and then a steam-boat whistle was blowing and seagulls blew across the water like torn shreds of paper, and Nina was standing over him in her nightgown and he was awake.

'Henry? Henry, wake up. Henry!'

He stared at her. It was morning. He couldn't think where he was.

'Henry,' she said, 'you were shouting out.'

He sat up. He was still fully dressed. Out of the window, the day looked blue and windy and unsettled; and across on Sixth Street he could see dust blowing, and a sign swinging backwards and forwards.

'Oh. . . Nina,' he said, thickly.

She sat beside him on the bed, and took hold of his hand. She looked pale, and her mouth was bruised, as if she had been crushingly and violently kissed. 'I'm sorry about what happened last night.'

'Well. . . no, that's all right. Nobody made any promises, did they? You didn't make any promises to me, any more than I made any promises to you.'

'Henry, I'm still sorry.'

'It's all right, you don't have to be.'

He stood up, feeling stiff and awkward, and went across to the washstand. He filled up the basin; and then he eased off his coat, and unbuttoned his waistcoat, and rolled up his sleeves. Nina sat watching him: he could see her in the looking-glass.

'I persuaded Charley not to do anything silly,' she volunteered.

'You mean, you prevailed on him not to pull my fingernails out, or cut my arms and legs off?'

'You shouldn't have called him a hog. I mean, anybody would have taken exception to that.'

Henry splashed his face, and then groped for his towel. Nina stood up and handed it to him, and watched him closely while he dried himself.

'I didn't marry you, simply because I went to bed with you,' said Nina. 'I have always been a free woman. I travel from town to town, how can I be anything else but free? I choose the men I want to sleep with because they are beautiful, or because they are ugly, or because they are wealthy. I choose exceptional men, whatever they look like. You are exceptional. You are so exceptional that you have no need of this ridiculous jealousy. Perhaps you are poor, and down on your luck, but you have a spirit in you which you do not even recognize yourself. You have a hardness in you, too; which you try to conceal. You are sentimental, yes; but when you find what you want, you will sweep anybody out of the way in order to make sure that it is yours. Do not condemn Charley Harrison so readily. Do not hate him. Quite often, the people we hate the most are the people who are most like ourselves.'

Henry stripped off his stale shirt, and hung it over the back of his chair. Then he began to unbutton his long johns. 'Are you going to stay, or are you too modest?' he asked her.

'Don't be cross with me,' she said; not pleading, not demanding, but calm.

'I'm not cross,' he told her. 'You can only be cross about people you care for.'

'Henry. . . .'

He took hold of Nina's wrists, and grasped them very tightly. 'Nina, I don't care. I'm not interested. If you want to go to bed with Charley Harrison, that's none of my business. As you say, you're a free woman. You can do whatever you want. *Ailleagan cumh nan neamh.*'

Nina said, with great softness, 'That also means "lady of easy virtue".'

'I see. Well, I should have guessed. More fool me.'

'Henry, I shall always remember you.'

'Well,' he said, swallowing, 'that's one consolation.'

He released her wrists; and she reached up on her toes and kissed his cheek, and then his lips. Then she turned and left the room without another word, leaving him standing there alone. He looked towards the window, towards the windy street. The swinging sign said H.V. Cram Novelty Store. He sat down on the bed again and felt that his whole world had collapsed around him like a balloon. He heard the door of

Nina's room closing; and voices in the corridor; and someone saying, 'How long do you think it's going to take us to get to Cheyenne?'

He wondered if he ought to think of going back East. Perhaps the frontier was more than he could take. Its greed for gold, its careless violence, and its loose morality. Perhaps, on the other hand, he was simply tired; and because he was tired, and a stranger, he was being more dependent on the people around him than he should have been. Back home in Bennington he wouldn't have been jealous of a girl like Nina. He probably wouldn't even have looked at her, let alone thought of taking her to bed. And as for bursting into her bedroom, and blustering away at Charley Harrison. . . . He flushed at the memory of it, and hoped very much that he wouldn't bump into Charley Harrison again.

He washed, and dressed in his second-best suit, and combed his hair. In the looking-glass, he was still handsome, still fashionable, still poised. He was beginning to think twice about the moustache, however. Sticking up like that, it looked mannered, and even effete; especially in comparison to the wealthiest men he had met in Denver, the really powerful figures behind the banks and the brothels and the dry-good stores, who all wore their whiskers heavy and drooping like walruses.

He left the boarding-house and walked across the street to the Rocky Mountain Dining Room. He still had $1.35 left, and he was determined to spend it on a good breakfast. The wind blew grit in his eyes, and he had to clutch the brim of his hat to keep it on. There was an awning in front of the dining-rooms reading Excellent Eats, Pies, Zang's Beer, Steaks, which ripped and thundered with every gust. He had almost reached the boardwalk on the far side of the street when three men in derby hats and dust-soiled suits came out of the shadow of the hardware store next to the dining-rooms and walked towards him with friendly smiles on their faces.

'Mr Henry Roberts, isn't it?' asked one of them. He had a big blue chin and a white scar across the bridge of his nose that looked like a caterpillar.

Henry hesitated, and looked from one man to the next. 'That's me,' he said, defensively. 'What of it?'

'Somebody wants a word, that's what of it?'

211

'Well, I'm going to take some breakfast. If somebody wants a word, they can come and have a word in the dining-room.'

One of the men circled around behind Henry, and stood there with his arms folded, grinning, one eye closed against the wind, and chewing a burned-down stub of cigar. Henry stayed where he was.

'Are you coming, or what?' asked the man with the blue chin.

There was a long, tight pause. Then Henry dodged to one side, and tried to make a run for the dining-rooms. At once, the man who had been standing behind him leaped on to his back, tugging his coat halfway down his back, and hitting him hard on the side of the neck. Henry staggered, lost his balance, and fell heavily on to the roadway.

They beat him up quickly, and very hard, and without any kind of emotion. They kicked him in the ribs, in the back, in the hip; and although he kept his hands clutched protectively between his legs, they kicked his fingers again and again, and still managed to bruise his stomach and his groin. One toecap cracked him straight in the nose, and his face was instantly smothered in blood.

When it was over, the man with the blue chin said, 'A special message for you from Mr Harrison. If it hadn't have been for the lady, you would have been sitting on your cloud by now. Mr Harrison says get out of town and stay out of town, that's if you don't want another kicking. Now, take my advice, do what he asks. I'm serious, Mr Harrison once said that he was going to make sure that he killed twelve men during his life-time, so that when he went to heaven he could be judged by a jury of his peers. As far as I know, there's nine to go, so don't be one of them.'

Henry hardly heard any of this terse, twanging address. His head was singing, and his ears felt as if they were stuffed up with cotton. But after a while he was conscious that the men had gone, and then he cautiously lifted himself up on to one bruised elbow and looked around. Several passers-by stared at him, but nobody attempted to come to his assistance. They didn't want the bummer beating them up too.

It took Henry almost a minute to get up on to his feet. Then, hobbling, he made his way back across the street to the boarding-house; and up the stairs. He had to lean for a while against the banisters on the landing, panting and coughing,

212

before he was able to continue down the corridor to his room. But at last he managed to reach the door, one shoulder sliding against the wallpaper, one foot dragging, and blood running out of his nose and all down his mouth and his chin.

There was a carpet-bag standing in the corridor outside his room. He pushed it aside with his foot, and opened up his door. And then, as he lurched towards the bed, he saw whose carpet-bag it was. Standing by the window, in a prim hat and a prim blouse and a long brown skirt, neat and smiling, was Augusta.

'Henry!' she exclaimed, as he collapsed on to the bed. 'Henry, what's happened?'

'Fight,' muttered Henry, through thick lips.

'Oh, Henry, how could anybody do such a thing? Wait, please, my dear, and I'll fetch some water, and a towel. Here, staunch your bleeding with this.'

She handed him her scarf, which he pressed against his nose. He coughed blood, and it splattered all over the comforter.

Gently, she washed his face, and dried him; and then eased him out of his torn coat and his bloodstained shirt and collar. He didn't resist. He didn't even look at her. But all the time she murmured to him, 'There, there you are, my darling. Everything is going to be wonderful now.'

BOOK TWO
BONANZA

*'A rich mine, vein, or pocket of ore;
from Spanish "fair weather", "prosperity".'*

EIGHT

She said, 'There are two men outside who want to talk to you.'

Henry looked up from the card-table, one eye squinting against the smoke of the cigar which was clenched between his teeth. 'I'm busy,' he said. 'Did they tell you what they wanted?'

'They don't speak very good English. Well, the one who seems to be doing all the talking doesn't. The other one doesn't say anything.'

'Sounds like the garbled leading the gobstruck,' remarked Jim Roelofs, and cackled like a chicken.

'Are we playing this hand or aren't we?' Billy Coren complained. 'I got 75 dollars riding on this.'

'Garbled leading the gobstruck,' Jim Roelofs repeated, and cackled again.

Henry laid his cards face-down on the table and eased himself out of his chair. Eighteen years of married life had changed him very little, except to make him heavier jowled; and to infuse one side of his hair with grey. He was still handsome, thickly-eyebrowed, well-built. The neatly-trimmed moustache was still there, although he no longer waxed it up into points. He was the kind of middle-aged man who attracted all the wives at the local socials, and made them speak more throatily than they had meant to; and who only had to compliment a spinster to make her blush brightly.

Augusta held back the door-curtain for him as he passed. 'I really couldn't understand a word,' she said. 'And I'm afraid they rather *alarmed* me.'

'That's all right,' Henry reassured her, touching her shoulder.

Augusta had become more angular; tighter, busier, sharper. But her sharpness had been brought about by years of happy hard work; of rising at five-thirty to sweep up and make pastry;

of baking pies and tidying shelves and serving customers all day; of mending and sewing; and of going to bed late at night when it was dark, after an hour of reading the Bible by lamplight, and of lying in contented silence clasping Henry's hand and thinking how lucky she was, and how perfect they were, and how everybody must admire them.

'Panhandlers, most like,' said Henry, to nobody in particular, as he walked through the corridor which separated the store and the post office from the living quarters at the back. On the wall of the corridor was a framed etching of Abraham Lincoln; and, next to it, an amateurish watercolour of an Irish wolfhound. Henry pushed his way out through the beaded curtain into the store itself; a wide room with a boarded floor and a low ceiling, densely but neatly stacked on either side with all the merchandise which the citizens of Leadville demanded: plum preserves, calico, canned salmon, bootjacks, bushel-baskets, kerosene jugs, Woolson's coffee, Union Leader cut plug, blankets, hats, crackers, and 'all the latest clothing, both nobby and modest'. At the far end of the store, behind a high mahogany counter and a decorative brass grille, was the post office and bank. For Leadville, all these years later, was what the rickety mining township of California Gulch had come to be; and this bank was the same bank which Henry had discussed with Plumb-Bobbs, on his very first visit.

The two men who wanted to talk with Henry were standing close to the doorway as if they had no confidence at all that they would be listened to; and that they would be asked to leave the store in pretty short order. This was hardly surprising, for they were the two sorriest-looking sourdoughs that Henry had ever seen. They were both bramble-bearded, and their clothes were so worn-out and patched and patched again that they looked as if they were wrapped up in quilts. One of them wore a peaked cap with a leather top that must once have been waterproof, but which now had the appearance of a shrivelled mushroom. The other wore a huge shapeless stetson. At his feet, a filthy mongrel shivered, and occasionally sneezed.

'Well, gentlemen,' said Henry, resting his hands on his hips. 'They tell me that one of you talks and one of you don't.'

'I am always being called August Rische,' said the man in the peaked cap, lifting the cap high off his head as if inviting an academic inspection of his small knobbly bald patch. 'And you are always the celebrated H. Roberts?'

'Who's this?' asked Henry, nodding towards the man in the stetson with the shivering dog.

'This gentleman is always being called George Hook.'

'I see,' said Henry, glancing towards Augusta, and raising his eyebrows. 'And what do you want of me?'

'We are in the way of prospecting, Mr Roberts. Mr Hook and I have been now for five years north and south, here and there, digging and searching, always with immense industry.'

'Not with immense success, though, by the look of it.'

August Rische lowered his eyes, as if he were ashamed of himself, and shuffled his feet, and sniffed. The dog sneezed twice, in accompaniment. For his part, George Hook looked vacantly around the store, as if he were nothing to do with any of this conversation whatever, and was simply here to decide at his leisure what brand of chewing-tobacco he wanted.

'The placer is not always presenting itself with obviosity,' said August Rische. 'Everyone has lucks; everyone has misfortunes. Mr Hook and I have not been more misfortunate than some adjacent prospectors; and now we sure feel that we are ready for finding gold.'

Henry drew slowly on his cigar, narrowing his eyes as he did so, and examining first August Rische and then George Hook.

'Well,' he said, 'at the risk of giving offence, I must say that you two are just about the most played-out pair I've ever seen, and considering I've been living here for eighteen years, that's really something.'

'Played-out?' asked August Rische, uncertainly. George Hook belched and August Rische gave him a quick nudge in the ribs.

'You do know that the gold ran out here, nearly sixteen years ago?' said Henry. 'Once the placer was gone, that was it. Every prospector was up stakes and off to Pike's Peak or Cripple Creek or Virginia City. There's silver, for sure. But every decent claim is already taken; and those that aren't taken aren't worth having. Everything else is played-out, just like you two.'

'Mr Roberts, we only look for slim pickings,' said August Rische. He tugged his cap back on to his head again, too tightly, and had to adjust it. 'We have kept together bodies and souls for all these five years by prospecting in mines that were always said to be done for.'

Henry shook his head in gentle exasperation. 'You might

218

have kept bodies and souls together, but not much else. Not even the seat of your pants.'

'We repeatedly implore you, Mr Roberts.'

'What do you want? A free handout? You won't get it here.'

'Mr Roberts, all we ask is a grubstake. Is a grubstake asking the moon from you? Twenty-five dollars, and maybe some flour, and whatever we dig up, you can have a third of it. A third for George Hook; a third for myself; and a third for you. There is no peculiarity in that, is there?'

Henry took the cigar out of his mouth, and paced around the boarded floor. All three of them watched him: August Rische, George Hook and the dog. Henry went up to the glass counter where the candies were displayed, and leaned forward with his hands in his pockets and peered into it. Fresh chocolate fudge, cut in squares, which Augusta had made yesterday afternoon; as well as pecan penuche; and caramels; and molasses taffy, which she had pulled with the help of the thin starved-looking woman who lived across the street and took in laundry, and sometimes miners, too.

Henry said, with his cigar clenched between his teeth, 'I've been living here and working here for eighteen years, Mr Rische. When I got here, I had nothing at all, except for eighty-one dollars left over from my wife's childhood savings, and enough good sense to realize that even a godforsaken place like California Gulch needed a bank, and a post office.'

He stood up straight, and faced the two sourdoughs with his hands in his pockets, his watch-chain stretched across his brown hound's-tooth vest. 'Everything you see around you here is the result of honest hard work. It may not be much to somebody like you, who wants to be a millionaire; but look at me and then look at yourself, and then tell me who's the better off. Here,' he said, and he drew around the cheval-glass which his customers used when they were trying on suits and bonnets. 'Take a look at yourself, what do you think?'

August Rische kept his eyes averted, although George Hook walked across to the mirror and peered into it from only two or three inches away, and then suddenly smiled at himself with benign lunacy.

August Rische said, in a quiet but persistent voice. 'I know how you are thinking of us, Mr Roberts. Bums and wastrels. Not worthy of any investing. But have some belief that whatever sum you care to give us for the purposes of grubstaking will be cherished and husbanded.'

'Spent on whiskey, more like,' said Henry. 'Now, take yourselves out of here. This is supposed to be a food store, hygienic. Do you think people are going to want to buy anything here if they walk in and see you two dungheaps and that mongrel of yours?'

'Henry, let them have some crackers,' Augusta implored. 'They're probably starving.'

Henry waved his hand impatiently. 'Go on, then, dip in. Take a handful.'

But August Rische remained where he was, frowning at Henry from beneath the peak of his cap, as if he would change Henry's mind by staring at him.

'Go on, get yourselves lost,' snapped Henry.

'Sir, all we are asking is twenty dollars,' begged August Rische. 'Two golden eagles, sent flying to bring back hundreds more. Throwing your bread at the water, sir, and expecting its return.'

'Just take your crackers and go, will you?' Henry told him. 'And, Augusta, give that dog something, there's a hambone out back.'

'Well, sir, if I am not persuading you to take a chance,' said August Rische, with an air of tremendous resignation.

The word 'chance' for some inexplicable reason caused the hair around the back of Henry's neck to prickle, as if he had been touched by the bare wires of a galvanometer. *Chance.* He couldn't think why it had such an extraordinary effect on him. He found himself standing with his hands in his pockets and his eyes focused on nothing at all; so that the sunny interior of the store became blurred, and the voices of the men in the back room suddenly seemed very distant; like men talking in another time. *Chance.*

Augusta said, 'Henry.'

'Yes,' he answered, his eyes still not focusing.

'Henry, Grover says he gave the hambone to Mrs McLintoch. But there's a pork-knuckle, if that's all right.'

'All right,' Henry said absent-mindedly; and then the wheels of the coffee-grinder began to turn against the sunlit window, as George Hook idly ran his hand around it; and the turning of those spokes unlocked for Henry the concealed memory of the word 'chance'.

220

The Colossal Whirler, turning against the sky. The sunlight of summer, eighteen years ago, in 1860, before the war; before Lincoln was President and before anybody had heard of Chickamauga or Chancellorsville; before bicycles and typewriters and suffragists; before linoleum and talking telephones. A young day at the end of an innocent era. And Madame Waldorf the fortune-teller had peered into his head and said, 'You will not become wealthy by talent; or by skill; but simply by chance. There will be two men who are looking for something. One of them speaks very little English. You will know them when you meet them, at least you will if you remember my words.'

August Rische and George Hook, their pockets crammed with Graham crackers, opened the door of the store and stepped out into the dusty sunshine. August Rische turned, and raised his cap, and said, 'With regrettability, we are taking our leave, Mr Roberts; but thank you for the small foods.'

Henry said, 'Wait.'

What Madame Waldorf had predicted for Doris, that had come true, hadn't it? That there was a cloud over her life, and that she would never marry? Now here were these two men whose arrival she had spoken about, all those years ago; and her forecast had been that they would make him rich.

August Rische didn't hear him, and closed the door. Henry crossed the store in three electrified steps, opened the door up again, and called, 'Wait! Mr Rische! Mr Hook!'

The two tattered prospectors turned around; as did almost everybody else in the street, Leadville, like most Western towns, was populated by the incurably inquisitive, and gossip was as staple as whiskey. Henry beckoned August Rische and George Hook back towards the store; and they shrugged at each other, and came, watched by half a dozen shoppers and prospectors and layabouts who were all patently wondering why a smart prosperous man like Henry Roberts should want to have anything to do with two run-down no-hopers like these.

Henry said, 'I've changed my mind.'

August Rische looked suspicious. 'You want back the crackers? The pig-bone?'

'Of course not. I've changed my mind about grubstaking you. Come on back inside.'

Cautiously, the two prospectors followed Henry back into the store. Augusta stared at Henry in perplexity, her hands

221

clasped in front of her apron, and said, 'Henry? Is something the matter?'

Henry went to the cash register, and rang up No Sale. As the newspaper pundit Finley Peter Dunne had recently written, 'th' cash raygister is th' crownin' wurruk iv our civilization,' and at no time had Henry agreed with that remark more than now. He handed August Rische two 10–dollar coins, minted in Denver; and August Rische took them and laid them side by side in the palm of his dirt-stained hand and stared at them as if they had materialized there by magic. George Hook kept his eyes on Henry; squinting and suspicious; quite obviously baffled and alarmed by anybody who should so freely give them money.

'There's just one thing,' said Henry, and walked around to the post office side of the counter; where he took out a sheet of vellum paper, and quickly scribbled on it, 'Rec'd of Henry Roberts, Twenty Dollars in Gold Specie, Being a Grubstake for Mining Exploration in the District of Leadville; in Return for which I Guarantee One-Third of All Ore Precious or Semi-Precious.' He waved the paper dry, and then brought it round for August Rische to sign and for Augusta to witness. August Rische signed his name in big, careful, kindergarten loops.

'Now then,' said Henry. 'If there's anything you need such as bacon, or vinegar, or beans, you can help yourselves to whatever you need; enough for a month, say. Augusta, will you help these gentlemen?'

Augusta, mystified by Henry's sudden change of mind, walked around the counter with her striped skirts swishing on the boards and her large bustle protruding aggressively. Bustles of such a size were already waning in popularity in New York and San Francisco, and had become much trimmer; but Henry had once told Augusta that her large bustle made her look 'most provocative', and so she made sure that she always wore it, and that she paraded it as ostentatiously as possible. 'You will need 33 pounds of bacon for two men for one month,' she announced. 'You will need 85 pounds of flour; and four pounds of salt; and 16 of sugar; and I suppose you had better have some dried beef, too, and some coffee.'

August Rische nodded, and kept on nodding, unable to believe his luck. Henry stood with his hand on the counter, alternately smiling and not smiling; and hoping very much that his feelings about Madame Waldorf would prove to be justified.

222

'If you have no cart,' he said, 'I will have one of the boys bring these provisions out to you. Where is your claim?'

'Ah,' said August Rische, carefully.

There was a pause. Augusta turned around from the sugar-sack, and looked first at August Rische and then at Henry, quite perplexed.

'You do *have* a claim?' asked Henry.

'We are always having intentions,' August Rische declared.

'You are always having intentions, but you don't have a claim, is that it?'

'Always before we were scraping wherever we found somewhere deserted,' August Rische explained.

'Oh, *Henry*,' said Augusta, exasperated, and putting down the sugar-scoop. 'These two are quite impossible.'

Henry rubbed his eyes. 'If you don't have a claim, there isn't any point in my giving you all these provisions, is there? Nor a grubstake, either. Now, listen, you've worried my wife, and you've taken me out of a poker game with my friends, just to be panhandled. I'm not going to be vindictive, and I'm not going to give you any trouble; but I think you'd better return those twenty dollars, don't you, and then we can forget about the whole business.'

August Rische stood up straight for a moment, and looked almost proud. Then he stiffly held out his hand, and offered Henry his two golden eagles.

'I am apologizing for any mendacity,' he said. His lip trembled, and Henry realized that he had been seriously defeated. He and George Hook had no money whatsoever; no claim; and no hope of finding one. Henry knew for himself how low a man could feel with no money and no chance of ever making any. He could remember as sharply as if it were only last week how Augusta had spread out her money on the bureau at the Cherry Creek Guest House, $98.27; and how he had peered at it with puffed-up eyes and realized that here was his only salvation. There was a time when every man had to give in; not willingly, not lightly, but simply for the sake of being able to eat tomorrow. That was why he had given in to Augusta, and eventually agreed to marry her. She had been willing, and sympathetic, and ready to do anything. And apart from that, she had been able to offer him $98.27; enough to get him away from Denver and Charley Harrison, and to set up his business in California Gulch. God, he thought; what a man can give away for $98.27.

He said, in a different voice, 'I do happen to have a claim myself.'

Augusta chipped in, 'Not the Little Pittsburgh?'

'Well, I was thinking about it.'

'But you own the Little Pittsburgh outright! You're not going to give away two-thirds of it to these tramps, are you?'

Henry raised both hands. 'Listen, Augusta, the Little Pittsburgh is barren; I never had a red cent out of it anyway. What's the harm if Mr Rische and Mr Hook have a crack at finding something up there? One-third of something is better than three-thirds of nothing at all.'

'I don't approve,' said Augusta.

'You don't approve? You don't approve of what? Of making a little money?'

'I don't approve of surrendering ownership of our property to men like these; vagrants.'

'I'm not talking about surrendering ownership. I'm simply talking about giving them the opportunity to mine up there, in the off-chance that they dig something up. Even a little zinc would be better than what we're getting at the moment, which is thin air.'

'I don't approve. Do I have to repeat myself?'

Henry took a deep breath. 'Well,' he said, 'I'm sorry about that. But I'm still going to grubstake these gentlemen, and give them a month up at the Little Pittsburgh to dig for whatever they can find. So would you measure out provisions for them; salt and bacon and whatever else they want; and I'll go get the deeds, so that they can see where they can dig.'

'No,' said Augusta.

Henry took the cigar out of his mouth and looked at Augusta with uncertainty. Augusta stood with her head lifted, her mouth tightened, her spectacles framing her eyes as if someone had pencilled ovals around them to emphasize how fixed they were; how challenging. She had startled Henry with this sudden show of defiance; not least because of the way in which she seemed to expect that he would give in to her without argument. There had somehow always been an unspoken understanding in their marriage that Augusta would do anything for Henry, and always agree with him, no matter what. It was a kind of silent acknowledgement that it had been

224

she who had pursued him, and suggested marriage; that it had been she, and only she, who had declared their coming-together to be 'a great romance'; and most secretly and most painfully of all, that she was plain and drew compliments for nothing more than her pastry, while he was unarguably handsome, and easy-mannered, and drew the women of Leadville into the store as much for his smile as he did for his groceries.

But now: she was insisting that he give these two prospectors nothing, and it was clear from the expression on her face that she meant it very seriously.

Henry said quietly, 'Gentlemen. . . here are your twenty dollars.' And without taking his eyes off Augusta, he dropped into August Rische's hand the two golden eagles which Rische had so hurtfully returned to him.

'Go up to the head of the gulch,' said Henry. 'Up on the left, you'll find a shoulder of rock, overlooked by a bluff, with an overhang. You can't miss it; there are pits and diggings all over the place. There's a sign, too, if nobody's taken it down, or used it for firewood.'

George Hook took off his drooping stetson for the first time; and the dog sneezed yet again, and yawned.

Henry said, 'We'll send provisions up later today; all the flour and beans that you're going to need for a month's hard work. But let me tell you this: that's rock-solid ground up there, and when I say hard work, I mean hard work. I'm not paying twenty dollars for anybody to lie down like Laurence's dog.'

August Rische looked quickly from Henry to Augusta, and cleared his throat, and then said, 'You are always being blessed, Mr Roberts. You also, Mrs Roberts.'

'You can go now,' said Henry.

August Rische and George Hook retreated, leaving the door open behind them, so that the light and the dust and the horse-chaff blew in across the floor. Augusta went punctiliously to close the door, while Henry made a note on an order-form for all the supplies that Rische and Hook would require. He hesitated at the end of the list, and then wrote in '1 bott. whiskey'. He could forfeit that much towards his future.

Augusta said, 'I hope that is the first and last time you humiliate me in front of others.'

Henry folded the order-form, and looked at Augusta narrowly through the smoke of his cigar. 'You think I humiliated you?'

225

'Of course you did. I specifically asked you not to let those two miners take a share of the Little Pittsburgh; and what did you do? You made me look like a foolish and interfering woman with no right to say anything at all in her own home.'

Henry said, 'You're beginning to sound like a suffragist.'

'I think I should be able to express my opinion, don't you, even if I don't have a vote?'

Henry shrugged, and walked back through the store towards the beaded curtain.

'Don't you have anything to say at all?' Augusta asked him.

Henry stopped, and turned around. 'What do you want me to say? That you're right; and that I shouldn't have let those two dig up at Little Pittsburgh? Well, I'm not going to say it, because you're wrong. Even if they don't find anything, they won't have cost us more than twenty dollars and a few pounds of bacon. If they do, we can share in whatever it is they come across, copper or zinc, fair shares for all, in thirds.'

'But supposing they find *gold*,' said Augusta, quite shrilly.

Henry paused, and looked at her carefully. She was so agitated that she was twisting the bow around the front of her skirt, around and around, as if she were strangling a chicken.

'If they find gold,' said Henry, 'well, we could be rich.'

He stayed where he was, in spite of the fact that he could hear Jim Roelofs calling, 'Come on, Henry, we've finished all the damned beer; and now we want to finish this damned game.' He could sense that he was getting very close to what was really upsetting Augusta, like a dentist who approaches a nerve.

'Don't you *want* to be rich?' he asked her.

Augusta shook her head. 'Haven't you ever realized Henry, that I am more contented with this store; more contented with the baking I do; with my candies and my pies; with getting up at dawn and going to bed tired at night; with you; and with the life we lead; than any of the riches in the wide world, Comstock or Ophir or Deadwood Gulch? If those vagrants find gold, what will it ever do to us, except upset us, and disturb our happiness? I don't want it, Henry; I want everything to stay as it is. I want that deed-of-claim to remain in the bureau drawer, the same as ever, until we die.'

Henry felt as if someone had hit him, uncompromisingly hard, on the side of the head. When he had married Augusta, he had believed that they could very well be contented with each other; but he had never realized that Augusta had regarded their business at the post office and general store not just as a way of making a living, but as a mantrap of sorts, in which she could keep Henry constricted for the rest of his life. It was just as much his fault as it was hers, he supposed. In the past eighteen years, he had grown lazier and lazier, and spent more and more of his time playing poker with miners and drifters and assorted gamblers, winning a little, losing a little, and smoking cigars, and serving his customers with camp-kettles and pepper and gun caps; writing less and less frequently to Fenchurch, and allowing Augusta to run things the way she wanted, more or less, because of his belief that he was always in charge. He was still in charge, in a manner of speaking, because he still felt less for Augusta than she did for him; but he saw now that she would do anything to prevent him from interfering with the life that she had arranged for them both; and, as always, she had the advantage of caring for their marriage far more than he did.

He felt like an innocent, compared to her. She had been working desperately hard at keeping him for all of these eighteen years; while he had been sitting back and thinking of nothing at all, but how the years rolled by, and how they had never managed to have any children, and what was the price of flour.

She shocked him. He felt as if he had been sleeping for the past eighteen years. Where had he been, the day that California Gulch had received the news that Lincoln was dead? What had he been doing, when Plumb-Bobbs had come into the store, and announced with smelly grandiloquence that the Central Pacific and Union Pacific Railroads had at last met, and joined the continent, east to west, in Utah? And when Will Stevens came into town, that wet Saturday afternoon, three years ago, and leaned on the counter, and smiled, with rainspots on the shoulders of his buffalo-skin coat, and displayed in the palm of his hand the crumbly black sand which had proved to be the making of Leadville? He could see Will Stevens now, smiling, with bright brown eyes. 'Carbonate of lead, Mr Roberts, and I've had it assayed; two and a half pounds of silver to the ton.'

He was 43; and eighteen years had passed him by since Doris had died at the Bennington Fair. Eighteen years, all gone, like a dream. But now Augusta had suddenly woken him up: like someone who grasps a sleep-walker's arm to prevent him from falling.

He said, 'I very much doubt if they'll find anything, my dear. But I don't see the harm in them trying. Do you really think that a little extra money would affect us that much? You could have a refrigerator; and a six-hole stove; and we could have the rig revarnished. Now, what would be so disturbing about that?'

Augusta took an unsteady breath. 'Nothing, I suppose,' she replied. 'You must think that I'm being ridiculous.'

Henry came over and held her arms. 'Come on, my dear; you're not being ridiculous at all. You're overworked, that's the truth of it. Giving yourself too much to do.'

'Well, somebody has to do it,' she retorted, in a fraught voice. 'Somebody has to bake and sweep and stock the shelves.'

Henry was beginning to feel exasperated with her. But he knew what would happen if he raised his voice to her; and told her to stop being so self-pitying and contradictory. One minute she was saying that she didn't want their life at the store to be altered in any way: the next she was complaining because she had too much to do. But if he tried to point that out to her, she would burst into tears, which always made her look uglier than ever, and then she would sulk for days in silence, until he had given her some special little present, and sworn to her again and again that he loved her, and that he would never leave her, and that she was the finest-looking woman in Leadville.

'Maybe, if we had a little extra money, we could afford to hire some help,' said Henry.

Augusta looked away. 'I'd better finish the palm cookies,' she said.

'And then you'll pack up some supplies for Mr Rische?'

'I suppose so.'

Henry kissed her on the cheek. 'You're a good woman, Augusta.'

'Is that all?' she asked him, turning back. 'A good woman? You make me sound like your mother.'

Henry tried to smile, without much success, but couldn't think what to say. From the back parlour, Jim Roelofs called out, 'Are you coming there, Henry, old fellow; or do we fold the game and take it down to Brannigan's?' Henry nodded towards the beaded curtain to indicate to Augusta that he ought to go and join them, and Augusta said, 'Very well, then,' and

228

went off to the kitchen, where her pastry was rolled up, ready for cutting.

'You took your sweet time,' said Billy Coren. 'I've got 75 dollars riding on this hand.'

'I'm sorry,' said Henry, and sat down, and picked up his cards.

Jim Roelofs frowned at him. 'You look like you just saw a ghost.'

'It's nothing,' Henry told him. 'I was thinking, that's all.'

'Thinking? That's a damned painful pastime.'

Henry slowly fanned out his cards. 'Yes,' he said. 'It can be.'

They played for the rest of the afternoon, but Henry's mind wasn't on the game, and he lost 26 dollars. Augusta would be upset about that: she only tolerated his poker-playing as long as he didn't lose too much money. Otherwise, she said, what was the point of her breaking her neck to make pennies out of pies? Usually, he came out ahead. He was a good player, with a natural instinct for cards. But today the Colossal Whirler kept turning in his head, and Doris kept saying, 'It's perfect. The day, the fair, you,' and he could picture that cream and burgundy dress so clearly as the day she had worn it; and even see the sunlight on those stray curls at the side of her neck. And then he thought of Augusta, and all these years of married life; and how often he turned over at night and pretended to be sleeping so that he could ignore her hand on his hip and her whispered question, 'Henry?'

The sadness of his life almost overwhelmed him; and yet it was all his fault. Was this all it was ever going to be? Playing cards, and serving customers, and watching the sun come up and go down again, faster and faster with each successive year, like a flickering zoetrope? What had Nina said to him, that night in Denver? 'You are a man who carves epitaphs, and always will be.'

He had just poured out a fresh pitcher of beer when there was a knock on the corridor wall, and Nat Starkey came in, all dapper and smiling in a bright green suit. Nat ran Starkey's Tasteful Saloon & Billiard Heaven on Second Street, and had long been a friend of Henry's, ever since the first days of the silver rush in '75. 'Afternoon, gents,' he said. 'How's life in hell?'

'Take a seat, Nat,' said Henry. 'There's beer in the jug, and a glass on the dresser.'

229

'Well, don't mind if I do,' replied Nat, and dragged up a chair and straddled it.

'Having a quiet afternoon?' Henry asked him.

'Not exactly. In fact, exactly the opposite. That's what I come to see you about.'

'Oh, yes?'

'It's them billiard balls you sold me, them newly-devised ones.'

'The Celluloid ones. What about them?'

'Well, darn it, every time one of my customers drops one on the floor, which is pretty darn often, if they're drinking steady, the darn thing explodes like a bomb. Bang! Just like that! The first time I heard it I nigh on shat myself.'

Henry laid down his cards, and told Jim Roelofs, 'I'm not,' then to Nat Starkey, 'Listen, you tell me how many explode, and I'll send back to J.W. Hyatt's for more.'

'Henry, it isn't the balls I'm worried about, it's the saloon. Every time one of them things goes off, every manjack in the whole darn place whips out his gun and hits the floor. Two shots fired already; and one of them broke a mirror.'

Later, as evening settled over the Colorado Rockies, Henry took a walk with Nat Starkey back along Chestnut Street to the Tasteful Saloon, on the pretext of inspecting his Celluloid billiard balls. In fact, he simply wanted to get away from the store and stretch his legs and think. As they walked along the boarded sidewalk in the grainy rose-coloured half-light, with waggons creaking and bouncing over the roadway beside them, Nat said good-naturedly, 'You seem glum, Henry. Never seen you so morbid.'

'I don't know,' said Henry. The mountain air was growing slightly chillier, and he pushed his hands into his pockets. There was a smell of pines in the air, and dust, and frying chicken. 'Did you ever wake up one day and look around you and think, what the hell am I doing here?'

'Every single day, Henry,' Nat declared. 'Every single day. Why, what's the matter?'

'Nothing. Just a mood I guess.'

'You're not having trouble with Augusta?'

Henry shook his head. 'I don't know. It's not what you'd call trouble.'

'She's a good woman, Henry. You won't find better.'

230

'I know. I think that's probably what's wrong. I sometimes feel like I need a bad woman. One with a bit of fire in her.'

They reached the entrance to the Tasteful Saloon, engraved-glass doors and fluted red-oak pillars. Through the window, Henry could see miners and gamblers laughing and smoking; and as Nat opened the door, cigar smoke whipped around it like an escaping ghost, mingled with piano music, and the high clear voice of a girl singing 'Over The River'.

'Last night I slept, last night I dreamed,
That life was running like a stream,
And that my love spanned o'er this tide,
Just like a bridge, from side to side. . . .'

Nat said, 'She's a nice girl, Sylvia. You'd like her. Plenty of fire, if it's fire you're after.'

Henry replied, 'Thanks, Nat, but no. I don't think that's going to solve anything. I think in fact I've left it eighteen years too late.'

Nat took hold of his shoulder, and squeezed it, and said, 'Listen, every man gets to feel offish, after he's been married for a while. Take a walk; have a few drinks. Get yourself into a card game. Go home late and roll into bed drunk and have an argument. Make an argument: tell Augusta she don't know shit from sarsaparilla. That's what I always do, when I'm feeling down. Because when the argument's forgotten about; and you've gotten over your hangover; the making-up is marvellous.'

'Supposing you don't *want* to make up?' asked Henry. 'Supposing you're looking for an excuse to walk out of the house and never come back?'

Nat paused, half in and half out of the saloon door. 'Is that the way you feel?' he asked. 'Naw, come on, Henry; not about Augusta. You and Augusta, the perfect couple, that's what Binnie always calls you. A marriage made in heaven. Maybe you're just bored.'

'Maybe I am,' said Henry.

He left Nat standing by the door of the saloon, and walked southwest along Chestnut Street, passing the Congregational Church, and then crossing over towards the Grand Hotel. Since Will Stevens had discovered that the soil beneath the gulch was so rich in silver, Leadville had prospered and expanded, and

231

now there were four churches, 60 saloons, over 80 gambling-houses, and more whores than anybody could count. In between, there were ramshackle huts, stone-built villas, stables, silver-mines, stores, and restaurants. The *Leadville Chronicle* proudly reported that 'we live in a community in which "Anything Goes".'

He carried on walking through the gathering evening to the small crowded street in the 300 Block that the locals called 'Paradise Alley'. It was here, on warm evenings like this, that the good-time girls clustered; dressed in their bustles and their lace and their bodices so low that one observer had said, 'one felt that they might put their leg through and step out of them.'

He chose the left-hand boardwalk; and was whistled and cooed at by girls from every window and doorway. Some of them recognized him, because they were customers at the bank; but none of them called out his name. It was all, 'come here, darling,' or 'kiss me, my dove.'

He stopped by a doorway where three girls were sitting on dining-chairs which they had taken out on to the boardwalk so that they could share a drink of whiskey and some evening air. They were all dressed in silks, of blues and bronzes and pale greens, with ruffles and ribbons and tassels; and each one of them had her hair fashionably tonged into tight circular curls. Their shoulders were bare; and their bosoms were cupped in lace, although one of them, the prettiest, had allowed her bodice to slip so low that her small pink nipples were exposed. Henry stood beside the girls, and touched his hat, and said, 'Evening, ladies. How's business?'

The pretty one sat up straight, and looked back at him with a slanting, defiant smile. She was bright blonde, with brown eyes, and a heart-shaped face. She couldn't have been very much older than sixteen or seventeen; and it was quite possible that she was younger. One of the brothels in Leadville boasted that not a single one of its fifteen girls was older than twelve. On the street corners, Henry had seen children who looked as young as nine; but there were rarely any takers. At that age, they were usually bait to lure a drink-fuddled miner into a back alley; where an outraged 'mother' would suddenly appear, and threaten to have the man arrested if he didn't instantly pay $20 consideration, and swear on the Book of Deuteronomy that he would never molest young girls again.

'It's early yet,' the blonde girl said. 'Most of the customers is window shopping, just now. It's later they'll come a-calling, when they've won a few dollars; or downed a quart of Old Sourmash. One fellow tells his wife he's walking the dog, and leaves the poor mutt tied up to the end of the bed, and it always howls something awful.'

'What's your name?' Henry asked her.

'Charity, what's yours?'

'Henry.'

'Well, well. Would you care for a drink, Henry?'

Henry looked at her for a long moment, eye to eye. He had the strongest feeling that she knew what was unsettling him; that she could sense quite clearly the disappointment and frustration that racked him like a toothache. He lowered his eyes then, and looked at her breasts, white as firm blancmanges; the areolas crinkled by the coolness of the breeze. Unhurriedly, provocatively, she lifted her bodice so that she was covered, one breast after the other; but all the time she kept her eyes fixed on him.

He accepted a drink, a small tot of stingingly harsh whiskey; and then he said, to all of the girls. 'What would you do, if you were me?'

The other two girls hooted with amusement, and one of them replied, 'Cut my moustache off, straight away, and no mistake.' But the blonde girl said in a quiet and knowing voice, 'I would keep my peace when at home; and do what I wanted when abroad.' Then she winked at Henry, slowly and obviously, and helped herself to some more whiskey.

'You don't even know what my problem is,' Henry told her.

She smiled. 'Every man has the same problem. There's only one problem in the whole world, and every man has it.'

'So, you're a philosopher,' said Henry.

'Not me,' she told him. 'All I do is straight sex; or gamming, if you want it, for five dollars more.

Henry put down his glass. 'Thanks for the drink,' he said, gently; and reached into his pocket and gave her a dollar. She took it into the palm of her hand, twirled her fingers, and it had disappeared.

'That's a good trick,' said Henry.

'Oh, I can do better than that,' she smiled. 'One man whose name you know gives me silver dollars, one by one, as many as I can walk across the room with, without them falling out.'

Henry amused, said, 'Goodnight,' and walked on; past the

crowded cribs and the cheap hotels and the $5 bawdy-houses; and now the night was beginning to stir with music and laughter and the sound of miners' boots drumming along the boardwalks; as well as roulette wheels clattering and dice tumbling. He found himself at last outside The Opportunity Saloon, a long low building crowded with prospectors and loafers and gamblers, and went inside.

There was a long pine bar, behind which were clustered dozens and dozens of elk's antlers; and enough bottles of whiskey to incapacitate the whole of Colorado for a week. The low room was unbreathable with thick cigar smoke, and crowded with pine tables, on which men were playing faro and poker and rummy. At one table, a pointy-nosed fellow in a tight city hat was rattling away at three-card monte. 'Here you are, gentlemen; this ace of hearts is the winning card. Watch it closely, follow it with your eyes as I shuffle. If you point it out the first time you win; but if you miss you lose. I take no bets from paupers, cripples, or orphan children. The ace of hearts. It is my regular trade, gentlemen, to move my hands quicker than your eyes. The ace of hearts. Who's going to go me twenty?'

Henry went to the bar and the barkeeper brought him a bottle of whiskey without even being asked for it. Henry paid, and filled up his glass, and drank. Everybody in a Western bar filled up his glass to the brim, because it was the accepted practice for the customer to pour his own; and each drink cost the same, no matter how full it was. Henry drank three, straight down, and then took his time over the fourth. A fat man in a striped shirt sat at the piano, and began to play 'The Girl I Left Behind Me.'

A lugubrious miner with a beard which he had parted in the middle and tied around the back of his neck leaned on the counter close to Henry, and said, 'If I don't strike paydirt tomorrow; tomorrow definite; I'm going to leave this goddamned town and head west. Due west, no stops; not for Mormons nor Indians nor nothing. You know what they've got at Calistoga, in California? Gold, in the water. Five dollars' worth the bucketful. All you have to do is strain it out.'

'Sure,' said Henry, 'and they've got gold in the air, too. Blowing in the wind. All you have to do is hang out a muslin sheet, and you'll catch yourself pounds of it.'

The miner peered at him with mottled eyes. 'Is that a fact?

You mean, you just hang out a muslin sheet, and that's all? No digging, no rocking, no nothing?'

'Help yourself to a drink, friend,' said Henry, and passed him the bottle.

Henry walked back to his store and post office very drunk. He was whistled at by whores, and propositioned by two seedy old panhandlers, but he took no notice, and plodded as steadily as he could manage along the street which led out towards California Gulch, and the two-storey building which for nearly twenty years he had been calling his home. Outside it took him a long time to find the right key; but at last he pushed open the door with a jangling of bells, and slammed it behind him with a juddering bang.

'Lock it,' he told himself blurrily, and locked it. Then he edged with exaggerated caution across the floor of the darkened store, shuffling his way between cracker-barrels and pot-bellied stoves and rows of kerosene lamps; hesitated; then dived through the glass-bead curtain, and stumbled into the corridor which led to the back parlour. He leaned against the wall on which the etching of President Lincoln hung, and allowed himself two or three deep breaths before attempting the stairs.

At that moment, however, Augusta appeared, in her long white nightgown. Henry jumped, and shouted out, and almost lost his balance, and toppled over.

'God damn it, you scared me! I thought you were a ghost!'

She stood halfway down the stairs, in darkness, looking at him. All he could see of her face was the occasional glint of light from her spectacles.

'You're drunk,' she said. Her voice was curiously tight, as if she were just about to burst into tears.

He glowered at her. 'Drunk?' he said, theatrically, swinging his arm. 'I have never been drunk in my life. Ever! And never wish to be. All you are witnessing now is a slight unsteadiness caused by grief.'

'Grief?' she said, cuttingly. 'What grief have you ever suffered?'

He covered his hand with his mouth. He was beginning to wonder if he was going to be sick. He had drunk nearly a fifth of whiskey, all on his own, and it was gliding and burning around in his stomach like oil, and giving off fumes that seemed to cling in the hairs of his nostrils and filter through the substance of his brain. God, he thought, if you were to wring out

235

my brain now, like a sea-sponge, you could pour it back in a glass, and drink it all over again. He belched at the thought of it.

Augusta said, 'You'd better go to bed.'

'That shounds – that *sounds* – as if you expect me to go to bed alone.' He beamed at her, and then immediately stopped beaming. Augusta was not the kind of wife who could be beamed at.

'I do expect you to go alone,' replied Augusta. 'I am not sleeping with a drunk. I can make up a bed for myself on the ottoman downstairs, and that will be quite adequate, thank you. In any case, I have to be up in three hours, to start the baking.'

'You mean to say . . .' said Henry, knowing all the time that he shouldn't be saying anything; that he should go to bed and keep quiet and wait until the morning, '. . . you mean to say. . . that you are denying me. . . the delights. . . .'

'Delights?' snapped Augusta. 'What on earth are you talking about?'

'The delights of your body, my dear! Your belly and your bum and all your other inestimable parts! Surely that is what we were married for, wasn't it? Not for children, obviously not, for we've never had any; although I dare say we could have tried harder. Not for money. Ho no! Certainly not for money! No, my love, we married for lust! Didn't we? Or didn't we? Or am I being objectionable? I see from your face that you think that I'm being objectionable.'

'Yes,' said Augusta. 'You're being objectionable.'

Henry nodded. 'You're right. I am. I'm drunk. I'm probably going to be sick, which will compound my disgustingness. But, what can a fellow do? H'm? Answer me that? The problem is universal, all men have it, and so do I. In eighteen years, I have never been able to escape it.'

'Go to bed,' Augusta commanded.

'No,' replied Henry, petulantly.

'You're revolting,' she said. 'I've never seen you like this. How could you?'

Henry swayed a little nearer to her. 'My dear,' he said, 'the reason why you have never seen me like this is because for eighteen years I have been asleep.'

'Go to bed,' she repeated. 'I won't hear any more of this.'

'Asleep!' he roared, at the top of his voice. 'Asleep, and damn well dreaming! A whole life gone by, dreaming! Damn you, Augusta, I've been asleep, tucked up in bed, like a child, or a cripple, or a lunatic! George Hook has had a better life than me! Damn it to hell, Augusta, damn it to hell, damn it to hell! I've been asleep!'

He beat his fists against the banisters, again and again and again, until they thundered. And then he bent double with his fist clenched tight and screeched so hard that he felt as if he were tearing the skin off his throat, 'Damn it to hell, Augusta! Damn all of it! Damn it to hell!'

She came down the last few stairs and tried to put her arms around him; but after this outburst he was quite calm. He pushed her away unsteadily and mounted the stairs himself, missing the second one, but managing with reasonable dignity to get to the top. Augusta stood in the corridor watching him with tears in her eyes. When he had reached the landing he turned around and looked down at her; and he knew then with chilly sobriety that he disliked her, very much. Not so much that he would do anything to harm her; not so much that he could leave her without any conscience; because after all it wasn't her fault that she was so plain; and that she felt so dependent on him; but enough to wish that there were some way in which he could be free of her; and that he would never again have to wake up in the morning and see her featureless white face lying on the pillow next to him, with those unplucked eyebrows, and that unbecoming bump on the bridge of her nose, and that open, dry-lipped mouth.

She said, 'Henry, I know you're drunk. Forgive me.'

'Forgive you? Why should I forgive you? What have you done?'

She came halfway up the stairs and held out her hand like a character in a stage romance, *The Fatal Wedding*, or *For Her Children's Sake:* 'If you strike my mother, I shall shoot!' Henry looked at her hand, and then turned away, shaking his head. The whiskey was churning around and around in his stomach like dirty washing; that, and the minced-beef pie that Augusta had given him for lunch. He said, 'I don't think I feel well enough for melodrama, Augusta,' and then he marched quickly into the bedroom, took the blue floral water-jug out of the basin on the washstand, and vomited into it noisily.

Augusta watched him from the doorway, half-disgusted,

half-sorrowful. When he had finished, she said, 'If you want me, I shall be sleeping downstairs.'

Henry wiped chilly sweat from his forehead with the back of his hand. 'Want you?' he said, but not loud enough for Augusta to be able to hear.

NINE

He woke before dawn when she was still asleep, and shaved by the light of the kerosene-lamp beside the bed. Then he dressed in a blue broadcloth suit, rubbed his moustache vigorously with Bellezaire brilliantine, and meticulously combed his hair. The sky outside was just beginning to fade into daylight as he packed his brown leather portmanteau with a spare coat and pants, two clean shirts, and two pairs of long johns; as well as socks, razor, and soap.

He made no attempt to go down the staircase quietly. If she woke up and asked where he was going, then he would tell her, but he would still go. But when he looked into the parlour, she was still huddled up on the ottoman, her mouth open, covered by a horse-blanket. He closed the door, and went through to the store, where he tore a page out of the order book, with the intention of writing her a note. But his pencil remained poised over the paper for almost a minute on end. He couldn't even bring himself to write the word 'Dear'; and so he crumpled up the torn page and tossed it into the shavings-barrel.

Outside, in the chilly mountain air, he began to feel distinctly grey, and very weary. If he hadn't been so determined to leave; and if he hadn't already packed; he probably would have gone back into the house and gone back to bed, to wake up later to hot coffee and crackled bacon and hashed potatoes, and sorrow, too.

But he harnessed up Belinda, their best grey mare; and then led her out of the dusty yard into the street, where he stood breathing fog as he mounted her; and then he rode out of Leadville while it was still silent and rimed with dew, a rough and ready town of smoke and mist and half-finished buildings. The dream continues, he thought to himself. Will I ever really wake up? Or will I dream until I die?

It took him most of the day to ride through the mountains to Denver. Through the pine trees, the sky was as blue as laundry. He planned to spend the night in Denver, and then take the narrow-gauge Denver & Rio Grande Railroad north-wards to Cheyenne, and change on to the transcontinental Union Pacific line for Omaha, and Council Bluffs. The days of waggon-trains and independent scouts like Edward McLowery were long since over; and even though the Sioux were still being troublesome in Dakota, travellers across the plains scarcely ever saw an Indian, let alone suffered a scalping.

Henry reached Denver early in the evening, when the city's gas-lights were just being lit, hundreds of tiny amber pinpricks sprinkled across the plain. Since he had first arrived here eighteen years ago, Denver had changed and grown beyond recognition. In the Spring of 1863, the whole of the town centre had been gutted by a ferocious fire started at the Cherokee Hotel; and in the spring of 1864, which had been as thunder-ously wet as the spring of the previous year had been dry, Cherry Creek had burst its banks and drowned 20 people, as well as causing over a million dollars' worth of damage. William Byers' *Rocky Mountain News* building, printing-presses and everything, had been completely swept away.

Since then, however, Denver had prospered: as the capital of the newly-established state of Colorado, and as the clearing-house for gold and silver, coal and iron, and the centre through which all of the state's farm produce and cattle were funnelled. The extravagant mansions of the rich were everywhere: the stone castle of John Edward Good, the pillared white marble creation of David Moffat, the house owned by real-estate king Charles Kitteredge, in which over a hundred people could be seated in the dining-room; and the palace of silver-miner Sam Hallett, whose wife Julia wrote her letters on a desk that had once belonged to Marie Antoinette. Solid gold doorknobs and solid silver bathtubs were so commonplace as not to be remark-able. The streets of Denver were served by horse-drawn streetcars; and forested with telegraph-poles; and almost every house was connected to mains water, brought up from deep artesian wells. Already, several of the richer houses were being connected up to the telephone.

Henry rode into the yard of the Front Range Hotel, where he usually stayed whenever he visited Denver, which was once or twice a year. The groom took Belinda, and the porter took his baggage, and he stiffly limped into the lobby to sign himself into a room. It was a warm evening, although a light wind was blowing over the mountains; and the first thing he did was to take a long hot bath. Augusta would be closing the store by now; putting out the lights, locking the takings in the safe, drawing down the calico blinds. He stood by the window and looked down into the street and smoked a cigar; and thought about Augusta with regret. But he knew that something had been awoken within him which would never again be quieted.

He dressed, and went down to the hotel restaurant for a supper of beef and home-fried potatoes. Then he hailed a horse-drawn tram and took the ride out to Brown's Bluff, where William Byers was living these days. Byers had sold the *Rocky Mountain News* only a month ago; with the intention of taking it easy for a while; but Henry had heard from their mutual friend Alvinus B. Wood that he was already fretting and trying to think up new ways of making money, not to mention new ways of industriously refusing to mind his own business.

Brown's Bluff was the local nickname for the high ground south east of the city; once the 160–acre homestead of builder Henry Brown. It was here that most of Denver's newly-wealthy citizens had settled and built their mansions, and the one-horse tram toiled up the hill between rows of elegant fences and stone sphinxes and wrought-iron gates.

Henry sat at the back of the tram, next to a giggly young couple who were just coming home from a party and a tired-faced woman who must have been a cook or a maid at one of the richer mansions. The tram reached the top of the Bluff, and everybody climbed out. From here, the tram would roll back down the hill again, with the horse riding on the rear platform, and the conductor steering and braking the vehicle from the front.

William Byers lived in a square, prosperous mansion of grey dressed granite, with rows of bright green bay trees standing in tubs on either side of the front path. There was a warm light shining from the parlour window, and as he walked up to the front door, Henry could see the back of William's head, as he sat in a chair talking.

The door was opened by the Byers' black butler Giltspur; who took Henry's hat and coat and showed him into the hallway. William came out almost immediately, a puffier and squatter-looking man than the young newspaper owner whom Henry had first met in Denver eighteen years ago, but still forceful and still direct and still undeniably charming. Henry had been friends with him, on and off, ever since he had moved out to Leadville. Henry's store had at one time been the only outlet in the district for the *Rocky Mountain News*, and Henry had taken advertisements for it and passed on mail and advertising revenue. William had even written an article about Henry's store and called it 'The Aladdin's Cave of Leadville.'

'Henry, this is unexpected!' William enthused, pumping his hand. 'I'm afraid we've eaten already; but there's some cold sausage if you're hungry, and I'm sure that Mary's got some soup.'

'It's all right, thank you,' said Henry. 'I ate at the Front Range. I'm sorry if I've interrupted anything. I can always come by tomorrow.'

'Not at all! Come on in, there are two gentlemen here that I'd like you to meet!'

Henry followed William into the huge, decoratively-carpeted parlour. The room was less crowded with statuettes and pianos and trailing plants than some of the houses on Brown's Bluff; but all the same it was very fashionably over-furnished with gigantic leather-covered armchairs, and potted ferns, and small tables covered with fringed velveteen cloths, and lamps, and cushioned stools, and a disproportionately enormous bust of Plato. Elizabeth Byers was sitting by the fireplace in a dark green lace-collared dress, looking dignified but rather duck-like, which she always did when she pursed her lips. By the window, with his hands clasped behind his back, stood a short, curly-haired man with a fresh, European appearance, and wildly sprouting side-whiskers. Sitting beside him, his legs crossed, smoking a pipe, was a darkly suntanned man of about 36, one of those cheerful, confident, pugnacious characters who look as if they can always top whatever anybody else has to say with a better story of his own.

241

The curly-haired man came forward, and bowed, and held out his hand.

'Henry, this is Baron Walter von Richthofen,' said William. 'The baron is thinking of building a kind of resort village, on the southern outskirts of town. With a spa, perhaps, and a beer garden.'

'What you might call Carlsbad in Colorado,' beamed the baron.

'And this is Mr Henry M. Stanley,' said William. 'You should know him by repute, if nothing else.'

'I'm honoured to meet you,' said Henry, shaking Stanley's hand. 'I thought you spent most of your days in Africa.'

'I expect to return next year,' replied Stanley, with an affable smile. 'But meanwhile I thought that I might explore the wilds of darkest Denver.'

'I've been talking to Mr Stanley about a steamer service along the Platte River,' William explained. 'A side-wheeler, perhaps, docking at Riverfront Park, and plying its way between Denver and the Missouri.'

'Is the Platte navigable, Mr Stanley?' asked Henry. 'I always thought it was too silted, and too shallow.'

'Well, I went down it once,' Stanley replied. 'That's one of the reasons your friend Mr Byers wanted me here today. And I'm sure if *I* can do it, then anybody can do it.'

'Oh, Mr Stanley, you're being too modest,' put in Elizabeth.

'I should say so,' laughed von Richthofen. 'The only man who could find Dr Livingstone was you. You can't expect everyone to be so daring.'

Giltspur brought in a silver tray with a decanter of wine, and poured a glass for each of them; although Stanley asked if he might have a glass of water as well, so that he could take his quinine powders. Then they sat and talked about the baron's plans for building himself and his wife an enormous Germanic castle as the centrepiece of his new suburb, and stocking the grounds with bears and wild boar and canaries.

'Imagine the delights of such a place,' von Richthofen exclaimed, slapping his tightly-trousered thigh. 'To sail by steamer all the way across the plains and into Denver, and then to come by carriage to a healthful mountain resort with every conceivable attraction! We shall be millionaires a hundred thousand times over!'

Later, Henry said to Stanley, 'I'm sure you've been asked

this question a thousand times before, but what did you actually say to Dr Livingstone when you first met him?'

Stanley was lighting his pipe. He sucked at it studiously for a moment or two, and then he blew out his match and settled back in his chair and laughed. 'Only about a dozen people in the whole world know the secret of that, apart from David Livingstone and myself, and James Gordon Bennett, of the *New York Herald*, who sent me to find Livingstone in the first place. Both Livingstone and I decided it should be reported as having been very calm, and very dignified, almost offhand. But in fact when I arrived in Ujiji, we simply clung on to each other and burst into tears.'

He paused, and then he said, 'I know that many people have accused me of being a publicity-seeker, and of gilding my exploits with exaggerated language. But none of those who criticize me have ever been to the jungles of Africa; and seen for themselves the wonders and the horrors of which that continent is almost equally composed.'

At midnight, Elizabeth curtseyed, and retired, and William handed round cigars. The four men smoked and talked of business, and money, and how Denver could one day become the financial and cultural capital of the west; more prominent than Chicago, more sophisticated than San Francisco, a shining city of wealth and health.

'You're a storekeeper, aren't you, Mr Roberts?' Stanley asked him.

'That's right,' said Henry. 'Stoves, dried beef, blankets, and a little banking, too.'

'Banking?' asked Stanley, waving aside a curl of smoke. 'Well, now, that sounds interesting.'

'I'm afraid that it isn't, in particular,' Henry told him. 'I only do it to protect those of my customers who would either lose their money, or drink it, or gamble it away.'

'Still, a bank is a bank,' said Stanley, and looked at William, who nodded slowly, as if this cryptic remark meant something of particular interest to him. Baron von Richthofen said, 'You're right, Mr Stanley. A bank is a bank, and the further away it is, the more of a bank it becomes. What is known in Leadville to be a general store, with stoves, dried beef and blankets, can be represented in New York and Chicago as a very solid financial institution; and in London and Berlin as a counting-house to rival Rothschild.'

Henry said, 'I don't quite see what you're getting at.'

'Well, nothing, not really,' smiled Stanley. 'The baron here is just remarking on the way in which distance lends enchantment to almost anything, including banks. We have been having some difficulty, you see, in finding a bank here in Denver to handle all the funds which our foreign and Eastern investors will be putting into our paddle-steamer enterprise, and into the baron's resort.'

'What's wrong with the First National?' asked Henry.

William made a face, and shrugged. 'David Moffat's all right, but he's always been too inquisitive, and to finance an enterprise like this, you have to move your funds around in rather unorthodox ways – ways of which I am quite certain David would not approve, for all that he was once a bankrupt himself.'

Baron von Richthofen laughed; a short, sharp, shout of a laugh, and then leaned forward to slap William in amusement on the knee.

'What do you mean by unorthodox?' asked Henry.

Stanley puffed out pipe smoke. 'Nothing worse than gambling with it a little; using some of it to buy up land; or mining stocks; and then selling them again to make a little extra profit. Nothing that a normal respectable bank doesn't do every single day of the year, except more ponderously.'

'But surely your investors will expect guarantees against that kind of use of their money? After all, you might make an extra profit; but on the other hand you might not.'

Stanley said, 'You're quite right. But it we advertise honestly for money, and people send it to us, then what can we possibly do? It is not as if we are robbing them at gunpoint. Yes, some may ask for a guarantee, but we are making no secret of the fact that to build the baron's village and to provide the Platte River with a steam-boat service are very risky enterprises, and that they might not see a return on their money for several years. You cannot help natural greed, Mr Roberts; neither can you do anything about natural stupidity.'

'*Mit der Dummheit kämpfen Götter selbst vergebens*,' Baron von Richthofen grinned. 'Against stupidity, even God wages war in vain. It would be a crime not to take advantage of people's naiveté. It would not be healthy.'

Henry eased himself back in his chair. He glanced from William to Baron von Richthofen to Henry Stanley, and he began to see why rich men got rich, and stayed that way.

Whether they were really planning to navigate the South Platte or not; whether they would really build a Germanic castle out at Mountclair or not, he found it impossible to judge. Perhaps they would: they both sounded like profitable ideas. But quite nakedly, these three gentlemen's first objective was to muster up as much capital as they possibly could, and put it somewhere accessible, where not too many difficult questions would be asked about whether it was being used both properly and legally.

'I suppose you're thinking that my little banking counter would be just the kind of depository that would suit you down to the spats,' he remarked, drawing on his cigar.

'You mean you're offering?' asked Stanley, as if the idea had never even occurred to him.

Henry glanced at William again, trying to seek at least a hint of reassurance. William said, 'It would certainly solve one of our most difficult problems. Of course, if it would cause you any inconvenience. . . .'

'Well, there shouldn't really be any inconvenience,' put in Stanley. 'Mr Roberts here would have to do very little more than sign the money in and out; and occasionally provide a certified statement to make our investors feel happy. Actually, all of this work could be done by one of your clerks, couldn't it, William? Mr Roberts would have to do nothing at all.'

'He would have to call himself something like the First Silver Bank of Leadville,' said William. 'And, of course, as bank president, he would have to be paid a reasonable salary, for appearance's sake.'

William turned to Henry and Henry knew then that he was being flagrantly bribed. The expression on William's face was calm and remote and non-committal, a poker-face *par excellence*, so that if Henry were to respond by saying no, the matter would be passed over without argument, and without recrimination.

William said, with his mouth as tight as a ventriloquist's doll, 'I thought one thousand dollars a year might do, to begin with.'

Eighteen hardscrabble years, thought Henry. Eighteen years of work and disappointment and tedium. Eighteen years of Augusta. Eighteen years that have left me 43 years old, and with nothing to show for my youth but a long-dead girl called Doris and a storeful of crackers and dried navy beans. And here tonight, in Denver, three famous and successful men are offering me one thousand dollars a year for doing nothing at all; and that's a deal that might lead to other deals; and more money. That fortune-teller had been right: I'll never make money by skill, nor by working, no matter how hard. The only way that I'll ever make money is by chance.

He said, 'I'm leaving for Council Bluffs tomorrow.'

'How long will you be there?' asked William. The baron began to fidget with his cigar, unwrapping the outside leaf and sticking it back again with spit. Stanley kept up an unrelenting smile, as if it were necessary for him to smile to stay alive. William said, 'You haven't had words with Augusta, have you?'

'Well, not exactly words,' said Henry. 'I guess we both get on each other's nerves sometimes, cooped up in that store in Leadville, with not very much else to do but drink, and serve customers, and count bags of corn-meal, and shout at each other.'

'She's a fine girl, Augusta,' said William.

'I never denied it,' Henry answered.

Stanley stood up, and walked around the back of his chair, raising his cigar-hand to move away the leaves of a hanging fern as he went past.

'You think about this, anyway, Mr Roberts,' he said, standing framed in the heavily-draped window, his cigar gripped between his teeth. 'You put your mind to what we've suggested. So, when you get back from Council Bluffs, you can drop in to see Mr Byers here and tell him yes or no. You won't be longer than a month, will you?'

Henry shook his head.

'That's excellent, then. I mean, you can send a telegraph from Council Bluffs if you wish, or a letter, but I think we'd prefer to keep this kind of arrangement verbal, if you know what I mean. In finance, a handshake is generally sufficient. Those who did it remember it; those who weren't there can never prove it.'

William clapped his hands smartly together, and wrung them in a quick gesture of satisfaction. 'Well, gentlemen,' he said, 'that appears to have been an extremely profitable evening, with no small thanks to *your* fortuitous visit, Henry. What say we open up the '72 cognac, and drink a toast or two.'

Giltspur was called for, and the brandy brought. It was almost one o'clock in the morning now, but they lit fresh cigars, and talked and told jokes. Stanley was quite unexpected, especially when he talked about Africa and David Livingstone.

For while he had plainly admired and respected Livingstone deeply, even loved him; and while he had dedicated several years of his life to completing Livingstone's explorations, and locating the source of the Nile, he could still speak amusingly about the old man's obsessions, and about his own mishaps as he travelled through what he always referred to as 'darkest Africa'.

'David Livingstone believed unshakeably that the Nile bubbled up out of four fountains, between two magic peaks called Crophi and Mophi. When he died, he still had with him a letter to Lord Russell with a complete description of how he had at last located the fountains. He had left gaps in the letter so that he could fill in the latitude and longitude when he actually got there. Poor dear old man, he was very sick towards the end. But one day in 1874, when I reached Lake Edward, south of the Mountains of the Moon, I happened to catch sight of four blackies standing on the shore, all of them relieving themselves into the lake. There! I said, David would be pleased with us, we've discovered them at last, the four sources of the Nile! And my companions laughed so desperately that we almost fell out of the boat.'

William coughed on his cigar; and even Baron von Richthofen had to smile.

'We shot them, of course,' said Stanley, matter-of-factly. 'Four shots with elephant guns, tremendous bangs they make.' He turned to Henry and smiled widely. 'I must have been wrong about them, of course, because even after they were dead, the Nile kept on flowing.'

Henry looked at William and frowned. He remembered reading that after Stanley's return from his last expedition, he had been widely censured in England for his ruthlessness, and the number of African aborigines he had slaughtered. And the matter of native massacres was still a highly sensitive point in Henry's long-standing association with William: ever since the Sand Creek massacre twelve years ago, in which 163 Cheyennes had been killed by Denver volunteers. It had been intended as a punishment for a spate of Indian attacks that had been hampering Denver's trade routes. But most of the Indian victims had been women and children, and the volunteers had scalped the women and sliced off their breasts. William had cheerfully called it a 'brilliant feat of arms', but Henry had been disgusted when he heard about it, and told William so, in one of the fiercest arguments they had ever had.

William could see tonight that Henry was not at all entertained by tales of shooting natives for the sport of it, and he clapped his hands together again, and said loudly, 'How about a game of poker before we turn in? Come on, Mr Stanley! Baron? How about you?'

Henry stood up. 'I have to get back to the hotel now, William. My train leaves at seven o'clock.'

'Surely one game of poker won't hurt? You can always sleep on the train!'

'No, no, thanks all the same,' said Henry. He shook Baron von Richthofen's hand, and then Stanley's; and said, 'I won't forget to let William know about the banking arrangements, Mr Stanley. It's been most interesting to meet you. When do you return to Africa?'

'Well, I'm not sure yet,' said Stanley, conscious that Henry had suddenly become much more abrupt, even prickly. He looked quickly at William, but all William could do was give him a scrambled smile that meant, I'll talk to you later, when Henry's gone.

William's black stable-boy Edwin drove Henry back to the Front Range Hotel in the family trap. It was a moonlit night, so with their usual thriftiness the lamplighters of Denver had been around to turn off the gas-lamps. Edwin said nothing all the way down the hill; and Henry was too tired to talk anyway. But when they were near to the Front Range Hotel, Edwin started to hum a sad Negro spiritual tune; and then to sing

'Lord, can't you hear me weeping
I'm crying out to You
My heart is filled with longing
And my eyes are filled with dew.'

And it would always seem to Henry in his memory that the low melancholy sound of Edwin's singing was interrupted not by their arrival at the hotel but by the wild shriek of the Union Pacific locomotive as it clanked into Cheyenne the following afternoon to pick up passengers for Omaha, Council Bluffs, and points east. It was a windy day out on the plains, and as the conductor shouted, 'Booaarrdd!' and the long transcontinental consist pulled slowly away from the depot, tumbleweeds and newspapers blew between its wheels, and the smoke fled from its bell-shaped stack as if someone were hurling coal-black cauliflowers, one after the other, towards the thundery-coloured horizon.

The train travelled at 20 miles an hour through a landscape of dry grass and threatening skies. In the far distance, a prairie fire was burning, lurid orange flames on the edge of the world. A good-looking woman in a green and white striped suit and a feathered hat sat opposite Henry, and smiled at him. Henry was still wondering what he should say to introduce himself when her husband came back from the observation car, where he had been having an outdoor smoke. He smiled at Henry too, and then held his wife's hand in one of those unconscious gestures of possessiveness.

It was late the following night before the train at last rumbled over the Missouri bridge, and hissed at a snail's pace into Council Bluffs. Henry was asleep, his head against the glass of the window. The woman in the green and white striped suit (who was now wearing a pale blue suit) touched him gently on the shoulder, and said, 'Sir, don't you get off here?'

'Doris?' he said. He could smell her perfume, feel her warmth. But then he opened his eyes and it wasn't Doris at all, just the two of them, husband and wife, sitting opposite him, smiling in their ownership of each other.

He climbed down from the train into the chilly night. A porter carried his bag for him, and led him through the gaslit depot to the yard outside where two sorry-looking cabs were waiting, their drivers shuffling and smoking and banging their hands together because of the cold.

'There's a house on the right-hand side of Depot Street, just past the druggist,' said Henry.

'You want to go there?' asked one of the cab-drivers, whose head was wrapped up like a swede in a scarf.

'That's the general idea.'

Henry climbed up on to the cracked leather seat, and the cab jerked and jolted uncomfortably as the driver turned it around in the yard, and then clicked at his horse to get walking. The town as they passed through it was completely silent, empty streets, darkened windows, deserted sidewalks, and hitching-rails where no horses were tied. Even the wind seemed to be silent, and the wheels of the cab. Henry felt that he must be visiting Council Bluffs in his sleep, or in his memory. It had changed, too, in the time that he had been away. There were solid new buildings, banks and offices brought by the prosperity of the trans-continental railroad, churches and stores. Here and there, in between the proud new brick buildings, one or two of the old wooden shacks still huddled, unpainted, looking shrunken with age; and he saw Deacon's Lunch Rooms, almost as it used to be, except that it was now Evans Stylish Restaurant. But the Old Misery Saloon was gone, and so was the druggist that he had remembered, and they had passed the small square building with the false facade and the outside staircase before he realized.

'Hey, stop, this is it!'

'This is what?'

'This is where I want to go.'

'Here? There ain't no drugstore here. Never has been.'

'Well, there was once.'

The driver sniffed, and spat into the roadway. 'Fifteen cents for you, two for the bag, five extra because it's past midnight. And I've been living in this dead-and-alive burg for ten years next Thanksgiving, and *I've* never seen no drugstore here.'

Henry climbed out of the cab and silently paid the driver a quarter. The driver waited for a minute or two, obviously curious to find out where Henry was going to go, at half after twelve on a breezy night in the derelict part of Depot Street. But Henry himself hardly knew where he was going: back into his memory or forward into his future. And he didn't know whether he ought to, either. Time changes more than faces, and buildings, and the texture of human skin.

At length, bored with hanging about, the cab-driver turned his rig around and clattered off slowly back towards the depot. Henry picked up his bag and crossed the street until he was standing at the foot of the wooden stairs. He could picture her now, a picture so clear in his mind that it almost made him ache, that small chubby girl in the white cotton nightdress, with the face like a painted German doll. Her hair wound up in rags, except for those two long plaits. And the way that her big breasts rose heavily beneath the cotton each time she lifted her arms to peg up her clothes, her nipples stiffened because of the morning wind.

'You're a bit early, aren't you?' she had said; and he had answered, 'Early for what?' And he could remember with sweet clarity the hot feeling of plunging himself deep between her

250

thighs, the room smelling pungently of sex and sweat and coffee.

Now that he had arrived here, he knew that he had made a mistake. She probably didn't even live here any more. She was probably dead. Golden-hearted or not, whores had short lives in the West; either from disease or drunkenness or crude abortions or suicide or violent customers. Julia Bulette, even though she was the favourite prostitute of Virginia City, in Nevada, had been strangled for her jewels a few years ago; and the Western newspapers were crowded every week with items about girls who had been flighty with a razor, or like 25–year-old Grace Fanshaw 'committed suicide by drinking laudanum during a fit of despondency brought on by blighted love, acute alcoholism, and bad investments.'

He climbed the stairs one by one, until he reached the rickety landing at the top. He hesitated again, but then he knocked loudly on the side of the door-frame; so loudly that he would be bound to wake her up, if she were there, and he would be committed to seeing her.

He waited for three whole minutes. He rubbed his hands to warm himself up, and shifted from one foot to the other, and sniffed because the cold had started his nose running. He was about to pick up his bag and go back down the stairs when a lamplight appeared through the curtained window in the door, and he heard feet dragging on the floor inside. The lamplight came very close to the door, and then an extraordinary voice called, 'Who's there? Is there anybody out there?' It sounded like a woman; but she seemed to have something over her head that distorted and muffled what she was saying.

Henry sniffed again, and cleared his throat, and then said, 'I'm looking for somebody who used to live here. A girl called Annabel.'

There was a long silence; and then at last Henry heard the bolts being nudged back, and a key turning. The door opened inwards, and so all he could see was a hand holding up an engraved-glass oil-lamp. He recognized the lamp with a peculiar shock as the same lamp that had stood on Annabel's bedside all those years ago. An offensive smell eddied out of the house, not just burning kerosene from the lamp, but stale food, and liniment, and some sweetish odour like urine-soaked clothing, only stronger. Henry stayed where he was, watching the hand holding the lamp.

251

'Do you know where Annabel is now?' he asked.

The strange voice hooted, 'Come in.'

'You don't know who I am.'

'It doesn't matter who you are. Come in.'

'Look, if Annabel isn't here, I don't really think – '

'Come in,' the voice insisted. And then, when Henry still hesitated, it said, 'She's here. Annabel's here. Never left; not ever.'

Henry took out his handkerchief, and blew his nose; but kept the handkerchief raised to his face to stifle some of the smell. He stepped cautiously in through the doorway, and into the small lobby which he remembered from before. Then he turned and looked at the woman who had so persistently invited him in.

She was a small, dwarfish figure, with grizzled grey hair. The lower part of her face was entirely smothered in a filthy white scarf, crusted with yellow. She was wearing a large Indian blanket wrapped around her, tied at the waist with a pair of old stockings. She looked less than half-human, and she stank appallingly, but to Henry's surprise the eyes which glittered above the face-bandage were alert and intelligent-looking.

'Come in,' said the woman, and led him into the parlour.

It was like a nightmare: a hideous denial of everything he had remembered. The occasional tables had gone, the chaise-longue had gone, the patent organ had been taken away to leave nothing but a mark on the wallpaper. Instead of lace and velvet at the windows, there were dirty lengths of calico, nailed into the frames. There was no carpet, no pictures, no tiger-skin. It was just a bare, cold, inhospitable cell; and it reeked of filth and medicine and slow suppurations that Henry couldn't even guess at.

'I think I'm going to have to go,' said Henry. Bile rose up in his throat and nastily flooded his mouth, and he had to swallow it again. 'I can't imagine Annabel living here. I'm sorry. It was all my fault. I shouldn't have woken you up.'

The eyes watched him above the face-bandage.

'Annabel is here,' the voice repeated.

Henry at last realized what she was telling him. He stood in the centre of the room and the cold crawled down his skin from head to toe as if he were connected to a slow, powerful, galvanic current. He couldn't bring himself to move: either to step towards her or to turn and run away. Because the horror of it was that not only had *she* been destroyed, her flesh and her beauty and everything she had once been; but one of Henry's most crucial beliefs had been destroyed with her. The secret belief that whatever happened, he could always go back to that hot, erotic morning; that if ever he left Augusta he could always find the same sly, provocative girl with the blue eyes and the soft, massive breasts, and the willing vagina that would open up for him whenever he wanted it. Destroyed: the memory and the fantasy and all the unspoken desire, like a bright sky-coloured window breaking into hundreds of pealing pieces.

He said, 'Annabel.'

Her eyes told him yes. Her voice said, with an odd thumping accompaniment, 'Which one are you? Did you ever have a name?'

'I visited you one morning. I didn't have any money.'

'No money? Did I throw you out?'

'No. You gave me coffee, and lace cookies.'

'Did we go to bed?'

He nodded. 'I remembered it all these years. I never forgot you.'

'Hmfff,' she breathed. She shuffled slowly across the room, and sat down on a broken bentwood chair. It was the only chair in the house, as far as he could see. The bedroom was in darkness, but he thought he could make out a heap of blankets in there, and an old flour-barrel.

'Everybody else forgot me,' she said.

Henry stood and watched her in silence. Far away, towards the depot, a train screamed. Union Pacific railroad, heading west.

'I was so beautiful, wasn't I?' Annabel said, not noticeably to Henry, but to someone behind the face-bandage. 'The men used to say that I looked like an angel. And a bosom, they said, like a mermaid. A mermaid who never saw the sea. Did I tell you that I've never seen the sea?'

'No, you didn't tell me,' said Henry. He was so depressed and yet so sickened that he didn't know whether he wanted to weep or choke. He knew that he wouldn't be able to stay here for very much longer.

'I was beautiful, wasn't I?' Annabel asked him, directly this time.

'Yes,' he said.

253

'The doctor gave me salts of mercury,' she told him. 'I don't take them now. I want to die, that's all. There isn't any point in living unless you're beautiful. My mouth is all full of sores; I can hardly walk. There are so many swellings between my legs I can't bear the pain of cleaning myself. All I want to do is die; but somehow I don't.'

She peered at him. 'What did you say your name was?'

'Henry.'

'Ah, Henry,' she snuffled. She thought for a while, and then she said, 'If I asked you, Henry, would you kill me?'

He swallowed. Even his saliva seemed to taste of her sickly decaying smell. 'No,' he said.

'If I begged you?'

He shook his head. 'You should take the salts of mercury. Some people are cured.'

'Hmmfff,' she said.

Without saying anything else, Henry took a gold ten-dollar eagle out of his wallet, and held it up so that Annabel could see it. Then he bent down and laid it carefully on the floor. He had heard how contagious syphilis could be; and he preferred to offend her, rather than catch it himself. She made no attempt to approach him, or to come forward and pick the coin up. He waited for one moment longer, and then turned around and walked quickly through the lobby, picked up his bag, opened the door, and was cantering down the outside stairs before he could allow himself to think what a coward he might be. He crossed the street, and began to stride back towards the depot, taking in deep breaths of cold night air, and shivering as he went.

On the corner, he turned around, and looked back. It was an eerie sight, that old-fashioned square-built Iowa house, under a sky that was luminous with hidden moonlight, with the muffled white figure of Annabel standing on the top of the stairs, watching him run away from her. He carried on walking, so fast that he was almost dog-trotting.

He walked as far as the Pottawattamie Hotel; or at least as far as the lot where the Pottawattamie Hotel had once stood. Now it had been replaced by a large brick-built hardware store, with shuttered windows, and enamelled advertisements for Henry H. Taylor's famous graining combs, and Seroco Floor Oil. Not far away, a clock struck one, and here he was standing on a strange street in Council Bluffs, cold and shocked, and

254

exiled from his own past by eighteen years that had gone by in reality, but not in his mind. But Mrs Newall had vanished, and so had Dat Apple, and the hidey-hole where they had laughed and eaten bacon.

Hefting up his bag again, he went back to the depot. The cab-drivers had gone now, and he was glad of that. He was humiliated enough by what he had tried to do without being stared at by insolent locals. He went into the waiting-room where the cast-iron stove had died out, but still retained some of its warmth, and he huddled himself up on a varnished wooden form and tried to doze.

It was a long, uncomfortable night. At four o'clock in the morning, a long goods train clattered and clashed into the sidings, and for the next ninety minutes, brakemen whistled and shouted as they broke the train up and connected new waggons. There was no hope of sleeping, so Henry went outside into the cold to watch them disconnecting the link-and-pin couplings, and marshalling the rolling-stock around with the grinding of brakes and the colliding of buffers. He struck up a conversation with one of the brakemen, a laconic Pennsylvanian with a mouthful of chewing-tobacco, and after the train had been made up, he was invited into the huge roundhouse to share a cup of hot stewed coffee and a smoke.

'Aside from fighting bears in nothin' but your long johns, being a brakeman is the world's most dangerous job,' the fellow told him, as the sun began to shine through the roundhouse windows as softly as if it were shining into a dark, greasy cathedral. 'Gettin' yourself pinned between the cars, that's the favourite. Friends of mine chopped in half, couldn't count 'em. Then there was Smith, he was a real close pal, never even knew his first name, neither. Last month he was workin' on a bridge, and a runaway locomotive comes wallopin' down the track, and there ain't no way he's goin' to outrun that locomotive down a 200–yard bridge, so he lays his neck on the rail just to make it quick.'

Henry had breakfast at the station when the depot diner opened. He sat alone at the end of the counter eating corned-beef hash and drinking coffee while a bustling woman in a long white apron polished up her glasses, and her cups and her urns, and occasionally flicked her tea-towel at the ears of her young black assistant, telling him to 'get some steam up,

Thomas.' Then Henry took up his bag again and ordered a cab to take him to Edward McLowery's house.

The house was gone, demolished and replaced by a savings bank. But Henry went to the saloon at the corner of the street, a dark smoky room which looked as if it might be the kind of place where Edward would have gone drinking; and he asked the portly proprietor if he knew where Edward was living these days. 'McLowery,' he said, everybody knew him; thin as a garden-rake; an old-time waggon-train guide.'

'Sure,' said the saloon proprietor. 'He used to come in here more or less every afternoon. I knew him, Edward McLowery. Died four years ago; that cough of his got him during the winter. Think it was four years ago, could have been five.'

Henry found Edward's grave-marker in the unkempt grass of the Episcopalian Church on the eastern side of the city. It was the simplest of stones, not more than seven or eight dollars' worth, and the lettering was poorly chiselled. It said nothing more than 'Edward Harold McLowery, Gone To God.' No date, no message of love or sympathy, just 'Gone To God.' Henry stood in the cemetery with his hat in his hand, the grass whipping at the legs of his trousers, and above him the sky was overcast and dark, and the clouds were running to the east in a hurried, mysterious army. Here it was then, the end of the dream, the final realization that the life he had lived had not remained crystallized for him, waiting for him to look happily through it all again like an album of living photographs.

'Edward,' he whispered. Then, 'Annabel.' Then he put on his hat and walked out of the cemetery to where the cab was waiting for him.

'Depot?' asked the driver, and Henry nodded.

He took the 10:15 train back to Cheyenne. He spent most of the journey talking to a salesman who had come out West to see if he couldn't interest the people of Denver in boudoir alarm clocks. 'I've heard there's a fair number of ladies in Denver who spend a good deal of their time in their boudoirs,' he remarked, passing Henry a silver flask of bourbon, and saying, 'Go on, take a pull.'

The weather had turned very hot and clear by the time Henry got back to Denver. He went straight away to the Front Range Hotel, and shaved and changed, and then went down to the bar and ordered up a bottle of whiskey, from which he drank two brimful glasses, one straight after the other. He felt hungry, but he didn't know what he wanted to eat. Slightly light-headed, he boarded the tram for Brown's Bluff, and sat in the back feeling as if he had no identity and no past. Even the letters he received from his father these days read like the letters of a stranger, describing a world which had become shrunken by distance and time and by unfamiliarity. It had never occurred to him before, but Fenchurch must look very old now; and Henry knew that he would never see him again before he died.

William Byers was sitting in a patent collapsible day-bed in his back garden, drinking Regent punch through a straw and reading *The Wasp*. The tree shading his sun-bed rustled in the afternoon wind. The principal ingredients of Regent punch were rum, strong tea, rye whiskey, lemon juice, and champagne. The principal ingredients of *The Wasp* were satire. William looked up as Henry cross the lawn, and raised his straw hat, and said, 'Well, you were quick! I thought you said you were going to Council Bluffs for a month!'

Henry had to shade his eyes against the sun. 'I changed my mind.'

'Sit down,' William invited. 'Bring over that chair.'

Henry said, 'I can't stay long. I want to finish up a couple of business arrangements downtown: then I'm leaving for Leadville in the morning.'

'Back to the fair Augusta?'

Henry didn't answer that. William said: 'I'm sorry about Stanley.'

'You don't have to be sorry,' Henry replied.

'Well, he's always rather full of himself,' William remarked. 'I suppose anyone would be, after discovering Livingstone and then finding the source of the Nile. He's an ambitious fellow, Stanley. What you might call a man of destiny. Or he believes he is, anyway.'

Henry nodded, and walked around the garden a little. William watched him, without getting up from his day-bed. Birds chirped, leaves blew. In the distance, snow glittered on Pike's Peak. Henry said, 'What kind of a tree is this?'

'A royal paulownia. Comes from Japan. What do you think of it?'

Henry shrugged.

'Are you here to say yes?' William asked him.

'I guess so.'

257

'Well, then, that's one load off of my mind. Why don't you have a drink?'

Henry said, 'I think I've had enough, thanks. I'll just get back to town and finish what I have to finish, and leave it at that. You can arrange the paperwork, can't you? The name of the bank, that kind of thing?'

'Of course I can,' William told him, carefully. 'Listen, you're not upset about anything are you? We don't want problems.'

'You won't get any.'

'Well, okay then,' said William. 'Just so long as we don't. We're talking about very large sums of money here. Tens of thousands of dollars. And I know Stanley wouldn't take very kindly to anything going wrong.'

'What will he do, shoot me with his elephant gun?' asked Henry, turning around so that the heel of his shoe crunched on the grass.

William's eyes sloped sideways in embarrassment. 'I don't think that what Stanley had to go through in Africa has very much to do with a plan to build a vacation resort at Mountclair and set up a regular side-wheeler service on the South Platte River.'

'I think it has everything to do with it,' said Henry. 'But, you're going to pay me one thousand dollars a year, so you say; and on those terms I believe that I can forget my own opinion. And, provided you keep up your payments, I see no reason why I shouldn't *continue* to forget it, year by year.'

'No,' William agreed, with a mask-like smile, 'I don't see any reason why you shouldn't, either.

Henry rubbed a paulownia leaf between his fingers, feeling the soft hairiness of its green under-surface, and smelling the dead-geranium smell of crushed chlorophyll. 'Can you give me the first thousand now?' he asked. 'How shall we put it, by way of advance?'

'I don't usually walk around with a thousand dollars in my pocket,' said William, 'even when I'm setting out to bribe the president of the First Silver Bank of Leadville, Colorado. But I'll see what I can do.'

Henry didn't even smile. 'I'm not leaving Denver until tomorrow morning,' he said, firmly. 'You know where I'm staying, the Front Range. You can leave the money at the desk if I'm not there.'

'Henry,' said William. The shadows of the shade tree flickered across his face.

'What is it?'

'We've always been friends, haven't we? You and I? We're not doing anything criminal here; we're not even doing anything unethical. We're only helping ourselves, and helping Denver at the same time. It's all for the good of the city, so you don't have to be so censorious. Nobody's twisting your arm, Henry; and if you don't want to act as our banker, then all I can say is that we'll have to find ourselves somebody else. But, there are tens of thousands of dollars involved, like I told you; and I would rather that you looked after them, than David Moffat, or Luther Kountze at the Colorado. It's all a question of discretion.'

Henry said, 'I understand.'

'Well, I hope you do,' William replied. 'Listen, why don't you have that glass of punch?'

Henry hesitated, and then he said, 'All right. Just one.' He brought over the white-painted cast-iron chair from under the oak tree, and sat on it with studied correctness, his hat on his lap, almost as if he were posing for his portrait. William reached around to the little side-table that was attached to his day-bed, where the glass jug of Regent punch quietly clinked, and poured him a long one, and topped it with mint.

'You seem to be feeling sorry for yourself for some reason,' said William. 'Now, that's not like you. If somebody were to ask me what kind of a man you are, I'd say carefree. Steady, not particularly ambitious, but a man who relishes the good and simple things in life, like a smoke, and a drink, and a game of cards, and hang whatever happens next Tuesday.'

'Well, that's not me at all,' said Henry.

William looked at him in perplexity. He could see by the expression on Henry's face that Henry was quite serious, and yet it was almost impossible for him to believe that he could be talking and acting like this.

'Listen,' William began, 'if it's anything to do with what happened at Sand Creek – '

Henry replied, 'No. It's nothing to do with Sand Creek. We've had our arguments about that, but I don't bear grudges. I think you all got what was coming to you in any case, when your man Chivington had to give up politics, and Governor Evans had to resign.'

259

Major John Chivington had been the leader of the Denver volunteers who had massacred the Indians at Sand Creek; and his attack had been part of a showy political campaign to get himself elected as one of Colorado's Territorial representatives. Governor Evans had helped him by pleading with Washington for permission to rout out the Cheyenne. Both men had been friends of William Byers. Both men had been ruined by the public revulsion and political scandal which the killings had aroused.

Henry, in all truthfulness, bore no malice against William for having supported Chivington so enthusiastically. Those had been different days in Denver – wilder, rougher, every man for himself, not the pretentious genteel society it affected to be today. But it had taught him what kind of a man William was; and what kind of men he liked to do business with: and he could not forget that, not ever.

He said, with his eyes lowered, stirring his punch with his sprig of mint, 'I left Augusta, years ago, when we were first travelling out here.'

'But you got back together again. You married.'

'I left her at Council Bluffs, and travelled on here, thinking that she had gone back to Vermont; back to her parents. She hadn't, in fact. She hadn't gone any further than Des Moines; and there she waited for me to come after her. She met every train that came in from Council Bluffs, and asked every conductor if he'd seen me. Finally, she decided that I wasn't coming after her, and so she came after me.'

'And she found you? And you married her?'

Henry nodded. 'That was the greatest single mistake of my whole life William. And the reason you think I'm carefree, and unambitious; the kind of man who lets life roll by and never worries about anything; is because I have to be, in order to live with Augusta, and to keep my sanity at the same time.'

William said nothing for a very long time. Then he sat back in his day-bed and looked at Henry with sympathy, but also with critical intentness. 'You can't blame Augusta, you know.'

'I don't. I blame only myself. Well, and circumstances. I was down to my lowest ebb when she caught up with me. No money; no friends; and Charley Harrison's bummers had just worked me over because I'd caught Charley in bed with some woman.'

Some woman! he thought to himself. Nina, with her poised

260

and elegant body, her strange erotic allure. And here he was, in William's garden, calling her 'some woman'.

'Well,' said William, 'I suppose what you did was understandable, although it seems to have taken you a very long time to regret it so deeply. By the way, did you know that Charley Harrison was back in town?'

'I thought he was dead.'

'Not on your life. He was out in southeast Kansas during the war, leading some raggle-taggle party of Confederate guerrillas. Apparently he was bushwhacked by Osage Indians riding with the Union Army, and wounded, but of course he was bald as an egg so they couldn't scalp him. Instead, they ripped his beard off. He's scarred, of course. Wears a false beard these days to hide his chin. But he's alive, and well, and fat as ever. Walter Cheesman saw him down at the Platte Hotel.'

Henry drank a little punch, and took out his handkerchief to wipe his mouth. 'I can't say that I welcome the news.'

William made a *moue*, as if to say, what did it matter? Then he asked, 'You're going back to Augusta, then, in spite of everything?'

'I don't think I have any place else to go. I went back to Council Bluffs to see if – well, I don't know. It's hard to describe it. To see if I could go back all those years and start again, I suppose. It wasn't a very logical thing to do.'

William said, 'I sometimes miss the old days, when we were dragging our printing-press out here on a waggon.'

'It was more than nostalgia,' Henry told him. 'It was – what can I say? – some sort of effort to rearrange my life, I suppose. To go back, and do it all over again. Fruitless, I know. But it wasn't just sentiment. It was a real try at going back.'

'What *you* need,' said William, pouring himself a little more punch, 'is a time-travelling machine.'

'There isn't any such thing,' Henry replied.

'Exactly,' said William.

After leaving the Byers' house, Henry spent the rest of the day visiting warehouses and wholesale suppliers, most of whom were long-standing friends of his; joining them in a smoke and a cup of coffee, and looking at some of the latest goods just in from the East, fire-extinguishing bombs in blue glass bottles, tubular hockey-skates, lavender-water, mirrors, and Harvard tennis-rackets. In the evening, when the air was growing colder and the mountain sky was stirring itself into

261

one of those sunsets that looked like blackcurrant jelly stirred into a bowl of tapioca, he went back to the Front Range Hotel and ate dinner alone in the large mahogany-panelled dining-hall: a pork chop, fresh peas, and a baked potato.

He hardly slept that night. He stood by the window of his room looking at the lights twinkling all across Denver, and he knew that his past life was left behind him for ever.

TEN

Augusta was serving a grey-bearded miner called Jake Giddings when Henry walked in through the door of the store. She said nothing, but bustled off along the counter to bring what the old man wanted: a paper of pins, and a reel of strong brown thread. Henry came across the boarded floor and laid his hand on Jake's shoulder, and smiled at him.

'How're you doing, Jake? Long time since anybody saw hide or hair of you.'

'How do, Mr Roberts. Not so bad; although my feet ain't what they used t'be. Been up over Basalt way, on the Frying Pan River, panning a little, not doing much, but scraping a living.'

'Mrs Roberts looking after you?' asked Henry, looking point-edly towards Augusta.

'As always,' said Jake.

Henry waited until Jake had been served, and had left the store and closed the door behind him. Augusta didn't even glance at him, but tidied up the counter, straightened the cards of buttons on the rack, and then walked briskly around to the marble-topped meat table where she had been slicing bacon, and started to slice up more, turning the flywheel of the Enterprise slicer with strong, even, aggressive strokes of her arm.

'Augusta?' said Henry. The slicer made a sharp ringing sound as each rasher of bacon was cut, and added to the stack.

'Augusta, I don't know what to say to you.'

'Then hold your peace.'

'I had to go, I'm sorry.'

Her mouth was set, pudgy and determined. Her glasses were marked with a fingerprint, on the left-hand lens. She turned and turned the wheel of the slicer, and the rashers of bacon kept stacking up.

'I've said, I'm sorry,' he repeated.

'I heard you.'

'Can you just understand that sometimes – sometimes, a man wants to be free – to feel that he isn't just a – well, I don't know what to call it. A prisoner, of his own life.'

Augusta stopped turning the handle of the slicer. She wrapped the bacon she had sliced in greaseproof paper, and laid it on the counter, under the curved glass display cabinet, next to the kielbasa and the salami and the goat's-milk cheese. 'Henry,' she said, wiping her hands, and still not looking at him, 'you were never a prisoner. You're not a prisoner now. You're free to go, whenever you want.'

'Augusta – '

She lifted her head now, proudly, fiercely, and stared at him. 'Henry, you were never a prisoner. I didn't force you to marry me, and I have never forced you to stay with me. But you chose to do so, and that choice brought with it certain obligations. The obligation to respect me, the obligations to treat me with consideration, and the obligation not to hurt me. Perhaps you don't love me, Henry, although I don't believe that for one moment; but at least you can treat me as a wife, and a woman, and someone whose fate you freely decided to take charge of.'

She wept now, trembling, and clutching herself in her arms. 'How do you think I felt that morning when I woke up and found that you had gone? How do you think I *felt?* Not a word, not a note. You could have been leaving me for ever, for all that I knew. You could have been going to kill yourself. If you could understand only a fraction of the pain and anxiety which I have been experiencing since last week, Henry; the tiniest fraction; well, then you would understand the meaning of true torment, and how unconditionally vicious one human being is capable of being to another.'

Henry listened to this, and then lowered his head. He felt

both sad and bored. He knew that she would take him back; he was regretful that he had upset her so much; but he was more regretful that they would have to go through the long and tedious performance of sulking, and arguing, and apportioning blame, until at last he could settle down to his poker games again, and running the store, and smiling at Augusta occasionally to keep her happy. He had tried to break away; and his attempt had failed. All he wanted to do now was to settle back into the dream which had kept him happy and vacant-minded ever since Augusta had turned up at his boarding-house door in Denver and said, 'Everything is going to be wonderful.'

'I should refuse to take you back,' said Augusta.

Henry raised his eyes. 'You won't, though, will you?'

She hesitated, and then she shook her head. 'I'm just pleased that you're back, Henry. It must have been terrible for you. I'm sorry. I thought about it again and again, what I'd do if you came walking in through that door. First of all I thought that I'd shout at you, and tell you to get out, and never come back; and then I thought that I'd run up and hold you in my arms. Oh, but Henry; you *have* come back. Henry, you have, and I'm so sorry for being so cross with you!'

Now she came rustling around the counter, and she opened her arms for him, and held him close, her hands raised because they still smelled of bacon, her spectacle-frames tight against his chin, and he stood in the middle of the floor and patted her back as if he were calming a large dog, and knew that he was home.

She pulled back from him. 'Where did you *go?*' she asked him. 'I was so worried about you. I thought you might have left me and gone on to San Francisco. You always said you wanted to. I really thought you were going to California and leave me here in Leadville.'

'I went down to Denver, that's all. Spent a few nights at the Front Range Hotel. Talked to William, and some of the warehouse people. That's all. Nothing much. I don't know, just getting myself straight.'

'And are you straight now, my darling?' she asked, reaching up and stroking his forehead with her fingers that smelled like bacon.

The question seemed so ludicrous that Henry found it almost impossible to answer. But he nodded, and kissed her forehead, and whispered, 'Don't worry. It wasn't your fault. It was something that I felt the need to do.'

During the early evening, Henry checked the stock in the store, beans and oil and corn-meal flour and looked quickly through the accounts of the banking counter; dressed in his long brown duster coat, with a stub of a pencil behind his ear. Augusta looked at him fondly, and he realized that he was going to be let off very lightly for his escapade at Council Bluffs, not that he had yet told Augusta that he had been there; or ever would. It was one thing to tell her that he had wanted a few days alone, a few days of peace and solitude in Denver; it would be quite another to admit that he had been searching for the freedom which he had known before he met her.

There was pan-fried chicken with mustard greens for supper, and they ate it late, sitting over the kitchen table by the light of the kerosene-lamp, while outside the sky was as black as glass. Henry felt exhausted, and not very talkative, but Augusta chattered on about the store, and how many fly-whisks they had sold, and how Mrs Ellis had given birth to her twins at last, and how old Keith Briggs had been locked up for a day and a half for firing a gun in the Jack of Spades gambling hall. At last, as she was clearing away the dishes, she said, 'Those two sourdoughs were down here yesterday.'

'Which two sourdoughs?'

'You know, Rische and the other one. The one who never says anything.'

'Oh, yes. What did they want?'

'I don't know. They said they wanted to talk to you. They wouldn't talk to anybody else. They said it was very important, though, and when you came back, if you did, could you go up to the Little Pittsburgh?'

Henry stared at Augusta's back, as she pumped up more water to wash the dishes.

'That was all they said? That it was very important?'

'They said that you'd know what it was all about; but they didn't want to talk to anybody else. They also told me not to confess to anyone at all that they had been here; or, if anybody had seen them here, and I couldn't pretend that they hadn't, to say that they had worked the Little Pittsburgh right down to the rocks, and there was nothing there but muck and gumbo.'

Henry said, 'It sounds like they've found something.'

Augusta turned around, and pushed the hair away from her

forehead with the back of her hand. 'It didn't sound that way to *me*, I must confess. They kept saying over and over again that they were still stony-broke, and that the mine had yielded nothing at all. Or at least Rische said that. The other one just looked at himself in the mirror and pulled faces.'

'I don't know', said Henry, getting up on to his feet. 'Sometimes the simplest of men can find the most extraordinary things. The whole of America was opened up by ordinary men and women. You think of those very early pioneers today. You think of the time when there was nothing but desert and prairie and mountain, and nobody to guide them through it all, and certainly no railroad to sleep on.'

'Well, what if they have found something?' asked Augusta.

Henry grasped her shoulders and kissed the parting at the back of her hair. 'If they have, we could be rich. You wouldn't mind that, would you? You could have a different carriage for every day of the week. Monday, a green one; Tuesday, something in bright red; Wednesday, a brown surrey; Thursday, a coal-black brougham.'

'Oh, stop it, Henry,' she said. 'We argued before because you said you wanted money, and I didn't.'

'You shouldn't work so hard,' Henry murmured, into her hair.

'That's rather hard when your husband and partner is either playing poker in the back parlour or taking unwarranted vacations in Denver.'

'You're not going to blame me for that, are you?'

'I don't know,' she said. 'I might. I might punish you for it.'

'Madam,' Henry replied, raising an eyebrow, and smiling. 'You're getting a little presumptuous, aren't you, especially on the first night that your husband and master comes home?'

She raised her face him, that big pale face, and hesitantly he kissed her. Suddenly, unexpectedly, all her cornered frustrations burst loose, and she seized the hair at the back of his neck and kissed him so savagely, teeth and tongue, that his lips bled, and he could taste salt in his mouth.

She began to pant, in high-pitched, unintelligible whines. She took off her spectacles, and laid them with incongruous care on the scrubbed kitchen table. Then, still panting, she tugged up her apron and her voluminous brown skirts, and pulled down her white layered bloomers, clutching the side of the kitchen sink for balance as she stepped out of them.

266

'Now, now, now, Henry,' she said, and scrabbled open his belt-buckle with bitten fingernails. Her eyes roamed wildly with astigmatism and apparently uncontrollable passion, although Henry as he looked down at her unbuttoning his britches thought: how much of this is real, and how much of it is what she thinks I expect from her? Her scalp where it showed through the parting of her hair looked so dead white.

She cupped her hand into his underwear, and brought out his softly-swollen penis. She kissed it as if it were an injured bird, and pressed it against her face. He had never seen her behave like this before. All of their sexual congress since they had been married had been decorous and ordinary, as if the acts of sodomy they had performed in Chicago had always to be atoned for. But she was breathing fiercely now, as if she were madly elated or hysterical, and she gripped his penis in her fist and beat it up and down until it stiffened, and then she kissed it again, and sucked at it, and rubbed it against her eyelids and her cheeks, and slavered and moaned and cried. Then, still grasping him, she lay back on the hard-tiled kitchen floor, pulling him after her, and lifted up her skirts, and cried, 'Henry! Henry! Henry! Henry, I love you Henry!' Releasing him, she plunged both of her hands up to the knuckles deep between her legs, and spread herself apart for him, a livid display of flesh and hair.

Henry leaned heavily on top of her, and pushed himself into her, and thrust at her, his knee caught on her skirt. The tiled floor pressed on his elbows; Augusta's white distraught face joggled beneath him. He thrust and thrust as deeply as he could, while she kept herself stretched wide apart for him, her heavy legs raised high in the air, as if somebody were slowly waving a thick white bedroll on either side of him.

'Oh, Henry, punish me!' she cried out, her eyes squeezed tight shut. 'Hurt me, Henry, it was all my fault!'

At that moment, Henry almost lost any desire at all; or any feeling. He could feel himself dying away inside her. But she lifted her buttocks from the floor, and pushed herself up at him, and he began to rise again, gradually, enough to keep her heaving and thumping and panting on the tiles.

He felt the tug of an unwanted climax, and drew himself back. Three or four white drops fell against pink stretched skin. Augusta realized that he was finished, and lay back shud-

dering, and then started to sob, humiliated by her own cata-
strophic desires.

Henry loomed over her and kissed her cold sweaty forehead.
'Get up now,' he said, taking her hand. But she snatched it
away, and hid her face, and stayed where she was, on the
floor.

'All right,' he said, awkwardly getting up. 'I'll go to bed
without you.'

He took one of the lamps upstairs. The bedroom looked
familiar but smelled cold: a bedroom meant for two in which
only one person had been sleeping. Over the bed was a
coloured lithograph of Jesus surrounded by children; the
imaginary children that Augusta had never been able to
conceive. Henry tiredly unbuttoned his waistcoat and loosened
the cuffs of his shirt. He hummed to himself the spiritual which
William's black stable-boy Edwin had been singing as he had
driven him down to the Denver depot,

'Lord, can't you hear me weeping
I'm crying out to You.'

He washed his face in the basin beside the bed; then shook
himself into his nightshirt, and climbed between the sheets. As
he did so, something cold and hard rolled across the bed from
Augusta's side, and lodged against his hip. He picked it up,
and saw that it was Augusta's glass pastry-pin, the decorative
one which he had given to her three years ago, and which at
the time had been filled with spices. He clasped it in the palm
of his hand, and turned it this way and that, and realized with
increasing pity what Augusta had been using it for. She hadn't
expected him home today, and so she had left it in the bed,
ready for tonight.

He felt suddenly sad, and very sorry for her; and he hated
himself for what he had done to her.

He was still awake when she came to bed, and lay down
next to him, tense and still, scarcely breathing. But after a
while, guessing that he was only pretending to sleep, she said,
'You can't imagine what it was like thinking that you'd gone
for ever.'

'Augusta – ' he said, and reached out to hold her shoulder,
but she slapped him away.

'You have hurt me so much,' she said, and the resentment

268

in her voice burned into his consciousness like a branding-iron into a steer. 'You really have hurt me so very much.'

He slept. It was still dark when he woke up again, and Augusta was crying. He tried to kiss her, but her face was salty and wet with tears, and she pushed him away. He lay next to her, resenting her, feeling sorry for her, hating her, pitying her, liking her, remembering all of the summers they had spent together and all of the Thanksgiving dinners, all of the days and all of the weeks, spilling off the calendar in an endless torrent of numbers. And was this all that it could lead to? Lying side by side in a narrow bed in Leadville, listening to her sobbing, not knowing what he could do to help her, not even knowing what he could do to hurt her?

Augusta was one of the most complicated and interesting women he had ever met, but the tragedy of Augusta was that she was too plain for him to want to know anything about how interesting she was, nor anything about her complexities. She wanted him to love her, but he couldn't.

In the morning, when she woke, she looked across with unfocused eyes and saw the glass pastry-pin, on Henry's bedside bureau, where he had left it. She said nothing, but after that day it disappeared, and Henry never saw it again. He guessed that Augusta had smashed it, and thrown the pieces away. He never mentioned it.

The morning was golden as they breakfasted in the kitchen on coffee and shirred eggs with crumbs. They said very little: only the brief, light, informative conversation of people who have decided to live with each other without loving each other. 'Dan Maskell's coming in later, with some of that cheese of his.' 'Oh, could you make sure that butter's still fresh?' 'Did you see Dick McCloskey when you were in Denver?'

Both of them knew that no intimacies would ever be spoken between them again; not that many ever had been; and that in every respect except that they were still living together, their marriage was over.

Henry finished his eggs and said, 'I think I'll take a ride up to the mine, see what Rische and Hook have got to say for themselves.'

'You won't be too long? It's been hard enough this past week, not having you here. I need you to bring up some barrels.'

'I won't be long. What is it, a twenty-minute ride?'

He saddled up Belinda, and rode up the steep-sided valley

where the hamlet of California Gulch now lay mostly abandoned, its houses deserted, its boardwalks stripped for mining-
props. The warm morning wind blew dust from the crest of
the gulch, and the pines nodded all around him like curtseying
girls.

When he reached the crest of the Little Pittsburgh mine, he
saw a large oddly-shaped tent pitched there, and a fire, and
sitting in front of the fire, brewing up coffee, August Rische
and George Hook, as shabby and as eccentric-looking as ever.
August Rische stood up as Henry approached, and waved,
even though Henry was only a few yards away. George Hook
took not the slightest notice of either of them, but continued
to drink his coffee and turn his flapjacks in a little blackened
pan. A little distance off, their dog yapped, and then sneezed.

'I see your dog's still sick,' said Henry, climbing down from
Belinda's saddle.

'Oh, he's not sick, Mr Roberts,' said August Rische, holding
Belinda's bridle. 'He sneezes when the flowers are coming out,
that is all.'

'How are things?' asked Henry. 'Where have you fellows
been digging?'

George Hook looked up now, his mouth full of flapjack, and
acknowledged Henry with a nod of his head. August Rische
said, 'We are trying to dig close to the original mining place,
first of all. But we are finding always that the effort of
penetrating the rock is too great for what equipments it is we
are having. Well, picks and shovels; no compressed-air drill;
and always very hot, too, in the sunshine.'

Henry said, 'Whiskey doesn't help, either.'

August Rische scratched at his thick wiry beard, and ducked
his head forward a little, as if to indicate that he wouldn't
entirely agree with that; but then he wouldn't entirely *disagree*
with it, either. 'As it was happening, we are choosing to dig
ourselves under the overshadowing place, close to the butte.'

He led Henry across the sloping ground to a small, untidy
diggings, where a bucket and a winch had been set up, and a
covering of sacking had been thrown over the excavated soil.
Henry peered down into the excavation, and it was dark and
smelled of urine. He presumed that neither Rische nor Hook
could usually be bothered to haul themselves thirty feet to the
surface when they wanted to relieve themselves.

'Well?' he asked, testily.

'Ah, well!' smiled August Rische. 'First of all we are digging with no success, which for us is the usual way; so, we are not despondent. But then we strike this.' He drew aside the sacking, and underneath it was a mound of black sand and black rock. He scooped his hand into the dirt, and held it up beneath Henry's nose, and his face suddenly broadened into a grin.

'Carbonate of lead,' he said. 'Just the same like Mr Stevens was finding, only finer.'

Henry knelt down and sifted some of the black sand and pebbles between his fingers. 'Have you had this assayed?' he asked, and his voice sounded as if it belonged to someone else.

August Rische kept on grinning, and nodded. 'Not here, though. George is taking some to Aurora, so that nobody here is knowing.'

'Do you have the report?' asked Henry.

Without a word, August Rische reached into the back pocket of his britches, and handed over a crumpled assay, creased and re-creased and stained with coffee. Henry read it, and in spite of himself, his hand was shaking. The assay was signed by A. Rosenblum, of Aurora, Colorado, and it certified that out of a ton of ore of 2,000 lbs, 2,325 ounces were silver, worth $2,999.00 at coin value.

'We are lucky, you see,' said August Rische, taking off his cap, and smoothing his bald head with his fingertips. 'If we are not digging in the shades here, beneath the butte, we are not discovering the top of this silver. It is a pipe downwards, straight down into the ground, only a few yards in wideness; and if we are digging *there*, or *there*, or anywhere else, we are missing it.'

'How deep do you think this pipe runs?' asked Henry.

August Rische held out his hand; and, rather confused, Henry took it. 'Mr Roberts,' he said, 'we are all very expensive men.'

'I'm sorry?'

'This pipe of silver is downwards, well, who can tell? But hundreds of feet. We are so expensive, Mr Roberts. It is diamonds and fur coats now.'

Henry looked down at the smelly hole in the ground, and then at August Rische, and then across the shoulder of rock at George Hook, who was calmly eating his flapjacks by the fire, and tearing off pieces to feed to their dog. George Hook nodded again, and abruptly broke into a smile. 'Not bad, huh?' he called, in a thick, Teutonic accent, the very first time that Henry had ever heard him speak.

'Are you kidding?' said Henry. And then he gripped August Rische by the arms, and laughed at him, 'You bastard! You lazy bastard! You wouldn't dig in the sun, would you? Too much whiskey, too much like hard work! And you've found it! You lazy, incredible bastard!'

He dug into the ore again, bare-handed. 'Silver, damn it!' he whooped. 'Silver! Look at this, you bastards, it's silver!' And then he tossed it into the air, rocks and sand, so that it scattered all around him, because Alby Monihan's mine had at last paid off, and at last he had achieved the revenge he had always wanted against those Southern bullies who had beaten him in New York, and taken all his money. And at last he had won against Augusta; and at last he was rich.

'Silver!' he shouted at August Rische, and August Rische chuckled and skipped around the camp-fire, and George Hook began to whistle, and clap, and even the dog began to dance.

'Silver! You bastards! It's silver!'

He shook their hands again and again; and then he mounted Belinda, and made his way back down the gulch to Leadville, stunned, delighted; and the whole world seemed different as he rode; as though the clock-hands that had been stuck for so long inside his brain had ticked forward at last, only a second, but a second that was sufficient to take him from hardscrabble to riches; from tedious day-to-day worrying to tremendous wealth.

He stabled Belinda and walked into the store just as Augusta was weighing out sugar for Mrs Pomfrey, the stout old widow who had lost her husband Stanley in a shooting incident last May, at the Mosquito Saloon, five miners dead, nine injured, eleven mirrors broken, six bottles of whiskey spilled. And he took hold of Mrs Pomfrey and whirled her around, a carousel in black, and said, 'How are you, Mrs Pomfrey? Still cheerful?'

'Still in mourning, Mr Roberts,' said Mrs Pomfrey, brushing the fringes of her black headscarf, and frowning at him in disapproval, all chins and eyebrows.

'Augusta,' called Henry, 'Mrs Pomfrey can take her groceries for free. In fact, everything can go for free for the rest of the day, to anybody.'

Augusta stared at him; her face long and big and disapproving. 'What's happened, Henry? Henry, are you drunk?'

'No,' said Henry. 'No, Augusta, not drunk. Better than drunk. Better than drunk!'

A whiskery old prospector who had been sitting in the corner of the store trying on boots cracked in, 'Better than drunk? What the fuck could be better than drunk?'

'Henry, you're being ridiculous again,' said Augusta, clutching her arms together and turning around and around like a clockwork figure of a woman without a key.

'Augusta!' he shouted, quite loudly; and then far more softly, and more persuasively, 'Augusta.'

She stared at him through her tiny spectacles. 'Henry, what's happened?'

'You know what's happened. You knew before.'

'It's those two sourdoughs, isn't it? They've found something.'

Henry smiled and nodded, and took off his hat.

'It's those two sourdoughs. You're absolutely right. They've struck the top of a pipe of silver which reaches so far down into the ground that they can't even guess where it's going to end; even if it ends at all.'

He couldn't read what was in her face. She stood where she was, her hands by her sides, as if he had hit her with a sledgehammer, and she was about to fall. But something more had come down on top of her, with Rische and Hook's discovery of silver. Her life, and all her hopes of keeping Henry; no matter what the terms were.

She said, 'That's marvellous.' But her face was as white as paper.

'Augusta,' he said, and he came around the counter and took hold of both of her hands. 'Augusta, whatever misunderstandings or arguments we've had; however unhappy things have been; let's forget them now. Let's at least be the best of friends.'

'Is it really silver?' she asked him.

He nodded, smiling at her, trying to get her to smile, too. 'A rich lode of carbonate of lead, the same kind of ore that Will Stevens dug up. And it was a miracle they found it. It's – what – only about as wide as this floor and it's right under the shadow of the butte. But they dug there because the sun was too hot.'

'We're rich, then,' she said.

273

'Not just rich, Augusta. Very rich. Rolling rich! That whole lode belongs to us.'

Augusta said, 'I think I'm going to have to sit down for a moment.'

He brought her a chair, and she sat down with her hands in her lap, staring at nothing at all. The sun came in through the window of the store and illuminated the candy counter, neatly arranged with Augusta's special fondants and penuches, and the shining glass covers over the cheeses.

'I have some pies in the oven,' she said, suddenly, and started to get up. But Henry took hold of her shoulders, and pressed her to sit down again.

'Let them burn. They don't matter any more. None of this matters any more. You're a wealthy lady now.'

'But I can't just leave them.'

'You can. And not just the pies, either. Everything. The sweeping, the cleaning, the stocktaking, the candy-making. We don't have to be storekeepers any more, Augusta. It's over; the work is over.'

'No, no,' she said, 'I can't let them burn. I have customers who buy them every day. I can't be selfish.'

He tried to seize her arm, but she twisted away from him and went hurrying through to the kitchen, where he could hear her clattering with her baking-sheets and banging the stove door. He remained where he was, in the centre of the store, and while she fussed around with her pies, he looked slowly around him at all the shelves of canned food, at all the neatly-wound ropes, at all the stoves and jars and bars of soap, at all the bottles of vinegar and patent hair-restorers. He had put up all of the shelves himself; and helped to construct most of the counters. What he saw around him was his life's work, crowded and meagre. And now he would never have to touch a single jar or bottle or can again; never have to slice another joint of bacon; never have to heave drums of kerosene in from the yard; or bring in wood at five o'clock on a freezing winter morning to help Augusta light up the stove.

'Chance,' he whispered to himself. And then he turned, and in turning, caught sight of himself in a looking-glass advertising Blanke's Mojav Coffee; a heavy-set, handsome man with a distinctive moustache, dressed in a clean-cut white collar and dark brown velvet necktie, and a worn but well-tailored coat of sandy-coloured corduroy. It surprised him, in a way, that

274

the man he could see in the looking-glass was him. He looked younger than he felt: more humorous, less marked by his years as a storekeeper, and by his marriage to Augusta. He smiled to himself, and said, 'Chance,' a second time.

He walked through the corridor, and into the kitchen. Augusta was trying to scrape a burned pie-crust off the edge of the baking-sheet, and crying.

'They're all spoiled,' she said, and her voice was a honk of pure misery. 'They're all spoiled. Everything's spoiled.'

He stood behind her and clasped his arms around her waist. 'Augusta, you don't have to worry any more. Throw them away. Throw the whole darned tin away.'

'Oh, yes? And what if this precious lode of silver only goes down two or three feet, and then gives out? Then what? Should I search in the trash for my thrown-away tin? And what about my thrown-away life?'

'Augusta, is there a single silver mine around here that hasn't produced a fortune? They've already dug ten feet into it, in any case, and the ore is the same quality through and through.'

'Henry,' said Augusta, 'we may be rich, but we should never forget our beginnings, nor what we have always been to each other. The smell of wealth always draws the devil, Henry; you know that. Both you and I have seen what kind of men come here to Leadville, to seek their fortunes; and both you and I have seen what happens to those who have struck gold, or silver. This mine is a curse, Henry; it has always been a curse, ever since you first took that deed-of-claim. It had lain in that drawer for all of our years together like an evil talisman, and blighted everything that we have done together. Henry, I beg you to close the mine at once. Give Rische and Hook whatever you can, and tell them to go on their way. *Please*, Henry, before it destroys us completely!'

'Now then,' said Henry, 'what's this? I've never seen anybody so upset by the thought of riches. I'll do no such thing. In fact, I'm going right across to Lenont's, to order up a crusher and an amalgamating plant; and all the tools and winding-gear we're going to need. And I'm going to have to take on some extra men, too, right away.'

'You won't listen, will you?' said Augusta. She unfastened his hands from around her waist as if she were releasing a belt.

'Listen to what?' he said, irritably. 'Listen to your feather-brained fears that money will ruin us, and drive us apart? Why do you suppose that we've been quarrelling so much? Eighteen years together and nothing to show for it but a general store, that's why! Eighteen years of working and arguing and no more pleasure in our lives than poker for me and Sunday-morning church for you! Let me tell you, Augusta, I'm going to excavate that mine as quickly as I can and on the grandest scale that I can afford.'

Augusta stood silent; and on the table in front of her lay her broken pies.

'Very well,' she said at last, 'it seems that I cannot persuade you. I am beginning to wonder what use I am to you at all; except as a servant to run your store for you. And what use will I be now, without even *that* menial task to perform? You never want me as a lover; I cannot bear you any children. We scarcely ever eat together any more. I love you, Henry, with all of my heart, and I would never willingly leave you. But you have made me the most wretched soul in all the world; and if I am fighting now for you to close that mine and turn your back on whatever riches it may contain, it is only for the sake of my own happiness. Henry, all I have to ask you is this: is my happiness worth that price?'

Henry said, 'You're tired, that's all. You've been working too hard.'

'No,' she told him. 'Not tired. Just wretched.'

He said nothing for a moment, but then leaned forward and kissed her on the cheek, a grazing kiss with no affection in it. She turned her head away as if she were frightened that he was going to brand her. He went out into the corridor and took down his hat. 'I'll see you later this afternoon,' he said, as matter-of-factly as if none of this conversation had taken place. But after he had left the store, and the door had jangled behind him, and he had crossed the street into the triangle of midday sunshine outside the T.G. Underhill clothing company, on the corner, he stopped and pressed the palm of his hand against his forehead, as if he had been stung by a bee. It was a gesture of fiercely-controlled despair; of anger that he had no capacity to express. He no longer wondered why respectable men could sometimes be moved to murder their wives; although he knew that if it ever came to it, he could never think of murdering Augusta. She was too defenceless, too large and too pale and too self-pitying. He said, 'Damn,' to himself, and then, 'damn,' and a small boy walking past turned and stared at him as if he were mad.

For the first few weeks after the discovery of silver in the Little Pittsburgh mine, Augusta's fears that their marriage would immediately be sundered and that their business at the store would be torn apart were considerably quieted by Henry's new dependence on her for ordering supplies, for keeping books, for taking messages, and for regular evening meals at which he would expect nothing more than hot food and silence. He spent all day every day up on the hill, wrapped in a large black bearskin coat as the weather grew sharper, supervising with unusually stern energy the building of a hoisting-house over the shaft, and the installation of steam-powered winding-gear and buckets to bring up the ore. Nat Starkey from the Tasteful Saloon introduced him to an experienced mining engineer called R.P. Grover who had once worked for the Chollar mine at Virginia City, excavating the Comstock Lode; and R.P. Grover in turn brought in 'Bully' Brett, a hard-rock miner whose talents with dynamite, which was colloquially called 'giant powder', were legendary. By the time the pines up on the mountains around Leadville were touched by the first silver-thaw of the winter, the Little Pittsburgh was producing nearly 15,500 ounces of silver a week, and bringing in over $20,000. Henry went up there at eight o'clock every morning, just after the sun had come up, and stood watching the smoke rising from the chimney of the amalgamating plant, his head now crowned by a huge black bearskin hat, his breath fuming from his nose and mouth.

The Little Pittsburgh was not as impressive a mine as any of the big excavations around the Comstock Lode in Nevada. There was only a shingle-roofed hoisting-house, and a rickety track for the trucks to carry the ore across to the building which housed the stamping-machines, and the amalgamating-pans; and a sorry collection of unpainted miners' houses close to the side of the butte. But there were twenty miners working in it now, including R.P. Grover, and every hour of every day, ton after ton of heavy black ore was being blasted out of the ground, and stamped, and processed, and every hour of every day Henry was growing richer.

Henry had only just arrived at the mine one morning in mid-

October when R.P. Grover came walking slowly across to talk to him, rubbing his hands against the cold. Behind him, in the hoisting-house, the steam-engine which powered the air-compressors was rattling; and behind the hoisting-house the hillside rose steep and frosty and slanted with early sunlight. Two hundred and seventy feet below the hillside, 'Bully' Brett was drilling the nine holes in the rockface in which he would set the next charges of giant powder. All day, the mountains around Leadville thumped with the regular explosion of dynamite charges; and they had grown so commonplace that even the timid pine warblers no longer scattered.

R.P. Grover's given name was Robustus; a name chosen by his father, who had been a self-taught schoolteacher in Oregon, in the early days of settlement. He looked today as he must have looked as a baby, and Henry could see just what his father had been thinking of when he had christened him. He had a large head, with a broad Slavic face, and red protruding ears whose interior whorls were as complicated as a puzzle. His torso was tremendous: deep-chested and broad-shouldered, like a beef carcass, but underneath it his legs were so short and curved that he walked everywhere with a low, speedy lope. He habitually wore the unmistakable headgear of a Comstock miner – the felt crown of a hat from which the brim had been cut off – and a thick checked jacket of red and blue wool.

'Another bright one, sir,' he remarked, his hands thrust deep in his jacket pockets, inclining his head towards the newly-risen sun.

'What time will you start blasting?' Henry asked him.

'No later than ten after, sir. Billy's just drilling out the last of the edgers.'

'Did he start late?'

'No, sir; but there's a diagonal layer of sand down there, sir, and he wanted to be careful not to choke up the tunnel when he fired the charge.'

'Hm,' said Henry. From the beginning, he had taken a detailed, almost obsessive interest in the Little Pittsburgh mine, following each foot of its sinking into the hillside with notes, and inspections, and diagrams; and making sure that every sample was assayed and assayed yet again, so that he could determine whether the ore was richer as they excavated deeper, or poorer. He had even tried to use one of the compressed-air drills himself, although he had given up after ten minutes

278

because of the dust. At the Comstock faces, the miners had already learned to call these drills 'the widow-makers', because they blew up a fine dust of sharp silica flakes as they penetrated the rock, eventually killing six out of ten of their operators from silicosis.

'At least we've no flooding as yet,' R.P. Grover said, with stolid optimism. 'Nor too much heat, neither.'

Henry nodded. The sun had just risen over the top of the ridge 'It was a serious matter at the Comstock, water,' R.P. Grover went on. 'Some of it was boiling, too. One hundred and sixty degrees, down at the nineteen-hundred-feet level. The air was so steamy we couldn't see the ore. Well, I left the Comstock after my friend John Exley died. He fell up to his waist into a sump of hot water, and even though we dragged him out quick, all the skin peeled off his legs, all of it, like two soft stockings, and he died before we got him up to the top.'

'You didn't come over here to tell me that,' said Henry.

R.P. hesitated, and looked embarrassed, and coughed. 'No, sir. Not exactly.'

'Well, then, what is it?'

'I don't like to be offensive, sir,' R.P. told him. 'But on the other hand, begging your pardon, I don't see what else I can do, having the interest of the mine at heart.'

'Go on,' said Henry.

'Well, sir, it's those partners of yours: Mr Rische and Mr Hook; and in particular Mr Rische.'

'Yes?'

'With every respect, sir; especially since it was Mr Rische that discovered the lode; he's nothing more than an old-fashioned sourdough, sir, with very little understanding of mining, the way that it's done these days, he's an old hand-jacking man, that doesn't know nothing of widow-makers or giant powder, or square-set props. And none of this would matter if he didn't try to impose himself on the men, sir, with such forcibility.'

Henry looked across to his left, out over the town of Leadville, with its wide rutted streets and its incongruous collection of churches and brothels and fine solid hotels and assorted houses, some mansions and some shacks; and beyond Leadville, to the bleak landscape of mines and stamping-mills and depots. Sometimes, when the wind was blowing in the right direction, it was possible to hear the sound of Leadville's stamping-mills for miles, champing away at the ore like the factories of Mammon. And then there were the pines, and the snow-streaked mountains, and the low grey clouds of an early winter.

'I thank you for your comments, Mr Grover,' said Henry. 'But you'll have to remember that Mr Rische is a third equal partner in this mine, along with myself and Mr Hook; and that he is entitled to equal respect.'

R.P. Grover wiped his eye with one crooked finger, where the cold wind had made it water.

Henry turned away from him, in a manner which made it clear that what he was about to say next was not to be repeated. 'I have however been watching him; and the manner in which he has been conducting himself, particularly with regard to the men at the face, and I would like to make it clear that you have my support.'

R.P. Grover said nothing for a long time, but Henry could hear him sniffing intermittently. 'Do I understand you right, sir?' he asked.

Henry turned. 'You heard what I said.'

R.P. Grover still hesitated. 'Yes, sir. But – well, I wanted to have it clear. On account of any trouble, sir; if you follow me.'

'Trouble?' frowned Henry. 'Why should there be any trouble?'

R.P. Grover respectfully whipped off his miner's hat, and nodded his head two or three times; and then scurried back across the shoulder of rock towards the mine, his bandy legs moving like two curved coathangers. Henry saw the hoisting engineer George Coombs come out of the hoisting-house and wave, and R.P. Grover change direction and go to talk to him. Hoisting engineers after all, were the aristocracy of the toplanders, the men who worked on the surface, and earned four dollars a day, which was a dollar more than the men who worked below ground. The face-workers never complained: it was up to the hoisting engineer to lift them up and down the shaft in safety, and it was in the shafts that most fatal mining accidents occurred. R.P. Grover, who relished stories of terrible disasters, in spite of the grieving way in which he always told them, would explain how men who fell down the mile-deep Comstock shafts would be smashed into pieces by the protruding timbers on all sides, and how the fragments of their bodies would have to be fished out of the hot-water sumps at the bottom of the shafts with special hooks, then packed into old dynamite boxes and sent up to the surface.

While R.P. Grover talked, Henry had seen Nat Starkey riding in a leisurely way up the hillside on his chestnut mare with the three white socks, the mare he called Trey. Henry had been expecting Nat, but not so early, since Nat hardly ever stirred until eleven o'clock in the morning, and then to do nothing more strenuous than pour himself a large glass of bourbon, and break a raw egg into it.

It was Nat who had helped Henry more than anyone else in the weeks after the quality of the Little Pittsburgh's silver had first been proved. Nat had underwritten Henry at Lenont's Mining Supplies for a steam-powered hoist, as well as building materials, and timber. He had then gone to five of Leadville's saloon-keepers, and formed a consortium to guarantee the costly heavyweight machinery which was needed for extracting silver out of the lead and other worthless materials with which it was mixed. Nat had asked for nothing in return except a lifetime two percent of the mine: a royalty which had already made him a moderately wealthy man.

Nat rode up to Henry and dismounted. His mare shook her head, and her breath clouded in the cold mountain air. The two men clasped hands, and then Henry said, 'Let's take a walk to the mill. I'll show you how we're getting along.'

'I came up early because I couldn't sleep,' said Nat. 'Don't ask me why, I've been having these dreams lately. I keep thinking I can hear my father talking to me.'

'I thought your father was dead.'

Nat sniffed. 'He is. That's what concerns me. I just hope it isn't an omen. I can tell you something, Henry, there's one thing I very much don't want to do, and that's to die in my sleep. I want to have the chance to say some last words. In fact, I've even got my last words ready.'

'Oh, yes?' asked Henry, abstractedly.

Nat held out his arm in a poetic gesture. 'I'm going to say, "Everything on the black, my friends!" What do you think of that?'

'Everything on the black? Well, I suppose it's quite neat, for a gaming-house keeper.'

'You don't like it? Don't tell me you've heard better!'

'It's not as bad as the epitaph that one farmer's widow wanted me to carve on her husband's tombstone. "Embracing At Last His Beloved Sod." '

Nat cackled.

281

'Here,' said Henry, 'you'd better tether Trey to this fence-post here. The noise of those crushers is going to spook her if you don't.'

Now they were close to the mill, the battering of metal on metal was deafening. One correspondent had said of mine-processing plants that they made 'Niagara sound like a whisper'. The Little Pittsburgh mill was built on five levels down the hillside, in what looked like an inter-connected series of five small shingle-roof barns, with weather-boarded sides, and rows of windows. On the very lowest level, where the steam-boilers were housed, two chimneys protruded, rolling out thick brown smoke. Large barrels of water were perched in rows along the ridge of every roof on the mill, in case a spark from one of these chimneys set the shingles alight. If a fire started, the nearest barrel would be toppled over by a tug on a rope, and its water would be sluiced across the roof.

Henry took Nat by the arm, and led him up the muddy, wheel-tracked hillside to the upper level. Here, they crossed the tracks used to bring up the carts of ore from the minehead, and entered the gloomy, thunderous, fuming interior of the mill. Nat had been up here several times before, but not when the mill was working at full capacity, as it was this morning.

Henry pointed out a waggon of ore being tipped into the Blake jaw-crushers: huge iron plates which ground the rock into pieces about the size of a man's fist. The crackling and grinding and crunching of stone always made Henry feel as if his skull was breaking; but it was the rhythmical beating of the stamps on the next level below that set up the unholy hammering that could be heard and felt so far away. The Little Pittsburgh had only three of them, because they had cost almost $30,000 each; but each of them was the size of a small house, and contained ten half-ton hammers, driven by eccentric cams, which smashed the ore down into iron batteries full of water and mercury.

'Here!' shouted Henry, and scooped up a handful of the paste which poured out of the stamps: a fine sloppy mixture of ore and water and mercury. If there was any silver or gold in the ore, it would be dissolved into the mercury. Then it could slip through the fine screens of the amalgamation tables on to the level below, where wide oscillating belts called vanners would shake out the lead and some of the silver.

'I think I'm going deaf!' screamed Nat, as they descended the wooden staircase which took them down to the fourth level.

'Don't worry!' Henry screamed back at him. 'The fumes will poison you first!'

The fourth level was thick with pungent, metallic steam. Here, there were rows of amalgamating pans, like huge pressurized saucepans, in which the mixture of ore and water and mercury was 'cooked' for eight hours with salt and bluestone. It was then piped down a further level, where it was allowed to settle, and where at last the tailings could be flushed out, leaving the pan heaped with pure silver.

As Nat and Henry reached the last level, their millman came out, wiping his hands on a filthy rag. He saluted Henry, and nodded to Nat, and then shouted in Henry's ear, 'I'm trying out a new process tomorrow. I was told that it worked a treat at the Santa Rita. It might work better here. They steep the ore in chlorine gas; to turn the silver into silver chloride; which will dissolve in water. Then they leach it out with a percolator.'

'Sounds interesting!' Henry shouted back. 'Talk to me tomorrow!'

At last they left the mill, and walked across to collect Nat's mare, and go on down to the mine itself.

'How's the finance?' asked Nat. 'I called in at the store, and Augusta told me you were going to Denver at the end of the week to talk to David Moffat.'

'We're making up accounts now for the last month's diggings,' said Henry. 'On a rough average, though, we've been bringing up $25,000 a week; and when we get that new winding-gear in, it could be very much more. In another two months, counting wages and supplies, we should have paid Lenont's back for everything – drills, stamp-mills, vanners, you name it. We'll be clear of debt, and every silver dollar we dig up from then will be pure profit.'

'You know something, Henry, we're very lucky men,' said Nat. 'And you, you're the luckiest of all of us.'

'God's will, Nat, no more,' replied Henry. 'Do you want to go down the shaft and take another look at the face? They should be blasting in just a while.'

Almost as soon as he spoke, there was a deep, suppressed thump below the ground, as 'Bully' Brett's charges went off. That would mean the end of the night-shift; for while the dust settled the men who had been down below since yesterday

283

evening would return to the surface, leaving the rubble-strewn face for the next shift to dig clear.

'If they're changing shifts, I'll pass for today,' said Nat. 'Besides, I'm meeting Johnny Brown for a drink about mid-morning, and my system is telling me that I could use a drink.'

Henry thrust his hands into the silk-lined pockets of his thick fur coat as he watched Nat ride off across the sloping hillside and down the gulch. Today, for the first time in a long time, he began to feel satisfied and reflective. Ever since the morning when August Rische had shown him the silver ore he had deliberately given himself no time to think about anything else but hiring miners and blacksmiths, ordering up drilling equipment and milling machinery; supervising the building of the hoisting-house and the mill; borrowing money; visiting assay offices; talking to bank presidents; and sitting up late in bed with the lamp burning low so that it wouldn't disturb Augusta, poring over books like *Silver Extraction: A Metallurgist's Guide* and *Mine Management*.

His preoccupation with the Little Pittsburgh had served the secondary but happy purpose of keeping Augusta reasonably satisfied; less tetchy, less sharp. If he had talked at all at the dinner-table during the past few months, he had talked about the mine. He had bored her, he knew, but he had kept her content, and co-operative, because as long as she felt that he was inextricably involved in day-to-day mining in Leadville, she was reassured that he would always come back to her every evening, for meals and rest and whatever affection he allowed her to give him; and at least she would continue to enjoy the dignity of having a husband. She was silently terrified of their accumulating wealth: the thought that they were rising higher and higher on a mountain of shining silver. But so far, the silver remained unspent and she kept her fears mostly to herself, even the ultimate terror that as soon as he was rich enough he would leave her for ever.

Henry had been modest in his purchases so far. Almost all of his share of the Little Pittsburgh diggings had gone for investment to David Moffat, the one-time bookseller who had founded the First National Bank of Denver. William Byers didn't trust David Moffat, but Henry did; and David Moffat had shown his trust in the Little Pittsburgh by coming out to Leadville in person, and insisting on being winched right down to the face, his bald head popping with perspiration. Henry's most extravagant acquisitions since the discovery of silver had been his fur coat, as well as a matching fur coat for Augusta which she rarely wore, and five pairs of handmade shoes. He had even kept the store open.

But his caution and his modesty and his intensive daily work up at the mine were nothing to do with thrift: they were nothing more than manifestations of his deep inner glee that he was now incredibly rich; that he could now do whatever he wanted, go wherever he wanted, and shower himself in diamonds, if the mood took him. Augusta should have been alarmed by his sudden diligence, rather than reassured; because even when he was cutting epitaphs in Carmington he had been flamboyant in his dress, and fond of showing-off. Now, as wealthy as he was, he was behaving almost meanly.

At night, when Augusta was breathing thickly through her open mouth, he would lie with his hands supporting his head, thinking of all the houses he was going to own, all the land he was going to buy; all the silk shirts and bespoke-tailored suits. But it was enough for now that he could afford it all, without having to go out and do it. He had set himself a target. When David Moffat called him, and told him that his bank account had reached $100,000; then, he would spend.

It was the anticipation of freedom that he relished so much. And perhaps, too, it was the slow punishment of Augusta; watching her face light up into a smile whenever he arrived home; seeing the way in which she grasped on to every tiny nuance in his conversation about the mine, anything that would give her hope that he was going to stay in Leadville, and stay with her, and always be careful with his money, and quiet. Praying that he wouldn't leave her, baking his favourite pies, running the store and the bank and the post office counter on her own, to please him. While all the time he knew that he would go, one day.

He wasn't completely free of guilt about Augusta; nor was he lacking in compassion. In other circumstances, they probably could have been the closest of friends. But Augusta wanted him to love her, which he was unable to do; and he believed that the only way in which he could ever be rid of her was through cruelty. Well: he believed it sometimes, when he was trying to rationalize his feelings towards her, or when she had spent two hours in the kitchen making him Philadelphia scrapple, which he particularly liked.

285

He watched Nat Starkey disappear behind an irregular row of dark serrated pines; and then he nodded his head to himself in a self-satisfied way, and began to walk towards the hoisting-house. He had almost reached it when there was yet another deep thumping noise under the ground. He paused, frowned, and then started to jog towards the hoisting-house with his heavy fur coat flaring out behind him.

'Mr Grover!' he called. 'Mr Grover! Who's blasting? Mr Grover!'

R.P. Grover appeared at the open doorway of the hoisting-house. 'No warning was called, sir! Don't know what happened!'

'Anybody down there?' Henry panted, as he reached the door. Two or three dusty-faced miners from the night-shift stood aside to let him pass, and said, respectfully, 'Mr Roberts, sir.'

'Don't know for sure,' said R.P. Grover. 'Most of the night-shift are up. None of the day-shift have gone down yet. Bully! Where's Bully?'

'Bully's still below,' called one miner.

'Bully! Who else?'

'Young Jim Pickings. He stayed behind with Bully, to help him pick up blasting-caps. Bully's particular about blasting-caps.'

'Nobody else? Just those two?'

'Far as I know, sir,' replied R.P. Grover; but he said it in an odd way, in a noticeably suggestive tone of voice; so that Henry turned and looked at him but didn't quite know what else he was trying to say.

'Come on, Mr Grover,' he said, tugging off his coat. 'You – and that fellow there, what's your name?'

'Jackson, sir, no relation to George Jackson.'

'Let's get down there and take a look,' said Henry.

'If that's what you want, sir,' said R.P. Grover. And at that moment, Henry guessed what might have happened; what must have happened; and he stared at R.P. Grover with a feeling of incredulity and dread which he hadn't felt since Doris had died.

ELEVEN

The Little Pittsburgh lode, for the first two hundred feet of its depth, was almost vertical; and so it had been mined simply by sinking a vertical shaft alongside the lode, and hammering into it with compressed-air drills and picks, and blasting it where necessary with giant powder, and sending the excavated ore straight up to the surface in buckets. Deeper down, however, the lode had begun to slope away, and so the miners had been obliged to dig beneath its slope, and support their excavations with square-sets, so that as they dug into the diagonal ceiling which loomed above them, it didn't collapse and crush them.

Henry climbed into the winding-cage with R. P. Grover and the young miner called Jackson, and with a rattling of steam and a high-pitched purring of steel cable, they were lowered down quickly to the hundred-foot station. It was hot and gloomy and chokingly dusty down there, and the flames of the few candles which burned on wall-brackets were vitiated and dim. Henry tied his handkerchief tightly around his mouth, and then said, 'Come on, let's go further down.'

They climbed out of the unsteadily-swaying cage, and crossed the rocky floor of the station until they reached the neck of the incline shaft. Henry took down a candle and peered into the incline, but all he could see was denser dust.

'Blown themselves up, most like,' said R. P. Grover.

'Bully wasn't careless, was he?' asked Henry. 'Not like some.'

'Oh, no,' agreed R. P. Grover. 'Not like some. Dan Scott tried to knock a piece of giant powder into a hole in the ceiling, thinking it was wood, and blew both his eyes out.'

'I think you can save us your horror stories,' said Henry.

Just then, the large flywheel at the head of the incline began to turn. It was connected by driving-belts to the hoisting-engine on the surface, and so someone down at the bottom of the incline must have tugged the bell-rope to have themselves brought up. After a few moments, the top of a giraffe-car appeared through the billowing dust, and inside it, staring up at them with grimy faces, were 'Bully' Brett and Jim Pickings. The young miner called Jackson let out a whoop, and said, 'Safe and sound, boys! Safe and sound!'

'Bully' Brett lifted himself out of the giraffe with a grunt, and dusted himself off with almost fastidious gestures. He was short, powerful, muscular, with a face as ugly as a gargoyle; but a body which would have delighted a sculptor. He wore nothing more than a tight woollen cap and a pair of long johns cut off at the knee; and his body gleamed with sweat. By comparison, Jim Pickings looked thin and runty, although his shoulders were well-built, and his hands were thick-fingered and strong.

Henry loosened the handkerchief around his mouth and pulled it down around his neck. 'What happened?' he asked. 'Are you both all right?'

'A little deaf, sir,' said Bully, banging his left ear with the flat of his hand. He glanced with piggy little deep-set eyes at R.P. Grover, and this time Henry caught the glance, and what it probably meant. *You didn't say that Mr Roberts would come down here, asking questions; not straight after.*

'There's been an accident, sir,' Jim Pickings put in.

'Accident? What kind of accident? Has the roof caved in?'

Bully gripped Jim Pickings' wrist: Henry could only guess how tightly, but the boy closed his mouth at once, and his mouth stayed closed. Bully put on an exaggeratedly mournful expression, and scooped his hat off his head so that his hair stuck out, and said, 'Mr Rische, sir. Fell bad luck, sir. Fell bad luck.'

'Mr Rische is down there?'

'What remains of him, sir.'

'In that case, I'm going to have a look. Mr Grover! You're coming too. Mr Brett – tell me what happened.'

Bully smeared his woollen hat all around his chest and under his arms, to mop up some of the sweat, although Henry guessed that it had probably reached saturation point long ago. 'Well, sir, nothing to it. We'd finished blasting, and we was ready to come upstairs, when Mr Rische said we had a miss-

288

fire; and that we dursn't leave it for the next shift to stick their drills into. I said right you are, Mr Rische, I'll pick it out, don't you have no fear of that; but he said that he was a miner, too, and that he could pick it out as well as anybody. And before I could utter a single word, sir, not the word of a warning, the poor damned fellow had thrust his pick into the charge-hole sir, and young Jim and me were lucky not to get what he got. The walls of that tunnel are red, sir, red as paint, and not a single sign of Mr Rische nowhere, so we was just coming up to get some lime, sir, to dress the tunnel with, before the next shift comes down; on account of not wanting to leave a mess.'

Henry said, 'I want to look,' but R.P. Grover caught his arm.

'If you've never seen the like of that before, Mr Roberts, it's probably better not to. I went down once after something like that, only the second time I was down in a mine, and I looked up, Mr Roberts, and there was a fellow's kidney hanging from the candle-bracket. So, better not to, sir, on the whole.'

Henry was trembling. The heat and the suffocating dust were more than he could stand. His clothes clung and slid around him, heavy and chafing with sweat, and every breath that he took smelled of dust and blood and giant powder. He said, throatily, 'You've killed him.'

R.P. Grover looked at Henry and almost imperceptibly shook his head. 'No, sir. Nothing like that. You heard what Bully had to say. It was just a consequence of inexperience, sir; Mr Rische not knowing much about giant powder. I've seen it before. And you know how particular Bully is with his explosives, sir, even down to his blasting-caps. Fellow I knew at the Yellow Jacket mine left his blasting-caps everywhere, and one day someone got one mixed up in his pipe-tobacco. Blew his pipe to pieces and the nose clean off his face. None of us stopped laughing for a week.'

Henry said, 'You've killed him.'

'No, sir,' said R.P. Grover, placidly. 'Not us.'

And it was the way in which he said 'not us' that made Henry think again about that conversation on the hillside this morning. R.P. Grover had been asking him for something: for support against August Rische. And R.P. Grover had made it patently clear in that peculiar sideways manner of his that he was going to deal with Mr Rische in the most effective possible way. Had it occurred to Henry that he intended to kill him? Henry sought through his conscience as frantically as a man

289

searching through a portmanteau for a vital paper which will save his life. Had Henry known that R.P. Grover would kill August Rische, if he were simply to show that he supported him; and that he would turn a blind eye? Or was it nothing more than an echo of guilt about Doris; and Augusta; and a feeling that luck would never be with him, no matter how ferociously he grasped for it?

'I want to see him,' Henry insisted. If he had murdered August Rische, by carelessness, by intention, by a nod or a wink, he wanted to witness what he had done.

'Not the best idea, sir,' said 'Bully' Brett.

'Nevertheless,' said Henry.

R.P. Grover indicated with a cursory nod of his head that Bully and Jim Pickings should make their way to the surface. 'You go, too,' he told young Jackson. 'There's nothing more that you can do now.'

Jackson hesitated, but Henry said, 'Go on, boy.'

Without a word, R.P. Grover helped Henry to climb into the battered, dusty giraffe; then swung himself in beside him. He tugged the rope which was the faceworker's only contact with the hoisting-house, and after a moment or two the flywheel began to turn, and Henry and he were lowered gradually down the steep incline into the choking lower levels of the Little Pittsburgh mine. Henry felt as if he were being slid into some giant's dark pocket, amongst the rubble and the rubbish and the snuff of death.

At the lower end of the incline, the shaft was blind with dust. It had stopped swirling now, but as R.P. Grover lifted his lamp, Henry could see that it hung suspended in the air like the silt from the bottom of a stirred-up pond. They listened for a moment, before climbing out of the giraffe, but all they could hear was the creaking of the square-sets which supported the sloping roof, and the endless running and rustling of the rats which inhabited every mine.

'Are you sure about this, sir?' asked R.P. Grover.

Henry said, 'Let's get it over with.'

They felt their way with shuffling, crunching footsteps through the fog. R.P. Grover kept the lamp aloft, but it illuminated very little except a halo of dust particles immediately around it; and the flame began to dip and gutter because of the lack of air. The explosion had consumed almost all the oxygen in the face-workings, and it would take time before fresh air would circulate down through the ventilation pipes.

Henry coughed. 'Where do you think he could be?' he asked R.P. Grover.

'Anywhere, Mr Roberts,' said R.P. Grover. 'Or everywhere.'

They cautiously shuffled along a little further. Henry said, 'This morning, on the hillside out there – ' But R.P. Grover touched his arm and said, 'Ssh! Don't you hear something?'

Henry listened, his hand held over his mouth to suppress his breathing. Nothing but rats running; and timbers deeply complaining; and dust settling and settling and settling in an endless whispered requiem for August Rische. And for something else, too: the death of Henry's innocence.

'There,' said R.P. Grover. 'Listen again.' And Henry listened again, but still heard nothing. He looked at Grover through the brown-tinted gloom, and Grover looked back at him for a moment or two, and then beckoned, silently, and began to make his way across the gallery in which they were now standing, stepping over the base-timbers of the square-sets with a practised hoist of his left leg that made him look as if he were limping.

Quite suddenly, they came across August Rische. The spectacle was so horrifying that Henry's legs seemed to lock at the knees, and he was unable to move. What made it even more frightening was that for one split second before Henry realized what they had found, he thought that August's body was a sack or a kitbag that had somehow become caught up in the pulley-ropes that looped from the ceiling of the gallery; and to realize then that it was the remains of a man was almost more than his mind could accept.

R.P. Grover held up his lamp. 'It's him all right,' he said, and although he was trying to be nonchalant about it, the veteran of a hundred grisly mining accidents, Henry could hear the constriction in his voice.

Henry at last managed to step forward, although his terror at what he was seeing was absolute. August must have been blown out of the face-tunnel, almost ninety feet away, and his body must then have been caught by these loops of rope. His arms were held out on either side of him like Christ crucified, and his head sagged down between his shoulders. His legs had both been blown off, however, and the lower half of his body was an incredibly complicated tangle of flesh and bone and

291

sinews, all mingled up with shreds of cotton and leather. He was bleeding on to the dusty floor of the gallery in a long black stream, like an emptying basin.

With a trembling hand, R.P. Grover raised August Rische's head. The body danced on the loops of rope like a marionette, and blood spattered all over Henry's shoes. Miraculously, Rische was still alive, although so close to death that it hardly mattered. The shock which so often killed miners after comparatively slight injuries had sustained him for a few minutes after the blast, numb, and unaware what had happened to him.

'August,' said Henry, in a voice dry with guilt and dust.

August opened his mouth. A bubble of blood glistened and then burst.

'August,' Henry repeated.

But R.P. Grover shook his head, and said, 'He's gone.'

'Can we cut him down from there?'

'If that's what you want.'

R.P. Grover took out his clasp knife, and while Henry supported the weight of the body, Grover quickly cut the tangled ropes. Between them they lowered the body on to the ground. Henry was sickened by how light it was: by the thought that this was how little a man weighed when he had no legs.

'Better to leave him here now,' suggested R.P. Grover, with undisguised distaste. 'I'll send two or three of the lads down, they'll bring him up, and – ' he glanced around the gallery, wiping his hands on his work-trousers ' – clear up the rest of him.'

He picked up the lamp; and both of them were about to leave when August Rische spoke. Henry was so startled by the voice that he shouted out, 'Ah!' and stumbled back against a floor-timber.

'Your wife, Mr Roberts,' breathed August Rische, in a bubbling whisper. 'Always taking the very best care of your wife. . . .'

Henry opened his mouth and then closed it again. But even if he had managed to say anything, it would have been too late, because August Rische let out a cockerel-crow gurgle, and died, his lungs flooded with his own blood. Henry stood where he was, staring at him; and then stared at R.P. Grover.

292

'I told you not to come looking for him,' said R.P. Grover, with the slightest hint of an accusation.

'I don't know what he meant about my wife.'

'Dying men say the strangest things,' R.P. Grover replied. 'Sometimes I think they purposely leave us with the most troublesome words they can think of, just to cause a disturbance once they're gone.'

'Did we kill him?' asked Henry. 'I want to know the truth, Mr Grover.'

'Accidents are a way of life, down in the mines, Mr Roberts. It's a very accidental profession.'

Henry turned away; and then he said, 'Let's get back to the surface. I think I've had enough of this.'

They retreated across the gallery, and then tugged the rope for the engineer to hoist them up the incline. Henry said nothing as they were winched upwards in the giraffe. The air in the shaft was beginning to clear now, and passing in front of his face he could see the chiselled surface of the rock, streaked here and there with black, the unalluring mixture of lead and silver which was now making him wealthier with every day that passed; although how many tons of ore would it have taken for him to gain as much wealth as he had fortuitously acquired today, with the death of August Rische? Rische had left no will; and had no known relatives; and so his third-share in the Little Pittsburgh had already reverted to Henry without the need for any legal argument at all.

Back on the surface, in the glare of the winter sun, the day-shift were waiting to go down, and R.P. Grover picked three of the most hardened of them and sent them on ahead to clear away August Rische's body. Somebody else was waiting there, too, outside the hoisting house: Augusta, in a plain coat of brown wool, with a feathery hat of brown ostrich feathers. She looked unusually severe; and her nose was as red as a grosbeak's breast with cold.

'You should have worn your fur, my dear,' Henry told her, taking her arm, and walking her away from the mine.

'I'm sorry, yes, I should,' she said. He was surprised by the apology in her voice. Then she twisted around looked back frowning towards the mine and asked, 'Has something happened? I heard one of the men talking about an accident. I asked him what it was, but he wouldn't tell me. Not rudely; or unkindly; but as if he felt that I oughtn't to know.'

293

Henry stopped, and held her hands. 'I'm afraid that it's quite bad news. Some giant powder went off by mistake, and August was standing close by.'

'August! Is he hurt?'

Henry squeezed her hands. They felt cold, even through the trim leather of her brown kid gloves. 'He's dead, I'm sorry to say.'

'Dead!' she cried, and both of her hands flew up to her face and clapped to her cheeks as if she were a kind of mousetrap.

'I'm afraid so. There was nothing that anybody could have done to save him. I don't suppose he felt anything.'

'Oh my God,' whispered Augusta. And then, without warning, she fell to her knees on the ground.

'Augusta!' Henry shouted. He seized her, under her arms, and tried to lift her up, but she was a heavy woman; and either she had fainted, or else she had simply decided to kneel there and lean against him with all the inert weight that she could bring to bear. Her feather hat fell off, and the cold wind caught it, and blew it fitfully across the rocky ground, until it caught in a tangle of bushes. Henry tried to heave her on to her feet again and again, but each time she dropped back into a kneeling position; and when he tried to appeal to her to stand up on her own, she simply stared at him with glassy hysterical eyes.

'Augusta, get up,' he ordered her.

She knelt where she was, swaying. Henry held her shoulders for a moment, then released one, then released both of them.

'For goodness' sake, Augusta, you look like the leaning tower of Pisa.'

She jerked her head up. 'That's a cruel thing to say to someone who has almost fainted.'

'You didn't almost faint. You simply decided to get down on your knees and make an exhibition of yourself.'

'I'm suffering from shock.'

'Because of August? A filthy old German sourdough you always greeted with your nose turned up?'

'Lately, he was much cleaner. He started asking for fresh shirts.'

'Just because he started asking for fresh shirts, that wasn't any excuse for you to – *kneel down*, damn it – and *sway*.'

Augusta was quiet, her hands clasped together, palm-to-palm, over her pudenda. It was the word that came into Henry's mind, for some inexplicable reason – pudenda. Yet how sexless she looked, in her brown coat and her spectacles, her hair scraped back from her big pale forehead, and braided into those elaborate Teutonic plaits that always reminded him of loaves of bread. He stepped away from her, then took one step back, and said, 'I'll fetch your hat. Get up. You can get up on your own, can't you?'

He started to walk across to the bushes, where the hat was teasingly lifting its brim in the wind, as if it intended to blow away as soon as he was nearly there. But Augusta called, 'Henry!' and he turned around to see her still kneeling there, one hand raised for him to help her.

Helpless, he thought, as he walked back to her, and held out his hand to lift her up. Helpless and plain and defenceless. Supposing I should incline my head to R.P. Grover, and silently suggest that *she* should meet with an accident down in the mines? But then he thought of August Rische, hanging in the loops, bloody, without legs, and the breakfast he had eaten that morning rose up in the back of his throat like thick dry oatmeal; and it was much as he could do to take Augusta's hand and stand there beside her while she struggled up on to her feet.

'Thank you,' she told him, cuttingly. 'Now you can bring my hat.'

He retrieved her hat and she put it on and adjusted it while she was staring straight into his eyes, as if his face were nothing more than a looking-glass. Then she said, in a busy impatient tone, 'A messenger came for you this morning from David Moffat.'

For several reasons, none of them important but all of them irritating, Henry disliked it when Augusta called David Moffat by his Christian name. He felt that David was *his* friend, *his* business acquaintance, *his* banker; and certainly not Augusta's, if even the least of her criticisms of him were to be taken even half-seriously. She called him Lerf, because of his shiny bald head ('lerf,' she always used to explain, 'is the French for egg.'). Or else she called him Mr W.B.B., which meant 'Wealth Before Beauty'. If only she had realized how ugly she was looking these days to Henry; so ugly, in fact, that if a friend ever commented on Augusta's appearance, Henry would feel that they were being patronizing to him. 'Poor old Henry, nice enough fellow, but have you seen that old burro of a wife of his?'

'What did he want?' asked Henry.

'To see you, that's all. He asked if you could go to Denver, as soon as possible.'

'Did you bring the rig up?' Henry asked, looking around for it.

'No, I walked.'

'You *walked*? And you're going to walk back?'

'I was hoping that you would give me a ride on Belinda.'

'Augusta, I'm busy up here. A man has just been killed. Apart from that, we have a new amalgamating-pan going in today.'

'And all of those things are more important than your wife?'

'I didn't say that.'

'You didn't have to.'

They walked down the hillside in silence for a while, and then Augusta said, 'You're not going to go to Denver, are you, just because Mr Wealth-Before-Beauty beckons?'

'David doesn't beckon, Augusta. He *asks*. He doesn't ask very often, but when he does, it's only because it's important.'

'He wants to tell you how rich you are, I suppose.'

'I know how rich I am, thank you.'

'And a good deal richer now, I suppose, with poor August dead?'

Henry gripped her arm, and stared at her with such violence in his eyes that she couldn't help flinching. 'I could hit you sometimes,' he told her.

'Well?' she challenged him, although he could tell by the slight catch in her voice that she was frightened. 'Here I am, my dear. Hit me.'

But he wouldn't. He couldn't. He released her arm, and stood where he was, with his hands on his hips, steadily breathing freezing cold air through his nostrils. The truth was that he didn't even care about her enough to hit her. To hit a woman, he knew, was an admission of failure; but to be unable to hit her whether he had failed or not, that was the secret and terrible measure of a marriage that knew no love at all. And never had done, he thought; and never will.

He rode Belinda down to the store, with Augusta sitting side-saddle in front of him, her brown ostrich feathers blowing against his face and sticking to his lips, her big bottom protruding over the side of the mare like a sack of washing. When they reached the store, she jumped down gracelessly and went straight in (so she said) to see to her candies. Henry swung himself slowly out of the saddle and tethered Belinda to the rail in front. A boy of about sixteen was waiting there, wearing a thick Mackinac jacket and a wide-awake cap, on which the frayed braiding of a Union cavalry badge could still be seen. He was a round-faced boy, spotty and awkward, but polite, because he touched his cap as Henry mounted the steps up to the boardwalk, and asked, 'Mr Roberts, sir? Begging your pardon.'

'What is it, son?'

'Mr Moffat, sir; he sent me to bring you back to Denver.'

Henry looked towards the closed door of the store, into which Augusta had just disappeared.

'How long have you been waiting out here, son?' he asked.

'I'm sorry, sir?'

'How long have you been sitting out here in the cold?'

'About an hour, sir. Mrs Roberts said she'd bring you back directly, sir; and that I had to wait.'

'Outside? She told you to wait outside?'

The boy bit his lip. Henry laid a hand on his shoulder and said, 'Come along in; get yourself warm by the stove and help yourself to some chocolate cookies. I won't be long; I just have to throw a couple of shirts into a bag.'

They went into the store. Augusta was standing by the candy counter, setting out rows of freshly-made fondants. She watched the boy with sun-blinded spectacles as he walked unsurely across to the stove, and stood there with his mittened hands held out over the top of it, but not too far, in case Augusta should accuse him of absorbing too much heat.

'Don't forget to take your cookies, too,' said Henry, looking at Augusta all the time.

'Are we a charity now?' asked Augusta.

'The boy has come here all the way from Denver, on his own, to fetch me for David Moffat. The very least we can give him is a few cookies.'

'And what if I were to start giving away a few cookies to *every* hungry young child who comes hanging around at the front of our door?'

'If you were to do that, my dear Augusta, it wouldn't make the slightest difference, because we are as wealthy as all hell – '

'Don't profane!' she snapped.

' – as all *hell*,' he repeated, with determination,' – as all damned hell – and we can afford to give away cookies to most of Colorado, if we feel like it – and I'm certainly not going to begrudge this boy!'

'That's right!' Augusta screeched suddenly, and the boy looked at Henry wide-eyed in alarm. She threw her candy-spoon across the store, and it seemed to tumble through the winter sunlight as slowly as if it had been thrown for a mile. 'Accuse me of meanness! Accuse me of starving young children! Accuse me of everything! You're never wrong, are you? Not you! Never, never, never! It's always me! I'm the one to blame, no matter what happens! Well, listen to me, Henry Roberts, I baked those cookies myself, and I worked hard to bake those cookies, and I expect to be paid for them, especially if they're going to be eaten by a brat who comes here running errands for David Moffat, of all people!'

Henry was silent. He knew his face was as rigid as an Indian mask, but he couldn't help himself. He said, in a voice that was very little more than a croak, 'How much is it for six cookies?'

Augusta stared back at him, quivering, her eyes seeming to fill the whole lenses of her spectacles.

'How much?' he demanded, louder this time, harsher.

'Nothing,' said Augusta. Her lips framed the word as if it were a toad from a Grimm's fairy story, crawling dangle-legged from the mouth of the unkind sister.

'You want money, don't you?' bellowed Henry. 'You want money! Tell me how much! How much, for six chocolate cookies? How much, Augusta? How much are they? Three for a penny? Ten for a nickel? Come on, my darling, tell me!'

Augusta opened her mouth again but this time nothing came out at all, and Henry knew that he had gone too far; that he had raged too much; that he had deliberately forced her into the position of having to explain not only to him but to herself the fright she felt about their wealth, and the agonies she felt about their marriage. That was why, in spite of his anger, in spite of the splintering revenge inside his head, he turned away from Augusta, and wrenched open the jar of cookies on the side of the polished counter, and crammed as many as he could into the boy's outstretched hands, and then stalked to the back of the store, and hammered up the stairs to get his bag packed; all this in jerky, tight, suppressed movements; choreographed by fury, scored by silence, and directed by inadequacy. And

298

stood there, in the bedroom, staring at himself in the looking-glass, and thinking only one question, the most fearful question of all human anguish: why me? Why me, oh God, why me?

He was still standing there when Augusta came into the room. Her reflected face in the looking-glass was as pale as a midsummer moon.

'Henry,' she said, quietly.

He didn't answer.

'Henry, I'm sorry. Henry, please forgive me.'

He turned around and faced her. She looked wounded and small.

'All right,' he said, 'I forgive you.'

'It's just that I'm frightened. I thought my future was so secure. Not wealthy, or important; but at least secure. Now it seems like a great yawning chasm, and I don't know what to do.'

Henry hesitated for a moment or two, and then took hold of her hands, turning her wedding-band around and around between his finger and thumb. 'There's nothing to be frightened of,' he told her, although he knew that he was lying. He was frightened himself.

Augusta lowered her head. 'Why did this have to happen to us?' she asked him. 'Of all the people it could have been. But no, it had to happen to us. Oh why was that man on the train?'

He knew that she meant Alby Monihan. She had made the same useless protest so many times before. He squeezed her hands, and kissed her on the forehead, and said, 'I won't be away for long. I'll bring you back a surprise. Something to make you understand how lucky we are.'

'I don't want anything but you, Henry.'

'You've got me.'

'But you're rich now. And you expect me to behave like a rich man's wife.'

'Is that so difficult for you?'

She turned her head away. He had always thought that age would improve her appearance; invest her with dignity; and strengthen the indeterminate lines of her face to make her handsome. But age had done nothing except make her look older, and older in a strange way: as if she had never been young.

She said, 'I'll try, Henry. I promise. But I will never be able to sleep easily again. Money that comes as easily as this. . .

well, it can't be counted on; it can't be honest. Henry, there has to be a penalty.'

He finished packing his bag, and clicked the clasps closed. 'If there is a penalty, Augusta, it will come in its own time. Meanwhile, let's be thankful for what we have. Whatever you think, that silver didn't come from the devil. It came from up there.'

Henry raised his finger and pointed up to Heaven.

'I hope you're right,' Augusta whispered. 'I hope that you're not taking His name in vain; nor misinterpreting His will.'

'No, Augusta,' he said; although there was an intonation in his voice which made her wonder to what question 'no, Augusta,' was the answer.

There was a thin whirl of snow in the air when Henry arrived in Denver the following day, and went into the First National Bank to see David Moffat. Genial, bald, and dressed in the smartest of dark frock-coats, David Moffat was talking on the telephone when Henry came in; but beckoned him to sit down, and opened the decanter of rum on his desk, and pushed it across for Henry to help himself.

'No,' he was saying, 'I don't want even a hundredth share of it; not even a thousandth. No. No, I won't be tempted, not any grounds at all.'

At last he hung up the mouthpiece, and sat back in his deep leather-buttoned chair, and smiled, and clasped his hands together, and smiled, and said, 'Well, now. How is life in salubrious Leadville these days?'

Henry finished pouring himself two fingers of rum, and stoppered the decanter and pushed it back. 'Full of incident,' he replied. 'One of my partners in the Little Pittsburgh was killed yesterday; Mr Rische.'

'Well! That's very tragic!'

'Yes,' said Henry. 'As far as I could discover, he was trying to pick out a charge of dynamite that had misfired. There was an explosion – and, well, he was blown in half. It was terrible.'

'My dear fellow,' said David. 'Well, I'm sorry to hear that. It must have been an appalling shock.'

He paused for a while, in order to show decent respect for August Rische, his hands still clasped together, his face exaggeratedly serious; but then he asked, 'I suppose this means that Mr Rische's share of the mine reverts to you? If I can be

300

so hasty in discussing the financial implications of such a recent tragedy.'

'Well, it has to be thought of,' said Henry. 'And, yes, his share does revert to me.'

David's eyebrows went up a little, and stayed there. 'Every cloud has a silver lining, so to speak,' he remarked. And then he smiled, and said, 'The reason I wanted to see you was because I have just received the latest accounts of your personal profits from the Little Pittsburgh, and you are now exactly half a millionaire.'

He handed over an open ledger, headed 'H. Roberts, Silver Proceeds', and there at the end of a long list of handwritten entries was the provisional total, '$532,106.23.'

Henry read the rows of entries with a growing sensation of lightheadedness. His head was a hot-air balloon, sailing off into unreality. He read the total again and again. Then he said, 'I can hardly believe it.'

'Ah, but it's *true*, my dear fellow! And, what's more, if you now own two-thirds of the Little Pittsburgh, then without any question at all, you are a whole millionaire, not just a half! Congratulations! A millionaire! And just for that, you can take me out to lunch!'

Henry closed the ledger and handed it back to David with a broad smile. 'Do you know what I'm going to do,' he said. 'I'm going to drag an architect back to Leadville with me, and I'm going to build a house. That's what I'm going to do! And not just any house, either. A mansion! A mansion with fifteen bedrooms and half a dozen drawing-rooms and a room for poker and a room for billiards and a room for dancing. And it's going to have a lobby like the Fifth Avenue Hotel in New York, only bigger; and chandeliers; and Oriental rugs; and real animal skins on the furniture. And it's going to have gardens, too, like a palace; you wait and see.'

'You're a rich man, Henry,' grinned David. 'You can do what you like, more or less. You want a house like that, you build one, that'll please that poor hardworking wife of yours. You'll be able to hire servants, dozens if you want to; and all she'll have to do is sit back and enjoy herself. What is it she likes best of all? A little embroidery? Music, maybe?'

'Oh, she'll find something,' said Henry. 'She's one of these ladies who always manage to keep themselves busy.' But even while he was smiling; even in the middle of all of his exhilar-

301

ation, he knew what Augusta would say. He could picture her disapproving face in his mind as clearly as if David were holding up a daguerreotype of her: eyes hard as creek-pebbles, mouth tight as vinegar. There has to be a penalty, Henry. There has to be a judgement. Money that comes as easily as this can't be counted on, you know.

'Let's go find ourselves a bottle of champagne,' David suggested. 'We can't celebrate an occasion like this with desktop rum. Have you tried Latham's Restaurant yet? Dennis Sheedy reckons they've got the finest grub in town. What do you think of braised tenderloin of beef? Hm? With hashed potatoes?'

They shrugged on their heavy fur coats; two big and affluent men; and walked across the street to Latham's, under a sky as green as corroded lead.

David said, 'That was your friend William Byers talking on the telephone when you came in. He's still trying to persuade me to invest in some gopher-brained scheme to send paddle-steamers up and down the Platte. I've told him no, more times than I can count on my hands and my feet and the hairs in my ears, but he still keeps on. Him and that fellow Henry Stanley; scalawags united.'

Henry thought of his conversation with William and Henry Stanley, the night he had visited Denver on his way to Council Bluffs; and of how expansively both of them had talked about the plans they had for Riverfront Park, and for starting up a side-wheeler service on the South Platte; and for the life of him he couldn't remember what arrangements they had made with him about banking. It was something to do with using the name of his bank at Leadville, but he couldn't quite recall what, or why; he had forgotten about it completely after going back to Council Bluffs, and encountering Annabel and then returning to Leadville to find that August Rische and George Hook had struck silver.

He decided it would probably be more prudent not to mention his involvement in William's scheme to David Moffat; particularly since he remembered that William had been moderately insulting about David's banking methods, and about David's baldness, too.

'You know William's trouble?' said David, as they reached the mahogany-framed entrance of Latham's Restaurant. 'William always wanted to be God. That's why he chose to be

302

a newspaper proprietor, rather than a politician. A politician has to be careful whom he insults; a newspaper proprietor has to make sure that he insults everybody, and as often as possible.'

The snow twisted between them like a bridal veil. Then David took Henry's arm, and said, 'Come on inside. No, after you. Multi-millionaires after millionaires, that's the usual rule.'

Latham's was warm and busy and noisy; a large wood-panelled room clad all around with large engraved mirrors, and decorated with crimson plush wallpapers and hothouse ferns and bronze statues of ladies with flowing hair and suggestively slipping drapery, an art-form that was highly popular west of the Missouri. David Moffat was greeted by Stephen Latham himself, a glossy bean-shaped man with a pinprick moustache and a face the colour of pink candlewax; and Stephen Latham twirled around them as he guided them across to one of the best tables, overlooking the entire floor of the restaurant, and tugged out their chairs for them, and snapped fresh napkins into their laps, and asked them what they would care to drink.

'Champagne is the order of the day,' said David, 'and we'll both have the braised tenderloin, with browned potatoes; and the creamed spinach, too.'

Stephen Latham brought them a magnum of French champagne, and a plateful of raw oysters, and said, 'Nice crowd we've got in today, Mr Moffat; and all the nicer for having you here.'

'This man's a flatterer,' joked David Moffat. 'But don't I adore being flattered; even by him.'

'Mr Moffat, a man of your distinction, it is almost impossible *not* to flatter you,' smiled Stephen Latham.

Henry's attention, however, had been caught by a jostling and a sudden commotion at the restaurant's doorway; and a dithering amongst some of the recently-arrived customers; as if something interesting and disturbing had happened. Someone cried, 'This way! This way! Come on, now, make some way there!' and Stephen Latham turned around at last, and then said quickly, 'Excuse me, there is somebody I have to greet. I do apologize. But, you know, with such a busy restaurant to run. . . .'

'What the blazes is going on?' asked David; but his question was answered almost immediately by the appearance through the crowds of customers of a very tall hawk-nosed man with his hair combed up into a high gingery cock's-comb; and on his arm, black-eyed, white-skinned, shy but smiling, a young woman whose appearance made Henry's stomach tighten as if somebody had actually squeezed it tight in their fist.

He watched her unswervingly as she was escorted across the room; and when she stopped behind Stephen Latham, in a position in which he was unable to see her, he threw down his napkin, and pushed back his chair, and unashamedly stood up to stare at her.

She was in her mid–20s, at least half his age. But she had a riveting composure about her, a way of carrying herself that told Henry that what he had originally taken for shyness was in fact a high degree of self-confidence. She was obviously used to being stared at, and used to being surrounded by admiring men, and so instead of acting skittishly, she stood quiet and assured, her head slightly lowered, her lips slightly parted, her liquid-dreamy eyes fixed on Stephen Latham as if she knew both nothing and everything: that devastating combination of innocence and seductiveness that could unbalance even the most sophisticated of men.

'Henry, for God's sake,' David Moffat chided him, and grasped his sleeve. 'You don't want to make an exhibition of yourself.'

But Henry brushed his hand away, and continued to stare at the woman like a man who has seen a ghost, not of anyone he has known in the past; but of someone out of a secret and unrealized dream; with a face and a bearing that was all the more disturbing because he had never believed that there actually could exist a woman who looked like this.

There was something of Doris in her; some heavy-lidded sleepiness about the eyes. But where Doris had been blonde, and fair-skinned, this woman was dark, with long caramel-coloured ringlets heaped up high on her head, under a plumed hat; and a dark complexion. She was more beautiful than Doris, too. She had a finely-formed chin, and a mouth that looked as if it would taste of strawberry wine (should you be allowed to taste it), and a small straight nose that was very slightly tipped. She was small: only an inch or two taller than five feet, but her green velvet day-gown revealed a deep, full bosom, and a tiny corseted waist.

The gingery man waited until Stephen Latham had seated this sleepy-eyed angel, and then sat down himself; and it was only then that Henry groped behind him for his own chair, and sat down again. The young woman had glanced once around the room, and Henry had attempted to smile at her, but if she had noticed him, she had given no indication of it. The sleepy eyes had turned away.

'Do you *know* that woman?' Henry asked David, in a breathless whisper.

'I know the man. That's Murray Holman, who owns the Majestic Theatre on 16th Street. But I can't say that I've ever seen her before. Quite a treat for sore eyes, wouldn't you say?'

'She's devastating. That's the only word for it.'

'Don't look so smitten; even if you *are* smitten. It always spoils my luncheon when people start looking smitten, even when they're smitten by me. Not that I get too much of that these days. These days, those other people are usually the smiters, and I'm nothing more than a very elderly smitee.'

'David, she's the kind of woman who can kill my appetite stone dead, just looking at her. I'm serious.'

'She's probably an actress, if she's having luncheon with Murray Holman.'

'What does that matter?'

'Come on, Henry, you know what reputations actresses can have. Anything in pants that hasn't forgotten to take a bath for less than three months, and actresses are after it like a turkey-vulture going for raw meat. No, you take my advice, Henry, old man, you're best off the way you are. Cosily married, comfortably off, and nothing to look forward to but more money. You would never survive the scandal that would break out if you had a love affair with a girl like that. They're undiluted arsenic: so keep away.'

'Is that the voice of experience talking?' Henry asked, with a sly smile.

'Is there any reason why it shouldn't be?' countered David. He took out his crumpled white handkerchief, and wiped it around the top of his bald head as if he were drying the lid of a large kitchen casserole. 'Even bankers are permitted a few hours out of the dog-kennel, once in a while.' He paused, and then he said, with unexpected frankness, 'Her name was Audrey. I knew her for years. We were very close. Friends, as well as lovers. But in the end I suppose we loved each other rather too much.'

'Well, you know what it says in Ecclesiasticus,' Henry

replied. 'How agree the kettle and the earthen pot together? For if the one be smitten against the other, it shall be broken.'

'That's it,' David agreed. 'That's what I mean by being smitten, and the consequences of it.'

'Still,' said Henry, with a surge of sudden decision, 'I have to go introduce myself. I can't sit here, four tables away from such a captivating woman, and me a millionaire, or at least half of one, and pretend that I don't want to get to know her.'

'You're making a mistake,' David told him, quite pragmatically.

'Yes,' said Henry. 'I expect I am.'

He threw down his napkin again, stood up, tugged down his waistcoat, and walked across to Murray Holman's table. Murray Holman had drawn his dining-chair very close to the young woman, and was inclining his gingery quiff towards her, and reciting something in a dry, croaky whisper, pausing and smiling from time to time to see what she thought of it, and then continuing, but apparently eliciting no response from the young woman whatsoever, since her face was as calm and as beautiful as ever, a face that needed no expression at all.

Henry looked down at Murray Holman's red hand resting on top of the young woman's white glove. Then he cleared his throat, and inclined his head, and said, 'My compliments, madam. Henry Roberts, of Leadville.'

Murray Holman frowned, and glared up at Henry through eyebrows that were like thickets of bright red thistly bee-balm. 'I'm sorry, sir, this lady is with me, and we're not welcoming any intrusions this afternoon.'

Henry smiled. 'My compliments nonetheless.'

To Murray Holman's obvious annoyance, the young woman lifted her hand up to Henry, so that he could take it and brush the back of her white net glove with his lips.

'If you'll forgive me for saying so,' he told her, 'I vow that you're by far the prettiest lady I've ever seen in Colorado; and Colorado is known for her pretty ladies.'

Henry didn't know if he was overtired, or overwrought, or slightly drunk. He could hear what he was saying, but he could scarcely believe that it was him. Could this really be Henry Roberts, the taciturn storekeeper and mine-owner, who spent most of his time drinking whiskey and playing poker with his old cronies in Leadville, or supervising his silver-mine, speaking to a strange young woman in a Denver restaurant with all the courteous smarm of a Southern gigolo?

But the young woman's response was warm and immediate. She blushed very slightly, and nodded her head, and said, 'You're most flattering, Mr Roberts.'

Murray Holman now had no alternative but to introduce her. 'Allow me to present Mrs Elizabeth McCourt Doe,' he snapped.

Mrs Doe put in, 'You may call me "Baby Doe" if you wish, Mr Roberts. Almost everybody else does.'

'Well, that's a very striking name,' said Henry. 'A striking name for a striking lady.'

Murray Holman pulled a grotesque face. 'Now, if you'll excuse us, Mr Roberts,' he said, testily, drumming the table sharply with his fingertips. 'It's really been a pleasure to, unh.'

'Are you here for long, Mrs Doe?' Henry asked Baby Doe, ignoring Murray Holman's elaborate display of impatience.

'She's appearing in my new play,' said Murray Holman. 'Her day-boo as an actress. *Hamlet*, complete with real lake for Ophelia to drown in. Mrs Doe here will be playing Ophelia.'

'I don't mind the water,' put in Baby Doe, helpfully.

Henry frowned at her, and then said, 'You don't?'

'Well, it's a wonderful opportunity. Mr Holman says that he can make me famous. The toast of the Rockies.'

She reached across the table and laid her hand on Murray Holman's wrist, and that to Henry was an unmistakable signal that however charming he might be; however attractive and however courteous; Baby Doe was interested above all in fame and fortune, and Murray Holman was going to remain her escort for just as long as he could promise her attention, and applause, and money. For all her sleepy-eyed look of girlish naiveté, Baby Doe was clearly ambitious, and proud, and acutely aware of her own allure.

'You like Shakespeare?' Henry asked Baby Doe.

Baby Doe blinked.

'You know,' Murray Holman prompted her. 'The fellow who wrote *Hamlet*.'

'Oh – oh, yes,' smiled Baby Doe. 'I think he's extraordinary. Did you know he wrote in poetry *all* the time? I've learned most of my lines.

'Do not, as some ungracious pastors do,
Show me the steep and thorny way to heaven,

307

Whil'st, like a puff'd and reckless libertine,
Himself the primrose path of dalliance treads
And recks not his own rede.'

She hesitated, and then turned to Murray Holman, and said, 'Do you know, I never understood that. What's a rede, and how do you reck it?'

'Search me,' replied Murray Holman. 'Now, Mr Roberts, you really must leave us be. I have some important business to discuss with Mrs Doe.'

'Well, now that I'm an actress of some note . . .' said Baby Doe, with a teasing and only half-apologetic smile.

Henry bowed his head, and then returned to his table. David Moffat was drinking turtle soup, his bald head bent forward, his napkin tucked into his collar; and there was a plate of San Francisco Bay shrimps waiting for Henry, brought from California on the Central Pacific Railroad, in chunks of ice. Henry sat down and said to the waiter, 'Bring me some sauce diable.'

'Well?' asked David, tearing sourdough bread. 'Did madam give you the brush-off?'

'Not at all,' said Henry. 'But Mr Holman is going to cast her in the part of Ophelia in his new production of *Hamlet*. Complete with real lake for Ophelia to drown in, he says. And just at the moment, that's all she's interested in. Fame, and money.'

'Show me a woman who isn't.'

The waiter brought Henry his devilled sauce, and he began to eat his shrimps, chewing slowly without tasting either the shellfish or the pepper. A trio began to play on piano and violin and double bass, 'The Song of the West', and the restaurant was noisy with laughter and clouded with tobacco smoke and busy with waiters and customers and revolving fans.

'You're smitten, that's your trouble,' said David Moffat, after a long while.

Henry asked, 'What other theatres are there?'

'What do you mean?'

'Apart from the Majestic. What about the Tremont?'

'What about it?'

'Well, is it for sale?'

'For sale?' asked David blankly. 'The Tremont? How should I know?'

'It's a good theatre, though, isn't it?'

'Sure it is. It's not as large as the Majestic, doesn't seat so many. But it's a luxury theatre, yes.'

'Who owns it? Do you know?'

'Of course I do. Willis Benn. I helped to finance his first three productions.'

'Would he sell?' asked Henry.

'You mean the whole theatre?' David wanted to know, but when Henry nodded, he shook his head, and said, 'Well. . . I'm not so sure. He may. His wife's sick, I know that much. But whether that will make any difference, that's anybody's guess. He loves his wife, but he loves that theatre, too.'

'Why not ask him?' Henry enthused.

'He wouldn't part with it for peanuts,' David warned.

'How much?'

'I don't know. Thirty-five thousand, at least.'

'Can I afford it?' Henry asked him.

'Well, of course you can afford it. But whether it's a worthwhile investment, that's a different question altogether. And, believe me, running a theatre isn't cheap these days. One failed production, and you're sunk. Or semi-sunk, anyway.'

'David,' said Henry, 'you get on that galvanic muttering-machine and call what's-his-name, Willis Benn, and tell him I want to buy his theatre, outright, cash, now.'

'What do you mean, now?' David Moffat's face was as bright as Henry's shrimps.

'*Now*, before luncheon is over.'

David turned in his seat and squinted across the restaurant at Baby Doe, who was laughing now at some remark that Murray Holman had made; or perhaps just to show Henry that she didn't care for his attentions at all; that charm alone was not enough. Then David turned back to Henry again, and said, 'Are you sure she's worth it? She looks pretty flighty to me.'

Henry leaned forward, pushing aside his half-finished shrimps. 'David,' he said intently, 'I have never asked anyone for much. I have never asked myself for anything. I lay back for most of my life and expected good fortune to walk in through my door; and when it didn't, I did nothing more than shrug and accept it. David, I have been selling picks and shovels and bags of flour for nearly twenty years, and living with a woman I neither love nor respect. Now that good fortune has at last arrived, don't think that I'm going to continue to expect

309

nothing out of my life but what I have already. I'm rich, David, and I'm going to be very much richer; and no matter whether I worked for my riches or not, I'm going to enjoy them.'

'And enjoying your riches includes. . ?' asked David, inclining his head towards Baby Doe.

Henry remained expressionless. David at last wiped his mouth, put down his soup-spoon, and said, 'Very well. I'll be back in a minute.'

By the time the wild duck on dirty rice was served, with a bottle of pale Fleurie and a side order of baked potato skins and new green peas, Willis Benn himself had arrived at the restaurant. He waved aside the cloakroom attendant who tried to take his fur-collared coat, and walked straight across to David Moffat with his hands in his pockets, his face pale, and his hair still sticking up at the back where his hat had tugged it as he took it off. He was a short, handsome man, rather theatrical in his manner, his face betraying the signs of worry and overwork and more gin than was good for him; but pugnacious, and determined.

'Well, Mr Moffat,' he said. 'Is this the gentleman who wants to buy my theatre?'

'Henry Roberts,' said Henry, standing up and holding out his hand.

Willis Benn ignored his hand, and said crisply, 'I hope very much that this isn't a practical joke.'

'Sit down,' said Henry. 'Have a potato skin.'

'I've eaten, thank you; and I'd rather stand. At least until I hear what it is that you have in mind.'

'Nothing complicated,' said Henry. 'I simply wish to buy the Tremont Theatre, for cash.'

'I see. And what do you intend to do with it? Demolish it, I shouldn't wonder, and build a hotel?'

Henry shook his head. 'Nothing of the kind. I want to buy the Tremont simply because I want a theatre. I want the Tremont to remain exactly as it is now; and I want you to go on running it, and whatever staff and company you have to continue to put on plays.'

Willis Benn stared at Henry for nearly half a minute without saying a word. Then he drew out a chair, and sat down. 'I'm not sure that I understand,' he said. 'The Tremont is a good theatre, of course; in fact, it's one of the finest theatres in the West. But I'd be lying to you if I pretended that it was a good

310

investment. Our last production of *Lucia di Lammermoor* made only $450 profit; and most of that we had to spend on new upholstery, and back wages for the set-builders.'

'Well, you're honest enough,' said Henry. 'Go on, have a potato skin, before they get cold. But the fact is that simply owning the theatre will be a worthwhile investment, as far as I'm concerned.'

Willis Benn looked across at David Moffat. 'Is this true?' he asked.

David Moffat squashed out his double chins over his collar, and tried to make a face that was both reassuring and non-committal. 'As far as I understand it,' he said. 'Mr Roberts here has what you might call personal reasons.'

Henry glanced across at Murray Holman's table, to make sure that Baby Doe was still there. A waiter was just setting down a *coupe de glace* in front of her, melon flavour, with Italian wafers, and Henry realized that he didn't have more than fifteen minutes to persuade Willis Benn to sell him the Tremont, if that.

'Are there any conditions?' asked Willis Benn. He picked up a potato skin, sniffed the yellow jack cheese on it, and then put it down again.

'Only two,' said Henry. 'Well, three, really. The first is that you give me an immediate answer, right here and now, yes or no. The second is that you make arrangements as soon as you can for putting on a production of *Hamlet*, with a real lake on the stage for the scene in which Ophelia drowns herself, and maybe a choir, and real performing dogs, and whatever else you can think of; and the third is that I get to choose who plays the part of Ophelia.'

Willis Benn sat with his lips pursed, and then said, 'So that's it. A woman. Wouldn't you know it.'

Henry said, 'That's my offer. What my motives are, well, they aren't any concern of yours. You can take the offer or not, whatever you want. But it won't be repeated; not ever.'

Willis Benn said, 'I couldn't accept less than $27,000. And the contract of sale would have to include guaranteed employment for myself as theatre director, and guaranteed employment for all of my staff and my principal company.'

Henry looked at David. He could see in David's eyes that David believed that Willis Benn would accept less. As subtly as he could, in the pretence of folding his napkin, David raised

311

both hands twice, and then three fingers on his right hand. Ten plus ten plus three.

Henry said, 'You'll put on *Hamlet*, too, just the way I want it?'

'I don't see why not,' Willis Benn replied. 'There's always room in the theatre for a little burlesque. That's as long as you pay for the lake and the dogs and whatever other circus performances you want to include. Yes, and the lady's salary, whoever she is.'

'You're pretty broke, aren't you, Willis?' David put in, sensing that Henry was too eager to settle the deal, now that he knew he could offer Baby Doe exactly what Murray Holman was offering her, and better.

Willis shrugged. 'I can't say that we've been doing spectacularly well.'

'So this sale could save your bacon for you?'

'It might not work out too badly, provided Mr Roberts is sympathetic to what the theatre is trying to do; and doesn't impose too many fancy productions on us. With all due respect, Mr Roberts.'

'Well,' said David, 'I'm sure that you'd find Mr Roberts the most sympathetic of proprietors. He's a great lover of the arts, aren't you, Henry? An aficionado. He paid for Inman's Viennese jugglers to visit Leadville once, didn't you, Henry? He's a cultured man.'

Henry saw that Baby Doe had almost finished her ice, and was licking her spoon with a tongue that was as pink and provocative as that of a white-furred kitten. Murray Holman was beckoning the waiter across to bring him a brandy and a cup of coffee, and it wouldn't be long before they left. Henry said to Willis Hunt, 'No arguments. I'll pay you thirty.'

Willis Hunt was in mid-conversation with David about their staging of *Il Trovatore*. He stopped, and stared at Henry in dramatic disbelief. 'Thirty?' he asked, pronouncing every letter with the clarity of a trained thespian. David echoed him. '*Thirty?*' but David's voice was strangled with a very different kind of disbelief.

'That's it. That's the offer. Thirty. You can have the cash as soon as the papers are signed. Now, make up your mind.'

The waiter came up to Willis Benn, and asked, 'Would you care for a drink, sir?'

Willis Benn tugged quickly at his nose: a nervous gesture

that Henry guessed must be habitual. Then he rubbed his hands together quickly, and smiled, and said, 'Champagne, I think, French. A magnum, if you have it.'

'Yes, sir, the Bollinger.'

Henry stood up, and shook Willis Benn's hand. Then he asked David, 'Look after the details, please, David,' and without saying anything else, walked back across the restaurant to Murray Holman's table. Murray Holman was leaning back with his thumbs in his waistcoat while the waiter lit a cigar for him, and Baby Doe was sipping coffee, the plumes on her hat blowing in the draught from the ceiling-fan above her head.

'You'll pardon a second intrusion,' said Henry, loudly.

'Do you really think so?' Murray Holman demanded, equally loudly. Baby Doe looked up and smiled at Henry, but she was clearly anxious that Murray Holman was going to be extremely irritated.

'Well, maybe you won't pardon it,' said Henry. 'But the fact of the matter is that I, too, am just about to stage a production of *Hamlet*, with a real lake; and not only with a real lake but with a choir as well, and a team of performing dogs, and Edwin Booth in the role of Hamlet.'

'*You* are about to stage a production of *Hamlet?*' Murray Holman asked, blowing out cigar smoke, and coughing, and waving aside the offer of a fourth match from the waiter standing beside him. '*You* are about to stage a production of *Hamlet?*'

'With Edwin Booth?' asked Baby Doe, deeply impressed. Edwin Booth was easily the most popular and best-paid touring actor in the West. His Romeo brought tears to the eyes of even the most hardened sourdoughs.

'That's correct,' replied Henry.

'*You*, as far as I know, are a mineral prospector,' said Murray Holman, tartly. 'So where are you going to stage a production of *Hamlet?* Two hundred feet down in the Little Pittsburgh mine?'

'Ah, you *do* know me, then,' said Henry.

'I've heard about you, I must confess. More's the pity.'

'Have you heard that I now own the Tremont Theatre, on West 14th Avenue?'

'No, I haven't, and I don't believe it. I met Willis Benn only this morning, and if Willis had sold the Tremont to you or to anyone else, he would have told me about it.'

'Do you want him to?' asked Henry.

'Do I want him to *what?*' Murray Holman demanded.

Henry smiled. 'To tell you about it. He's right over there, talking to David Moffat. They're working out a contract of sale.'

Murray Holman peered at Henry through the flat blue layers of his cigar smoke, like a man peering through shutters. He didn't believe Henry at first: wouldn't. But then he slowly eased himself around in his chair, and stared across the restaurant towards David Moffat's table. He stared for a long time, and then he eased himself back again, and took the cigar out of his mouth.

'Did you have to do *Hamlet?*' he asked, with a rasp in his voice. 'I've already spent a king's ransom on that production; nearly $12,000.'

'I had to do *Hamlet*,' said Henry. He looked down at Baby Doe, and couldn't help grinning with the knowledge that he had almost won her. 'It's the only play for which Mrs Doe is already prepared.'

He held out his hand to Baby Doe, and said, gently, 'You're the most remarkable-looking lady, Mrs Doe, if you'll forgive me; and I very much want to get to know you. That's why, this lunchtime, I've bought you a theatre, and an actor-manager, and a company of players, so that you can play Ophelia the way she ought to be played, and play her for me.'

'You bought me a theatre?' said Baby Doe, in a haunted, inquiring, whisper. Then, 'Did you hear that, Murray? Mr Roberts has bought me a theatre!'

'Is Mrs Doe under a contract to you, Mr Holman?' asked Henry, bluntly.

'Of course,' snapped Murray Holman. He was confused, and irate.

'But, Murray,' cooed Baby Doe, reaching over the table and touching his hand. 'You know that I haven't signed the paper yet. That was why you were taking me to lunch. I haven't signed the paper yet.' She looked up at Henry and gave him an admiring smile. 'You don't even know me, Mr Roberts. You don't even know me at all. How could you buy me a *theatre?*'

'Let's just say that I recognize grace when I see it,' said Henry, and then laughed out loud, because the power of his money had suddenly become apparent to him. The power not only to buy what he wanted, but to be able quite wilfully and promiscuously to change the course of other people's lives. In

314

the space of a single lunch-hour, he had altered Willis Benn's future, irrevocably; and thwarted Murray Holman; and won himself the most desirable girl that he had ever seen in his life, changing her destiny, too, forever. The power of wealth. He could almost feel it in his muscles.

'Pardon me,' he said to Murray Holman, 'but as soon as you've finished your luncheon, perhaps Mrs Doe would like to come over and talk to me.' He inclined his head respectfully to Baby Doe, and said, 'We do have a great deal to discuss now, after all.'

'Mrs Doe will be leaving with me, thank you,' replied Murray Holman, his nostrils widening aggressively.

'Well, I don't think so,' said Henry, and took Baby Doe's hand, and kissed it again, and then retreated from the table in the certain knowledge that Baby Doe was quite capable of making it clear to Murray Holman herself that she was not going anywhere at all, at least not with *him*.

As he sat down again at his own table, David said, 'We seem to have most of the basic agreement worked out, Henry. I've suggested to Willis here that we all meet some time tomorrow morning to exchange the necessary papers.'

'All right,' said Henry, and shook Willis Benn's hand. 'Good to do business with you, Mr Benn.'

'My pleasure, Mr Roberts. And – er – is that the young lady, over there? The one sitting with Murray Holman?'

Henry gave away nothing; except perhaps a flicker of his eyes.

'You could do yourself a darn sight worse,' smiled Willis Benn. 'She's a choice young lady, worth fighting for. Don't ask me if she's worth all of thirty thousand dollars, because I wouldn't know. But I hope that you'll discover that for yourself.'

After he had left, the waiter brought their tenderloin steaks; and now Henry ate with an appetite. He didn't look over at Baby Doe, but David did, and shook his head from time to time as if he couldn't believe that any of this meal was really happening.

'We're friends, aren't we?' he asked Henry.

'I like to think so,' Henry told him.

'Well, in that case, let me be frank with you. You're a rich man now, but you're only going to *stay* rich if you observe the fundamental tenets of good business. Today, you just broke three of those tenets in one crack.'

Henry chewed steak, watched David, and said nothing.

'First of all, you should never pay a man more than he's asking. He'll be pleased to get what he had in mind, he doesn't need any more. If you give him any more, you'll only earn yourself a reputation for extravagance and then you'll find that nobody will ever offer you anything for a fair price, ever; and you'll have every free-loader and panhandler and confidence artist from here to Bangor, Maine, coming clustering around you looking for whatever they can get. And the business community won't take you too seriously, either.'

David paused, embarrassed at what he had felt obliged to say, but Henry told him, 'Go on.'

'Well, second of all, you should never make a bad investment, not for any reason at all. Now, I'm not saying that the Tremont Theatre is all *that* bad a buy; but if you'd wanted to put money into it, you'd have been better off from an investment point of view doing what I did: laying out capital for individual productions, judging each production on its financial possibilities.'

'Anything else?' asked Henry. He had stopped chewing now, and swallowed, and set down his fork.

'Only one more thing. You can kick me if you like, tell me to mind my own business. But, Henry, you should never make any business decision on account of a woman. Or any decision, come to that. I mean, you think back on history. History is littered with sorry examples of men who were brought low by a pretty face and a creamy frontage. Mark Antony. Samson. Jim Fisk.'

'Jim Fisk?' asked Henry. Jim Fisk had been the flamboyant partner of Jay Gould, and together they had made themselves a fortune by forging Erie railroad stock and selling nearly $6 million of it to Cornelius Vanderbilt. Fisk had been shot in 1872 by a rival for the affections of a lady called Josie Mansfield. Henry said, 'I hope you're not going to compare me with him.'

'I'm just giving a word to the wise,' replied David. 'It wasn't meant to be personal.'

'In that case, I won't take it personal.'

Just then, followed by murmurs of appreciation and a great turning-around of heads, Baby Doe came across the restaurant, her skirts slightly raised, and approached Henry's table. Behind her, glowering, his gingery quiff leaping from the top of his head like an angry exclamation point, came Murray Holman, obliged to escort her by the rules of etiquette, but manifestly fizzing with jealousy.

Henry and David stood up. 'David,' said Henry, 'allow me to introduce Mrs Elizabeth McCourt Doe. Mrs Doe is going to be my very first leading lady.'

'Charmed,' said David, taking Baby Doe's hand.

Baby Doe said, in an affected whisper, 'We must meet later, Mr Roberts, to talk about the play.'

'Perhaps you'll do me the honour of having dinner with me,' said Henry.

'Not tonight, I regret,' she told him. There was a whole encyclopedia of romantic and erotic allures in the way she spoke, the way she held her head, the way her hair curled around her neck, the glistening light on her lips, the faraway look in her eyes. Henry felt almost as if his lunch had been drugged with sticky opium, as if he were heavy-limbed and helpless.

'Tomorrow?' he asked her; and when she nodded, he said, 'Where are you staying?'

'At the Corona,' she said, 'on Broadway.'

'Seven o'clock, then,' he told her.

Murray Holman, as he escorted Baby Doe away, leaned forward to Henry and lifted one threatening finger, and said, 'I won't forget this, Mr Henry Roberts. You mark my words, I'll have your scalp for this, and I'll hang it on my goddamned lodge-pole, along with all the other scalps of interfering amateurs.'

'You're welcome to try,' Henry replied, as gently as he could. But he could see Baby Doe stop and turn and smile at him over Murray Holman's shoulder, and he knew just what it was that Murray Holman was fighting for, and how hard he would fight for it.

TWELVE

That afternoon, he went out and he spent over $45,000. He went to Ischart's the Jewellers on 15th Street and bought a pair of matching diamond solitaire rings: one for himself of over 59 carats, and one for Augusta of over 32 carats. Buying the rings was an attempt both to placate Augusta and to defy her. He did genuinely feel that she deserved a reward for all the years of work she had put into the store, and what else did a man give his hard-working wife but a diamond ring? On the other hand, he knew that she would vigorously disapprove of his having spent so much money on something so ostentatious. She would find it more threatening than flattering: a bright and sure sign that their old life was over, that her security had literally been mined away from under her feet.

The jeweller laid the rings side by side on the dustless black velvet of his display tray, while the afternoon sunlight came softly in through the clerestory windows and illuminated the sapphires and the pearls, the silver and the gilt, a new world of new reflections which Henry wanted to relish to the very utmost. He was rich now, and he wanted to look rich, and behave rich, and live rich.

'There is a legend that this diamond once belonged to Marie Antoinette,' said the jeweller. He held up the ring, and the stone suddenly flashed, as brightly and as abruptly as a lighthouse on a clear winter's night. 'You know that every large diamond has its story. Now, you're going to become part of this diamond's story.'

'I don't think so,' smiled Henry. 'This diamond is going to become part of *my* story.'

'Whatever you say, sir; of course.'

Later, he went to Kilgore's, and ordered four new suits, as

well as a dozen shirts, and fifteen new silk neckties. He went to Reed and Sherman on 12th Street, not far from Cherry Creek, and bought two pairs of ready-made shoes, and had his foot measured so that in future he could order his own handbuilt shoes. He bought a pair of diamond and ruby cufflinks in the pattern of chessboards; and silk underwear; and six cases of French champagne; and cologne; and two English shotguns by Holland & Holland, with silver-engraved sideplates and exhibition-grade walnut stocks.

He intended to buy himself a new carriage, too, but by the time he had left Manning's Shotguns, the sun was already well down behind the cold purple frieze of the Rockies, and he was feeling tired and in need of a drink. He went back by cab through the brightly-lit streets of Denver, feeling both elated and unreal. Every now and then he raised his hand, and turned it from side to side, so that the huge diamond on his middle finger caught the flare from the gas-lamps and the glitter from the shop-windows that flanked the street. The evening was sharp and clear and dry, a fine Denver evening, and the stars prickled high above him, diamonds in their own right.

'You're going to wear it now, sir?' the jewellery salesman had asked him, momentarily disconcerted, even though he was obviously used to the eccentric ways of the suddenly wealthy.

'Anything wrong in that?' Henry had replied.

'Nothing at all, sir, except that you haven't insured it yet.'

Henry had admired the ring sparkling on his finger, and said, 'Well, if I lose it, I can always buy another.'

He had intended to go straight back to David Moffat's house, where he was supposed to be staying the night. But he kept finding himself thinking again and again about Baby Doe; and he was reluctant to spend the evening small-talking to David about money and investments when he still hadn't had time to churn over in his mind the dramatic way in which she had affected him. He kept glimpsing her face, again and again, in his mind's eye; he kept thinking about her hair, and how it strayed in those soft and wayward curls around the nape of her neck. He kept seeing her eyes, and the deep warm shadow between her breasts; and somehow those images became intermingled with memories of Nina, balancing athletically over his bed, and even further back, to Doris, and that summer's day in Carmington, so long ago now that it seemed to have shrunk

319

to the size of a tiny animated picture, in which the characters spoke in tinny, barely distinguishable voices.

Thinking about Baby Doe made him think about the tragedy of his own life. It was not a tragedy in the theatrical sense; even though he was now the owner of a theatre. It wasn't a *King Lear* or a *Macbeth*. It was simply the plain tragedy that affects those ordinary people who are never lucky enough to find someone who inspires them, either to love and be loved, or to realize the best out of themselves; but although it is an ordinary tragedy, the kind of tragedy you meet with every day, it is no less heartrending, no less dramatic, and the sadness of it cuts no less deep.

Instead of David's house, he directed the cab to the Corona Hotel, on Broadway between 8th and 9th, on Arlington Heights; a small stocky building in the Queen Anne style, from whose upper windows the lilac sunlight was still reflected so that it looked like nothing more than a decorative facade, the shell of a building through which he could see the sky. For one unbalancing moment, Henry was reminded of the time when he had gone back to Council Bluffs to find Annabel and Edward McLowery, a time when past and present had overlapped, like two voices speaking at the same time. Standing over Edward McLower's grave-marker, closing Annabel's door, it had seemed to him that only a few minutes had passed since he had first met them; that time had somehow closed itself like a folding mirror. For one moment, he saw the Corona Hotel as a skeleton of itself; and was sharply reminded of the mortality both of buildings and lovers. You never get time for a second chance, he thought to himself. You have to seize your time and seize it tight; and that was why he was here on Broadway at the Corona Hotel looking for Baby Doe a day earlier than he was supposed to.

'Mrs Doe?' he asked the desk-clerk. The man's face was as smooth as beeswax. He picked up the telephone, and said, 'I'll inquire. Who shall I say is calling?'

'Say, the new owner of the Tremont Theatre.'

The desk-clerk stared at him for a moment, but then picked up his telephone, and wound the handle with a tight little whirl, and said, 'Mrs Doe? There's a gentleman here in the lobby. Yes, he wishes to see you. The new owner of the Tremont Theatre. Does that make any sense?'

There was a pause; then, 'Yes, it seems to make sense, sir.

320

Please go up. Mrs Doe's room is on the third floor, number 313.'

She was waiting for him at her open door as he came quickly along the carpeted corridor. She was already dressed for dinner, in a low-necked silk dress of dark dove-grey, with lace-frilled cuffs, and a beribboned bustle tied up with bouquets of small grey-and-white silk flowers. Her hair was drawn up tightly, into shining brunette curls, and pinned with tortoiseshell combs. Her perfume was distilled from gardenias. She said, 'I didn't expect you,' and her voice was as soft as the lilac evening air.

'Didn't you? Didn't you think that a man who cared about you enough to buy you a theatre would want to pay some attention to you at the earliest possible opportunity?'

She lowered her head, but he could tell that she was smiling. 'Don't tell me that you're going to see anyone so crucially important that you can't put them off until tomorrow,' Henry went on.

'You're awfully direct, Mr Roberts,' she said. 'I scarcely even know you; for all of your attentions.'

Henry rested his hand against the lintel and watched her in amusement and appreciation. 'In that case, I shall do everything I can to make sure that you do. Especially since you're going to be my Ophelia.'

She looked up at him with those slanting, hypnotic eyes. 'You *assume* that I'm going to be your Ophelia.'

'Why shouldn't you? Whatever Murray Holman offers you, I'll offer you double.'

'Murray Holman's furious. I mean he's really, really furious. He kicked a newsboy on the way out of the restaurant.'

'Then I shall pay the newsboy double, too.'

'You're funny.'

Henry shook his head. 'No, I'm not funny. I just appreciate a jewel when I see it; and want to have it for myself.'

'Are you drunk?' she asked.

'Not even slightly. You will be my Ophelia, won't you?'

'Do you know what kind of girl Ophelia was?'

Henry said nothing. His father had read him some of Shakespeare's sonnets and part of *Titus Andronicus*, but that was all the Shakespeare he knew. '*Why, there they are both, baked in that pie, whereof their mother daintily hath fed, eating the flesh that she herself hath bred.*'

Baby Doe said, 'Ophelia was fey, that was what Murray said.'

'Fey? What does that mean?'

She shrugged. 'I don't know. Precious, I guess; something like that.'

There was a silence between them; one of those awkward but eager silences between two people who don't know each other well enough to be able to carry on a fluent conversation; and yet like each other enough not to want to say goodnight.

Baby Doe said, 'We were supposed to be having dinner with the Cheesmans.'

'Can't you call Murray on the telephone, tell him you've suddenly developed a headache? He'd understand, wouldn't he?'

'I don't know,' said Baby Doe. 'It really means a lot to him, this dinner. The Cheesmans are putting up most of the money for *Hamlet*. And I did promise.'

'How much did you promise?'

'Cut my throat and hope to die; go to Hell and hope to fry.'

'*That* much?'

Baby Doe smiled. 'Well, nearly that much.'

Again, that silence, relished as slowly as clear molasses. Then Baby Doe opened wide the door of her room, and immediately walked away from him, into the foggy lilac light of the early evening, her shoulders and back a bare white triangle, as bare as ivory, as white as Star-of-Bethlehem flowers, her head turned so that he could see her profile, the light touching her lashes; and he felt then that he entered the room on a wave, rather than walking, a wave that surged him forward until he was standing close beside her.

'Will this make up for breaking your promise?' he asked her, and he took out of his pocket the small navy-blue ring box which contained Augusta's ring; although he didn't open it. Baby Doe stared at him, and the evening light on her lower lip was an angel's-bow, just as Doris' had been; and then she reached up and clasped Henry's wrist.

'You mustn't spoil me until you know me,' she said.

'I won't get to know you unless I spoil you.'

'I'm a woman, that's all.'

'I know. But you're a dream too. And even dreams have obligations. Especially to the people who dream them.'

'No,' she said, and walked a little further away, towards the grey chaise-longue, her grey skirts rustling. The windows

322

suddenly lost their light: the sun had gone down over the mountains, and Denver was steeped in the shadow of its greatest glory. Baby Doe looked up at Henry, and there was a complicated expression on her face; an expression which the twilight made almost malevolent. She was gentle, and she was beautiful; but she was very strong, too. And that was what she wanted him to know.

'I'll order something to drink,' she said. 'Is there anything you like?'

'Whiskey's very acceptable, thank you.'

'Hm. I would have thought rum, looking at you.'

'Do I really look that uncouth?'

'No, not uncouth. Just – I don't know – *homespun*, if you know what I mean.'

'Homespun? You're the first person who's ever said that.' Henry felt peculiarly inadequate, and embarrassed. He didn't expect women to criticize him so directly, and yet so lightly. She wasn't being insulting; only accurate, and somehow that hurt all the more. It hurt, too, because he liked her so much. He thrust his hands into his pockets, and went to the window, and lifted the curtains, and looked out at the lights of Denver, like lanterns drowned in a lilac lake, 15th Street and Broadway and Capitol Hill, which had once been Brown's Bluff; all sparkling now with electricity, and spun with telephone wires.

Henry said, 'I suppose you'd better go. Murray will be waiting for you.'

Baby Doe hesitated, and then replied quietly, 'I don't have to, you know. I'm my own woman.'

Henry let the curtains fall back. On the opposite wall, there was a large melancholy lithograph of Wind River, during a thunderstorm; and on the black walnut sideboard just below it, a brass domed clock ticked, almost six hours wrong. Somebody next door flushed a noisy lavatory, and down in the street there was a rumble of wheels on the paved roadway.

Henry said, 'I didn't think that anybody could say that they were completely their own, whether they were man or woman. Everybody has obligations, after all, if only to be peaceable to his friends and neighbours, and nothing else.'

In reply, Baby Doe asked, 'Show me what you have in that box.'

'Do you really want to see? Or are you teasing me?'

'Perhaps I'm teasing you; perhaps I'm not. But show me.

You can't offer it to me and then take it back again, without my having seen it. You're not cruel, are you, as well as sentimental?'

'I didn't say that I was sentimental.'

'You didn't have to. You have it sewn on your sleeves. A heart on one side, and tears on the other.'

Henry took out the ring box again and approached her across the room. It was so dark now that they could scarcely see each other, yet neither of them had proposed lighting a gas-mantle (the Corona was still awaiting belated conversion to electric light). He stood in front of her for a moment, and then he placed the ring box in the palm of his right hand, and opened up the lid, and held it out for her to look at as cautiously as if it were actually dangerous; which in a strange way it was.

'Look,' he said; and she picked it up.

It caught the dimmest of lights, and concentrated them all into one violent lilac spark. Then, she slipped it on to her middle finger, and it was dark again, suppressing its fire until the morning.

'It's flawless,' said Henry, in the darkness. 'Thirty-two carats, from South Africa, guaranteed.'

'It's perfect,' said Baby Doe. She clasped her hand over it, as if it were a bird or a crystallized butterfly that might escape. Then she asked, 'Why? Why did you give it to me? I'm only an actress; not even that yet, not properly. I'm nobody special.'

'You don't believe that any more than I do,' said Henry.

There was another pause, and then Baby Doe said, 'No. But I'd really like to.'

'You must go,' he told her. 'What time is your dinner?'

'No,' she said. 'I'm not going now. What on earth could happen tonight to compare with this?'

'Dinner with the Cheesmans? Mrs Cheesman makes a wonderful dish of scrambled eggs and calves' brains.'

Baby Doe reached across and held Henry's hand. 'You wouldn't call for me, would you, and tell them I'm sick? A sudden headache. You could always pretend that you were the hotel doctor.'

'And then what?' said Henry.

'I don't understand.'

'Well, I couldn't take you out to dinner, could I, in case you were seen by anybody who knew the Cheesmans, or Murray Holman.'

'That doesn't matter.'

'Not to you, perhaps, but it does to me. Walter Cheesman's a big noise in Denver, and I don't particularly want to upset him; not for the sake of a dinner, anyway.'

Baby Doe hesitated for a long while, and then she started to stroke the back of Henry's hand with a gentle, insistent, circular motion, around and around, and the lightness of her touch and the closeness of her perfume and the warmth of her presence in the darkness made him close his eyes and feel for one strange lightheaded moment as if he were completely contented; as if this was all he ever wanted to do for the rest of his life.

'I was born in Oshkosh, in Wisconsin,' whispered Baby Doe; 'and when I was only young I married Bill. Well, William, that was his name. William Harvey Doe. He could never make money at anything, so in the end we sold everything we owned, which wasn't much, and came West to Central City, to mine for gold. Bill never had any luck, but all the miners liked me, and called me "baby"; and that was how I got the name of Baby Doe.'

Henry was silent, listening, feeling the endless circling movement of Baby Doe's fingertip on the back of his hand. In spite of himself, he was beginning to feel aroused, and he kept thinking of kissing those angel's-bow lips, and feeling those full breasts pressing against his chest. He hadn't allowed himself to be tempted by a woman like this for as long as he could remember; but then he had tended to treat most pretty women stand-offishly, since he had accepted that he was always going to be loyal to Augusta, no matter how much he despised her, and that for some reason which he still failed to understand, God had ordained their marriage in heaven above.

Baby Doe murmured, 'I divorced Bill four years ago. He used to beat me, although I never found out why. He couldn't love me, and so he beat me instead. I think in a funny sort of way he was trying to show me how much he cared; but if anybody cares for you so much that they want to kill you, then I think it's time to leave, don't you? And so that's what I did; and came to Denver, looking for glamour.'

She smiled, and said, 'Sparkle, and money, and champagne; and now I've found them all. Well, the sparkle, anyway. I haven't seen very much money yet, except for the thickness of Walter Cheesman's bankroll, and as for champagne – well, they're taking their own sweet time with that rum, aren't they?'

325

Her manners were suddenly far less formal; more country than city.

'You didn't order it yet.'

She blinked at him. 'I think you'd better light the gas. I don't believe I can see very well. I've been drinking with Murray Holman all afternoon; and believe me, when Murray's upset, he certainly drinks; and when I see him drinking, I have to join in, it has that effect on me; so you can bet that Murray's feeling worse than terrible, and you can bet that I'm nearly feeling worse than terrible, too.'

'Is that the real reason you don't want to go to the Cheesmans' dinner party?' asked Henry, knowing very well that it wasn't. 'You drank too much with Murray this afternoon?'

Baby Doe raised her hand, and touched the huge diamond mounted on her ring with the tip of her nose. 'How much did this cost?' she wanted to know.

'Don't ask.'

'But a lot?'

'It wasn't cheap, I'll admit. But then neither are you. Not one thing about you; with the single and distinct exception of Murray Holman.'

'Oh, Murray's quite kind,' she said. 'He's kinder than most men, anyway. It's just that he's duller than he looks, and I guess that's an awful disadvantage, to be duller than you look.'

Henry had now lit the gas-mantles beside the fireplace; and Baby Doe lifted her hand again, as Henry had done in the cab, and inspected her diamond ring more closely. 'It's the most beautiful thing I've ever seen,' she said. 'Don't you think to yourself, how can a stone be so beautiful?'

Henry stood with his arms folded, watching her possessively. She looked up at him, and said, 'You do understand that I can't accept it, don't you?'

'Of course you can,' he told her. 'It's a gift. You're going to be my leading lady, in my very first stage production.'

'But it must have cost thousands and thousands,' Baby Doe protested, 'and what will people think?'

'What people? Murray Holman? Walter Cheesman? The Sheedys? Why should you worry yourself about what they think?'

'But they're so respectable.'

'They weren't once. Just because they've taken to putting on airs; and sitting in their drawing-rooms on Brown's Bluff

326

playing whist, and cocking their noses up at anybody who isn't a member of the Sacred 36, those self-adoring three-dozen who think they're the cream of Denver society, that doesn't mean they're respectable. You ask Cheesman where that fat bankroll of his first came from; you ask Dennis Sheedy about his cattle deals. Listen to me, Mrs Doe – in Denver, you can be as spotless as your last dollar, but that doesn't ever clean the dirt off your first.' He put down the box of matches, and then he said, 'Anyway, I didn't think that actresses worried very much about respectability. Not respectability of *that* kind. The whist and Kensington kind.'

Baby Doe stood up, and came across to the fireplace. 'Actually,' she said, 'I'm not really an actress at all. I'm not like Louie Lord or Adah Isaacs Menken. I mean, I'm simply *me*, and that's all. I've never acted in a play before, nor even recited.'

'So why were you going to appear as Ophelia?'

'I don't know. Murray asked me. It just seemed like an exciting thing to do. And everybody at the theatre said I had natural charm. Especially Murray. He was always saying it.'

Henry reached out and took her hand, the hand on which she was wearing the diamond ring, and smiled at her. 'For once I agree with him. Now, shall we order some dinner? What will you have?'

They ordered pepper-pot soup, with cheese and hot bread; and while they were waiting for the bellman to bring it up, Henry telephoned Murray Holman and said that he was Dr McKirdy, consulting physician to the Corona Hotel, and that Mrs Doe was running a fever. The telephone lines were very crackly and indistinct, but eventually Murray Holman seemed to understand, and said that he would come around to see her in the morning.

'She's running hot and cold!' Henry assured Murray, in a fake Scottish accent.

'You're making me sound like a hotel room,' Baby Doe laughed.

It was a strange supper. As they sat at the table overlooking the traffic of Broadway, eating their soup, Henry found that Baby Doe was a complicated mixture of innocence and experience, vanity and uncertainty, self-assurance and complete artlessness. He began to see why a man as straightforward as her husband William might have beaten her: she could be frustratingly stubborn and obtuse, and when they started

327

talking about Denver society, she said so much for the virtues of calling-cards, and the unsuitability of fish-knives, that he put down his soup-spoon and stared at her in friendly wonderment; unable to believe that a woman so alluring could be so determinedly petty about manners. The simple trouble was that for all of her looks, for all that she had learned, she was afraid. She knew that she was admired, and she delighted in it; but she was still unsure of her place in society, and whether it was better to be risqué and adored, or cool and acceptable. This was a world in which there were scores of whorehouses and illicit gaming dens, and yet a world in which a woman could be 'cut' for picking up too large a piece of pigeon-wing at table. 'If the woman to whom you are talking should lift too large a piece of food from her plate, you should immediately cease all intercourse and stare steadfastly into an opposite corner of the room.'

But Henry adored her. Adored her looks, and relished her company; because in spite of her anxiety about social niceties, she was funny and provocative and endlessly flattering.

'You shouldn't have bought me this ring. You *shouldn't*,' she said.

'Give me one good reason why,' he challenged her.

'Because it will make me suspect your motives,' she smiled. 'It will make me think, when I look at it, that your thoughts are not entirely honourable.'

Henry sat back, and wiped his mouth. 'Perhaps they're not. But that's no reason why you shouldn't accept it.'

She said, 'I don't know how to. And quite apart from that, I don't know whether I ought to.'

'You think that I'm seducing you, is that it? And that by giving you this ring, I'm trying to make it impossible for you to say no?'

She didn't answer. But Henry stood up, and came across to her, and took hold of her wrist, feeling silk over skin over narrow delicate bones, and said, 'I'm going to go now. I'm going to leave. Not because I'm angry with you, or upset with you; but simply because I don't want you to feel that you're compromised. I want you to keep the ring, but I don't want you to feel that you have to give me anything in return. Nothing at all: not friendship, not affection, not money, not love. I've given it to you because I like the look of you, because it looks well on you; and because the very first moment I saw you at

328

the restaurant today with Murray Holman, I thought to myself, God, there's a dazzling star, if ever there was one; and a dazzling star deserves a dazzling star.'

He paused, and then he smiled; quite aware what a calculated speech he was making. More gently, he said, 'If you never want to see me again, that's your choice. How can I force you? But you and this diamond have always been destined to meet each other; it's part of the life-force that every diamond possesses, and which every human possesses. Before you were even thought of, this diamond was already waiting in the ground; but when you were born, it stirred, and now it's sitting on your finger. It's magical, don't you see, just like you are.'

Baby Doe reached out and tugged at his sleeve, and said, 'It's just so much; and you don't even know me. It's just so *much*. You've made me frightened. I keep thinking to myself, what does he want from me, to pay him back for a present like this? Because, Henry, *please*, if we're going to be realistic, who gives away a diamond ring to girls they've never met before? And not just an ordinary diamond ring. This: it's enormous! If I hadn't seen it flash for myself, I would have thought it was glass.'

'Don't think anything of it,' he told her. 'I'll see you tomorrow night, for dinner.' He went to the door, and picked up his hat.

His hand was already on the doorknob when she said, 'Don't go.'

'I must. It wouldn't be right.'

'I said, don't go,' she repeated; and stood up, and came towards him with her skirts whispering on the carpet like cautioning friends.

At that moment, there was a polite knock at the door. It was the bellman inquiring if they had finished their dinner, and would it be possible for him to remove their dishes. This was Henry's chance to go; to play the game the way he wanted to. But when he looked again at Baby Doe, and the gas-light in her eyes, he went against his poker-playing instincts and put down his hat, and stood and waited in silence while the bellman collected the plates and the cutlery, watching Baby Doe while she, in return, watched him.

When the bellman had gone, and closed the door behind him, Baby Doe said, 'You couldn't have gone. You haven't told me anything about yourself at all. If I'm going to accept your ring, at least I have to know who you are.'

329

He said, 'I don't think I'm anybody.'

'You must be.'

He came forward and he put his arms around her waist and he held her close. She didn't resist at all: in fact she laid her head against his starched shirtfront as if she had known him for ever, instead of less than a day.

'My name is Henry Roberts,' he said, quietly. Beside him, the gas-mantle hissed and flared. 'I come from Bennington, south Vermont, where I used to carve gravestones. I fell in love, lost my love, fell in love again and lost her too. I married eighteen years ago out of practicality and pity; yes, and defeat, too. A lack of fire. Today I'm very rich, and growing richer by the minute. That gentleman I was talking to today, David Moffat, he's my banker and he was telling me the news that I'm a millionaire, or almost. But I discovered something else today, too: that it's even better being a millionaire if you have someone who enchants you to spend your money on.'

'Murray told me you were married,' whispered Baby Doe, against his shirtfront.

'Well, yes, I am. But I don't think we care for each other very much. It's just what I said it was. A marriage of practicality. A business arrangement, more than anything else. Augusta manages the store and I manage the silver-mine and at least in the evenings we have somebody to talk to.'

'Augusta? That's her name?'

Henry nodded.

'What does she look like?' asked Baby Doe.

'Not like you,' he told her. 'Nothing at all like you.'

She raised her head to him, and he held her face in his hands as if he were holding the Grail; the one true light, discovered at last. The irises of her eyes were the pale blue of fragile china; a touch of rouge highlighted her cheekbones. He bent forward and he kissed her, without invitation and without hesitation, and that kiss seemed to last for no longer than a single beat of his heart, or a single tick of the domed brass clock, which was six hours wrong; and yet it was the most disturbing kiss of his life; a kiss of eroticism and treachery, a taste of what might have been and hadn't; a taste like red wine and black sins.

A breath, and she gently pulled away from him; her skirts still whispering. He said nothing, stood where he was. The tiny curls on the back of her neck; her profile lost in the shadow from the gas-mantles. She said, 'You shouldn't have put a name to her. Now I know who it is that I'm going to betray.'

He came forward and held her shoulders, warm hands on bare white skin. 'You would have known sooner or later.'

'I shouldn't trust you. How could you possibly buy me a theatre? What kind of man buys a woman a theatre?'

'What kind of woman deserves one?'

She leaned her head back so that it rested against his shoulder. He ran his fingertips down the long arch of her neck, and touched her, so softly that she scarcely felt it, in the deep cleavage between her breasts.

'You're playing a game with me,' she said.

He smiled, kissed her hair. 'If I am, you're winning.'

Hand in hand, almost formally, they walked through to the bedroom. The affair was going to commence by mutual understanding; no words were necessary. Perhaps it had been inevitable from the moment Henry had walked up to Murray Holman's table and introduced himself. Perhaps they had both been conniving at it all evening long; testing each other, teasing. But he took off his grey coat, and hung it on the hook on the back of the door; and then in his silk-backed waistcoat came over to her and unfastened the hooks and eyes at the back of her gown, revealing inch by inch the pink and white embroidery of her corset-cover, kissing as he did so her neck and her ears.

She sat on the edge of the high brass bed, her back straight, to slip off her corset-cover and to unlace her tight silk and whalebone basque; and he watched her, unbuttoning his cuffs and his shirtfront, prising off his boots, and loosening his embroidered satin suspenders. At last she stood in front of him, naked except for her grey silk stockings and white ruffled garters; her head raised provocatively and unashamedly, her full breasts cupped in her hands, the dark raspberry nipples tightened. On her softly rounded stomach there were the marks of her whalebone stiffeners, but her waist was slim, and her hips were narrow, and her thighs were so slim that even although she was keeping her legs tight together, there was a perfect inverted triangle between them. Her pubic hair curled up from between her thighs like a dark wisp of smoke, through which the crimson flame could just be glimpsed.

Henry stepped out of his silk long johns, the new ones he had bought today on 16th Street. His body was as white as

331

hers, but in twenty years of storekeeping he still hadn't lost his muscularity, the heavy framework of a man trained in cutting stone. Between his thighs he was rearing up, and with each beat of his heart he reared a little more; and the skin was already peeled back to reveal a proud and glistening head.

Baby Doe approached him without a word, and laid both of her hands flat against his chest. He kissed the curls around her forehead, and then her eyelids, and then smoothed the palm of his hand all the way down the warm curve of her back, running just the tips of his fingers in the cleft of her bottom. Her heavy breasts swayed against him, and he felt the touch of her nipples, and he closed his eyes to control the breathlessness that was tightening his lungs. He hadn't felt such an upheaval of emotions for years and years; he hadn't felt such urges ever. Her stomach pressed against his jutting penis, and the sensation was electric; so that he felt his hair prickle up on the back of his neck; and his fingernails itch as if they were going to crawl off the ends of his fingers; and such an explosive tightness between his legs that he couldn't have spoken, even if he had wanted to.

He stooped a little, and picked her up in his arms. She was so small and warm and light compared to Augusta; her skin was so soft. He kissed her and laid her on the satin comforter, and as he climbed on to the bed beside him she clung to him, and began to kiss him back, murmuring now in words that he was unable to understand.

'You're so *tight*,' she whispered at last; her hot breath crowding his ear. 'You're so tense! Feel your arms. Your shoulders. All your muscles are tight as springs.'

He kissed her again and again, and caressed and squeezed her breasts, stimulating her nipples with his tongue and his teeth. She ran her hands into his hair, and hummed with pleasure; but when at last he started to slide his hands down her stomach, and kiss her between her breasts, she firmly but gently raised his head up, and said, 'Too tense, my sweetheart! Too tight! Too anxious!'

'What – ?' he began, but she shushed him, and reached down to grasp his penis in her fist.

'This first,' she said, and although she said it gently it was an unmistakable order. She began to rub him, up and down, clutching him tightly and without fear; while her other hand, the hand on which she still wore the diamond ring, cupped and played with his scrotum. He felt the cold diamond scratch against his skin.

She lay back on the slippery comforter and he raised himself over her, every muscle in his body so taut that he looked like a Greek sculpture of a fallen warrior; deltoids and dorsals and quadriceps quaking with frustration and outlined in the lamplight as if they had been carved and polished from the whitest hardest marble. She rubbed him more quickly, and his head dropped down between his shoulders with a jerk, and he gasped for breath.

'My sweetheart,' she breathed, and from then on she would always call him that. He heard her but he couldn't see her; the bedroom seemed to have contracted smaller and smaller until it was a shrunken spot of infinite tension and infinite weight. He forgot time, and space, and where he was, and who he was; and then abruptly the tension broke and the bedroom rushed back to its normal size, and light and images came sparkling back, and there was Baby Doe lying beneath him, her face flushed with affection and amusement and actual joy, her neck and her breasts necklaced with shining pearls of white.

Now, he made love to her; and what she had done had enabled him to make love to her with such slowness and peace that he could concentrate on nothing but pleasing her, and honouring her beauty. He was soft at first, after the satisfaction she had given him, but she was so well-anointed that he was able to slip inside her, and gradually grow again until he filled her completely. Already, he thought, he had done something with Baby Doe that he would have been unable to do with Augusta. To Augusta, softness had always been unquestionable evidence that he no longer loved her.

Baby Doe was a sexual revelation to him: after all these years. She made love warmly and vigorously and with simple generosity; and when at last she clasped her legs tightly around his waist, slippery in dove-grey silk, and held him tight, and whispered, 'Enough, enough, you're beautiful, my sweetheart,' he felt as if the whole world had changed, as if he had emerged from the past into the future. It was her giving which had surprised him so much; her continuous attention to *his* pleasure, rather than hers, although it was out of that giving that most of her pleasure had come. And somehow she had made it quite clear that she wasn't trying to settle her account for the theatre, and for the diamond; but that she had wanted

Henry to make love to her, and that was all, and that she always made love with such directness, and with such enthusiasm.

They lay side by side on the comforter for a long time, almost an hour. They heard the noises of the Corona Hotel all around them, trolleys coming and going, voices, rattling plumbing. Outside in the street, they heard the light grinding of carriage wheels, and the clatter of horses. Somebody whistled. Somebody shouted. Somebody knocked at Baby Doe's door, but they didn't answer, and so their caller went away.

Henry stroked Baby Doe's hair, and felt her face with his fingertips as if it were impossible for him to believe that she was real. She lay and looked at him and said nothing while he outlined her shoulders, and the hollows of her collarbone, and the curve of her breasts. He held his flattened hand an inch or two over her mound of Venus, so that the crest of pubic hair just tickled him; and then with almost dreamlike slowness ran his finger down the moist divide of her sex, gently entering her at the very end of the caress.

There was another interlude of love; of Henry's fingers deep inside her, of Baby Doe's sharp teeth biting the muscle beside his neck as he made her tremble; and released *her* tension at last. They lay back again, very close arms awkwardly twined, breathing the same breath, sharing the same tiredness. Henry knew already that he had passed through the stage of being infatuated with her; he was already in love with her. Not that he was going to admit it yet, not even to himself. How could he? To fall in love with Baby Doe would mean that the best two decades of his life had been wasted on whiskey and poker and a good plain woman who had never shown him what a marriage could really be. A clock struck twelve midnight, and Henry sat up in bed.

'You're not going?' Baby Doe asked him.

He shook his head. 'I think I'm hungry, as a matter of fact.'

'We can ask the kitchen to send up some sandwiches.'

He eased himself off the bed and walked across to the window. Baby Doe lay with her arm angled behind her head, watching him.

'I feel as if everything's changed,' he said. He turned around. 'Do you understand what I'm trying to say? I feel as if everything's different.'

'It *is* different.'

She got up from the bed and padded on bare feet across the

carpet to stand beside him, and put her arms around him. Her hair strayed across his shoulder and her nipple, still sticky, touched against his arm. She smelled of gardenias and the sweetness of sex. He put his arm around her shoulders and held her even tighter; and kissed her.

'You're my third lover,' she said. She was looking down at the darkened streets, where only carriage-lamps bobbed, now that the city's electricity had been frugally switched off for the night.

Henry didn't reply, but waited for Baby Doe to tell him more. Unusually for him, he felt no jealousy that Baby Doe had slept with other men. Perhaps it was because she had given him so much, and he felt no need of any extra reassurance.

Baby Doe said, 'Bill McCourt was the first. I was only seventeen. I don't think he knew anything more about making love than I did; and on our wedding night he couldn't even work out where he was supposed to put it. You don't mind me talking like this, do you? I've never been able to talk about it to anybody else.'

Henry said, 'Go on,' in a voice as soft as a leaf falling on to a wet sidewalk.

'Then there was Jeremy Morgan, he was the owner of a men's clothing store in Central City. He and Bill were friends, sort of; but when Bill started to hit me it was Jeremy who always came to help out. So when I left Bill, he was the first person I turned to. I liked him; I still do. I think you would have liked him, too. The only thing wrong with him was that he was completely vain. Always dressing up like a dandy, always preening himself in the looking-glass; and you'd say something, like, "I think you're a marvellous fellow, Jeremy," and he'd blink at you and say, "What?" because he'd been so busy prettying up his necktie that he hadn't heard you.'

'How long did you stay with Jeremy?' asked Henry.

'On and off, two or three years. I liked him, though. He was vain, but he was always kind. I think that vain people often are. Kind, you know.'

She squeezed Henry tight, and said, 'And you're the third. And the best so far.'

'Why did you come to bed with me?' he asked her. 'One minute you seemed to be so worried about respectability; about playing whist on Brown's Bluff, and not using a fish-knife.

335

Then you came to bed with me and made love as if you had no qualms or conscience at all.'

She smiled. She knew that he was half-teasing her; but she also recognized that he seriously wanted to understand why.

'I'm too old for courtships,' she said.

'That's not the reason.'

She looked up at him. 'I saw you in the restaurant and I thought you looked like just the kind of man I wanted. Is that so wrong? I do want to be respectable, Henry; it's very important to me. But when I saw you today I looked at you and thought, he's beautiful.'

'Too old to be beautiful.'

'Don't be so ridiculous. You're *mature*, that's all. And that's what I want. Somebody who can take care of me; but won't smother me. And when you bought me that theatre, that was the perfect way of showing me that you could do both. You took care of me, by buying it, but at the same time you gave me something which would allow me to make my own name, to do something for myself, and be a little bit independent.'

Henry kissed her forehead. 'And that's why you went to bed with me?'

'That's why I decided I liked you. I went to bed with you because I needed you.' She hesitated, and then she said, 'I still do, Henry. I need you very much. I mean, if it isn't you, if it *can't* be you, then it will have to be somebody else. You're married, after all; and I don't even know what your wife looks like. She could be a ravishing beauty. But I'd prefer it to be you; you and me; for as long as we possibly can.'

Henry gave her a fleeting smile. 'Let me think about Augusta tomorrow. Tonight, I could do with some sandwiches.'

'Order some more wine, too,' said Baby Doe. 'I love that wine. It makes me feel as if I'm dreaming.'

'Perhaps you are,' replied Henry. 'Perhaps *I* am, too.'

They spent the rest of the night together, sleeping, then waking up again and making love in the darkness; touching each other; exploring each other's faces and bodies as if they were the maps to their new and as yet unimaginable future. The morning was grey and overcast; from their window the mountains were almost invisible, and the air felt humid with impending rain. They took breakfast in their room (to the undisguised amusement of the bellboy): black coffee and muffins and scrambled eggs; and then they dressed. But after they had

336

dressed, they undressed again, and went urgently back to bed, and Henry thrust and thrust into Baby Doe until she clutched the sheet tightly in her fists and panted *tuh – tuh – tuh – tuh*, the silk of her stockings already stained dark with juice.

After that, they spent the rest of the day lying in bed, or washing, or simply sitting together naked, kissing and talking and sometimes not talking at all. The morning went by; they ordered steaks for lunch and ate them cross-legged on the bed, drinking champagne from tall flared glasses and toasting each other with every swallow. 'To you, my sweetheart.' 'To you.' 'To yesterday.' 'To Hamlet.' '*And* Ophelia.'

They did not emerge from their room until it was dark again. They were dressed up like fully-fledged members of the Sacred 36: Henry in a formal evening suit for which he had sent out to Wallman's the Society Costumiers on Welton Street, white tie, white collar, and a shirtfront as white as a migraine; Baby Doe in a cream silk evening gown with a low décolletage edged with a foam of Brussels lace, and an extravagant bustle decorated with bouquets of yellow lace and satin flowers; and long cream evening gloves. She had asked Henry to help her put up her hair; and, clumsily, he had held her pins for her, and fastened her curls, and although she had scolded him for pinning one side of her hair lower than the other, he had found this small experience both pleasing and erotic, for no woman had ever asked him to help her so intimately with her toilet before. He had stood by the window watching her as she powdered her face and sprayed on her eau de cologne, and the pain of what he had missed in a lifetime of marriage to Augusta was so sharp that he had almost felt like groaning out loud.

Heads turned in the lobby of the Corona Hotel as Henry and Baby Doe crossed through the crowds and stepped outside to ask for a cab. Henry asked for La Différence Restaurant, and tipped the doorman a dollar.

At La Différence, they were seated prominently next to the three-tier ornamental fountain in the centre of the room, and attended by the maître d' and two commis waiters, as well as the wine waiter. La Différence that season was one of Denver's most fashionable eating-houses; and it glittered with candlelight and jewellery and solid silver cutlery, and with such wealthy and celebrated Denverites as Lawrence Phipps and Charles Kitteredge. The walls of the restaurant were hung with French tapestries, showing 17th-century hunting scenes around the

Loire Valley; and in one corner there was a marble statue of Diana, even more magnificently bosomed than Baby Doe, which had once belonged to Louis XIV.

Henry had only just ordered a bottle of champagne when there was a cheerful cry of, 'Well, Henry!' and William Byers came over, with a new curly moustache, and shook him by the hand.

'And goodness me,' he said, 'who's this? How did such a startling lady arrive in Denver without my knowing about her? Please, Henry, introduce me.'

'This is Mrs Elizabeth Doe,' said Henry, with a small smile. 'Mrs Doe is a very old friend of the family.'

'My dear Mrs Doe,' said William, and took her gloved hand, and kissed it as if he were trying to suck the dye from out of the fabric. 'I must compliment Henry on his family friends.'

'You're very sweet,' replied Baby Doe. Only Henry noticed that her lips were slightly swollen from crushing kisses, and that there was a tiny crimson mark on the side of her neck: the amorous wounds of a day and a night in bed.

'Mr Byers used to own the *Rocky Mountain News*,' said Henry. 'He's a businessman now, and occasional politician.'

'Occasional being the word for it,' said William. 'By the way, Henry, did you know that we were planning to try out our side-wheeler service down the South Platte River, first week in March? We've got the boat, she's moored up by Water Street; and the fitters start work on her next week.'

'Well, I'm pleased for you,' said Henry.

'Oh, she'll be a dream!' William enthused, rubbing his hands together. 'Brass fittings throughout, red plush seating; a dining-room three times the size of this restaurant; as well as a billiard-hall and a fifty-foot bar. Regular service, up and down the Platte, once a week; we'll make ourselves a million. You're still getting your commission, of course?' he asked, in a lower voice.

'I expect so, William. I really haven't looked, recently. Augusta handles all the bank books in Leadville; and David Moffat handles all the mining accounts here in Denver.'

'And Mrs Doe?' asked William, mischievously. 'What does Mrs Doe handle?'

Henry gave William a sharp look, and William raised his hands in self-defence. 'I really have to get back to my party,' he grinned. 'But do give me a call before you leave Denver; I must tell you what plans we have for the side-wheeler service, and for the resort town, too. Now that you're such a wealthy fellow, perhaps I can persuade you to invest some money in them. You know, just a few hundred thousand.'

While they ate (poached trout, followed by thin-sliced bear steaks with juniper sauce), Henry pointed out to Baby Doe the famous and the rich: the men who had made their money out of cornering the city's water supply, the men who had gambled everything they owned on buying up cement, the men who had dragged printing-presses and steam-engines and refrigeration plants all the way across the Great Plains, at a time when Denver was nothing more than a collection of shacks, and they had been unable to tell for certain whether it would ever be anything more.

'People blame them now for profiteering and price-fixing,' said Henry. 'But you just think of the faith it took to come all the way from Omaha with a ten-ton steam-engine when there was nothing here but mud and dust and a creek that kept overflowing itself.'

Henry saw another face he knew: a face that he didn't like at all. On the far side of the restaurant, his bald head shining, his chin covered by a brown false beard, sat Charley Harrison, one-time owner of the Criterion Saloon, and leader of Denver's 'bummers'. Harrison didn't look their way, but Henry was fairly sure that he must have seen them when they arrived. Harrison was now the owner of a liquor business in West Denver, and an important figure in the Denver Democratic party. In spite of his past unpopularity, and his scalped-off chin, he was still as noisy and as demanding and as offensively ebullient as ever.

Henry was just about to look away when Harrison turned and caught his eye. He grinned, behind his unlikely brown beard. Then Henry saw him mouth 'excuse me' to his dinner companions, and come across the restaurant buttoning up his evening coat over his huge belly.

'Well, now,' he said, fatly, wiping sweat from his neck with his crumpled napkin. 'Look what the wind's blown in. How do you do, my dear, I'm Charles Harrison. And how are you, Mr Roberts?'

'Well recovered, thank you, from our last encounter,' said Henry, tartly.

Uninvited, Charley Harrison dragged out a chair and sat down beside them, as close as he could to Baby Doe. 'Did this fellow tell you what happened when he and I had a contra-tom over a lady tightrope walker?' he beamed. The elastic which held his beard was absurdly tight, and underneath his chin Henry could see the edges of what must have been a hideous red scar. William had told him that the Indians had cut Charley Harrison's chin right to the bone.

Baby Doe glanced unsurely at Henry, and said, 'Mr Roberts and I are only friends, Mr Harrison.'

'And with that, I'll oblige you to leave us, please,' put in Henry.

'Leave you? What nonsense! I wouldn't be so bad-mannered, especially to a young lady as divine as this one! I'll have to hand it to you, Mr Roberts, you can sure pick 'em; but your problem is that you can't keep 'em. Hee-hee! Friends, indeed! Who could stay friends with a lady like this? Not me, and that's for sure! Sooner or later, that friendship would blossom into blissful conjugation, and everything that goes with it!'

Henry was fiercely tempted for one uncontrolled second to punch Charley Harrison right in the beard. But he could see that Baby Doe was not upset by his attentions; she had been slobbered over by enough drunks and wooed by enough middle-aged satyrs to be able to keep her composure; although she looked pale. Henry turned, and beckoned to Guido, the immaculate hook-nosed maître d', and simply reached into the pocket of his white evening waistcoat and took out $50 in gold, which he slipped into Guido's unerringly-positioned palm. He nodded towards Charley Harrison, the very slightest inclination of the head, and Guido closed his eyes momentarily to show that he understood.

Guido laid his hand on Charley Harrison's massive shoulder, and said, *sotto voce*, as if he were explaining that his aunt had died, 'I regret, sir, that you must return to your own table. We would prefer if you could do so without any undue disturbance.'

Charley Harrison had been taking a deep breath in order to recite Baby Doe a love poem called 'Your Face Is Like The Washoe'; and he let it out explosively. 'You take your hand off of me, you greasebelly, or by God I'll break your back over my knee.'

'I apologize, Mr Harrison,' Guido persisted, 'but you are unwelcome here, and I must ask you again to return to your own table.'

'Unwelcome?' Charley Harrison roared out loud, silencing the entire restaurant. 'Who says I'm unwelcome? Does this lady say I'm unwelcome? No she does not! Do you say that, ma'am? There now! Unless this lady wants me to go, then by God I'm staying, and don't you ever dare to touch me like that again, you crook-nosed apology for a corkscrew!'

Baby Doe glanced quickly and anxiously at Henry, and then at Guido, and finally at Charley Harrison. The restaurant remained silent; not a single knife scraped on a single plate; nobody spoke; the orchestra was frozen like the courtiers in *The Sleeping Beauty*. Only the silent approach of two of La Différence's burlier waiters, moving with the grace and speed of sharks, gave any indication of the latent violence that now threatened the restaurant's elegant poise.

But it was Baby Doe who broke the spell. Without a word, she picked up the silver boat of juniper sauce, which had been served with their bear-steak, and poured it slowly down Charley Harrison's shirtfront. Charley Harrison stared down at himself apoplectically, unable to speak, scarcely able to breathe. The sauce slid greasily on to his thighs, and between his legs.

'That sauce is supposed to go with anything,' Baby Doe said, in an uneven voice. 'I was just wondering whether it would go with you.'

From the table next to them, where the cement king Charles Boettcher was sitting, there came a delighted yelp of laughter. Then more diners joined in, and there was applause, and the banging of knives and forks on the table; and the orchestra played 'Where the Columbines Grow'', Colorado's state song; and with huge fury Charley Harrison rose from his seat and stormed out of the restaurant, quickly followed by the two perplexed-looking men with whom he had been having dinner.

Henry reached across the table and grasped Baby Doe's hand; and if he hadn't loved her before, he certainly loved her now. He had never known such a woman; for all of her complicated character, for all of her uncertainties.

'Keep the ring,' he said, laying his hand over it. 'Now you really deserve it.'

THIRTEEN

When Henry called in at David Moffat's house that evening, there was a message from Augusta, from Leadville, imploring Henry to return home at once. David, standing at the top of the staircase, his bald head illuminated in a variety of brilliant colours from the $25,000 stained-glass window which he had imported from Tiffany, his hands thrust into the pockets of his quilted satin smoking robe, said, 'That was all she said. "I beg you to come home at once." '

Henry picked up the telegraph message, read it twice, and then dropped it back on to the silver tray on the bureau in the hall. He had arranged to meet Baby Doe again tomorrow, and take her to see the Tremont Theatre; and then in the evening to the opera. After that, they were invited to a house-party at the Byers'.

'Would you care for a drink?' asked David. 'I've just opened a bottle of Macon. It's rather fine.'

Henry said, 'You managed to sort out the theatre?'

'The papers are ready, if that's what you mean.'

Henry nodded. He wished to God he didn't feel so twisted up with guilt. Why should he feel guilty, just because Augusta had asked him to come home? He didn't feel anything for her, did he? He didn't love her, he didn't even like her. And yet the burden of it was that he had lived with her for eighteen years, accepting her dependence; and by accepting her dependence he had also assumed responsibility for keeping her happy; or at the very least contented; and to ignore her now without warning would be cruel, to say the least, and dishonourable, to say the most.

David came down the stairs holding the bottle of Macon by the neck. 'Here. There are glasses in the library.'

342

They sat down among the ranks and ranks of leather-bound books, most of them financial, *The Wealth of Nations* and *Das Kapital* and the *Principles of Political Economy*. David offered Henry a half-corona, and they both lit up in silence, filling the room with strata of fragrant smoke.

'I expected you back yesterday, of course,' said David, meaningfully. 'We had the papers ready by six o'clock.'

'I don't think there's any particular hurry, not now.'

David crossed his legs, and rhythmically flapped the heel of his loose-backed slipper. 'I suppose you spent the night with Mrs Doe; not that it's really my business.'

Henry nodded.

'Is it anything serious?' asked David.

'I don't know. I hope so.'

'Hm,' said David. 'I told you that you were smitten. I could see it in your eyes at the restaurant. You looked as if somebody had struck you in the face with a paving-stone. You still do.'

Henry smiled, and lifted his glass. 'Here's to all paving-stones, wherever they are.'

'You'll have to be careful, you know,' David advised him. 'If Augusta gets wind of this, and decides to divorce you, you could end up paying a very pretty penny indeed.'

'Augusta won't divorce me.'

'You don't think so? I shouldn't be too sure. Maybe not straight away, but as soon as she's found herself a sympathetic man-friend; and there's no shortage of those in Leadville, not for a good hardworking woman who can cook. She may not be a Baby Doe, not to look at, but there's plenty of men who prefer their women on the homely side.'

'David,' said Henry, 'I'm not talking about divorce.'

'That's all right, then,' David replied. 'But in that case, have your fun and have it discreetly, and be prepared for it all to end abruptly, with no recriminations and no tears. Let me warn you, that's the way it has to be.'

'What about Audrey?' Henry asked him, rather too sharply. 'Is that the way it ended with her?'

David blew out cigar smoke, and drummed his fingers on the arm of his chair. 'I'm trying to save you some pain, Henry.'

Henry stood up, and went over to the the ashtray, and over-punctiliously rounded the ash of his cigar. 'No, David,' he said, 'you can't do that. Whatever I'm in for, I'm in for; painful or not.'

343

David raised an eyebrow. 'You like her as much as that, then?'

'I love her.'

'How can you? You've only known her a day.'

'And a night. And I love her. There isn't any question about it.' David blew out his cheeks in soft exasperation. 'You haven't told her, I hope?'

'Not yet. But I will.'

'I see,' said David. Then, 'What's that on your finger?'

'What?'

'That ring. Is that a diamond?'

Henry held out his hand. David took it in disbelief, and stared at the enormous glittering stone with smoke leaking out of his nose and mouth as if he were a deflating hot-air balloon. After a while, he said, 'It's real,' although there was a slight interrogative hint in his voice, as if he would still like to be reassured that it wasn't.

'Yes, it's real. Do you want to see the valuation? I bought it from Ischart's. I bought another one, too; not quite as big.'

'Oh, not quite as big. That's reassuring.'

'Well, this one if fifty-nine carats. The other one was a little over thirty-two. I gave that one to Baby Doe.'

David was silent for a moment. Then he said, 'Jesus.'

'What's wrong?'

'You gave Baby Doe a thirty-two carat diamond, and you expect me not to say Jesus?'

'I told you, David. I love her.'

'Whew,' David replied. He shook his head so briskly that his cheeks flapped. 'Whew, you love her, all right. You sure do love her, something special, I mean it.'

'Listen, I'm going to see her tomorrow,' said Henry. 'I have to, I promised. But then I'm going to go straight back to Leadville, to talk to Augusta. I don't want to deceive her, Henry, whatever I feel about her.'

'You've already done that, haven't you?'

'David,' Henry protested, 'Baby Doe walked into that restaurant and from that moment on, it was fate. I didn't know she was going to be there. I didn't know that I was going to fall in love with her. I'm trying to do the best I can. You can understand that, can't you?'

'Sure,' said David. 'Have another glass of wine.'

They stayed up until two o'clock in the morning, talking

344

about business, but again and again the conversation returned to the topic of Baby Doe. For if Henry intended to go on seeing her, his business life could be affected just as radically as his marriage. Eventually, after the long-case clock had chimed in the hallway, David drained the last of his wine, and said, 'Go back to Leadville, that's my advice. Think about it.'

'And supposing, while I'm thinking about it, some other man elbows in and takes Baby Doe?'

'If that happens, then she isn't worth having, especially after everything you've given her. And, Henry, don't give her any more. No more diamonds, no more theatres. Not just for the moment. She won't respect you any the more for it. And, believe me, it's very easy to run through a million dollars, when you're spending it like that.'

Henry said nothing, but helped himself to the last of the Macon. David stood looking at him for a while, and then said, 'Goodnight, Henry. I hope you sleep well.'

'Thank you,' replied Henry. 'You too.'

The next morning, after a short and heavy night's sleep, and a breakfast of steak and grits, Henry went to the offices of Kenneth Abrams, the architects, on Arapahoe Street; and spent an hour with Josiah Dunkley, who had the reputation of being the most expensive and most flamboyant designer of luxury residences in the whole of Colorado. Dunkley invited him into a high, bright office, with a distant view of Pike's Peak wreathed in clouds. There was a vast table of polished mahogany in the middle of the office, spread rather too tidily with drawings and plans and elevations, and in a glass case on the far side of the room there was a scale model of the mansion that Dunkley had built for Roger Woodbury, the silver king, with Doric columns and spires and courtyards.

Dunkley himself was short and loud and round, with wild grey moustaches and a way of squinting at his clients with one eye, as if he doubted both their sanity and their bank balance. He wore a buff day-coat and a violently checked waistcoat, across which was draped a collection of chains and baubles: a gold seal, a monocle, a rabbit's foot mounted in gold, and a one-inch ruler made of solid silver.

He poured Henry a breakfast bourbon, and then stood facing him with his hands propped up on his hips. 'When a man comes into money,' he said, in his thick, whiskey-matured voice, 'a man wants to show his friends and his neighbours what he's made of. He does it by dressing lavish; by wearing lavish jewellery – couldn't help noticing that ring of yours, Mr Roberts – and he does it by riding around in expensive carriages. He buys racehorses. Fur coats. Yachts; and works of art. But all of these gewgaws are secondary to the building of his dream mansion. The house, Mr Roberts, is the embodiment of all ambition. When you step inside a man's house; by Jiminy you step inside his soul.'

Henry said, 'I want something very special, Mr Dunkley. I want a house that's going to stand out. But, all the same, respectable; and in good taste.'

'Taste? What does taste have to do with it?' Josiah Dunkley demanded. 'You're a millionaire now, Mr Roberts, and *you* set the style. What *you* decide, that's taste. If you've always wanted colonnades, then you shall have your colonnades. If you've always hankered for towers and battlements, then it's towers and battlements. And fountains, if you wish. And a suspended staircase that sweeps down like the Niagara Falls on either side of your hallway; can you imagine that? And a marble floor so polished you could drown yourself in it?'

He stepped forward, and grasped the lapel of Henry's coat. His squinting eye glittered up at Henry like a hawk's; avaricious and excitable. 'When I look at you, Mr Roberts, do you know what I see? I see a tall, wealthy man, standing in the grounds of a house that looks like Versailles. Formal, dignified, classical; but lavish, too. Whatever else, we're talking lavish.'

He pulled open a drawer in a large mahogany plan-chest, and sorted through heaps of engravings. At last he came up with a drawing of the Palace of Versailles from 1668, with its courtyards and orangery and huge flights of steps. Henry studied it for a while, his hand on his chin, and then he smiled and nodded.

'You see,' said Dunkley, 'I thought you'd like it. Your version will have to be smaller, I'm afraid. Louis XIV practically bankrupted France to put this little cottage together. But I'm sure I can draw something up which will tickle your fancy. And I can get you the very best landscape gardener.'

'And you can build something like this in Leadville?'

'My dear Mr Roberts, I can build something like this on top of Long's Peak, given the finance.'

'Well, I'm returning to Leadville later today,' said Henry.

'Perhaps you could come along with me, and take a look around, and see if you can't pick out a suitable site.'

'Will your wife be returning with us?' asked Dunkley. 'I do like to discuss my plans with the wife. All the domestic offices, and suchlike.'

'My wife is already in Leadville; you can talk to her there.'

'Oh, I'm sorry,' said Dunkley, 'I saw you at La Différence last night, with a very striking young lady, and I naturally assumed – '

'A cousin,' said Henry, in a challenging tone. But he wished almost as soon as he had spoken the words that he hadn't. Baby Doe was his lover; his lady companion; his mistress, and his intimate friend. Why didn't he have the courage to say so? And why had he made an arrangement to take Josiah Dunkley back to Leadville later today when he had already promised Baby Doe that he would take her to see the Tremont, and then to the opera, and afterwards to the Byers' house for a late-night party?

He was betraying Baby Doe already; in the same way that he was betraying Augusta. And yet somehow it seemed that his betrayal of Baby Doe was worse, because she expected nothing from him but his affection and his trust. She had given herself quite freely and generously to him; that was what he loved about her. Why couldn't he do the same for her in return?

He shook hands with Josiah Dunkley and left the office with a smile, promising to call him later in the day to fix a time of departure. But down in the street, as he buttoned up his overcoat against the fresh fall wind from the Rockies, his smile quickly faded, and he walked southeast along 17th Street with an expression of worry and perplexity.

What could he do? Augusta had urgently asked him to come back to Leadville, and he was after all her husband. Yet he wanted more than anything else he could think of to stay here in Denver with Baby Doe. He stood on the corner of 17th Street and Champa, while the horse-drawn trams jangled past, and the wind whipped up rubbish in the entrance to Womack's Hardware & Tools. An old woman with voluminous skirts was struggling down from a cab, and so he went over to help her, and then asked the cab to take him to the Corona Hotel. The old woman said, 'Bless you, sir. You have the face of a fortunate man.'

Baby Doe was waiting for him in the Ladies' Parlour at the

back of the hotel, dressed in a dark blue high-necked gown with a large bow tied at the side. Her hair was drawn back with combs and she looked both severe and elegant, but devastatingly pretty. Henry took her hands as she came out of the parlour, and kissed her, and said, 'You look exquisite.'

'Did you see the architect?' she asked him.

He nodded. 'I'll have to take him out to Leadville to look for a suitable site. He showed me one or two ideas. But, within reason, I can have anything I want. If I've got the money, I can even have anything *without* reason.'

'When will you be going?' she asked him, as they walked through the Corona's crowded lobby.

He said, 'I'm not sure yet. It'll have to be soon; I have to get back to the mine. And, well, there's the store, too.'

'And Augusta?'

He gave her a smile that wasn't really a smile at all. 'You have a way of making my marriage sound like a particularly unpleasant disease.'

'I'm sorry, I didn't mean to.'

'No, I know you didn't,' he told her. 'I can't help being married to her, that's all. And I do have certain responsibilities, whether I like her or not.'

'I'm sorry, I spoke out of place,' said Baby Doe. She took his hand, and squeezed his fingers. 'Henry . . . please don't think that I'm trying to make things difficult for you. Because if I am, I'll just go, if that's what you want. I won't be a burden to you.'

He stopped, and turned, and held her shoulders, and looked straight into her eyes. 'My darling, I don't want you to go.'

'But your business, Henry; and your reputation, and everything.'

'Hang my business. Hang my reputation.'

'What are you saying? You can't say that.'

Henry swallowed a breath, and looked around him, and then looked back at Baby Doe, and said, in a quiet and level voice, 'I love you. That's what I'm saying.'

Baby Doe stared at him; and suddenly her eyes sparkled with tears. She pressed her dark blue glove over her mouth to stop herself from sobbing out loud.

'I know it's ridiculous,' said Henry. 'I know that nobody can fall in love in a day and a night. I know all of that. It's nothing more than infatuation, that's all. A rush of blood to the head.

348

The last desperate fling of a middle-aged man, almost twice your age. If I were you, I'd ignore it. I'd pretend you hadn't heard, if I were you. I'd keep on walking out of that door and forget to come back. Put me out of my misery as quickly and as kindly as possible. You said I was sentimental. A heart on one sleeve, and tears on the other. Well, that's all it is. Sentimentality, and the world has quite enough of that already.'

Baby Doe bowed her head forward so that her forehead was pressed against his coat, and he was almost suffocated in the plumes of her hat. She wept silently; and all that betrayed her weeping was the shaking of her shoulders. Hardly anybody in the hotel lobby paid them any attention; they looked like nothing more unusual than a couple exchanging an affectionate embrace.

At last, however, she looked up; and her eyes were smudged with crying. 'Henry, I love you, too. Not for the diamond. Not for the theatre. For you, that's all. Just for you.'

Henry held her tight for a moment. Then he said, 'You go bathe your eyes. I have a call to make. Then we'll go down to the Tremont Theatre and take a look.'

While Baby Doe returned to her room, Henry went to the Corona's front desk and asked to use the telephone. He called Josiah Dunkley's secretary, and left a message that he would be unable to return to Leadville today; but that he would call again later and make a definite appointment for the weekend. And could Mr Dunkley remember that he would need his furs when he visited Leadville; it was always colder than Denver.

The Tremont Theatre was small, but very gilded, an essay in Western rococo. Henry sat up in the circle, while Baby Doe stood on the empty stage and recited her lines from *Hamlet*, in a high, clear, faltering voice.

'My honour'd lord, you know right well you did;
And with them words of so sweet breath composed
As made the things more rich: their perfume lost,
Take these again; for to the noble mind
Rich gifts wax poor when givers prove unkind.'

Henry didn't know whether she had chosen that particular exchange to make a point; or whether it was accidental. He had decided not to return to Leadville today, but the guilt of having ignored Augusta's telegraph sat in the back of his mind like a tattered crow, clawing its way from side to side along its perch: and it would stay there, he knew, until he went back. Then, of course, his conscience would have to deal with the problem of having abandoned Baby Doe.

He applauded her, in the empty theatre, and his applause echoed and echoed again like trapped birds flapping against a window.

They went to the opera, Mozart's *Idomeneo*, and Baby Doe sat tensely beside him during the whole performance; so that by the time they left for the Byers' party, Henry was anxious and off-key. In the cab, he said, 'Let's go back to the Corona. I don't feel like facing the Byers again.'

Baby Doe said, 'Something's wrong, isn't it?'

'Nothing's wrong. Why should anything be wrong? I just don't feel like facing the Byers.'

Baby Doe was silent for a while, as the cab drove past one street-light after another. But at last she laid her hand on his thigh, and said, 'All right.'

They went back to her room at the Corona and ordered a bottle of champagne. They sat on opposite sides of the room; and for some reason the gas-light tonight seemed flat and harsh. Henry smoked a small cigar, although he crushed it out halfway through. Baby Doe drank her champagne in small, regular sips, and watched him with the unaccusing look of someone who knows that their love affair is beginning to come apart. How could she accuse the man who had suddenly swept into her life with a theatre and a diamond ring, and had treated her right from the very beginning with care and passion and extraordinary wonderment? All the middle-aged men she had met before had been devious and self-serving and emotionally callused. But Henry had somehow managed to retain a youthful sense of romance; almost a sense of innocence; as though his mind was still in Bennington, in sunny days before the war, when the girls giggled and the Colossal Whirler turned and nobody had ever heard of Chickamauga.

She said, as flatly as she could, 'I know you have to go back to Leadville. You mustn't feel guilty about it.'

'Guilty?' he asked, looking up as if she had been flicking iced water at him.

'You can't decide, can you? Between her and me? Between your past and your future? And I don't expect you to. Not right away. Come on, Henry, we met by surprise. I didn't know that

350

I was going to fall in love with you; and you didn't know that you were going to fall in love with me. So you have to go back and rearrange your life. At the very least, you have to go back and face Augusta.'

Henry, in shirt and suspenders, his collar hanging loose, came across the room and laid his hand on Baby Doe's naked shoulder. 'I just want to be sure that you'll still be here when I get back,' he said, and his voice was hoarse.

'Are you frightened that I won't be? After everything you've given me?'

'That diamond wasn't meant to be an insurance policy,' he told her; and then he smiled, and bent forward to kiss her on the forehead, and said, 'I don't want you to love me for my diamonds alone.'

Without taking her eyes off him, Baby Doe slipped one shoulder-strap from her creamy-coloured evening gown, and then the other. She reached behind her, and unclasped it, and unbuttoned it, and let it fall forward, and beneath it, lifted high by her tightly-laced basque, her breasts were bare.

'Kiss my breasts,' she whispered, with tears in her eyes. And Henry knelt in front of her, waist-deep in the satin of her gown, and took her breasts one after the other in his hands, and kissed them, and sucked her nipples hard against the roof of his mouth, until she clutched his shoulders and said, 'I love you, Henry, no matter how sudden it's been. I love you! So you can go to Leadville, and talk to Augusta, and deal with all of your business problems; and I'll still be here, waiting for you. Do you understand that? You have nothing to fear.'

They went to the bedroom and made love: differently this time, thoughtfully and almost sadly, because they knew they were going to have to part for a while. But when their lovemaking was over, Henry held Baby Doe very tightly in his arms, and whispered in her ear all those words of trust and passion that he had never been able to whisper to Augusta; telling her that he was devoted to her, and that he adored her, and that when he made love to her she felt as if she were part of him, as if he didn't know where his body ended and hers began. And silently he swore to himself that he would never lie to her, never again, and that he would never deceive her. My God, he thought: there has to be one person in your life, just one, to whom you can tell the truth, the whole truth, and nothing but the truth.

Morning came like an unwelcome acquaintance, and there was rain in the air, freckling the windows and slicking the streets. The Front Range mountains had sulkily wrapped themselves up again in cold and tumbling cloud; and the barometer in the hotel lobby was falling steadily. Henry sat on the edge of the bed, with no pants on, tying his necktie, and said, 'I'll be back by Monday. If there's anything you need, call David Moffat; or go up to his house and see him. I've left word with him to give you whatever you want.'

'I'll survive,' smiled Baby Doe. 'I've done it before.'

They parted as if they were lovers who had known each other for years; and it felt to both of them that they had. For as much as Henry had felt when he had first met her that Baby Doe was the living embodiment of all of his ideals of what a woman should look like, and what a woman should be; Henry to Baby Doe was like no man she had ever imagined possible, a man whose gentility and whose gentleness had been preserved by years of being married to the wrong woman. They kissed on the sidewalk, with the cold rain falling in their faces, and then Henry took a cab around to Arapahoe Street to collect Josiah Dunkley.

Henry and Josiah Dunkley arrived in Leadville the following afternoon; and the city and all the tree-lined mountains around it were skimmed with a thin layer of melting snow. They tied up outside the store under a sky the colour of Bible paper, and Henry walked straight in, slapping his gloves together, while Josiah Dunkley followed him with trepidation. He had heard something of Leadville's reputation for being violent and wild; and Henry's taciturnity had done nothing to reassure him. It was only the prospect of a $12,000 fee that had kept him smiling as they travelled to Leadville in increasingly bitter weather: that, and the chance to build one of the most extravagant houses that the West had ever seen. 'Versailles,' Josiah Dunkley had said to himself, with satisfaction, sitting in his office, with etchings and engravings of Louis XIV's palace laid out in front of him. 'Versailles in Leadville!'

Augusta was serving mint humbugs when Henry walked into the store. She looked up at him, with suspicion and relief. 'You're back,' she said. 'You got my message, then.'

'Yes,' replied Henry, in a dry voice. At that moment he wished more than anything that he was back in Denver, in the Corona Hotel, with Baby Doe. He had imagined this store so romantically, with its candies and its bags of flour, and its smoked hams hanging from the rafters; but now he was back he could see how cramped and ordinary it was; and how Augusta hadn't changed at all. In a few days, his view of life in Leadville had been turned inside out. He had stepped through a mirror, into another place and another time and another life; and all this was only a dim reflection of what Henry Roberts had once been, and once been content with.

'This is Mr Dunkley,' said Henry. 'He came back here to design us a new house. You may as well know that I'm a millionaire now. Well, so David says. We're rich. We can give up the store.'

Augusta made no attempt to acknowledge Josiah Dunkley; and instead took the three pennies she was paid for the humbugs and rang it up noisily on the upright cash-register. 'Do we really need a new house?' she wanted to know. 'Is there anything wrong with this one?'

'Augusta, millionaires don't live in general stores.'

'Why not?'

'Because they don't. Because it isn't right.'

'Is it right to flaunt money which you did nothing to earn?' Augusta demanded.

'Don't say I did nothing to earn it. I suffered as much as anybody.'

'Oh, did you? All those years of drinking whiskey and playing poker. What purgatory!'

'Augusta – '

Augusta faced him sternly. 'Don't "Augusta" me, Henry. Ever since you've been gone, I've had George Hook down here, once or twice every day, demanding to see you. I've been very frightened. He seems to think that August Rische was killed on purpose; that it wasn't an accident at all; and he wants to have it out with you.'

'Is that why you called me back?'

Augusta stood up straight behind the candy counter, where she had been putting the humbugs away. She took off her spectacles, and stared at Henry with myopic eyes. 'No,' she said.

'Then why?' he asked.

She glanced at Josiah Dunkley; but Josiah was doing his best to look interested in a display of Old Hickory Babbitt metal. The most extravagant and most expensive of Denver architects

353

was completely confused and dismayed by his arrival in Leadville, and was already trying to think of a way of making his excuses and returning as soon as possible to Denver. As he had frequently told his backgammon partners, 'I am never enthused by discomfort, nor by emotional stress,' and here in Leadville he had immediately encountered both.

Augusta lowered her head. 'I called you back because I missed you,' she told Henry.

Henry rubbed his forehead in exasperation. 'But, my dear – I was only going to be gone for a week or two. No more than that.'

'Nevertheless,' said Augusta. 'You're my husband, Henry; and whatever has passed between us, I love you still, and will always be devoted to you; and I miss you when you're away.'

Henry didn't know what to say. He took Josiah Dunkley by the arm, and led him through to the parlour, and said, 'Sit down, please. Let me get you a drink. Anything you like.'

'A large whiskey, I think, if that's not too much to ask for,' said Josiah Dunkley, looking around for a comfortable chair in which to rest his ample bottom. He had expected a kind of rough luxury in Leadville; big old-fashioned armchairs, perhaps, and sawn-oak beds. But these mean surroundings were most discouraging. Stained wallpaper, prints of Abraham Lincoln, Windsor chairs, and a smell that betrayed that particular kind of good plain food which Josiah Dunkley loathed. Boiled gammon, and onions; or braised lamb shanks; or corn pone pie.

Augusta came into the kitchen as Henry was looking for the whiskey. She untied her apron and hung it over the back of the chair. She was wearing a home-made dress with a high collar, and her hair was tied back and streaked with grey. There was dust on her spectacles; and she wore no jewellery at all.

'I had to telegraph,' she said. 'George Hook keeps asking where you are, and threatening to break up the store. He says you murdered August Rische; that you had him dynamited on purpose.'

'Do you think that's true?' asked Henry, calmly.

'I don't know,' said Augusta. 'I'm afraid.'

He had been crouching down, searching through the back of the spice cupboard. At last he stood up, and said, 'Where did you hide the whiskey this time?'

'I'll get you another bottle from the store.'

'But there was a bottle in the parlour, only a third empty.'

She hesitated, bit her lip.

'You drank it?' he asked her, disbelievingly.

She looked back at him with pain and defiance. 'Well, what else was I supposed to do, left here on my own, not knowing when you were going to come back? And two or three times a day, that awful George Hook knocking at the door, demanding to know when you were coming back?'

Henry stood up, and closed the spice cupboard doors. He was suddenly aware that this store, which had been his home for nearly twenty years, his and Augusta's, was forfeit now; that by making love to Baby Doe he had surrendered his past, and everything that was part of it, including this business, and this house. He had alienated himself from Augusta, and from their marriage-bed, and even from the things that belonged to him, his books and his playing-cards and his bone-handled razor, resting upstairs in the rose-patterned mug. Not that he would miss any of it, not seriously. This house felt as crowded and as uncomfortable to him as it probably did to Josiah Dunkley; and for all of Augusta's fussy supervision, for all of her fervid domesticity, it seemed dingy, and shabby, and it smelled of polish, and stale air.

'You haven't even kissed me yet,' said Augusta.

He looked at her steadily, but he knew that his eyes were giving nothing away. He didn't allow them to. His hands remained by his sides.

She stood waiting. But Henry knew that if he kissed her, it would be proof to her at least that he still felt some affection for her; and he couldn't afford for his own sake to give her even that much hope. She stepped forward, and took off her spectacles, and said, 'Do you still love me, Henry?'

He looked at her thick unplucked eyebrows. The small red spot just above her left eye.

'Kiss me,' she breathed.

There was a long moment's pause. Then he closed his eyes and bent forward and kissed her, on the cheek. When he opened his eyes again she was weeping. Quite silently, quite defiantly; but with tears running down her cheeks and dropping on to the collar of her dress.

'How can you be so cruel to me?' she sobbed.

'Augusta – '

'We're supposed to be man and wife. We've lived together

for all of these years. I've given you everything, Henry. Every-thing. And you can't even kiss me.'

'I've – I'm – ' he hesitated, and then he said it. He hadn't meant to; at least not so soon. But she with that sensitivity of hers had known at once that something was different; that his usual off-handedness had somehow altered. Perhaps it was more studied, more deliberate. Perhaps it was invested now with genuine guilt. But he said, bluntly, in words that fell through the room like half-pound weights, 'I've fallen in love with somebody else.'

Augusta touched the sides of her mouth with her fingertips as if she could feel a cold-sore developing. 'What?' she said. Then, 'Who? How could you have done? Henry, what are you talking about?'

He dragged out one of the kitchen chairs and sat down. He was crying now like her. He didn't know why. Perhaps it was pity; not just for Augusta, but for himself, too, that it had taken him all these years to find somebody he really adored. 'I met her in Denver. I didn't mean to, but I did. And I fell in love; and she fell in love with me.'

'Have you been. . . intimate with her?' Augusta asked stiffly.

'Yes,' he said.

'Well,' said Augusta, at once, turning her face away. 'I forgive you.'

Henry jolted his head up. 'You forgive me?' he shouted at her. 'You forgive me? You don't even understand what I'm saying to you, do you? I said, I've fallen in love. I've fallen in *love*, Augusta, in *love*! Do you know what that means? And you don't even know what she looks like, or who she is, and you forgive me? Augusta, I don't want your forgiveness! I don't *need* your forgiveness! I'm simply saying – I've fallen in love – and that's all!'

His face was smothered with tears. She glanced at him, and said, 'You're talking like a boy.'

'Well, yes,' he said, 'perhaps I am. But I'm not ashamed of it. And I'm not ashamed of what's happened. I can't be. After all these years, Augusta, how can I be?'

Augusta drew a long, shuddering breath. 'Well . . .' she said, with deep sarcasm and terrible pain, 'the faithful husband; the honest storekeeper; the man of his word.'

He said, 'I'm sorry.'

'No, you're not,' she told him, her eyes blinded. 'You're not sorry at all. You're glad. Not because you've fallen in love. My God, Henry, you wouldn't recognize love if it came up behind you and smacked you on the back of the head with a truncheon. You're not in love, and never will be. You're just pleased to have another excuse to inflict hurt on me, that's what it is. You're cruel, and vicious, and small-minded; and in return for everything I've done for you, all you've been able to give me is constant humiliation, constant agony, constant despair.'

She let out a wild hooting noise, and crossed the kitchen floor in two ungainly lurches, and clung on to him, pulling and tugging at him as if he were a breakwater covered with slippery weed, and the sea was sucking and dragging her away from him; as if her life depended on her gripping his coat and his shirt and never letting go.

At that moment, however, there was an embarrassed cough at the doorway, and Henry looked up to Josiah Dunkley standing in the hall, one hand raised as if he wanted to say something. 'I'm so sorry to interrupt . . .' he began. 'But there's a gentleman here . . . a Mr Cook. He says he urgently needs to talk to you.'

Henry stood up, but Augusta kept on clinging to him. 'Promise me you won't leave me,' she hissed, under her breath.

He grasped her wrists, tried to pull himself free.

'Promise me you'll never leave me,' she repeated, that same hysterical hiss; and he knew that if he didn't promise, she would probably screech and cry and throw herself on to the floor. He bit his lip, and then he said, 'We can talk. We can discuss it.'

'*Promise.*'

Henry nodded. 'All right,' he said.

'All right what?' she persisted.

'All right, I'll never leave you. Now, please.'

She lifted her face to him, and it was clear she expected him to kiss her. That big, pale face, wet with tears. He closed his eyes and did as she demanded, although it was like nothing more than bending forward at table and pressing his face into a cold white blancmange. Then he moved her away from him, and said, 'Why don't you change . . . put on that pink gown I bought you in Denver . . . then we can go to the Grand for something to eat . . . you know – and Mr Dunkley here can tell us what ideas he has in mind for a house.'

'You promised,' she reminded him.

'Yes,' he said, and gave her a smile that was actually painful to put on. She curtseyed with an off-balance tilt to Josiah Dunkley and said, 'Excuse me,' and left the room as if nothing had happened at all; as if she were still the mistress of the house; and still in charge of her husband's heart.

Josiah Dunkley raised his eyebrows at Henry but made no remark. He had built dozens of houses before for the newly wealthy, and with each commission he had seen yet another example of how a huge and sudden influx of riches could break apart a marriage which poverty and dedication had for years kept together. The greatest and most dangerous freedom which wealth brought with it was freedom of emotional expression.

'Mr Cook's waiting for you in the store,' he said; and then let out a little '*ha!*' which might have been nothing more than a cough, or an explosive clearing of the throat.

Henry said, 'Thank you,' and went through; but when he came out from behind the counter it was not Mr Cook who was standing in the dusty sunlight but Mr Hook; in a large black bearskin coat; holding a rifle. His face looked drained and mean and bemused. He could have been a lunatic Russian count, or the owner of a large and dangerous travelling-circus.

'I came looking for you,' he said, in a high, accusing contralto.

'Well, I'm here now,' Henry told him.

'But you ran away before, when August was killed.'

'I didn't run away, George; I was called to Denver on business.'

'You ran away, Mr Roberts. You ran away because you were guilty.'

Henry walked into the centre of the floor and stood facing George Hook with his hands in his pockets, his chin confidently tilted upwards. George Hook took one step back, but then remained where he was, staring balefully. He kept the rifle pointed towards the floor, but Henry was in no doubt that if he were to be provoked enough, he would use it. No man went to settle an argument in Leadville, Colorado, carrying a gun: not unless he seriously meant to shoot somebody. It was a wild, raucous, ridiculously wealthy city; and more men and women were killed there in one night than in the rest of the state of Colorado in a month. That was why, when you took your gun with you, you were generally considered to mean business; and you could only expect business in return.

'It's my opinion that August was killed on puppus,' said

358

George. 'It's my opinion that he was blowed up deliberate, by you; and by that snake-in-the-grass R.P. Grover.'

'I hope you realize the gravity of what you're suggesting,' said Henry.

'Oh, you don't have to talk to me about gravity,' warned George. He raised his rifle at last, and waved the muzzle about two inches in front of Henry's nose. 'Don't you talk to me about gravity. I'm a prospector, Mr Roberts, and I know all about gravity. Gravity adhesive, gravity specific, and gravity grave. And I know too that what R.P. Grover had to say about August was damned lies and that's all, on account of August being the least incautious man that ever was, and determined to live to one hundred.'

Henry reached out and grasped the muzzle of the rifle, and directed it away from his face. 'George,' he said, quietly, 'however incautious August was, or wasn't, the fact remains that he took a risk and blew himself up. Now I'm as sorry as you are; and as grieved as you are; and remember it was me who found his body first, what there was of it. But it was still an accident, whatever you say, and although I stood to gain if August died, believe me I would rather have lost a ninety percent share in the Little Pittsburgh, than lose August; and that's the whole truth of it.'

George Hook stared at him for a long time, and then at last lowered the rifle. 'The poor dog died, too, you know. Pined for August, and wouldn't eat. Then died, that's all. Within two days, keeled over and died.'

'I'm sorry,' said Henry. He began to feel as if he was going to be saying 'sorry' forever, for everything. But all those accusing faces, Augusta's and George's and Josiah Dunkley's and Murray Holman's and Annabel's and Edward McLowery's; all the way back to Mr Paterson, and Doris. How could he have done so little, and yet have to apologize for so much? All he had wanted, really, was to have a quiet life, and a reasonably pretty wife, and enough money to play poker.

George Hook said, 'You mark my words, Mr Roberts; and mark them good. I'm going to find out the truth of this, whether you killed August or not, whether you knew that he was going to die. And if I find out that you did, then you can also mark my promise that you're going to suffer; and when I say suffer I mean suffer real bad, the way that August did.'

He said no more; but turned and walked out of the store,

leaving the door open behind him. Henry stood where he was for a very long time, but then at last stepped forward and closed the door in much the same quiet, proprietorial way that any shopkeeper would have done. But then he rested his back against the door, and stood there with his hand covering the lower part of his face, and neither moved nor spoke for nearly a minute, his eyes clouded with indecision, and guilt, and perplexity that this should all have happened to him.

Josiah Dunkley was standing not far away, eating roasted peanuts.

'These are fine,' he remarked when Henry turned and caught him with his mouth full.

'You go ahead and take as many as you want,' said Henry, without even hearing himself. 'Right now, I'm going to get changed for dinner. I want you to tell Augusta everything you told me about the house.'

'You mean Roberts Lodge, Mr Roberts?'

Henry came over and slapped him quite hard on the back. Josiah wheezed, but then smiled. 'Please don't do that again,' he said. 'It always brings on my coughing.' Henry resisted the urge to say 'I'm sorry,' but simply grimaced. 'We all have afflictions, Mr Dunkley. If you ask me, they're sent down by God, in order to make us better people.'

'I'd still prefer it, sir, if you wouldn't slap me on the back.'

Henry didn't know what to say to that, but grasped Josiah Dunkley's fat padded shoulder, and squeezed it in what he hoped what would be taken as a gesture of professional intimacy. 'Tempt her with it, won't you?' he urged. 'Make it sound grand, but practical. She's not the kind of woman who holds with anything lavish. Tell her how modest it's going to be, compared with the Phipps' house; or Sam Hallett's place. Talk about taste, and discretion. She's a plain woman, Mr Dunkley.'

'Yes,' replied Josiah Dunkley. 'I see that.'

Henry pursed his lips uneasily, and then said, 'I still haven't found you a whiskey, have I?'

Josiah Dunkley said nothing, but crushed another peanut shell between finger and thumb, and regarded Henry with suspicious steadiness.

'There's, umh, a bottle around here someplace,' said Henry.

The three of them dined that evening at the Grand Hotel on Chestnut Street; and while Augusta prissily filleted a sole, and Henry toyed with a steak that he hadn't wanted to begin with,

Josiah Dunkley dismantled a brace of squab with one greasy hand while with the other hand he shuffled through the sketches and plans which he had prepared for the eventual creation of Roberts Lodge. 'Or Roberts Hall, or Trebizond, or whatever you wish to call it.'

Although the underlying theme of the house was strongly Versailles, Dunkley had gratuitously introduced an eclectic assembly of parapets and porticoes and cupolas to embellish it; and the result was so thickly over-decorated that even Henry sat back in his seat and examined it with growing disquiet. Hadn't Fenchurch always advised him to be 'sober, and modest, and tasteful if you can'? But here was a house that shouted 'money' through a megaphone. To display his wealth with a huge diamond ring was one thing (and he had guiltily taken the precaution of concealing his ring in his valise before his arrival back in Leadville, in case of upsetting Augusta); but to build a mansion like this was beyond any extravagance that he could ever have dreamed of. It was probably a bargain, at an estimated cost of $276,000, especially since it included a galleried library, an orangery, a ballroom, a summer and winter kitchen, and a master bedroom which stretched for over 100 feet, with a balcony outside wide enough to accommodate an orchestra; and especially since the price would also provide for a fully-landscaped garden with orchards, and tiers of marble steps, and rose-bowers, and stone gryphons spouting water, and a fair-sized artificial lake (kidney-shaped, of course) with Venetian bridge. But Henry, for all of his love of showy jewellery and well-cut coats, was still a plain man from Carmington, Vermont, who had never known money; and he couldn't help feeling unsettled by the blatancy of Josiah Dunkley's designs. To build this place would be one thing; but to *live* in it, that would be something else; to step outside each morning into a fantasy of statues and fountains, of topiary and flowers, and to turn and see behind him a palace of gargoyles and urns and sweeping stairs and a thousand glittering windows. . . .

At length, however, it was his hatred of Augusta that decided him. For twenty minutes now, she had been picking at her fish; and what with that, and the bourbon, and the cigar smoke, Henry had been growing increasingly irritable. He leaned forward on the figured-damask tablecloth, and said 'Mr Dunkley, your designs are choice. Loud, perhaps. But then Leadville herself is loud. A loud city, that deserves loud houses.

361

All we have to remember is that Mrs Roberts here will have to run the house; and make sure that it's tidy, and organized, and that the silver gets polished. Our *present* home, as far as I'm concerned, is hers. She cleans it, decorates it, keeps it; yes, and runs the business, too. So if we're building a *new* house, one to replace it, then I think that hers should be the final word, don't you?'

Josiah Dunkley frowned at Henry, and then turned to Augusta and gave her a watery smile. He couldn't understand for the life of him why Henry was turning over the final decision on 'Roberts Lodge' to Augusta; especially after the weeping and the arguments that he had witnessed this afternoon. What he didn't understand was that Henry was seeking any way in which he could openly split their marriage; any way in which he could show that Augusta failed to understand his ambitions and to appreciate his tastes. Henry knew that Augusta hated the plans for the house. He had lived with her for nearly twenty years, and whenever she looked at something out of the corner of her eyes, gave it that particular shifty sideways glance, she detested it; and she detested these designs. They were vulgar; they were pompous; they were absurdly arrogant. They were designs fit for a miner with too much money, and that miner's wife.

Josiah Dunkley unhappily shuffled the principal elevations across the dinner-table so that Augusta could see them more clearly. 'What do you say Mrs Roberts?' he asked, without taking his worried eyes off Henry.

August slowly unwired her spectacles from around her ears, and peered at the drawings from two to three inches away, her eyes bulging and myopic. She sniffed once loudly, and wiped her nose on her napkin. Henry felt himself wince from his mouth all the way down to his toenails.

'Well,' she said, at length, peering unfocused at Henry and Josiah Dunkley, and sniffing again. Taking her glasses off always made her nose fill up. 'I think the plans are rather pretty. Yes; if you like them, Henry, let's build.'

Henry stared at Augusta and showed her by his rigid expression what he was thinking. You're trying to keep me, Augusta; you're trying to give yourself the false appearance of a broad-minded and agreeable wife, a wife in tune with her husband's ambitions, just in case I try to make an issue of your insensitivity, and your selfishness. He could almost hear the words being spoken in the divorce court, even now; and he was quite sure that Augusta could, too. 'Your honour – Mrs Roberts always bent over backwards to accommodate her husband's tastes – in this case agreeing to the construction of a huge and ostentatious mansion – even though she secretly disliked it – in order to keep him happy.'

Josiah Dunkley slowly and precisely folded up his papers and restored them to his briefcase, switching his eyes first on to Augusta and then on to Henry.

'Do I, unh, take it then, that – '

Henry nodded. 'Go look around Leadville tomorrow; find us a suitable site; then build. If you want a contract, talk to David Moffat.'

Josiah Dunkley said, 'This could do with a toast, don't you think? A small celebration? What we're going to see here is the finest mansion ever built between Denver and San Francisco, bar none.'

But Henry scarcely heard him. He waited for as long as he could; until the rushing noise inside his head seemed to have died down a little, and then he threw his napkin on the floor, and stood up, and walked away from the dinner-table without a word. Augusta hesitated, and then hurried after him. Josiah Dunkley pulled a face, looked around at his abandoned table, and then waved to the wine waiter to bring him a half-bottle of champagne.

At the cloakroom, Augusta caught hold of Henry's sleeve, and said, 'Wait. I'm not going home on my own.'

Henry looked around him. He had drunk too much, and he kept seeing the hotel lobby in a succession of details. The potted plant with the cigar-like curved black leeches the feet of diners passing by; the chipped beige paint on the architrave over the cloakroom door. And a babble of voices and noises, as if he were under water, drowning in tinkly bubbles and nonsense.

'You promised.'

'What?'

'Henry, you promised. Take me home.'

His chin dropped down on to his starched shirtfront. His eyes closed. He might well have been dead. That would solve a few problems, wouldn't it, to die here, in the lobby of the Grand Hotel, standing up, already attired for the grave in full evening dress, no smiles, no farewells, no flags, no kisses, no regrets? But he opened his eyes again and he was still alive,

363

and Augusta was clutching his hand and staring at him through fish-eye lenses, concentrating on nothing but *him*, and his loyalty.

He took her home, and said nothing all the way west along Front Street, back to California Gulch, past the Engelbach Foundry and the James B. Grant smelter, with their red fires roaring in the night; past the desolate baseball diamond on which the moon shone with cold and kindly light, waiting for tomorrow's children; and out to the store again, on the Malta Road, just past Washington, the low dark building in which they had spent so many years together, and to which they again returned; neither of them knowing which one was chained to which.

In the early hours of the morning, as the moon passed their bedroom window, he said, in a haunted voice, 'You don't really want that mansion, do you?'

There was a pause, during which she breathed loudly and regularly, not sure whether she ought to admit that she was awake or not. But at last she said, 'I do. Yes. I like it very much.'

'You don't. You hate it. I saw it in your face.'

'No,' she said, evenly. 'I like it.'

He propped himself up on one elbow. 'You hate it. You don't think that I've lived with you for twenty years without knowing when you hate something? And you hate that mansion. You really hate it.'

'I do not hate it either. I like it. I think it has charm.'

'Charm?' roared Henry, throwing back the comforter and leaping out of bed in sheer frustrated fury. 'How can you say it has charm? It has extravagance, yes, I'll give you that. It has vulgarity. It has pomp. It has show. But *charm*? What are you trying to do to me, Augusta? Charm? Charm! God Almighty!'

'Don't blaspheme.'

'And don't – for Christ's sake – say that something has charm – when for Christ's sake – it's hideous! And you know it's hideous! And I know it is! And the only reason it's ever going to get built is because it's the one way that we can show all the people round here in Leadville that we're really rich. And it's grotesque! And you have the face to lie there in bed and tell me it has *charm!*'

She said, tight-mouthed, 'You're drunk.'

He sat down on the edge of the bed, naked, middle-aged,

grey-haired, grey pubic-haired, bulging around the waist, handsome but long past youth; skin thicker, touch coarser, rich but despairing. And too rich, really, to have to despair for too long. Because none of these arguments with Augusta were really necessary, except for the purely internal purpose of irrigating his guilt. He was already free, financially. All he had to do now was disentangle himself from his marriage. But he was discovering just how much harder it is to abandon the weak than it is to turn your back on the strong.

He said, 'I wish you were dead.'

There was a silence as cold as an uncut tombstone; a grave-marker without any message on it. Then Augusta turned over in bed, and huddled herself up in her comforter, and pushed him away whenever he tried to put his arm around her, and covered her ears whenever he tried to speak.

At last he stood by the window watching the moon over the west side of Leadville; listening to the distant singing of drunken miners; and wishing to God that he was hot and close in the arms of Baby Doe. Eventually though, he eased himself back into bed, keeping well away from Augusta's plump and chilly back, and slept; but soon after dawn he was woken up by someone pounding at the front door of the store, and yelling, 'Mistah Roberts! Mistah Roberts! By Cracky you got to come quick! Mistah Roberts, you up there?'

FOURTEEN

R.P. Grover said, 'He's crazy. I said that right from the very start, now didn't I?'

Henry peered down the shaft. 'Do you think he's serious?'

'I didn't at first, sir. But then he dropped that stick of dynamite down the shaft; and then I believed him; he's crazy. He

365

could do anything. Set us back six months' production. Maybe worse, depending on how much damage he does.'

Henry listened for a moment to the strange hollow singing that comes out of every mine-shaft, as underground draughts blow, and men whisper and hundreds of rats rush, and water drips like grandfather clocks. It was an extraordinary chorus, eight hundred feet below the surface of the earth, and often deeper. Echoing, deceptive, the voices of the voluntary tomb. But from George Hook there was no sound at all.

'Where is he?' Henry asked. 'I mean, not exactly. But approximately.'

'About two hundred feet down, sir. Just below gallery fifteen, as far as we can judge it. He's sitting in that bucket, and he's jammed the pulley-wheels with something; screwdrivers, probably, so that we can't wind him up and we can't lower him down. And from what he's been shouting out, he's got himself sixty or seventy sticks of giant powder sitting right in that bucket alongside of him, and he isn't afraid to let the whole lot off, himself, too.'

Henry dusted his hands and stood up straight. It was dark inside the winding-house, but thin knives of bright grey daylight shone through the cracks in the hastily constructed shake roof. One of the men offered him a flask of whiskey, and said, ' Take a pull, sir? Breakfast.'

Henry shook his head. 'What did Mr Hook say before he went down? Did anybody hear?'

'Just me, sir,' put in the winding-engineer, already white-faced with tiredness. 'Lower me down to sixteen, that's what he said, and that's what I did; and then the bucket jammed. That's when I called out to ask him what was wrong, and that's when he said he'd stuck himself fast on purpose, and that he was going to blow the whole mine up, sir, kit and boodle, if you and Mr Grover wasn't brung.'

R.P. Grover added, 'I was the first one here, sir and shouted down at him to hear what it was he wanted.'

'And?' asked Henry. 'What does he want?'

'Confession, sir,' R.P. Grover muttered, out of the corner of his mouth.

'What?'

'Confession, sir; to Mr Rische. That's what he wants.'

Henry took out his handkerchief and blew his nose. It was cold up here this morning, up at the top of California Gulch, and their breath blew from their lips like dirty rags. A heavy mass of grey cloud was rolling in from the northwest, over the jagged pines; and some of the older men were talking about a blizzard. The mine was at a standstill, because George Hook had jammed up the winding-gear, and the men stood around in shivering clusters, kicking their heels and clapping their hands as if they were applauding their misfortune.

Henry was offered a cup of hot black coffee, which he drank all at once, blistering the roof of his mouth. Then he went back to the top of the mineshaft, and knelt down, and at length called out, 'George! Is that you, George? This is Henry Roberts!'

There was a long, distorted, echoing yowl. Then a voice came back, surprisingly clear, as if George Hook were standing only a few yards away, and it said, '*Murderer.*'

'Come on up,' yelled Henry.

'No,' came the reply. 'Not until you say it was you that killed August.'

'Don't be ridiculous. I didn't kill him. It was an accident. Now, take out those screwdrivers, or whatever it is you're using to jam those wires, and let us wind you up. Come on, George, this isn't doing anybody any good.

'Confess first,' George Hook demanded.

Henry looked over at R.P. Grover, but R.P. Grover tersely shook his head. 'Don't say a word, sir. Any confession, and they'll be bound to send for the sheriff, just to investigate; they'll have to; and who knows what clues he might turf up? Come on, sir, better safe.'

Henry asked, 'He's set off one stick of dynamite already?'

'Yes, sir,' said R.P. Grover. 'As far as I can tell, it didn't do too much damage; but he's sitting on two hundred times more. If he lets that off, sir, he won't only be blowing himself to kingdom come; he'll be blowing the heart from this mine. The square-sets will be bound to give in; and then the lode will collapse in on top of them. And – '

'Yes?' asked Henry, lifting his head from a diagram of the mine.

'Well, sir, there's thirty-one men still down there, sir. Finishing off the night-shift; but now they can't get up.'

'Why didn't you tell me this before?' Henry demanded. 'You mean to say there are thirty-one men down there; all at risk from this single ridiculous lunatic?'

R.P. Grover looked embarrassed. 'Well, sir, I'm sorry; but the truth is that we *can't* confess.'

'Even though thirty-one men will have to be crushed to death?'

'Sir – '

'Wait,' said Henry, and went back to the top of the shaft. He hesitated, drew a huge breath, and then shouted, 'George! Can you hear me?'

Echoes, pause, and then George shouting, 'Yes; is that you, Mr Roberts?'

'That's right, George, it's me. 'George, listen, there are some men down there, thirty-one of them. You don't want to hurt any of them, do you? They're prospectors, just like you. Good old boys from the times gone by. Most of them you probably know. But if you set off that giant powder, well, you won't know any of them for very much longer. And you'll be facing a charge of mass murder, George, when we wind you up.'

'You killed August, Mr Roberts, and if you want to save those men, and this mine, well then, you'd better confess.'

'I was nowhere near this mine when August was killed.'

'Maybe not. But you gived out that instruction, didn't you? You of all people.'

'George, you're making this up. This is all in your mind. Now, for God's sake take out those screwdrivers and let us haul you up. We can talk, then, I promise; and if you have any grievance, you can air it with the sheriff, and anybody else you want to talk to. George, I didn't kill August, that's the truth, and all you have to do now is come on up, and we won't say anything more about it. Do you hear me?'

There was a second's silence, and then a shattering boom, and after a moment or two a billowing cloud of blinding grey dust blew out of the top of the winding-shaft and choked into the shed, making everybody cough and wheeze and cover their eyes.

'He's serious,' R.P. Grover said, laconically.

'You bet your ass,' spat the winding-engineer. 'Serious? *Jesus!*'

Henry took R.P. Grover aside, leading him by the elbow. 'Didn't you mention an accident once, at the Comstock Lode; something about drillbits?'

R.P. Grover sniffed, and wiped his nose with the back of his index finger. 'Are you trying to suggest what I think you're trying to suggest?'

'What choice do we have? We can't wind him up, we can't get down to him, and he's threatening the lives of thirty-one of our men. There's no point in trying to shoot him, either; there's more risk of hitting the giant powder than him.'

Uncomfortably, R.P. Grover turned around and looked back at the head of the mine-shaft. The dust was just beginning to settle now, although the men standing close to the shaft were still nothing but dim shadows. Then he turned back to Henry, and said, 'They were winching up a bucket full of drillbits, that's all, and one of them caught on a timber, so that the bucket tipped and the whole lot of them fell out. They fell for half a mile, and hit eight men in a car coming up. Five was killed instant.'

Henry said, 'All right, then. Clear the winding-shed, tell the boys that everything's under control. Then wheel up a barrow-load of steels; and hammers, too, whatever you can find.'

R.P. Grover hesitated for a moment; but then he shrugged, and returned to his men, shrilling his whistle. 'Let's clear the shed, boys, let's get ourselves out in the air, now. Let's give Mr Roberts a chance to talk this man out of the shaft. Look alive now, let's go.'

Soon the winding-shed was empty except for the engineer, and R.P. Grover, and two of R.P. Grover's most experienced hands, and Henry. The miners filled up a wooden wheelbarrow with more than twenty worn-down drills, mostly three-foot change drills of three-quarters of an inch diameter, although R.P. Grover added five or six bull steels, about a foot long, with 1¼-inch tips.

'I think you have to give him one last chance,' said R.P. Grover. His two assistants stood back, their eyes wide in their grimy faces, quite aware of what Henry was proposing to do, and frightened by it.

Henry approached the shaft again. 'George!' he shouted. 'George, can you hear me?' The echoes were muffled by the dust; but at last George shouted up at him, 'I can hear you, you murderer. And all I've got to say to you is this: you've got five minutes to confess; and if by that time you haven't, then believe me this mine is going up and your fortune is going to be lost for ever.'

'George, this is insane. There are thirty-one men down there.'

'You can save them, Mr Roberts. All you have to do is admit that you done it.'

Henry stood back from the shaft. R.P. Grover said, 'Shall we wait the whole five minutes, Mr Roberts?'

Henry shook his head. 'He's not going to change his mind. The longer we wait, the more danger those men are in.'

R.P. Grover beckoned to one of his miners, but the man folded his arms tightly and violently shook his head. 'I ain't tipping no steels down that shaft, not with a man down there.'

Henry turned, and looked at the other miner. 'How about you?'

'No, sir. Not me. My ma was a Cathlick.'

Henry turned at last to R.P. Grover and R.P. Grover stared back at him with an expression that said, if you order me, I'll do it; but by God I don't want to.

'Can you think of a better way?' asked Henry. He could feel perspiration prickling his moustache,

'I don't know, sir. It's not for me to say.'

'You worked out a way before, with Mr Rische.'

'That was an accident, sir.'

'Three minutes, Mr Roberts!' cried the distorted voice from the shaft.

Henry tugged out his handkerchief and wiped his face and his hands. Then, his heart banging, he bent down and grasped the handles of the wheelbarrow, and pushed it slowly towards the very brink of the shaft. George was at level fifteen, deep down in the new vertical shaft they had excavated to penetrate even further into the mountain; a good two hundred feet below the surface. Even so, the steels would take only two seconds to reach him, and by the time they struck him they would be dropping at nearly a hundred feet per second.

'Mr Roberts!' came the faint garbled cry.

Henry didn't wait any longer. With a grunt of effort that hurt his chest, he tipped up the wheelbarrow's handles; and with a ringing clatter the whole load of drills went cascading down the shaft, banging and tumbling as they struck protruding timbers, setting up a hellish cacophony that seemed to echo on and on and on. Henry set down the barrow, and then remained where he was, listening. There was nothing now, only the sighing of the draught through the ventilators. R.P. Grover came up and stood close behind him, listening too, and holding his pocket-watch open as the five-minute deadline approached.

'Five minutes,' he said, in a hoarse voice.

They waited for the great explosion; but as the second hand crept silently around the watch-face yet again, no explosion came. Henry turned to the winding-engineer, and said, 'See if you can jerk the bucket free.'

The winding-engineer engaged the gears, and the engine sputtered and chugged, but then the cables jerked to a halt again. They might have succeeded in disposing of George Hook, but the gear was still jammed. Until it was freed, thirty-one miners would be trapped below ground, and work at the Little Pittsburgh would have to remain at a standstill.

Henry didn't hesitate. 'Give me your gloves,' he said to R.P. Grover.

'You're not climbing down there, Mr Roberts?'

'It's my mine, Mr Grover, and I shall do what I wish. Now, give me your gloves.'

Reluctantly, R.P. Grover handed over his heavy leather work-ing-gloves, which he always kept jammed in his belt. Although they were a size too small for him, Henry tugged them on, and then approached the shaft again, standing right on the very brink. He might as well have been balancing on the parapet of a tall building; except that there wasn't a single building in America, not even in New York, which was eight hundred feet high.

'Take your time, sir,' said R.P. Grover. Henry looked down into the darkness, and nodded. 'I intend to.'

He reached across the open shaft and nervously snatched the hoisting cable in his right hand. The cables had been invented by A.S. Hallidie, the designer of the San Francisco cable-car system, and they were flat, more like tapes than ropes, five inches wide and almost an inch thick, made of braided steel wire. They were strong and durable, and they allowed buckets and cars to be hoisted up and down the shaft at terrific speeds, but they were awkward to grip on to, and greasy, and as Henry reached over and grasped the cable in his left hand, too, he felt a lurch of fear in his stomach that he was going to slip.

'I'll help you back, sir, if you change your mind,' called R.P. Grover.

'No,' said Henry. Then, less breathlessly, 'No. I'll be all right.'

He swung his legs out and gripped on to the hoisting cable

371

like a well-dressed monkey. He slid down two or three feet, and the sole of his handmade shoe was torn at the side; but at last he managed to get a satisfactory grip, and began to lower himself down into the shaft, half-climbing, half-sliding, stopping every now and then to re-adjust his handhold, and take a breath.

Gradually, the light of day began to fade, and he found himself descending into darkness. Some of the lower galleries were lit, and when he looked down he could see dim flickering lights shining on to the wall of the shaft; but after a while he began to feel that the whole world was closing in on him, and that he was bound to lose his grip on the cable and fall. Even when he passed the 80–ft mark, he was suffocatingly aware that there were still more than 100 feet to go, deeper and deeper into the heart of the mountain; into that hot, oppressive, whispering asylum of pain and hammers and sudden death.

He had known that the descent was going to be difficult; but he hadn't anticipated for a moment that it was going to be such hell. By the time he had climbed down 100 feet he was whining for breath, and his hands were clenched with cramp. His waistcoat and coat were drenched with sweat, and the abrasive edges of the hoisting cable had already torn through his trousers. He closed his eyes and kept on making his way down, sliding in intermittent jerks, trying to prevent himself from gathering so much momentum that he tore his way through his gloves; because once he did that there would be nothing to save him but the flesh and bone of his bare hands. R.P. Grover had told him plenty of horror stories about men climbing down cables: sliding so fast that they had been faced with the instantaneous choice of letting go and falling two hundred feet, or losing their hands and half of their forearms in a gory attempt to slow themselves down.

Somewhere that must have been nearly three-quarters of the way down, he gripped the cable as tightly as he could, and spun there, his head lowered, sweating and wheezing and coughing, keeping his hands clenched around the wire by bitter willpower, and nothing else.

'You have to go on,' he told himself. Then, 'Henry, why the *hell* did you do this?' He could only climb down. There wasn't even the remotest possibility of climbing back to the surface. He doubted if his muscles had the strength to take him up more than two or three handholds, let alone two hundred feet.

He went on down. His thighs began to bleed, lacerated by the braided wire. His leather gloves were in shreds, and in places he could feel the wire rubbing against his hands. He closed his eyes and tried to think of something else, of anything else, of mountains and plains and meals at the Grand Hotel; of Baby Doe reaching out to touch him. But all he could hear was the clanking of the jammed-up winding-gear, and the deathly murmuring of the ventilation, and the voices of R.P. Grover and all of the miners who were standing at the top of the shaft, amplified but curiously altered, like the voices of men who had been magically turned into bulls, and bears, and growling dogs.

' – *kill himself, going down there* – '
' – *climbed? Is he crazy?* – '
' – *do now?* – '

Unexpectedly, his foot touched something; a curved metal rim that swayed, and banged against the sides of the shaft. With an extraordinary feeling of terror and relief, Henry realized that he had actually reached the bucket in which George Hook had been suspended, and that his climb down the hoisting wire was over. Carefully, biting his lip, sweating hot sweat over cold sweat, he lifted one leg into the bucket, and then the other; and at last was able to crouch down in the corner, feeling the bucket sway and tilt beneath him, breathing harshly, his legs torn, but his hands intact, and safe.

There was very little light in the shaft, but enough to show Henry what had happened. George Hook was sitting in the opposite corner of the bucket bundled in his black fur coat, his face lifted aloft, as if he were still looking up to see what that clanging noise could be. A three-foot change steel had fallen like a spear, and struck him directly in the right eye, driving directly through his brain, down his neck, into his chest, out through his back just above his right buttock, and embedded itself in the metal floor of the bucket, holding him there, pinioned, in an oddly childish crouch. The fur of his coat was sticky with blood; the bedraggled plumage of a prospector who should have been wealthy, but never was. Henry wiped blood from his hand and thought to himself: this man lived for loyalty, and died for it, too; and not for gold, after all, nor for silver, nor for any kind of riches which could be excavated out of the ground. And the sadness of it was that Henry had liked him,

George Hook, and August Rische too, and their fleabitten dog, and now all three of them were gone.

On the bottom of the bucket, there were only two more single sticks of dynamite. George had been bluffing, in order to force Henry and R.P. Grover to confess. He couldn't have blown up the Little Pittsburgh at all.

Henry wiped the sweat from his face with his sleeve, and then stood up in the bucket to release the winding-pulleys. George had twisted wire around them, right through the spokes, to prevent them from turning; but it was a simple job to release them; and as soon as he had done so, Henry called up, 'Grover! Can you hear me? Wind me up!'

He was hoisted up slowly; and when he was swung out into the daylight, with George Hook's body huddled up beside him, R.P. Grover and the rest of the day-shift crossed themselves, and said, 'Amen,' and looked away. They all knew what had happened, in spite of the fact that Henry had ordered them out of the winding-shed. But the sight of George Hook, impaled by a change steel from skull to pelvis, was enough to convince them that this was still a hard world, without pity or compromise, and that a hard-rock miner's lot was still the meanest.

Henry was bloodied and shaking. R.P. Grover threw his fur coat around his shoulders, and said, 'They'll talk about this, sir.'

'Well, let them talk,' Henry replied sharply. 'Where's that whiskey?'

'No, Mr Roberts, you don't understand me. They'll talk about this with respect. They know that Mr Hook crossed you, sir; and that he threatened the lives of their workmates; and that you did the best you could. You redeemed yourself, sir, with that climb. There isn't a single man here who would have taken your place; myself included. Two hundred feet on a hoisting cable, sir, that's a climb you wouldn't readily do for money; nor for any other reason that I can think of.'

Henry stood where he was, shaking. 'No,' he said. 'You're quite right.' He was offered a pewter flask of whiskey, and he grimaced his thanks at the miner who had given it to him, and pulled at the neck, quickly, three or four times, coughing.

'He couldn't have done it,' he said.

'What?' asked R.P. Grover. Then, confused, 'Couldn't have done what, sir?'

'He couldn't have blown up the mine,' Henry told him, flatly.

'You see what he had there? Two sticks of dynamite, that's all. Hardly enough to blow out the lamps.'

'A rum type,' R.P. Grover decided.

'Yes,' said Henry, with conspicuous sharpness. 'But not entirely unjustified, wouldn't you say?'

R.P. Grover looked blank. 'Can't do with rumness; not down a silver-mine.'

Rumness, thought Henry, as one of the miners drove him back down to Oro Junction in his navy-blue carriage. Who can define rumness, and who can condemn it? For if rumness means eccentricity; and a sense of honour so deep that it appears to be odd; then George Hook was certainly rum; but martyred, too. For when that three-foot steel came lancing out of the darkness above him and penetrated his eye, killing him instantly – instantly, it must have been – so fast and silent that he probably didn't have time to realize that he was fatally injured – nor even to begin to comprehend what had happened to him – aaaahhh, and three feet of coldness right through him, instantaneous coldness, quicker than being struck by lightning – when that had happened he had been doing nothing more rum than demanding an admission of the truth, which itself is probably the definitive interpretation of rumness, but in its perversity the most honourable of all pursuits.

George Hook had died for the truth. Actually died. And when I killed him, I killed the truth, too. And here I am, going back to Augusta, and what truth can there be in that? No rumness, certainly, no honour, no perversity. I love Baby Doe, or at least I say that I do, I pretend that I do, I delude myself that I do. But how can I, when I can still talk to Augusta about building a mansion; when I can still discuss our future together, as if it were all anniversary cakes and smiling relatives? How can I think of staying with her, why do I even consider it, when Baby Doe is back in Denver, beautiful and understanding and willing; the Ophelia of the Rockies?

Guilt? Stupidity? Or the feeling that God has given me too much for nothing at all; and that if I try to tempt fate; and take Baby Doe; then I'll be punished for it?

He arrived back at the store and climbed down from the carriage. Up in the gulch, the whistle on top of the winding-shed blew, to tell the miners that the shaft was clear, and that they could start the next shift. Henry tipped the miner a dollar for bringing him back, and said, 'Tie the horses up in the stable,

375

would you?' Then he crossed the yard, and went into the back door, which gave straight into the kitchen.

Augusta was there, baking. Her nose was smudged with flour. She put down her pastry-pin, and said, 'Henry! My dear! What's happened to you? Henry, you're covered in blood!'

Henry sat down. 'Not mine, most of it,' he said.

She knew at once whose it was. 'George Hook,' she whispered.

Henry nodded, and sniffed. 'He's dead,' he said.

Augusta said nothing. Henry brushed flour across the table with the palm of his hand, and then he said, 'I'm going back to Denver, to talk to David Moffat. I've decided to sell the Little Pittsburgh.'

'Oh, Henry, you don't know how pleased that makes me.'

'Well,' he said, and then shrugged. 'The Little Pittsburgh doesn't have very happy associations, does it?'

Augusta knelt down beside him, and held his hands. 'You don't have to go back to Denver to sell the mine, do you? You could always send David a telegraph.'

'No, Augusta; I have to go in person.'

'But why? Look, it's starting to snow. Supposing the Fremont Pass is closed?'

'August, selling a silver-mine is a complicated business. I'll have to sign dozens of papers; and besides that, I'll have to meet any prospective buyers in person.'

Augusta said, 'Can't you stay, just for a while?'

Henry eased off his coat, and then began to unbutton his waistcoat.

'It's that girl, isn't it? Augusta demanded. 'That's why you want to go back.'

'I think I ought to talk to her, yes,' said Henry.

'And then you'll tell her what you promised? You'll tell her it's all finished between you; and that you've given your word to come back to me, and never leave me?'

Henry reached out and stroked her hair. She really wasn't as bitter and ugly as he always imagined. In fact, she had a grace about her that was almost religious. She had a kind and generous heart, Augusta; she always had done ever since she was a girl in Bennington; and it was only fear of losing him that had made her so anxious, and so shrill. He had married her, after all: and she did have the right to expect some kind of care. He didn't love her, but how could he leave her?

376

'Are you hurt?' she asked him, tenderly.

'Just a few scratches on my legs, that's all.'

'I'll draw you a hot bath. Have a rest today; you can go to Denver tomorrow, if the snow holds off. How would you like tripe in batter? And a winter-apple pudding?'

Henry gave her a pale smile of acknowledgement. He was beginning to feel shocked now, after what had happened up at the mine. 'Come on, my dear,' she said, and helped him up, and fussed him upstairs to the bedroom, where she made him lie down on the bed while she unlaced his ruined shoes, and unbuttoned his shirt, and massaged his chest and his stomach with hands that still smelled of shortening.

'You're right,' she said; 'you *should* go and see her. Tell her straight to her face that everything's over. Tell her how happy we are; and that it was wrong of her to interfere in a married man's life, no matter how much she wanted you.'

Henry lay back on the pillow. He thought of the steel falling down the mine-shaft, and hitting George Hook in the eye. He closed his own eyes, tight. He could almost feel the pain of it.

Augusta stopped massaging him, and said, 'Henry? Henry, my dearest, are you all right?'

The next day was crisp and sunny with no sign of snow, except on the peaks of the mountains that crowded in on Leadville like solicitous nuns. Henry was awakened by the sound of Augusta coming upstairs, and the warm smell of coffee. He rubbed his eyes. His hands were swollen and red, and his back was aching, but at least he felt rested.

Augusta set the cup of coffee down on the bedside table, next to the clock.

'Well, good morning,' smiled Henry. 'It looks like a good day for travelling.'

'Yes; you could say so,' replied Augusta. She stood with her hands folded over her apron, and her tone was distinctly chilly.

'Is there something wrong?' Henry asked her. He propped himself up on one elbow, and picked up his cup of coffee. 'Could you put less cream in it next time? You're making me as fat as a prize pig.'

Augusta said, 'I packed your case for you.'

'Yes? Well, thank you.'

'I found this,' she said, and opened her hand. Henry didn't even have to look at it to know that it was his diamond ring.

'I bought it in Denver,' he said off-handedly. 'I didn't wear it because I didn't think you would particularly care for it.'

'I don't. But I suppose you're entitled to waste your money in any way you wish.'

'Then why are you looking so upset?'

'Because – ' she said, and reached into the pocket of her apron, ' – because I found this, too.' She produced the receipt from Ischart's the jewellers, and unfolded it, and held it under Henry's nose.

'Well?'

'There are two diamond rings; one for a gentleman, and the other for a lady.'

'Yes, that's right.'

'Where is the lady's ring?'

'I, er, took it back. I only had it on approval.'

'You took it back without even showing it to me?'

Henry sipped coffee without tasting it, and shrugged one shoulder. 'I didn't think you'd like it, on reflection.'

'Perhaps I might. How could you tell?'

'It just didn't look as though it would have suited you. It was too showy. Listen, Augusta, you don't have to turn this into a performance. I bought two rings and took one back and that's all there was to it. When we go to Denver together, you can choose one that you really like.'

Augusta dropped Henry's ring down on the bed. 'You gave it to *her*, didn't you?' she said, softly.

'What are you talking about? That ring cost me a fortune. I wouldn't have given it to a woman I hardly know.'

'Henry, don't lie to me, as well as betray me. Don't you think that it's enough to have insulted me, and to have treated me with neither affection nor respect, and to have slept with another woman, without lying to me as well?'

'Augusta – '

'I don't want to hear another word, Henry. Not another excuse; not another invention. I simply want you to treat me as your wife, as I deserve. And you can begin by bringing me back from Denver that diamond ring, that exact ring, as described here, and putting it on to my finger, where it belongs.'

Henry banged his coffee cup so hard on to the saucer that it was a miracle it didn't break, and swung fiercely out of bed. Augusta retreated towards the door, afraid of his anger, but still determined.

'I want it, Henry, no matter what you might think of it.'

He splashed water into the basin on top of the washstand. 'All right! I can hear you! You want the ring back! I'll get it!'

'Henry, you don't have to be so angry. It's a compliment to you that I want it. Just like I want the house.'

Henry towelled his face dry, and then glowered at himself in the mirror Augusta's face appeared in the corner of the frame like a pale mask hanging on the bedroom wall. 'I'll get it,' he repeated doggedly.

He met David Moffat early the following, morning, for breakfast. They sat in the morning-room, which faced east, and which was discreetly decorated with eau de nil silk and faux bamboo furniture. The rug was eau de nil, too, thick and silent, pure wool specially woven in England. David's butler poured Darjeeling tea, and served out hot croissants and seven different types of jelly; as well as cold beef, devilled ribs, pickled eggs, and *sopocka*.

'I'm sorry to hear about your friend Mr Hook,' said David, stirring his tea with measured clinks of his spoon. 'I hear that such accidents are all too frequent in hard-rock mines.'

'There was nothing that anybody could do,' Henry told him. 'He was killed outright. The same thing happened at the Comstock, so I was told.'

'So now you want to sell? Well, it's understandable, after such a tragedy. You and he were tolerably good friends, I suppose?'

'You could say that; although most of the time he kept himself to himself.'

'Mm. Well, I have some buyers in mind. I was approached only last week by a consortium of Philadelphia bankers. They were quite anxious to get some of their money into silver, especially with the price going up so steadily. I'll telegraph them today, and see if they're still in the market.'

'How much would you ask?'

David Moffat carefully spread a piece of croissant with kumquat preserve and bit into it with teeth that were too white and too even to be real.

'Certainly no less than $850,000,' he said; and then added, 'cash, of course.'

379

'That's a great deal of money,' said Henry. His tea remained untouched.

'Yes, it is,' replied David, 'and it will all be yours. Now that your two partners have so regrettably. . . .' He swallowed his mouthful of croissant, and pointed heavenwards with his butter-knife.

Henry stood up, and walked across to the sunlit windows with his napkin still tucked into his belt. 'What would I do with it?' he asked. 'Buy up land? Or gold? Or railroad stocks?'

'What business do you know best?' David asked, rhetorically.

'Silver-mining, I guess; after running a general store and post-office.'

'In that case, to begin with, I suggest you buy up shares in a selection of different silver-mines. You know better than anybody which are the most profitable mines, don't you, since all of their miners come and shop at your store? I'll take care of selling the Little Pittsburgh; you put your ear to the ground back in Leadville, and draw me up a list of the twelve most likely silver-mines. Then, as soon as we've disposed of the Little Pittsburgh, we can start to buy.'

Before lunch, Henry went to the Corona Hotel to see Baby Doe. The morning was cold and snappy, and there was grit flying in the air. The clerk at the desk said that Mrs McCourt Doe was out shopping, but that he expected her back shortly. Henry went into the bar to wait for her, and nervously drank two measures of whiskey and smoked a cigar. In the looking-glass behind the bar he could see a heavy-looking man with a thick moustache; a man who kept glancing towards him as if he were lost, or as if he couldn't quite decide who he was.

Baby Doe arrived back at the hotel half an hour later, in a white fur coat with frogged buttons, and a white fur busby. She was accompanied by a tall, handsome girl in a green over-coat, and both of them were carrying parcels of shopping from Weston's and LaSalle's and Maquette's the Milliner. Henry could see right through the lobby to the front desk from where he was sitting; and he watched as the desk-clerk called out to Baby Doe, and beckoned her over, and then pointed towards the bar.

Baby Doe smiled disbelievingly, and then crammed all of her parcels into her friend's hands, and came hurrying through the hotel lobby in excitement. Henry winked to the barman, gave him two dollars, and then climbed off his barstool to greet her.

380

'Baby Doe,' he said, gently.

'Henry, my sweetheart,' she gasped, and seized the lapels of his coat as if she wanted to shake him out of sheer pleasure. He held her tight, and kissed her, and even though her nose was cold, she was just as warm as before, and her cheeks were just as soft, and she was just as fragrant and just as startlingly pretty. God, he had forgotten how pretty!

'You came back so quickly!' she said. They linked arms, and she led him back across the lobby to meet her friend.

'I couldn't wait to see you again,' he told her. 'And anyway, I had some important business to do; I've decided to sell the mine.'

'You're going to sell the mine? Does that mean you won't be rich any more?'

Henry laughed. 'Not at all, my darling. Exactly the opposite. It means that I'm going to be the wealthiest man in the whole of Colorado.'

'Here,' said Baby Doe, 'this is my friend Agnes Clarke. We met at the theatre, and we've decided to find rooms together.'

'You can have more than rooms,' said Henry. 'I'll buy you a house. Yes, and a maid, too, to wash out your linens.'

'My goodness,' said Agnes, in surprise, dipping Henry a little curtsey. 'You *are* rich?'

'Yes, and not afraid of it,' replied Henry. 'Would you girls care for some lunch?'

'I'll have to change,' said Agnes.

'Well, go right ahead,' Henry told her. 'Let's meet here in half an hour, if that's sufficient time for you. Tell me, Agnes, are you an actress, too?'

Agnes shook her head. 'I work for the *Ladies' Home Adviser*. I suppose you wouldn't think much of it. It's mostly to do with embroidery, and ladies' interests; like cookery, and how to cure the croup, and sometimes a little poetry.'

'Do you write any of the poetry?'

Agnes coloured. 'A little, sometimes. It isn't very good.'

'Tell me some,' Henry urged her. 'Go on, if you can remember any of it.'

'Now?' asked Agnes, flustered.

'If you want to. But don't let me embarrass you.'

'Oh do, Agnes,' encouraged Baby Doe, her eyes sparkling. 'She's so clever, Henry, you'd scarcely believe it.'

Agnes lowered her head and clasped her hands together. 'Very well, then, she said, 'but only a very short one.

'Under the linden trees,
Full many a glad eye sees
Treading the path, strewn with late autumn flowers.
The maiden pass before
To enter at the door,
And beaming bright,
With wreath of orange-flower and robe of white;
While by her side
He walks who soon shall claim her for his bride,
His own, whate'er of weal or woe betide.'

Baby Doe clapped her hands, and hugged Henry's arm. 'Isn't she marvellous!' she cried. 'She always makes me cry, with her peotry! Oh, Agnes, thank you!'

Henry smiled, and bowed to Agnes courteously. 'My compliments,' he told her. 'That was very sentimental.'

Agnes said, 'I do try to suit my verses to the occasion.'

'Ah, well,' said Henry, unsure if Agnes might not be making a prickly little point about him being married already. He took out his watch. 'It's six minutes to twelve now; let's meet here at half after.'

'I'd be honoured,' replied Agnes.

Henry helped Baby Doe to carry her parcels up to her room, and to spread them all out on the bed. She had bought a pair of indigo-coloured shoes, soft and small, with tiny heels; a winter hat of rusty-coloured velvet, with a bow, and a spray of moonstones; three pairs of embroidered linen bloomers, so fine that when she held them up, Henry could see her hand through them; and countless bottles and jars of face-cream and hand-softener and salve – Myrka's Powder, perfumed scalp food, hair-curling fluid, and violet essence. Henry sat on the end of the bed and picked all the cosmetics up one by one in fascination, and read the labels.

'Gives that velvet softness to the skin so much admired by all,' he said, and then put the jar down again, shaking his head. Augusta had never used any preparations like these: her vainest indulgence had been a jar of rice-powder which she had bought four years ago and which was still only half-empty.

Henry found them all mysterious and alluring, almost erotic, because they were so feminine.

Baby Doe hung up her coat and came into the bedroom wearing a simple black velvet dress with panels of black silk, and a ribboned bustle.

'You're not in mourning?' he asked her, with a smile.

She stood beside him, and stroked his cheek, and ran her fingers into his hair, tangling it. 'I missed you,' she whispered. 'That was almost like mourning.'

'I missed you, too.'

She reached down and kissed the top of his head. 'How was Leadville?'

'Leaden.'

She laughed. 'How was your wife?'

He made a face.

'Did you tell her anything? About us, I mean?' Her fingers stopped stroking while she waited for an answer.

Henry took a breath, and nodded. 'A little. I didn't tell her your name. I simply said that – I simply said that I'd met somebody else.'

'And she was upset, of course?' Baby Doe's voice sounded brittle.

'Upset isn't the word. But – you know – she has this extra-ordinary ability to pretend that everything is quite all right – that it doesn't matter. She asked me – well, she asked me if we'd been intimate. I'm sorry – but I suppose that's the first question that anybody asks – and when I said yes, that we had – she said, 'Oh, I forgive you,' just like that, as though it didn't matter at all.'

Baby Doe said, 'Can't you see? That's Augusta's way of making you admit that it's unimportant.'

'I told her I didn't want her forgiveness.'

'I'm pleased,' said Baby Doe, hugging him close. 'If you had have done, my sweetheart, that would have meant that our lovemaking didn't mean anything to you; that you considered it wrong, something for which you had to make amends.'

Henry raised his head, and kissed her, long and deep. Then, as silently as before, he stood up, and kissed her again, holding her face in his hands. Their kisses, when their lips parted, clicked as softly as leaves falling on to the meniscus of a winter pool. His hand smoothed down the narrow curve of her back; his left hand cupped her breast.

'Make love to me,' she said.

'But we have to meet Agnes in ten minutes. Don't you want to change?'

She pressed a finger against his lips. 'Ssh. Agnes will understand. Agnes will probably write a poem about it.'

She lifted her black velvet skirts and her black broderie anglaise petticoats, and gathered them up in her arms, baring her bottom to him, as white as Italian marble, and her black silk hose. Her bustle-pad perched on top of her bottom, but when he tried to untie it, she kissed him, and said, 'It doesn't matter, don't let's wait.'

He laid her back on the bed, amongst the wrapping-paper and the ribbons and the linen underwear and the shoes, and in three or four quick movements he had tugged off his coat, unbuttoned his waistcoat, and pulled down his pants. As he mounted her, she grasped him in her hand, and gripped him so tight that the head of his penis looked black with swollen blood. Then she guided him in between her thighs, without any preliminaries at all, except those of having thought about him every waking hour since he had left her and of having dreamed about him every hour when she was asleep. She was so hot and slippery that he was able to push himself into her right up as far as he could go, and she clutched at his shoulders through his shirt and cried out like a bird.

They thrust and thrust at each other, both of them unashamedly panting and grunting, while all of Baby Doe's shopping seemed to gravitate towards them, cosmetic jars clacking together, paper rustling, shoes and hats and underwear entangling themselves around them. Henry didn't know if minutes passed, or days, or even weeks. But suddenly Baby Doe began to moan softly under her breath, over and over again, almost as if she were grieving; and then her thighs and her stomach shook and shook, and she bent her head forward and said something that sounded as if it could have been a curse.

After a long pause, Henry withdrew from her, and stood up.

'You look so elegant,' smiled Baby Doe, 'with your pants around your knees. The great millionaire!'

Henry grinned, and blew her a kiss; which she pretended to catch in her hand and press between her legs. The gesture was both sweet and scandalous, and that was what he loved about Baby Doe.

384

'We'd better get ready,' he said. 'Agnes will be wondering what we're up to.'

'She can only guess right,' replied Baby Doe. She stood up, and brushed her skirts straight, and then said, 'I won't be long. All I need to do is powder my face.'

Henry glanced down towards her skirts. 'You're not going to – ?'

'Wash?' She shook her head. 'I love the smell of you, my sweetheart; and I'm not going to wash that away. Besides, I might be washing away your son and heir. Or even your daughter.'

He was so accustomed to Augusta, who rarely wanted to make love and who could never have children, that it hadn't occurred to Henry that he could quite easily make Baby Doe pregnant. He tugged at his collar uncomfortably, and said, 'But if you had our child – ?'

'If I did, my adorable Henry, I would love it, whatever it was, boy or girl, and I would bring it up to be happy and wise, and never to marry the wrong person. You're not worried, are you? You shouldn't be worried. I would never burden you, Henry; not ever. Not with guilt, not with responsibility, not with anything. All that I would ask from you would be just enough money to keep the child properly dressed, and fed, and sent to school.'

Henry said, 'You're talking as if we're going to break up.'

She lowered her eyes. 'I don't know. You can't predict the future, can you?'

He stood behind her and wrapped his arms around her waist, and hugged her. 'Baby Doe, I want to be with you for ever.'

'For ever is for ever, my sweetheart. And there's your wife to think of.'

He let go of her, and pressed the heel of his hand against his forehead. 'Yes, you're quite right, there's my wife to think of.'

'You don't want to hurt her, do you?'

'I think I've hurt her enough.'

'So you don't want to walk out on her straight away? Not after twenty years of marriage?'

Henry turned and looked at her. She was challenging him, rather than sympathizing with him. She was saying: if you want me, and especially if you want me for ever, then you've got to leave her. He slowly buttoned up his waistcoat again and reached for his coat. He said, 'It isn't going to be easy, you know. She's a very dependent sort of a person. Very weak. I just have to mention the idea of leaving her, and she collapses.'

Baby Doe said nothing, but stood against the light of the window with her face in shadow, and waited for him to say what he was going to do. You're the man, my sweetheart, you decide. It's your life, your wife. You decide.

'I – ah – have to make her comfortable, that's all.'

There was a long pause. Then Baby Doe said, 'Yes?'

'Well, you can see what my problem is. She's living and working in a general store; and I think at the very least I should finish the house, before I actually walk out on her. Give her somewhere decent to live. It's been twenty years, nearly. You can't just – ' he made a quick, stunted gesture with his hand, ' – throw it away – leave her with nothing.'

'I see.'

'I don't think you do. I don't think you realize how completely dependent Augusta is on me. She depends on me for everything; her whole living and breathing. You can't just turn around and walk out on somebody like that; you have to pull them off you, one sucker at a time, like ivy. I'm sorry. I can't tell you how dearly I love you. But, Baby Doe, it's going to take time.'

She turned her profile to him. He would have done anything then for a detective camera, to be able to catch the entrancing curve of her forehead, her slightly-open lips. Why is life so crowded with beauty and punishment? Why do we have to live out these terrible destinies? He could have wept for the woeful frustration of it.

'How long?' asked Baby Doe.

'Four months, not very much longer. Can you wait four months? I can get to Denver once every week to see you. And you've got the play, too. That's plenty to keep you busy.'

'And who shall I talk to, if I wake up crying in the very small hours of the night?'

Henry said, 'Don't punish me, my darling. I'm trying to do the very best that I can.'

'But you're going to go back to your wife, at least until you've built her a house?'

'Darling, I can't – I'm not able to – '

Baby Doe stared at him, vexed. 'You can, Henry! You *can*! You're a millionaire!'

'Only on paper.'

'Oh, don't make excuses; you're a rich and powerful man. You can do anything you want.'

'I've been thinking of getting into politics, too,' said Henry.' I was talking to Nat Starkey about running for mayor.'

'I don't understand. What difference can that make to us?'

'It means that I can't afford to have any scandal in my background, that's all. I have to be discreet. Not *offend* people. That's what politics is all about.'

Baby Doe raised her arms wide, in an unknowing imitation of the way in which August Rische had been crucified on the wires in the Little Pittsburgh mine. She said, in a chokey voice, 'I know what you're asking of me, my sweetheart; you're asking for time to make up your mind. You don't have to make excuses.'

'They're not excuses, Baby Doe; they're reasons.'

She lowered her arms again. 'Well, perhaps they are. But I love you, and I can't wait for ever, knowing that you belong to somebody else.'

'Believe me – ' he began, but then he tugged his hand through his hair and looked away from her, and said, 'Just believe me, please.'

FIFTEEN

The snow came early to Leadville that year; and since Leadville was and remains at 10,188 feet above mean sea-level the highest incorporated city in the United States of America, that meant earlier and deeper than any other place nearby, including Denver.

Josiah Dunkley had selected a site for Henry's mansion, between East 10th Street and East 9th Street, on the northern slope of Capitol Hill; and most of the provisional plans and elevations had been completed: entire cloth-bound books of drawings of staircases and balconies, towers and porticoes, all in colour, and all in exquisite detail. The snow, however, had closed the Fremont Pass five times; and with no railroad link to the outside world, all practical work on the mansion had to be postponed until the early spring. Three railroad companies, the Denver & Rio Grande, the Santa Fe, and the Denver & South Park, were battling each other ferociously for the right to serve Leadville's transportation needs, but so far no decision had been reached, and no railroad ran.

For all of its wealth, for all that it was built on huge beds of silver carbonate, as well as rich deposits of zinc, copper, iron, bismuth, and manganese; for all of its smelters and foundries and silver-mines, and the millionaires who owned them, Leadville was still isolated and wild, and its snowy streets still crackled from time to time with the sound of gunfire.

Henry struggled through to Denver seven times during the deepest winter months to visit Baby Doe. She and Agnes were sharing the neat grey-painted house on Larimer Street that Henry had bought for them; and they were comfortable enough; although Baby Doe was growing tired of spending days on her own, and many of Henry's visits would end in silence, with them sitting apart, and the snow outside the window falling on to Denver and its scores and scores of telegraph poles until the city looked like a snowed-in fleet of whalers, with frozen masts and rigging. Henry no longer gave excuses why he hadn't yet left Augusta; Baby Doe no longer asked him for any.

There was a sadness and a sweetness about those months which would remain with Henry for the rest of his life. Their affair grew more mature: they no longer shed tears for each other. He touched her, and she no longer shivered. But they were far more profoundly in love. They waited for the spring with a strange pensive calmness, as if they were afraid to admit their superstitious fear that the winter might never end.

In late November, David Moffat sold the Little Pittsburgh mine to a consortium of three Eastern mining companies for one million dollars, in cash. Henry went up to see the mine one last time, and to shake hands with all of the men, but the snow was so thick that all he could make out was the chimney-stacks, and some dark depressions in the snow. Inside the winding-shed, R.P. Grover was stalking impatiently up and down while the steam-engine was being repaired; the same old faulty valves about which he had complained to Henry so often.

'Well, then, Mr Roberts,' said R.P. Grover, over the noise.

Henry pulled off his gloves. 'I just came up to say goodbye.'

'You were probably right to sell, sir. There always comes a time when a man has to move on; and forget about his beginnings. Nobody should dwell on their beginnings, if you ask me.'

Henry looked around. The winding-shed was filled with fragmented clouds of steam. 'Do you think there are any ghosts here?' he asked. R.P. Grover didn't answer at first, so Henry looked at him, straight and serious, and said, 'Well?'

'No ghosts, sir. No more than most mines. Although one of the fellows swears that he can hear Mr Rische's dog barking, sir, right down in the lower levels. Barking for his master, so to speak.'

'Timber, I expect,' said Henry, with a grimace, although for some reason the story unnerved him. 'You know how those square-sets can creak.'

R.P. Grover grasped Henry's hand. 'Oh, I wouldn't credit ghosts, sir. Not me. You and me will be off to meet our Maker soon enough, won't we, and I'm sure that Mr Rische and Mr Hook can wait until then, can't they, if'n they've got some bone to pick.'

Henry pulled on his gloves again, and trudged down the hill on snow-shoes, back to the store. Augusta was waiting for him there as usual; quiet, big-faced, uncomplaining, happy that the snow had come so early, and even happier that it was lasting so long. On her right hand she wore her only symbol of the Roberts' new riches: a 32–carat diamond ring. Actually, to Augusta, it was less of a symbol of riches than a symbol of triumph. She had obliged Henry to give up his mistress, so she believed; and to bring her back the wanton woman's ring, as proof. Henry, of course, never mentioned Baby Doe now, and as far as Augusta was concerned, all his journeys to Denver were to do with the selling of the Little Pittsburgh, and the acquisition of stock in other silver-mines.

Henry often sat reading during the evenings; only to look up at her and think to himself, if only you knew. And if only you knew how relieved I was when I went desperately to Ischart's and found as if by magic that they had kept in their vaults a strass copy of the ring I first bought from them, for wearing at banquets and anywhere else where the risk of theft might be high. It cost me exactly $38.17, that ring. And that, my dear, is all that you are worth: because look at you, how you gloat over it, how you keep admiring its vulgarity, hating it for what it is, and adoring it for what it represents.'

As the winter began to break, however, Augusta's hold on Henry began to break with it. She had held on to him too long and too tightly; and as soon as the Fremont Pass was clear, he began to visit Denver every weekend on 'business'; and to take Baby Doe for snowy promenades along the banks of the frozen Platte, or for dinners at Walter's or Brown's, champagne and baked trout and in February, on her birthday, a whipped dessert of cream and pecans and feathery sponge which the chef at Walter's named 'Baby Doe Surprise', in her honour. Henry bought Baby Doe silk dresses and sapphire necklaces and scarves, and there were so many pairs of shoes in her cupboard that she had to keep some of them under her bed. Her housemate Agnes learned to be discreet at weekends, and to knock on doors before she entered, although Henry would often cheerfully invite her to join them for dinner, and afterwards the three of them would visit the Byers, or the Kitteredges, and the girls would talk and laugh and play the piano while the men sat in the library to discuss money, or silver carbonate, or play poker.

Henry was now very rich; even David Moffat wasn't sure how rich. Over $911,000 of the one million dollars which he had received from the sale of the Little Pittsburgh mine had been selectively invested in other silver-mines around Leadville, the Chrysolite, the May Queen, the Elk, the Little Willie, the Wheel of Fortune, the Tam o' Shanter, the Union Emma, the Scooper, and the Matchless. The Eastern consortium who had bought up the Little Pittsburgh had offered stock in the mine for public sale, and Henry, on his own inspiration, had bought back a large part of it, as $5 the share. Already, the consortium had introduced better drilling equipment and extra ore-crushers in the extracting works, and the shares had risen to $17.50 – which meant that in four months Henry had already made himself another half-million from the same mine. David estimated Henry's fortune at 'something around $4 million', although he always repeated those words that Henry had said so sharply to Baby Doe – 'on paper'. There was no telling how long the price of silver would continue to rise, or how long the

390

government would continue to buy 4.5 million ounces of silver every month for the minting of Federal coinage.

Over a game of poker one evening in March David said, 'I've warned you before, Henry, it's very much easier to *lose* a million than it is to acquire it. You've been lucky. Not many men have anything like your luck. But the only way you're going to hold on to that luck is if you keep down your spending; and make sensible investments; and after a while, diversify. You could think of going into railroad stock now; and maybe milling.'

'Let me see how I get on with the politics first,' replied Henry. His huge diamond ring flashed in the lamplight, and his cufflinks followed up the display with a quiet glitter of pavé-set diamonds and rubies. He was smoking a huge cigar of Havana tobacco, the size of one of Denver's telegraph-poles. He had grown his moustache longer, and taken to waxing up the ends again. He loved the wealth: he loved the ostentatiousness of it. He loved to see passers-by turn their heads in amazement as he and Baby Doe stepped down from their black shiny landau when they were driven to the theatre; Baby Doe in her furs and her feathers and her dazzling necklaces, and he in his glossy opera-hat and swirling black vicuna cloak.

'I never thought of you as being particularly political,' said David, in a careful tone.

'Why not?' asked Henry, dealing cards. He took the cigar out of his mouth and looked at David with a grin that wasn't entirely humorous. 'Money is power, didn't you always tell me that? With money, you can make waves.'

'It depends, Henry,' said David, uneasily.

'It depends on what? Go on, tell me. We've been friends for long enough. You don't have to be shy.'

'It depends on what kind of waves you want to make.'

'David,' said Henry, leaning forward over the green baize card-table and speaking softly so that the ladies on the other side of the drawing-room couldn't hear him. 'For all of my life, I've been floating along with the current, allowing myself to be taken wherever chance or fate or God's will or whatever you call it has decided to take me. I've kicked and struggled sometimes, but I've kept on floating. Now I've begun to see that if I go on floating for very much longer, my whole existence from the moment I was born to the moment when they cover my face with that sheet – my whole life will have been floating.

391

From birth to death floating, without leaving a ripple. What will I leave, for people to remember me by?'

David picked up his cards and carefully inspected them. Without raising his eyes, he said, 'It isn't generally advisable to make waves just for the *sake* of making waves. It could damage your business interests. It could even put your life at risk. Remember that politicians always have enemies.'

'Enemies? What enemies have I got?'

'Quite a few, already.'

Henry felt a prickly shock of perplexity, as if he had suddenly and accidentally caught his hand on a hidden tangle of barbed-wire. 'What do you mean? I don't have any enemies! Enemies? Me? Who?'

'You've been talking about standing for mayor of Leadville, haven't you?'

'Well?'

'There are those in Leadville who feel that the city needs greater respectability, rather than less.'

'David, what are you talking about?' Henry demanded.

David put down his cards. 'I'm just trying to tell you, Henry, in the friendliest possible way, that the most influential men in Colorado are also some of the most puritanical. You can recognize them by their bulging wallets and their blue noses. You've already created an incredible stir in Denver, dressing up in diamonds and opera-cloaks and walking out with the prettiest woman for five hundred miles around. Aren't you aware of the furore you're creating? Look at that ring on your finger, Henry, and tell me if that isn't guaranteed to stop anybody dead in their tracks. And look at this.'

David stood up, and walked across to the magazine rack by the fireplace, and came back with a recent copy of the *News*. 'I don't know whether you've seen this. I didn't show it to you before, but you might as well realize what kind of an impression you and Baby Doe have been making on this backward little town of ours.'

Henry took the newspaper with increasing bewilderment. David pointed with a steady finger to an article headed 'Mrs Elizabeth Doe – An "Ophelia Beyond Compare"; Beauty Of Beauties To Play Shakespearean Role in Mr Roberts' *Hamlet* Opening Next Month.' The reporter had been careful to avoid saying directly that Henry and Baby Doe were lovers, but all the way through the item there was a subtle but persistent implication that 'Mrs Doe and her wealthy sponsor' were more than professionally intimate.

Henry read the article from top to bottom, then handed the paper back to David, and said, 'You can put it on the fire now. That's where it belongs.'

David slowly folded it up. 'Henry, you can't ignore public opinion, not if you want to be a politician; and not if you want to become one of Denver's really influential elite. Money alone isn't enough. That's what I've been trying to explain to you. If you're going to get on, if you're going to make those waves you keep talking about, then I'm sorry – but you've got to finish matters with Baby Doe.'

'What are you trying to tell me?' Henry retorted, aggressively. 'You're trying to tell me that Mrs Doe isn't respectable enough for you? That you object to having a married man's mistress in your house? Is that it?'

'Henry, that isn't the problem at all. I adore Baby Doe. I think she's pretty and amusing and I know exactly what it is that you see in her. But you can't go on flaunting your adultery and still expect to get political and popular support.'

Henry sat silent for an uncomfortably long time. My God, he thought. I've suffered all these years with Augusta, scratching for money; and now that I'm rich, it's going to be just as bad. Where did that day in Bennington go, that day with all its sunshine and freedom? Where did my life go? Is this all there is to it, being nagged at by wives and cautious colleagues and moralistic busybodies who care more for respectability than they do for happiness? My God, he thought, if *this* is what the proper and acceptable way of leading your life is like, then it isn't worth living. I might as well have thrown myself down that shaft on top of George Hook, instead of a barrow-load of steels, and killed both of us together, to put us out of our misery.

He had always been dutifully conscious that a would-be politician should scrupulously avoid getting himself involved in sexual scandal; in fact, he had repeatedly told Baby Doe that he couldn't leave Augusta, not just yet, for fear of spoiling his chances of being elected mayor. Yet somehow, during the winter, as more and more money had accumulated in his bank account, and he had begun to realize that he was not just rich, but a millionaire several times over, his perception of what was scandalous and what was proper had radically changed. He

393

was rich: what he did was proper. It was only what poor people and Democrats did that was scandalous.

He stood up. He rubbed his hands together. He told David, 'This is it. You've decided me.'

'This is *what*? asked David.

Henry stalked into the centre of the drawing-room, and held out his hand towards Baby Doe.

'This is *what*, Henry?' David repeated anxiously, hurrying after him.

'David – this is where I stop lying – stop deceiving myself – and stop deceiving everybody else. That article shocked me, that article in the *News* about Baby Doe. It was cheap and it was smutty. If people are going to gossip about us, if people are going to snigger and moralize, well then, let them do it in front of us, where we can see them. I'm leaving Augusta.'

'What?'

Henry stood with his fists on his hips and bent forward and glared directly into David's bright pink face. 'I'm leaving Augusta. For good. She can have the mansion, she can keep the store. I'm leaving her. She's had eighteen years of my life, no, nineteen, and that's all the time she's going to get. She came to my door begging to be married, and I married her; but when I stood in that chapel and said that I'd honour and keep her, for richer, for poorer, that didn't mean that I promised to crush myself up for her, and live the rest of my life in boredom and frustration and pain. Happiness is a God-given right, David; and there's my happiness, sitting there, and I'm damned if anybody's going to stop me taking it, for any reason, political or moral or financial or social or any damned reason that you can think of.'

David raised both hands cautiously. 'Henry, come on, you've had three glasses of brandy – '

But Henry slowly and melodramatically shook his head. 'Maybe the brandy has loosened my tongue, David; but it hasn't affected my heart. All of you think that Baby Doe is a passing fancy, don't you? You've all been tolerating her here because you think she won't last long; oh, now that Henry's come into money, he has to have his little fling, it won't last long. Let's just hope that he's going to be civilized about it, and not flaunt it too much. You hypocrites. You, David, of all people. And me, worst of all, for not acting sooner; for making Baby Doe suffer all winter long; because I listened to you, and

394

because I didn't have the courage to leave Augusta when I first met her. Baby Doe isn't only beautiful, David, she's brave; and she's stayed loyal to me, and honest, when all of the rest of you have been doing everything you can to make sure that I remained respectable. Well – let me tell you what the price of respectability is, for me – and that's Augusta – and that is more than I am prepared to pay.'

He looked around the drawing-room, flushed, and then he said, in the clearest, best-enunciated voice that he could manage, 'I would give a million dollars, in cash, to be rid of Augusta, right this minute. I would give everything I own. Not that I consider it necessary, or just. Augusta will get what Augusta truly deserves. But let me tell you here and now that I shall be rid of her; and that I will stay with Baby Doe, and that I will still run for mayor, and damn it, I will run for senator, too, and anybody who doesn't like the idea of it can be damned.'

David was silent for a moment or two. He stood with his hands in his pockets looking down at the carpet. Then he raised his head, and said, 'Well, Henry, you just lost something this evening.'

'What was that, David?'

David said sadly, 'You lost a friend. Please, go get your coats, and leave. And whatever arrangements you want to make for handling your business – well, just let me know when you're ready. I don't want to have anything further to do with it.'

Henry said, 'This is the way you've been feeling all along, isn't it?'

David nodded.

'All right, then,' said Henry. He went over to Baby Doe and took her hand. 'Come on,' he told her. 'This is where the old life really ends, and the new life really begins.'

They left David Moffat's house without saying anything more. Henry and David still liked each other, and neither of them wanted to risk losing his temper, and hurting the other more than he had to. Henry turned around at the doorway, but they didn't shake hands.

'What are you going to do now?' Baby Doe asked Henry, as she snuggled up close to him in the carriage.

Henry leaned towards her as he reached into his pocket for his matches, to relight his cigar. 'You don't mind if I smoke this thing?'

She shook her head.

He struck a match, and sucked. 'The first thing I'm going to do is go back to Leadville,' he said. 'This time, I'm going to have it out with Augusta, straight and quick. It's the only way. "Augusta," I'm going to tell her, "I can't take the sight of your face any longer and that's the end of it." Then, I'm going to go round to Nat Starkey and the rest of the Leadville city administrators, and I'm going to offer them the following: an opera house, which they sorely need for their ears, and a street railroad, which they sorely need for their feet; and electric street lighting, which they sorely need for their eyes. And I'm going to tell them: if you don't elect me for mayor now, you need your brains tested!'

Henry was in great high spirits. He sat up straight in the back of the carriage, and clapped his hands, his cigar clenched between his teeth, one eye closed against the smoke. 'Then,' he said, 'I'm going to go to the judge and ask for a legal divorce, on the grounds of something-or-other, cruelty more than likely; and by God my love I'm going to marry you, as soon as the law permits.'

Baby Doe held him close. But she said, quietly, 'You're drunk now, my sweetheart. Tell me again in the morning.'

He took out his cigar, and breathed smoke, and looked at her with unfocused eyes. 'You don't think I'm going to do it, do you?'

Baby Doe said nothing, but leaned against his starched white shirtfront with its real pearl buttons and watched the street-lights dancing by as if they were will-o'-the-wisps, fiery entrancing goblins who led you to nowhere.

Early the following afternoon, his face grey, his moustache unwaxed, his coat-collar turned up against the wind, Henry set off for Leadville. When he arrived the next day, he went first to the store, but Hetty Larsen, who often helped Augusta to serve behind the counter these days, told him that Augusta had gone to the 'big house' as she called it, to watch the grand staircase being put in.

It was a cold day in Leadville. The streets were thick with icy mud, and a thin drizzle poured relentlessly down from the mountains. Waggons struggled through the ooze; carters whipped and cursed; and loafers leaned on the hitching-rails with water dripping steadily from the brims of their hats. In the Pioneer Saloon, on State Street, someone was playing 'Sweet Betsy From Pike' on the piano.

The house on East 10th Street was enormous, although it was still a shell. It was the talk of Leadville, and there were weekly reports on its construction in the local newspaper. At the moment, it was nothing more than a towering arrangement of brick walls and Doric pillars, with empty window-frames and empty doors, and the ground all around it was churned up by builder's waggons and wheelbarrows, and cross-trenched with excavations for the drains. Henry climbed down from his carriage and crossed the muddy ground in his $55 shoes, scaling the marble steps, which were crunchy with black grit and plaster, and entered the hallway, roofless still, so that the rain fell softly on to the floor.

Augusta was standing alone in front of the grand staircase; in a black cape, and holding a black umbrella. She must have heard Henry approaching across the hallway, but she didn't turn around; nor did she look at him when at last he stood beside her.

The grand staircase was almost complete: a magnificent sweep of marble stairs that curved around the side wall of the hallway, wet and dirty now, but all ready to be polished so that they would reflect the sparkle of chandeliers, and the silk of ladies' slippers, and the taffetas and velvets of evening gowns.

'Very impressive,' said Henry.

'I suppose so,' Augusta replied.

'Are they working today?' asked Henry, looking around.

'It's too wet. They'll come back tomorrow.'

Henry walked around her, and looked at her.

'Have you been here long?' he asked her.

'About an hour.'

'Any – ' he paused ' – particular reason? I mean, is there anything you particularly wanted to see? I mean, it's going all right, isn't it? No problems with the builders?'

'No,' she said, almost inaudibly. 'No problems with the builders.'

'Do you, um – do you want to go back to the store?'

She suddenly turned and stared at him, her face rigid under her plain black bonnet. 'Do you know what you've done?' she demanded. 'Do you understand at all just how *immorally* – just how *carelessly* – you've been behaving?'

'Augusta, this really isn't the place to – '

'You are so *weak*,' she barked at him. 'Henry, you are so weak!'

'*Weak?*' he repeated. He was baffled. That was the very last thing he had expected her to say. Treacherous, yes. Callous, perhaps. But weak? What on earth did she mean? Weak?

But Augusta was furious, and in full unstoppable spate. 'Since they've started building the house, and since I've been thinking of giving up the store, Henry I've been going through the books. The bank books, Henry, all of them; and all the correspondence; and all the transactions; all the things that *you* were supposed to be taking care of. It's your precious friend William Byers, isn't it? Him, and von Richthofen, and that ridiculous Henry Stanley. Those elite Denverites you keep boasting about. Well, do you know what they've done, with your collusion, or perhaps with your carelessness, and your unbelievable innocence?'

Henry had been right on the pitch of telling Augusta that their marriage was over; that he loved Baby Doe and that he wanted a divorce, so that he could marry her. Suddenly, in the rain, he found himself having to defend a casual financial arrangement that he had made with William Byers, for no reason that he could think of, and he couldn't even find the words to explain what he had done, or why. William had asked him if he could use his bank to finance a side-wheeler service on the Platte River, and a resort city for all of those Easterners who wanted a breath of mountain air; and that was all that he knew about it. The money had come and gone; and William had made him regular payments of commission; that was all he knew.

Augusta said, 'William Byers has been using our bank not to accumulate capital, Henry, but to disperse it. At no time in the past year has the Platte River Transportation account had more than $500 in it; except when a large deposit was made, and even then the funds were immediately transferred to other banks. I may be foolish, Henry, I may be ridiculous; and I may be a nagging wife. But I am not so foolish or ridiculous that I cannot recognize a blatant fraud when I see it; and I think that I am entitled to nag. In fact I think that I am entitled to report this whole affair to the sheriff.'

Henry stood silent, and looked at Augusta through the soft, cold rain, and knew that this, at last, was the very end. He

398

said, 'You can go to the sheriff if you want to, my dear; if you think that it will make you feel better; if you need some kind of revenge.'

'Henry,' she said, quite loudly, gathering up her damp skirts and walking towards him as if she meant to hit him, or embrace him. 'Henry, I don't want to go to the sheriff at all. But what have you done? What have you done to our name, and our reputation? Henry, I'm not talking about revenge! I'm talking about justice, about Christian virtue! You can't just let this matter go, as if it never happened! Henry, there were hundreds and thousands of dollars; and our bank was used to spirit it all away!'

Henry said, 'I'll look into it. Will that satisfy you? I'll investigate. Now, shall we go back to the store? It's wet.'

'Henry – '

'I'm not going to discuss it any longer, damn it! Now, I'm going back to the store, and I want to know if you're going to come with me.'

She looked at him defiantly, her tiny oval spectacles beaded with rain. 'No,' she said. 'I'm going to go see Harriet Henderson first, and have a talk, and some tea. I'll see you later, if you're back for the night. If not, well, I don't really care when I see you; since you're hardly ever here anyway, and when you are you seem to be far too tired even to talk.'

Henry didn't even try to persuade her to change her mind. He knew that it was no use. Augusta walked past him with her chin raised sternly, and made her way through the doorless entrance, and down the steps which led to East 9th Street. He followed her as far as the doorway; and when she reached the muddy street she turned and looked at him, her dark bonnet outlined against the silvery-grey puddles, her spectacles shining.

He said, 'Augusta,' and it was then for the first time that she hesitated, her hems raised above the mud. Perhaps she knew intuitively what he was going to say, because she waited with unusual patience, silent, her face white and unfocused. The wind blew the rain across the street in thick, persistent curtains, ruffling the surface of the puddles, and causing Henry's horse to whuffle, and toss its dripping head.

'Augusta,' he said, 'I'm leaving you.'

She received the news with unsurprised pain. She lowered her head, and then she lowered her umbrella. If you have just lost your husband, what difference does it make if your hat gets wet? She said something which he couldn't hear; and so he called out, 'What?'

She raised her head again. 'I said, I've been expecting this all winter. Is it the girl they call Baby Doe?'

'You know about her?'

'Henry, everybody knows about her. It's in all the newspapers almost every week; even the *Leadville Chronicle*. I've just been closing my eyes and waiting for you to tell me.'

'I see,' he said. He felt rather disappointed that Baby Doe was not a surprise.

'I did think that you had stopped seeing her,' said Augusta. 'After all, you brought me her ring.'

'Yes,' he said. He came down the steps, slowly, one at a time. 'But, well, it's easier said than done, isn't it, breaking up with somebody you really love?'

'You don't have to tell me that,' said Augusta, with agonized ferocity.

Henry said, 'I'm sorry. I was talking about myself, I meant me, not you; but I suppose it's just as hard for you. Look, I'm sorry.'

'If you were genuinely sorry, you wouldn't leave me. But you will.'

'Augusta, I'm *sorry*! But the fact is that I love her; that she makes me feel happy; and confident; and free.'

'I see,' said Augusta. 'Then you're more of a fool than I thought you were. I pity her. And I pity you, too.'

Without another word, Augusta began to walk away down Harrison Avenue, allowing her skirts to trail in the mud; while waggons and carriages struggled past her, and the shower started suddenly to fall much more heavily; so that gutterings gurgled, and water-barrels began to overflow, and the puddles in the streets were circled and circled with the dreary hoop-la rings of rain. Henry knew that it was a shower, that it wouldn't last, but somehow that made it all the sadder; that Augusta would soon look out of her window and see that the rain had stopped; and yet she was still deserted.

Henry remained where he was, with his hands in his pockets, staring at the half-finished ruins of his lavish mansion, 'Versailles' in Leadville. He was still there when a thin man with a dark drooping moustache and a black high-crowned hat came walking towards him from the direction of St Vincent's Hospital; his coat-collar turned up, coughing.

The man stopped, and coughed, and looked up at 'Roberts Lodge'. 'This your place?' he asked.

Henry nodded.

'It's going to be some house, when it's finished.'

'Yes.'

The man coughed again, and sniffed, and coughed again. 'This wet weather doesn't do my lungs no good; and I only came up here for the dry mountain air.'

Henry held out his hand. 'Henry Roberts,' he said.

'Ah, so you're Henry Roberts. Well, I've heard about you. I have a friend in Tombstone, Arizona, who knows a lady-friend of yours.'

Henry frowned at him. 'Mrs Doe?' he asked, puzzled.

The man shook his head. 'Nina Somebody, used to be a circus dancer. Ring any bells? Well, maybe it wouldn't. You're a famous man these days, aren't you? I was reading about that theatre you bought in Denver.'

'Your friend knows Nina? Mademoiselle Carolista?'

'That's it (cough) that's what she calls herself. Mademoiselle Carolista. Used to be a circus dancer. Not much use to anybody now. Fell off a wire in Helena, Montana, and broke her neck. Wyatt took her in for a while, don't know why; but I met her a couple of times; and she's a sweet lady.'

'Is she still there now? In Tombstone?'

The man shrugged. 'Who knows? I haven't seen Wyatt in a while; nor any of the Earps. But he was fond of that Nina, that Mademoiselle Carolista, and took good care of her, for some reason. She talked about you once in a while, that's how I know you were friends.'

Henry asked, 'Do you want a drink? I was just about to go down to the Tasteful Saloon.'

'That sounds like a gentlemanly suggestion,' the man replied. He shook Henry's hand again, and said, 'John Holliday, dentist. Most people generally call me Doc.'

Henry returned to the store later that evening, reasonably drunk. Augusta wasn't there; and there was no sign that she had been there since the morning. The stove was cold, and her breakfast bowl was still beside the sink, washed, but not put away. Augusta had eaten a bowl of oats for breakfast for eighteen years; one bowl every morning. Henry stood in the

401

darkened kitchen and looked at her bowl and felt immeasurably sorry for her; but also relieved. The guilt was over. He had faced her, and told her; and however hurt and lonely she might be, she was well provided for; and well-liked, and in time her hurt and loneliness would pass. At least, he hoped it would.

It was a strange experience, to walk around the house and know that he would never come here again. He went upstairs, to the bedroom and looked at the neatly-made bed in which he and Augusta had slept for all those years; at the jug and the basin in which he had so often washed himself; at the lithograph of Jesus on the wall, at the cheap ornaments and the shabby furniture. He sat down on the edge of the bed, and burped because of all the beer he had been drinking with his whiskey, and reached into the pocket of his coat for his white-gold cigar case.

He was just lighting up when he heard the front door of the store open, and the bell jangle. After a while, the light of an oil-lamp came up the stairs and along the landing, and Augusta appeared, very pale-faced. Her eyes were swollen as if she had been crying, and for the first time since he had known her, her hair was untidy.

She said, 'I thought you would have left by now. Back to your Baby Doe.'

'I, er, had a few drinks at the Tasteful Saloon. I met somebody, that's all. I just came back to take a look.'

'Yes,' Augusta said busily, walking across the room, and setting the lamp down on the bureau. 'I met your drinking companion outside. He was sitting on the boardwalk, coughing.'

'He's an interesting man. Plays a good game of cards, too.'

'He's been pointed out to me before,' said Augusta. 'I understand that he's killed people.' She unpinned her hair, and turned around. 'Just the right sort of company for you, I would have thought.'

Henry blew out smoke, and then stood up, shuffling with one foot to get his balance. 'Augusta – ' he said, spreading his arms as if an innocent gesture alone was sufficient proof of his innocence. 'Augusta, this had to happen, sooner or later. We couldn't go on.'

'*You*, apparently, couldn't go on. Don't speak for me.'

'Augusta, I never made you happy.'

402

'You don't know anything about happiness, Henry, especially mine.'

'But Augusta – '

'You *fool!*' she snapped at him. 'Don't you see that our life together wasn't concerned with happiness at all? If it had have been, I would have walked out on you; and years ago, too.'

Henry stood staring at her with his cigar twiddling smoke into the darkness of the room. 'Then what?' he asked her, in bewilderment. 'Then *why?*'

Augusta let down her hair. It was kinky and wavy from having been plaited when it was wet, and in the lamplight it shone with streaks of silver.

She said, in a flat, toneless whisper, 'God visits a certain destiny on all of us. Mine was to serve, and to suffer. That was all I asked of you, ever, that you should allow me to serve you. But it seems that even that was too much for you to give me.'

There was a long, painful silence. Henry felt as if he had an iron hook in his heart. He tried to think of something to say, but couldn't. The burden of Augusta's martyrdom was too great; a burden which he had never asked to shoulder, yet which now seemed almost impossible to put down.

'I suppose you have to go now,' she said.

'About the Platts River Transportation account – ' he told her. 'Believe me, you don't have to do anything about that. I'm sure it's all above board. I'll go back to William and Henry Stanley and look into it personally.'

Augusta folded her arms, said nothing.

'Believe me,' he insisted.

'It's a fraud,' she said. 'Anybody can see that it's a fraud. You've allowed them to use you as a stooge and a dummy. And you were either too simple or too careless or too vain to take any notice.'

'Augusta, I warn you, if you try to take this matter any further – these are influential people.'

'And what will they do to me? What will they take away from me that you haven't taken away from me already? You've taken my pride, my dignity, my very soul. What does my life matter?'

Henry said with almost hysterical firmness, 'You must not mention anything about these matters to anyone. I'm serious, Augusta. Listen – you can have the house, as soon as it's completed. You can have as much money as you need. But you will never, ever, disclose anything about the Platte River Transportation account to *anyone*. And especially not to the law.'

Augusta stared at him with pain and contempt. 'I've never seen you frightened before. It almost makes me glad that you're going.'

Henry clasped both hands behind his neck, and pressed with a grimace at his tension-tightened muscles. Slowly, without taking her eyes off him, Augusta moved around the end of the bed, until she was standing very close.

'This would ruin you, wouldn't it, if it ever came out?'

He didn't answer. She kept on watching him, plain and short-sighted, her silver hairs shining, her face bruised with grief.

'I will only say this,' she told him. 'I will keep these matters confidential, if that is what you want; but only for as long as you remain my husband. You cannot expect any allegiance beyond that.'

Henry stared at her. 'Why did you come back?' he asked her, and his voice was shaking. 'Why didn't you stay on that train and go all the way on to Bennington, and marry somebody else?'

Augusta smiled, a strange smile that made Henry feel as if someone with cold hands was cupping his testicles. 'Because I was always meant to be Mrs Henry Roberts,' she said. 'And I always will be, until the day I die.'

Henry spent the night at Nat Starkey's house on James Street. Frederick Maynard was there, and so was Thos Rogers, and from time to time other wealthy and robust members of Leadville's Republican party would call by and take a glass of whiskey or two; and some of Mrs Starkey's chicken-wings and hush puppies, dipped in green-pepper sauce. Henry enjoyed the Starkey house: it was warm and noisy and ostentatiously furnished, with palms and bookcases and pianos and sofas, and gilded oil-paintings of the Rocky Mountains in spring, and prairie fires, and the Starkey family looking florid and proud. It always seemed to be open house here, especially to Leadville's several millionaires; and they would bring in their extravagant moustaches and their gleaming shirt-fronts and their pretty wives and prettier mistresses, and slap their overfed thighs and tell off-colour stories which Mrs Starkey was lady enough to disregard.

404

With his diamond rings and his handmade shoes and his emerald necktie pin, Henry felt at home here, in the company of rich self-made men who didn't mind showing off their money. He drank more whiskey, laughed too loudly, and sweated into his tight white evening waistcoat.

'Mr Roberts has offered us an opera house, and a fire house, and electrified lighting for the streets,' said Frederick Maynard, standing with his large bottom to the fire, and a glass of brandy in his hand. There was general applause. 'I believe the least we can do for him in return is make sure that he's elected mayor.'

There was more applause, and everybody raised their glasses. 'By the way,' Thos Rogers shouted out. 'Henry will no doubt be satisfied to hear that he can afford to donate all these generous gifts and services. The Matchless Mine announced this afternoon that its shares have risen to $56; and that they believe they've struck another bed of carbonate, which could prove even richer than the first.'

'Well, now, I'll drink to that,' shouted Henry, far too loudly, and got up on to his feet. 'I'll drink to that, $56 the share; well, considering I bought them at $10.' He laughed, and then he raised his glass again, and said to the pink blurry faces all around him; all those smiling expectant faces as bright as jelly-babies, 'I also want to drink – to – '

He paused. He lowered his glass again. Somebody said, 'What is it, Henry?' but Henry knew what it was. It was a brief, sharp, briny-tasting image of this afternoon, when he had been drinking at the bar of the Tasteful Saloon with John Holliday; and Holliday had leaned close to him, and coughed, and then said, 'There's only one thing worth drinking to, my friend, and that's your own mortality. *I* know it, *you* know it. We're all going to die. I've been living my life in a constant flight from death. That's why I'm here, now; and I can only tell you this, that you must never let your life pass you by. If something's wrong in your life, then change it, and change it quick, because you haven't got long to go. You've found yourself a woman you love; then you go get her; and you forget about guilt, and you forget about morality, and conscience, because that Grim Reaper isn't going to worry about it when he carries you away, he's not going to care if you've been happy or sad, or guilty or frightened, or anything at all. How old are you friend? And this is the first woman you've ever loved? By all that's powerful,

405

my friend, you go get her; you marry her; you keep her close; and let's drink to mortality, because there ain't anything ever that's worth drinking to more.'

In Nat Starkey's suddenly-silenced drawing-room, Henry lifted his glass, and said, 'Mortality.'

Thos Rogers frowned, and hiccuped, and said, 'Mortality? *Mortality?* What the blue blazes is that?'

'*More* tality?' said Frederick Maynard, befuddled. 'I'd rather drink to *less* tality.'

Nat Starkey came up to Henry and put an arm around his shoulder. 'Let's drink to the mayor-to-be,' he declared. 'His health, and his money, and his happiness.'

He lifted his glass to Henry; and very quietly, so that nobody else in the room could distinctly hear what he was saying, murmured, 'You're a politician now, Henry. All millionaires have to be, in their way. So forget the past. Politicians and millionaires never have pasts. Not pasts that they should be seen to care about, anyway.'

'The mayor!' cried Thos Rogers; and then everybody stood, and clinked their glasses together, and laughed, and clapped, and shouted out, 'The mayor!'

SIXTEEN

She said, 'I want to be married.'

Henry had been standing by the window, looking out over the mountains. He said, abstractedly, 'Yes, my dear; I guess that you do.'

'No, really,' she told him, and came up behind him across the Persian carpet, her pink silk dress rustling, and put her arms around his waist. 'I love you, Henry. I want to be your wife.'

He patted her hands, and sipped his whiskey. 'You know

406

something,' he said, 'I love Denver at this time of the afternoon, just when the sun's getting low. It has a kind of golden shine about it that you never see anywhere else. Bright and golden, and clear as creek-water.'

'If you gave her more money, would she agree to divorce you?' asked Baby Doe.

Henry shrugged. 'I don't know. Whenever she writes, she never says. It's always about business.'

'Is there any way at all that *you* could divorce *her?*'

He shook his head. 'Not that I know of. In two years, she hasn't even walked out with anybody else.'

'But, Henry; I want to be your wife. Surely there has to be a way.'

'Maybe,' said Henry. They had been through this conversation almost every week for the past eighteen months, and he always ended it by saying 'maybe'. Sometimes he said, 'What does it matter, being married? We're living together, aren't we? You see much more of me than Augusta ever did.' But he knew that to Baby Doe it wasn't the same. She wanted more than anything else to be respectable, to be his wife, Mrs Henry Roberts, and join the Sacred 36. She had every right to: her lover could buy and sell most of the Sacred 36 in the same afternoon.

The light began to fail, and the fifth-floor suite in the Windsor Hotel began gradually to darken. Baby Doe asked, 'Shall I turn on the lights?' but Henry shook his head. He liked the twilight; the sight of the dying day. He swallowed the last of his whiskey and held out his empty glass for another one. A black servant in a white tunic appeared as if he had been conjured out of the shadows, and took the glass to refill it. Baby Doe never asked them how they always knew exactly the right moment to appear; and they rather disturbed her, like having rats in the house always coming and going.

He had promised Baby Doe a wedding as soon as he had walked out on Augusta. A wedding to end all weddings. Flowers, veils, choirs, orchestras; carriages and kings. But again and again he had asked her to 'please be patient'. He couldn't find a way of divorcing Augusta and Augusta was adamant that she wasn't going to divorce him, no matter what he did, no matter how blatantly he paraded his affections for Baby Doe. And he couldn't be too blatant about her, because the Republican Party of Denver seemed set to put him forward for a term as United States senator, and so far his separation from Augusta and his courtship of Baby Doe had escaped any really intensive gossip in the public prints.

In spite of everything, however, he made a determined effort to enjoy himself. He took Baby Doe to racetrack meetings; to parties; to restaurants. On Sundays, he promenaded with her in Riverfront Park, and raised his hat to anyone who looked respectable. He drank, he gambled, and he worked hard at what David Moffat had called 'diversifying' – investing his money in lumber, insurance, real estate, water, and gas. He had already spent $1.2 million in building a new harbour and factory town on the shores of Lake Michigan, which he believed would rival Chicago.

'I have bad memories of Chicago,' he always used to tell people. 'That's why I've made up my mind to build another city on the lake, and let Chicago die.'

He had been true to his word to the citizens of Leadville, and built an opera house, a fire department, a street railroad system, an electric light company, and a school. The opera house, on Harrison Avenue at St Louis Street, was considered by Nat Starkey to be a 'treat beyond belief'; and Henry had been elected mayor of Leadville with almost no opposition.

Only the house on East 9th Street remained uncompleted. Work had ceased on the day that Henry had told Augusta that he was going to leave her; on Augusta's instructions. It remained as a ruin, a folly; one man's unfinished tribute to the wife he didn't love. Children said it was haunted; and prospectors came in and stole the bricks. Shortly before Christmas, 1881, Henry ordered it demolished. He was not to know that Augusta stood in the snow and watched it being knocked down.

Henry gave Baby Doe everything but marriage. He bought her an ermine cloak that swept the floor; he bought her so many pearl necklaces that when once she had tried them all on together, she was unable to stand up under the weight. He bought her diamonds, sapphires, and rubies. He had her portrait painted, three times larger than life-size. He had sold her house on Larimer Street and bought her an Italianate villa called Casa Blanca on the outskirts of Denver, complete with silk hangings and tapestries and ancient Egyptian busts and peacocks moaning on the lawns. He worshipped her; he would have done anything for her; but he hadn't yet married her.

It wasn't only a question of Augusta's refusal to seek a divorce. It was the fact that in every letter she wrote to him, she managed somehow to make a mention of the Platte River Transportation company. He wasn't so simple that he didn't see that she was warning him, and after every letter from Leadville he became irritable and morose, and went down to the taproom of the Windsor Hotel, and drank more Whiskey than was good for him, in the company of fat and noisy men.

The Windsor Hotel was his. All five storeys of it, brand-new; with towers, and parapets, and flags, like a French château, and one of the most luxurious hotels in the world. It had cost $350,000 to build; and after that Henry had spent another $200,000 on putting in three elevators, 60 bathtubs, a swimming-pool, and steam-baths complete with 'Sudsatorium, Frigidorium, and Lavatorium'. Every one of the 300 rooms was lit by gas; over half the rooms had a marble fireplace. Downstairs, there was a gourmet restaurant serving trout, venison, bearmeat, and prairie chicken, and a steam-powered refrigerator to supply ice-cream.

He kept this one top-floor suite for himself; for private evenings with Baby Doe; for gambling with his Republican Party cronies; for working; and for thinking. He was very rich now. His fortune was probably more than $9 million, although it was impossible to assess it with complete accuracy. It was probably very much more. The Matchless Mine alone was bringing him in $1,000 a day, which he used as pocket-money; and he would occasionally amuse Baby Doe by standing on the balcony outside their room to throw silver dollars to the crowded street below, and to watch people scramble for them.

Not satisfied with having endowed Leadville with an opera house, he had also built one in Denver, 'The Roberts Grand Opera House', with carved cherrywood fittings from Japan, gilded mirrors from France, a crystal gasolier with one hundred gas jets, and silk draperies that had cost over $50 the yard. The theatre had cost him $750,000; and had opened early last September. His own box, however, had been empty on opening night. He had received a letter from Augusta, earlier in the day, and he had been too drunk to go. Instead, he had been sitting in the bar at the Windsor, where there were 3,000 silver dollars studded into the floor for decoration, drinking Old Hilltop Ten-Year Old bourbon and talking about baseball with another gentleman who was as drunk as he was. These were early days for Denver's baseball team, and Henry and some of his millionaire chums had taken to encouraging the home players by offering $20 in gold for stolen bases and home runs, and stationing beer-barrels at every base.

Henry patted Baby Doe's hand. 'We'll get married, don't you worry about it. I'll find a way.'

But just as Henry had seemed to be floating in a dream through all of his hard-scrabble years with Augusta, he seemed now to be floating even faster and even less effectually through his years of affluence. Rich as he was, he never felt that he was in control of his own destiny. Days would go by, weeks, months, as quickly as if somebody were whipping the door of his room open and shut, open and shut. Voices seemed to blur all around him; friends came and smiled and took a drink and went; games of cards flickered in front of him as if the pack were being blown across the baize by sudden draughts. The Windsor Hotel had risen as if by magic: scaffolding; foundations; brownstone cladding, towers, tiles, windows, and roof. The opera house had risen just as swiftly. All he seemed to be able to remember of its construction was when the decorators had shown him the large portrait of Shakespeare in the lobby.

'Who's that?' he had demanded.

'Shakespeare.'

He had sucked his cigar; and then blown out smoke; and waved his hand. 'Take it down. What did Shakespeare ever do for Denver? You can put up a picture of me there, instead.'

He seemed to spend more and more time sitting here in his suite in the Windsor; not because he enjoyed the isolation; quite often he was bored; but because it seemed to be the only way in which he could slow the days down. He would look across at Baby Doe sometimes, as she embroidered, or read a magazine, and the sun would be shining on those soft perfect cheeks of hers, and he would think: you don't know how old I'm getting, how quickly my life is disappearing. He wanted to marry her more than anything else he could think of; but the Denver Republicans were already talking of putting him up for the United States senate; and he didn't dare risk any revelations from Augusta about the Platte River Transportation company. So he kept her close, his Baby Doe, and tried to keep the days as long and as graceful as possible.

He had ordered her a carriage, varnished in dark blue and

410

striped with gold, with upholstery of pale blue satin. He had decided that it should always be drawn by four black horses. He would spend whole afternoons talking about how beautiful she would look in it, as she drove around Denver. She stared out of the hotel window, and said, 'It's snowing again. Didn't you say you had to go back to Leadville?'

'Business, that's all,' replied Henry. 'And that Oscar Wilde fellow is supposed to be appearing at the opera house. Do you want to come to that?'

Baby Doe said nothing, but watched the snow tumbling into the muddy streets as if it were the confetti at somebody else's wedding. When she turned around and looked at Henry there were tears in her eyes but he didn't see them; he was staring blindly at the wall, as if his mind was fixed a long way away and a very long time ago. *'You will become very wealthy one day,'* the fortune-teller had told him. But what had Nina said? *'You are a man who carves epitaphs, and always will be.'*

'Hm?' asked Henry, suddenly looking up.

'No,' said Baby Doe, 'I think I'll go out to the house. Agnes has been missing me.'

'Ah,' said Henry. Then, 'Yes.'

He left Denver the following afternoon in a wild snowstorm; sitting warm and well-fed in his private railroad car with its thick brown velvet curtains and its brown sofas and crystal lamps. Now that the Denver & Rio Grande Railroad had laid a track through to Leadville, Henry's frequent to-ing and fro-ing between the two cities had become very much more comfortable; and as the train clanked its way slowly up towards Idaho Springs, with the snow whirling against its windows, he sat back and daydreamed of Doris and summers long ago, although he found it impossible now to separate Doris in his mind's eye from Baby Doe, and he began to wonder if in some mysterious way they were related. Was it possible for spirits to find their way into other people's bodies, and seek out the lovers they had left behind when they died? The snow softly touched the glass of the railroad car window; and outside, although it was only lunchtime, the sky was as dark as ink.

'Mr Roberts?' his secretary asked him, uncertainly. His secretary was a young man straight out from law school in New York; a clean young man with large ears called Price. He had only been working for Henry for three weeks, and he still seemed to find his employer bizarre and baffling.

411

'What is it?' asked Henry.

'There's a message, sir, from Leadville. It seems that Mr Wilde is expected to arrive on Thursday, as promised.'

'Did you read what they said about Mr Wilde in the papers?' asked Henry.

'Well, sir, not much.' Young Price went pink.

'He seems to like sunflowers,' said Henry.

'Yes, sir.'

'He talks pretty effeminate, too. All this "too utterly-utter". Did you read about that?'

'Yes, sir.'

'Well,' said Henry, 'you'll have the chance to meet him this week. Just make sure he doesn't get the idea that *you're* "too utterly-utter." '

Henry laughed, the first time he'd laughed in a week. He didn't know why. Young Price gave him a lopsided smile of distress, and retreated to the tiny brightly-lit office in which he worked; at the very end of the railroad car, next to the lavatory.

Henry was superstitious about Leadville; perhaps because Augusta was there. He was unsteady on his feet when he arrived. He had drunk half a bottle of whiskey while the train had waited at Loveland Pass, over 11,000 feet above sea-level, for gangers to dig snow away from the tracks. He had sat staring at the snow, his glass in his hand; and by the time they had brought him his supper (chicken with lemon sauce) he had been slurring his words and almost snow-blind.

All the way down to Leadville from Fremont Pass he had tapped his huge diamond ring against the window, an irritating tapping that had set young Price's teeth on edge. It had seemed to carry all the way around the railroad car, penetrating and impatient and sharp.

Henry slept badly that night, at his special suite at the Clarendon Hotel, on the opposite side of St Louis Street from the Roberts Opera House. At half-past three in the morning he called for seltzer and cheese, and sat in his nightshirt eating it. It had stopped snowing. Leadville lay sparkling under a clear, black sky, gritted with stars. He finished the cheese and then he went back to bed and lay there with the cover drawn up tight under his chin, staring at the edge of the mahogany bedside table and trying to think of nothing at all; not money; not Baby Doe; not Augusta; not anything. He dreamed of

412

running. He woke up thinking, when was the last time I actually *ran?*

He was busy for the next two days. He visited the Matchless No. 3 shaft, where excavations into the new lode were progressing well; he also went down the Weldon No 2 shaft, off Monroe Street on Chicken Hill; and was shown around Meyer Sampling Works on Front Street. He talked to Nat Starkey and Thos Rogers about the electric light works, and the possibility of starting up a telephone company. He was told by Price late on Wednesday afternoon that Oscar Wilde had arrived in Leadville, but all he could say was 'good'. There were four shootings that evening: one at the Pioneer Saloon, one on Harrison Avenue, right outside the courthouse, and two in a brothel on Leiter, in the 300 Block.

He kept thinking: one day I'm going to walk into Augusta on the street, and then what am I going to say? Good morning? Are you all right? I'm sorry? For God's sake, why were you ever born?

On Thursday evening, in formal dress, he went to the opera house with Nat Starkey and his wife Olive to see Oscar Wilde. He was pleased to see that the auditorium was packed; and that all of Leadville's richest citizens had turned up, in evening dress and satin gowns, to occupy their gilded boxes. There was an excited hubbub of conversation and laughter; and even the miners in the stalls were stamping their feet impatiently, and calling out, 'Where is he? Let's get a look at the feller.'

Henry settled down in his box; and the theatre manager came in to shake his hand; and to offer him a bottle of champagne, bobbing noisily in a stupendous solid silver cooler which was valiantly carried by a red-faced boy.

At last, the theatre lights were dimmed down to tiny specks of gas; and the footlights brightened, and the rich crimson curtains were drawn back.

There were hoots of derision and cheers of surprise when Oscar Wilde walked on to the boards. He was dressed in a braided velvet jacket and silk knee-britches, and he was carrying a tall lily in one hand. His hair reached down to his shoulders, and was fluffed up on either side of his face. But he was not the languid fop that the miners of Leadville had expected him to be. He was bigger, and burlier, and instead of affecting the 'languid, dreamy walk' for which he had been derided by the Denver *Times*, he strode up to the footlights and

413

faced his laughing audience 'like a giant backwoodsman', as the Leadville *Herald* later reported.

He waved his lily, and that brought more laughter; then he tossed it into the stalls, amongst the miners, who didn't know whether they ought to catch it or stamp on it.

'I exhort you,' Wilde cried, in a clear and compelling voice, which immediately hushed the auditorium, from the miners up to the millionaires, 'I exhort you – all of you – to study when you can and as soon as you can the Gothic school of Pisan art. You will discover in it aesthetic principles which will illuminate both your minds and your souls. It represents the height of natural sensitivity; combined with the height of intellectual stylization.'

There was baffled silence. Somebody coughed; and that set off a whole fusillade of coughs.

'However,' Wilde said, 'I wish to speak to you first tonight of gold, and of silver, those precious metals which occupy your whole existence; from miner to mine-owner; and, most importantly, I wish to speak of those who worship gold and silver not simply as wealth, but as the raw material of great art. All of you know the *market* value of gold and silver, or else you would not be here, but its *aesthetic* value far outshines its commercial worth. Let us take one of the greatest of those who have created works of art out of precious metal – Benvenuto Cellini.'

Henry sat in silence as Wilde recounted the outrageous life of Cellini; how he had killed the Constable de Bourbon with his own hand, and fatally wounded the Prince of Orange; how he had accidentally slain a rival goldsmith and been thrown into prison for embezzling pontifical jewels; how at last he had returned to Florence to create some of the finest masterpieces of gold and silver that the world has ever seen.

In the front rows of the opera house, the miners sat enthralled; and when Wilde had finished they rose to their feet and applauded loudly, whistling and cheering.

'This Cellini,' one of them called out, 'if he's that good, and he's that tough, why didn't you bring him with you?'

Wilde raised a large, pale hand. 'I regret to have to tell you,' he said, with the faintest of smiles, 'that Signor Benvenuto Cellini is dead.'

'Who shot him?' another miner demanded.

After the lecture, Henry went down to the lobby, and there

414

Oscar Wilde was brought forward, surrounded by applauding well-wishers and curious miners, to shake Henry's hand.

'Mr Wilde, I very much enjoyed your lecture,' said Henry.

'I am most gratified,' said Wilde. He took out a handkerchief and dabbed at his forehead. 'I was warned that Leadville was the toughest as well as the richest city in the world, and I have to admit that I was looking forward to this evening with some trepidation.'

'Not all of us carry revolvers, Mr Wilde,' Henry assured him.

'I'm relieved to hear it,' Wilde replied. 'They said that if I didn't give a good account of myself, they would shoot myself or my travelling manager or both of us. Fortunately – ' he added, and here his voice rose a little, in case anybody should miss what he was going to say, ' – fortunately, nothing they could do to my travelling manager would intimidate me.'

Henry said, 'I understand that Mr Starkey and Mr Rogers have something of a reception arranged for you. A tour of the dance-halls, and the gambling saloons.'

'So I believe,' said Wilde, not altogether enthusiastically. Henry thought he looked tired.

'Well, when they've finished with you; if you're still on your feet; why don't you let me take you down one of my mines? Let's make it one o'clock, you should have seen the sights by then. I'll take you down the No. 3 shaft at the Matchless, and you can see where all these riches come from.' Henry smiled, and added, as a joke against Leadville's miners, 'Maybe you can go back to Europe and tell Mr Cellini's widow all about it.'

Henry went back to the Clarendon and ate a light supper of cured ham and eggs. He called the barber up, and sat in silence while he was shaved. There was no sound but the clink of the barber's razor in the basin, and the steady scratching of his blade against Henry's chin. Afterwards, Henry changed into a fresh evening suit, and sat by the window, drinking a large glass of undiluted whiskey.

At a quarter to two, Oscar Wilde and his reception party finally arrived at the head of the Matchless Mine; where Henry was waiting in his carriage with a thick rug around his knees. The night was very cold, and Henry had been taking regular nips from a flask of whiskey, and smoked two cigars. Young Price stood beside his carriage, clapping his hands from time to time, and looking as if he would much rather be back in bed.

415

Wilde was in tremendous spirits. 'Aha!' he cried, when he caught sight of Henry. 'We have had an evening to remember! Brass bands, piano players, an act in which a woman disappeared and failed to reappear, to the relief of all watching; a little faro; a little poker; a very great quantity of whiskey; some terpsichorean antics by some ladies who were unfortunate enough not to be able to afford very many clothes; followed by more whiskey; and some sporadic singing.'

Henry climbed down from his carriage. 'Well, then,' he said, 'let's finish the evening by having some supper down the mine. Price, did you bring that whiskey?'

'More whiskey!' Wilde exclaimed, polishing the palms of his hands in enthusiasm. 'That sounds like a capital idea!'

The Matchless was far larger and far more impressive than the Little Pittsburgh had been. Inside the cavernous winding-shed there were three banks of hoists, and the winding-engines were enormous; huge steam-breathing contraptions of green enamel and gleaming brass. Henry and Oscar Wilde were led towards the first of the cages; and accompanied by Nat Starkey and the night foreman, they were quickly lowered into the darkness of the mine.

'Deep into the heart of the mountain, my word,' remarked Wilde, as at last they were brought to a jarring halt, and allowed out on to the dimly-lit fifth level. Three or four car pushers turned around to stare at them.

Henry said, 'The foreman will show you around, Mr Wilde. Then come back here and have a drink.'

'Excellent,' replied Wilde. 'I must say that your whiskey appeals to me. What it lacks in refinement, it certainly makes up for in strength.'

Wilde, still chattering and posturing, was led away along the tunnel. Henry waited for him beside the shaft, and talked for a while to Nat Starkey. Nat said, 'Quite a character, isn't he? And not at all pious, like I'd expected.'

Henry shrugged. 'It seems to me that he's either a genius, or an out-and-out rogue; or maybe a little of both.'

It was almost twenty minutes before they heard Wilde's distinctive voice returning along the gallery. He was accompanied now not only by the foreman but by six or seven delighted miners, who hung on to everything he said, and toasted him repeatedly in whiskey, which they drank out of their tinplate coffee-mugs. Wilde himself was carrying a glass tumbler in one hand as delicately as if it were the sick primrose with which he had once stayed up all night; but a full bottle of rye in the other, to replenish the tumbler as often as required, which was quite often.

'Well, Mr Wilde, what do you say to the Matchless?' said Henry, stepping forward.

Wilde turned around on his slippered heel. 'A most vivacious mine, as mines go,' he replied. 'But very noisy. America is really a very noisy place; in fact I think it must be the noisiest country that ever existed. And noise, you know, is never conducive to poetry or to romance.'

He must have drunk a great deal by now; but he seemed to be refreshed more than stupefied; and he spoke more brightly, and his pale blue eyes were glittering with amusement.

Henry took a drink; and while the foreman chivvied the miners back to the face; and Nat Starkey talked to Thos Rogers; Henry sat with Wilde on the side of an ore-cart (over which Wilde had fastidiously spread a handkerchief, in case his silk knee-britches should be stained).

'Has this trip been a success for you?' asked Henry. 'Financially, I mean?'

'Only sporadically,' said Wilde, and drank, and unexpectedly sniffed. 'But then if one could *afford* to come to America, one would not come at all.'

'You don't think we're very, what is it, aesthetic?'

'My dear Mr Roberts, the best-dressed men that I have seen in the West are your miners. I adore their red flannel shirts, and their corduroy trousers, and their high leather boots. I shall make absolutely certain that I purchase a miner's ensemble myself, to wear in the drawing-rooms of Bloomsbury. But as for the rest of the country. . . well, it would be charitable to say that it is barbarous.'

Henry said, 'Let me ask you something, Mr Wilde. You seem like a man who might have an opinion on a matter like this. If you were ever torn between beauty and duty, which would you choose?'

For all of his affectations, Wilde was a sensitive man, and instead of answering Henry with a witty remark, or an epigram, or teasing him for his rhyme of 'beauty and duty', Wilde looked at him seriously, and brushed back his long brown hair, and when one of the miners approached them to ask for his autograph, waved the man away.

'There can't be any question about it,' he replied. 'At least, not as far as I'm concerned. I would have to choose beauty. The mark of civilization is the love of beauty.'

Henry said, 'This whole damned thing is tearing me apart.'

Wilde looked at him with care. Henry was very rich, and that may have made him more interesting to the poet than anyone else down at the bottom of the Matchless Mine; but he appeared to sense that Henry's struggle was a tragedy of classic qualities; and he said, in the gentlest of tones, 'Explain what you mean, Mr Roberts. What "damned thing"?'

They filled their glasses again, and drank more whiskey; and in his usual blunt but discursive way, Henry told Wilde about Augusta, and Baby Doe, and what had happened to August Rische and George Hook. Wilde was particularly interested in Henry's description of Baby Doe; and the way in which she drove about Denver in her carriage. He saw an exact parallel with Lily Langtry in London, for whom he had developed a mad passion from the very beginning. Lily Langtry, he had said, 'owes it to herself and us' to drive through Hyde Park in a black victoria, drawn by black horses, in a black bonnet emblazoned with sapphires.

At last, Henry told Wilde about Doc Holliday, and his views on death, and Wilde commented, 'Hm. Coarse, but sensible; especially from a dying man. All I can say is that when the Last Trumpet sounds, I shall turn over in my porphyry tomb and pretend that I haven't heard it.'

Henry said, 'I've bored you.'

Wilde put his arm around Henry's shoulder, and replied 'On the contrary, my dear sir, you have fascinated me. You have frightened me rather, too: because it seems to me that you cannot make your choice until you have confronted your own mortality. You are a man cursed by good fortune, Mr Roberts. You must go to your Baby Doe, and marry her, of course. But before that, you must stare your own existence unflinchingly in the face. You have never been tested by life, Mr Roberts. Now must be the time.'

Henry said, 'I don't think I understand what you mean. What kind of test?'

Wilde laughed, no longer serious. 'You must devise your own, Mr Roberts. What is it that you fear most? Rush out and embrace it, and see if you survive.'

The hoisting-gear rattled and sang, and another car-load of

guests and miners came down, brandishing fresh bottles of whiskey. There was singing and laughing, and now Nat Starkey joined them and said to Henry, 'Come on now, Henry; you mustn't monopolize our guest here. How about some more whiskey, Mr Wilde? And some of the men would like to hear a poem or two.'

'More whiskey? What a good idea!' smiled Wilde. He squeezed Henry's shoulder just once, and said, 'Remember, Mr Roberts: it is better to be beautiful than to be good.'

Henry returned to the Clarendon Hotel an hour later and went straight to bed. He told young Price not to disturb him, for any reason, until two o'clock in the afternoon. He lay on his bed in his nightshirt and felt that he was sweating whiskey. The bed dipped and rolled beneath him, but when he sat up, the room tilted. He went to the bathroom and drank a large glass of water, but even that tasted like whiskey. After five or ten minutes, he was wretchedly sick; sicker than he had ever been on alcohol for years. He sat on the lavatory seat with tears in his eyes and reckoned that he must have drunk nearly a bottle and a half of straight whiskey since yesterday evening.

Wiping his face with a towel, he walked slowly back into his bedroom. What had Wilde said to him? 'You must go to your Baby Doe, and marry her, of course. But before that, you must stare your own existence unflinchingly in the face.'

He hadn't understood at the time what it was that Wilde had been trying to tell him; but he knew now. He had always kept himself away from confrontation; he had always taken the easy way out. He had married Augusta because it had been easier to say yes to her than no. He had allowed August Rische to be blown up with an easy, casual nod. And he had killed George Hook himself because it was easier to kill him than to persuade him to come up.

He had no courage. He had been floating through life because he had never attempted to swim against the current. All he had was his money; and that had come to him by accident. Without his money, what was he? That was what Oscar Wilde had been telling him. Confront your own terrors; stare them in the face. Unless at some time in your life you have risked everything you care about, then your whole existence has no meaning.

At nine o'clock, he ordered breakfast. Two boiled eggs, and a glass of beer. Then he shaved himself, and dressed himself;

and looked at himself in the mirror. Tired, white, but smart. He brushed the sleeve of his brown checked day suit, and remembered with a smile what Oscar Wilde had said about the miners, and the way they dressed.

He found John Holliday in the Tasteful Saloon, in the back room, still finishing a game which had started the previous night. The Tasteful Saloon was dense with flat-smelling cigar-smoke, and a scrub-woman was mopping up the wooden floor with wet, wide strokes of her mop. Henry nodded a salute to the barkeep, Ted Johnson, whom he had known since the days when he ran the Leadville store and post office. Ted Johnson asked, 'Fix you a drink, Mr Roberts?'

'Just a beer, please, Ted,' said Henry.

John Holliday's game was on the point of breaking up. As Henry approached, one of the other players stood up, scratched himself, hooked up his coat from the back of his chair with his finger, and said, 'That's it for me, Doc. I'm turning in before you clean me out completely.'

Holliday coughed and shrugged. 'Nice to play with you, Samuel. Always nice to play with a gent.'

He looked up, and saw Henry standing in the morning sunlight. 'Well, if it isn't Mr Roberts. Good day to you, Mr Roberts. Don't tell me you came by for another drink. I don't think my liver could take any more; not until somebody's fed me.'

Henry drew out a chair and sat down. 'As a matter of fact,' he said, 'I came by for a game.'

Doc Holliday collected up the cards and shuffled them; no fancy shuffling but very quick. 'You want a game, hunh?' he asked, closing one eye against his cigar smoke. 'At ten o'clock in the morning, you came looking for a game?'

'That's right.'

'Any of you mugs want to play?' Holliday asked his departing acquaintances. The three of them looked at each other. The one called Samuel shook his head, and said, 'My wife's going to cut my lights out if'n I don't get home, and fry 'em up for breakfast.' But the other two, a tall thin man with a pencil moustache, and a broad, ruddy-faced man who looked like a farmer, both came back to the table.

'Be a privilege to take some money off Henry Roberts,' smiled the ruddy-faced man. He held out his hand. 'Name's Bill Potter, from Soda Springs.'

'Rugby,' said the tall thin man. 'Hayward Rugby. Used to work for the Hibschle Mine, sampling. Struck it reasonable rich out at Stray Horse Gulch.'

'How about some beers here, Ted?' called Doc Holliday. 'And maybe some hash, too, if anybody's hungry.'

They played a few hands for the fun of it, only bidding a few dollars. Then, when the saloon clock struck eleven, and the first of the day's regulars started drifting in, Holliday cracked his knuckles like pistol-shots, and said, 'All right then, gentlemen. What do you say that we really get to it? Mr Roberts here came looking for a game; let's give him one.'

They played for another hour; and this time the bidding went up in hundreds of dollars. Bill Potter and Hayward Rugby began to grow tense and hesitant; and threw in their hands more frequently and a great deal earlier as the pot grew larger.

Henry was badly off form. Maybe it was his hangover; maybe it was his nerves. But he misjudged the cards in game after game, and by the time the clock struck one, he was nearly ten thousand dollars down. Doc Holliday coughed, and smiled, and sat behind his mounting heap of IOUs with obvious pleasure.

Holliday dealt another round. One card face down to each of them, the hole card; one card face up. Henry's face-up card was the eight of spades. He eased up his hole card. The eight of hearts. He said nothing, but asked Ted to bring him another beer. Bill Potter, with the ace of diamonds, started the bidding. One thousand dollars. Henry raised the stake to two thousand dollars. Hayward Rugby bet two thousand dollars, too; and so did Doc Holliday.

A third card was dealt. Henry felt his stomach tighten up. The eight of diamonds. He raised the stake to five thousand dollars. Holliday glanced up at him, and coughed. Hayward Rugby said, 'I'm out,' and put down his cards, face down.

Doc Holliday examined his hand for a moment, and then said, quite calmly, without taking his cigar out of his mouth, 'I'll raise you. Ten thousand dollars.'

A fourth card was dealt. Henry wiped his mouth with the back of his hand. The ten of hearts. Bill Potter said, 'That's it for me, gentlemen,' and threw in his cards. Henry looked at Doc Holliday and said, 'Twenty-five thousand dollars.'

Holliday nodded his acceptance. Henry was concerned now. Twenty-five thousand dollars was a great deal of money to

421

Holliday; five thousand more than he had won so far. He must have the makings of a very good hand, or else he wouldn't have risked going on so long. Henry had learned three things about Holliday already this morning: that he wasn't a rash card-player, that he didn't bluff, and that he would throw in a poor hand straight away.

Holliday dealt a fifth card. Henry, reaching for his fresh glass of beer, looked down at it and tried not to flinch, or even flicker his eyes. The king of hearts. That meant he was holding a handful of fours, the second highest hand in poker. All that could beat him now was a straight flush.

He drank his beer, picked up his card, arranged it in his hand. This was the moment that Oscar Wilde had told him about. This was the time to see whether his luck was genuinely God-given or not; whether he really deserved his destiny. The regulars in the saloon somehow sensed that the game was nearing its climax, because they began to gather around the table; shuffling and pushing; curious faces with heavy moustaches, fascinated by the prospect of easy money and desperate failure. Someone called over to the piano-player to stop your goddamned tinkling, will you, this is serious.

Henry said, 'I came here for a game today, John; a game that would raise really raise the prickles on the back of my neck.'

Holliday said nothing; but watched him with eyes like pale glazed marbles.

'I'm a very wealthy man these days,' Henry went on. 'All of these fellows know me; I struck it lucky and now I'm rich. Well, I want to test that luck. Do you understand me?'

'Your voice is shaking,' said Holliday, with supreme calmness. He coughed.

'I want to test that luck,' Henry repeated, ignoring him. 'And that's why I want to make a special bet with you now, if you'll take it; a bet on this hand.'

'You must be pretty sure of what you've got there,' Holliday remarked.

Henry said, 'This is the bet. Everything *I've* got, against everything *you've* got.'

Holliday frowned at him; the first betrayal of expression since the game had begun. Somebody in the assembled crush of miners called out, '*Yaahooo!*' and tossed up his hat. There were shouts, and screeches, and then a burst of applause and a stamping of boot-heels.

Holliday said, 'I never heard of such a bet.'

'You did now,' said Henry. 'You win this hand, you get it all. The mining stock, the horses, the property, the money. Nine million dollars, or thereabouts. These gentlemen here are all witnesses.'

'Well, damn it, I can't offer you too much in return,' laughed Holliday. 'A greasy deck of cards, and a medicinal inhaler, and two fancy vests from France. Hardly seems like a fair bet to me.'

'Nonetheless, that's the bet. You want to take it, or concede?'

Holliday stopped laughing and stared at Henry narrowly. 'You mean it, don't you?' he said.

Henry nodded. He felt completely unreal, as if he were someone else altogether, a man that he had dreamed about; or remembered from another time and another place. For the first time in his life, everything was on the line. Not just the diamonds, not just the mining stock, not just the houses; but all the respect which his money had earned for him; and Baby Doe, too. He had no illusions that Baby Doe would stay with him if he were suddenly to lose everything he had.

There was silence in the Tasteful Saloon. Henry hesitated for a moment, and then tugged off his huge diamond ring and laid it on the beer-circled table. The miners and gamblers stared at it as if they expected it to do something magical, like rise up into the air of its own accord. Henry said, 'Here's proof. This ring represents my fortune. Here it is on the table.'

Holliday coughed once, but sucked in his cheeks to suppress another one. He reached into his pocket and produced a small cardboard pill-box, Dr Charles Broadbent's Famous Tubercular Lozenges. He rattled them, and put them down next to the ring. 'There you are, Mr Roberts. This represents *my* fortune.'

Henry said, quietly and immediately, 'I'll see you.'

Without another word, Holliday spread out his cards on the table, and the miners gasped like women. A full house, three aces and two tens. Nothing that Henry held in his hand could top that. The odds of two hands being dealt in the same game that were both higher than a flush were something ridiculous, like ten million to one.

Holliday raised both hands to Henry, and smiled, as if to say, 'I'm sorry, but it was your idea.' The miners shouted and whooped, and Holliday snapped his fingers to Ted Johnson for drinks all around. Then he reached across the table, and picked

423

up Henry's ring, and said, loudly, 'With this ring, good fortune, I thee wed; and kiss poverty goodbye.' He slipped the ring on to his finger, and then waggled his hand so that everybody could see it. There were more whoops, and somebody fired a revolver into the ceiling with a deafening bang, and they were all showered in plaster dust.

'Wowee,' shouted one miner, kicking the bar with his boot, again and again, 'wowee, never saw the like. Never saw the darn like.'

Ted Johnson was already coming across with a dozen brimming glasses of beer when Henry laid out his own hand of cards. Everybody in the saloon was so excited that very few of them took any notice. But Doc Holliday peered over, his hand still raised in the air to show off the diamond ring; and the transformation that went over his face was extraordinary. He looked up at Henry and his cheeks were as grey as a burned-out hearth.

'Fours,' said Henry.

An unnatural quiet fell over the saloon. Somebody said, 'Fours?'

Doc Holliday held back another coughing spasm, although his cheeks kept blowing out, and his throat rattled. He took off the diamond ring, and held it out to Henry on the palm of his hand.

'Keep it,' said Henry, quietly. 'Buy yourself some treatment. You gave me what I needed. You deserve something in return.'

He stood up, straightened his necktie, and walked wearily out of the saloon into the afternoon sunlight. The snow was dazzling; but the thaw had already begun, and the rooftops were decorated with musically-dripping icicles.

Henry walked all the way back to the Clarendon Hotel. Young Price was anxiously waiting for him in his suite. 'Mrs Doe's here, sir. She's been here for an hour. I didn't know what to tell her.'

Baby Doe was standing in the window, looking out at the Roberts Opera House. There was a luncheon tray on the table, chicken breasts and salad, most of it untouched. When Henry came into the room, she turned at once and came quickly over to greet him. She was wearing an elegantly cut spring suit in beige wool, with chocolate-coloured piping, and a large feathery hat.

'Henry, my sweetheart.'

424

He held her close, squeezed her, smiled.

'You smell of drink,' she said. 'You haven't been drinking?'

'A little,' he told her.

She said, abashed, 'I missed you, Henry. I caught the first train from Denver this morning. Henry, I missed you. I don't know. I was worried about you. I felt that you needed me. Is that silly?'

He couldn't stop smiling. He picked up the bottle of chilled white wine from the luncheon tray and poured himself a glass.

'We're going to be married,' he told her.

She came across the hotel room and the sun shone in the plumes of her hat as if she were a queen; or a queen-to-be.

'Henry,' she whispered. 'Oh, Henry, I love you so much.'

Henry kissed her, and then lifted his glass of wine, and walked around the room, and smiled at her. 'That's it,' he said. 'No buts. No delays. We're going to be married.'

He lifted his glass of wine again, in a silent toast, then he turned away and faced the window. Baby Doe hesitated for a moment; but then she came across and put her arms around his waist, from behind, resting her head against his broad back.

She didn't see that he was looking blindly out at the Rocky Mountain sunshine, his face wet with tears.

Epilogue

'I couldn't believe it when I found out that you were still living here,' said the young reporter, frowning into the darkness.

The old woman lifted her hand, as if to say that she didn't particularly care whether he could believe it or not. The shack was cold and sparsely furnished, and smelled of cooking-fat. The wind kept shuddering at the shutters.

'Can you tell me something about your wedding?' the young reporter asked her. 'Do you remember it at all?'

'Of course I remember it,' the old woman said, in the dryest of voices. She was very shrivelled, and crunched-up in her chair, and her silver hair was parted in the middle, and topped with a small black bonnet, of the kind that Victorian widows used to wear. 'It was the most spectacular wedding of the year. Even the President came.'

'That would be President – ?'

'Chester A. Arthur, of course. He was very charming. He said that I was the most beautiful bride that he had ever seen. And I was, too. You should have seen my dress. It was white lace, layers and layers of white lace. It cost $7,000, which in those days was a fortune. I swept down the stairs – I swept down the stairs – and there was Henry, waiting for me, looking as proud as a king. Poor Henry.'

'That was at – ?'

The old woman coughed thickly. 'Willard's Hotel, in Washington. The finest wedding that Washington had ever seen. You should have seen me. You should have seen me!'

'I wish I had,' the young reporter told her. He was beginning to grow uncomfortable. The old woman smelled very strongly of urine, and the wind kept banging at the shutter as if it was warning him that a hurricane was getting up. He was only

426

eighteen, a cub reporter on the *Leadville Herald*. His editor had lifted up his horn-rimmed glasses and peered at him with a with watery eyes, and said, 'Did you know that Baby Doe is still alive?'

'Who the hell is Baby Doe?' he had wanted to know.

Anybody less like anybody's baby was hard to imagine. A wrinkly old woman living in a shack by the dilapidated winding-shed of the Matchless Mine. His colleagues on the paper had teased him that he was going out to interview a ghost; so watch out – *wooooo!*

The old woman said, 'It wasn't fair, of course; it wasn't just. We could only stay in Washington for just a month. Henry had given those Denver party officials nearly a quarter of a million dollars, one way and another; but they sold him short. They took the money and still wouldn't respect him. There were two vacancies for senator – one for a full term, and one just for thirty days. There were 97 ballots, but in the end they said that his divorce weighed against him; and he lost. All he got was the thirty-day term.'

'That was more or less the finish of his political career, wasn't it?' the young reporter asked her.

'He tried again for the senatorial nomination in '86; but failed; and then for the governorship of Colorado, in '88, but he didn't get that either. They kept telling him that he was too ostentatious, that he shouldn't have married a younger woman like me, but I never believed them; I always thought that there was something else. David Moffat always used to say that it was "the Platte River" but I never understood what that meant, and he never explained it.'

The young reporter said, 'When did his business problems begin?'

The old woman was silent for a long time, and then she replied, 'I don't know. I can scarcely remember now. It all happened so gradually. It was his political failure that discouraged him the most; and I think that after that he lost his interest in life. It was all very well to be rich, but what was the point of it, if you couldn't have any effect on the world around you?'

She asked then, 'Would you care for some coffee?'

The young reporter glanced across at the grease-caked stove, and shook his head. 'Thanks all the same.'

The old woman snuffled, and shifted herself in her chair, and then she said, 'The mines began to peter out first, one after

427

the other. He tried to finance new diggings; and he had to mortgage all of our property to raise enough money; but we never hit it rich again. Then there was all that financial panic in '93, tom foolery, most of it, but half the banks in Denver were forced to close, and if it hadn't been for David Moffat, we would have been wiped out then. In the end we had scarcely anything left but the Matchless, which was still producing a little silver; but then they repealed the Sherman Act in '93, and the government stopped buying silver for coinage, and that was the finish.'

She said nothing for almost a minute. She had recited her piece. The young reporter didn't know what to ask next, and sat uncomfortably opposite her, watching her as she sniffed and rocked in her chair and reminisced.

'Henry went through such *bewilderment*,' she said. 'He went through such *pain*. He kept saying, "I won this luck." '

'What did he mean by that? Do you know?'

She shook her head, looked away, coughed. 'He just kept saying, "I won this luck. I won it." I didn't know what he meant.'

The young reporter looked down at his notes. 'He divorced his first wife in 1883, is that right?'

The old woman nodded. 'She divorced him; but he forced her. He told her that he was never coming back to her; and that if she didn't sue for divorce, he wouldn't give her a penny. She took in lodgers for a while, to make money; but then he sent miners around to threaten the lodgers; and so she gave in. I can't remember what the settlement was; but it was more than a quarter of a million dollars.'

She licked her cracked lips, and said, 'She asked the judge if she could keep the name Roberts; and the judge said of course you can, it's yours by right. And then he said, I want to have put on record that this divorce was *not willingly asked for*. Then she left the court, and she was crying.'

The young reporter scribbled and scribbled. Then he stopped scribbling, and said, 'My editor was surprised that you were still here.'

She shook her head. 'No, he wasn't; he was surprised that I was still alive.'

'But what are you doing here? I mean, surely you could have found some place – well, more comfortable.'

The old woman sat up straight in her chair. 'Henry died in

1899, my boy; a few months before the new century began. I so much wanted him to see 1900, but he never did. But, do you know, out of everything that we were forced to sell, he always kept hold of his stock in the Matchless; I don't know why. He said something had happened in the Matchless that changed his life. And over and over again, he told me, "Hang on to the Matchless," "Hang on to the Matchless." And so I did. And that's why I'm here today.'

The young reporter said, 'The Matchless mine is flooded, you know; and as far as I understand it, it's completely worked out.'

The old woman shook her head. ' "Hang on to the Matchless," that's what he told me. His dying words. Well, his last but dying words. His actual dying words were, "Who can cut my epitaph?" but I didn't understand that, either.'

Late in the afternoon, with the sky piled high with cumulus clouds, the young reporter left the Matchless Mine and returned to his office. He spent the rest of the day in the newspaper morgue, reading up about Henry Roberts and Baby Doe and the days when Leadville's streets had been crowded with celebrities and millionaires and famous criminals, and a man could be shot for laughing too loud.

He wrote a bright, human-interest story about Baby Doe; headlined 'Silver Baron's Widow Still Lives In Hope of Lucky Strike.'

It wasn't until two years later, when he was working on the Denver *Times*, that he came across a cutting that said, 'Henry Roberts Denies Platte River Involvement.' He had been working on a story about local government corruption, and he had been looking back in the files to check the last time that any Denver notables had been accused of taking bribes.

The cutting was annotated February 8, 1885. It said: 'Silver millionaire Mr Henry Roberts emphatically denied a suggestion made last week by the Colorado Democratic committee that he had taken $1,000 a month commission from certain unnamed parties in payment for allowing his Leadville bank to be used for the purposes of perpetrating "an extraordinary fraud".

'The Democrats accuse Mr Roberts of knowingly permitting his bank to be used illegally to disperse hundreds of thousands of dollars which Eastern and European businessmen had expected to be invested in a steamer-service on the Platte River, and a new resort city close to Denver.

'Mr George Osprey, of the Democratic committee, said, "In my view, Mr Roberts should be indicted for fraud. The evidence is clear. The Platte River is not navigable, nor ever will be, not even by side-wheeler; and the steamer that was actually built for the purpose has ended up as a showboat on the artificial lake at Riverfront Park, under the mocking name of *HMS Pinafore*."

'Mr Osprey said that the source of his information was "unimpeachable". He added, "You will not find a closer source of evidence on this matter; nor a truer." '

The young reporter vainly looked for any further mention of the Platte River affair; but there was none. The Democrats had apparently been satisfied with the effect of their allegations on Henry Roberts' political career. No mention was made of William Byers ever having been involved; nor Henry Stanley; nor Walter von Richthofen.

Eighteen months later, however, the young reporter's editor called him into his partitioned office, and said, 'Didn't you once write a piece on Baby Doe?'

The young reporter nodded. 'I went out to see her. I talked to her.'

'Well, here you are,' his editor told him, pushing a telegraph message across the desk. 'They found her yesterday, dead. Frozen solid, in that cabin of hers. The police said that she'd been dead for two weeks.'

The young reporter took the message and left his editor's office. He collected his coat, and his notebook, and went down in the elevator to the lobby; then out into the street. It was 1935: the year of *Porgy and Bess*; the year that the CIO was formed, to expand America's trades unions; the year that the Social Security Act was passed; and that Huey Long was assassinated in Louisiana. Ginger Rogers and Fred Astaire had just released their first picture together, and Walt Disney was hard at work on *Snow White*.

The Leadville coroner told the young reporter that Baby Doe had been found with a notebook of poems, apparently written by somebody called 'Agnes'. He showed the reporter the page at which the book had been left open beside her chair.

It read:

'Under the linden trees,
When blasts of winter freeze
Each sparkling dew-drop to a pearly gem,

The mourners slowly tread,
And weep their loved one dead;
While that blest word
"The resurrection and the life", is heard,
And they repeat
The hopes of those who trust in heaven to meet,
And rest for ever at their Redeemer's feet.'

The young reporter read it, and then handed it back. The coroner said, 'What do you think? Do you want to quote it?'

The young reporter shrugged. 'I don't know. I don't think so. I don't really know what it means.'

The coroner said, 'Don't ask me. It sounds like an epitaph.'